M000318024

ACKNOWLEDGMENTS

Daddy had explained that playing and working are part of that cycle of life. You had to find the balance of each. Satisfaction in either one depended on you and how much of yourself you put into it. Sit back and let the world flow by and you only see one spot in the river. Jump in and work the current and your visions are ever changing and exciting. You only had to put your hand out to let the current take you.

Ethel Koontz O'Connor, Gone Fishing The Hook

I put my hand out to Ethel and the people of Piney Bluffs and they have taken me into this wonderful world of telling their story. I jumped in after listening to a friend, Les, talk about his love of fishing. Those conversations led me to create the first Fishing Weekly. The current next brought me to a chance meeting with Susanne, my mentor, who found and nurtured the eager student within me. Special thanks to all the friends and family who were my encouraging reading team and kept the current alive. And with more appreciation than he'll ever know, to my husband, Ed, who listened to countless nights of fireside readings about these people who will forever be in my soul.

1

That was the last of it. I was closing the office door on forty years' worth of "literary genius" as Caleb used to say. The new owners would be moving in, putting their signature on the place, hanging a new sign. I just hope they might someday realize what had happened within those walls. They were changing the name of the *Piney Bluffs Bugle* to the *Piney Bluffs Blog*. A sign of the times I suspect. I'm sure some folks would confuse its name and think it was going to be about cranberries. But that's just the way some of the folks in town are. They had a comforting kind of hometown ways and simple honesty that made you shake your head and smile and made you glad that you had known them.

The office hadn't changed much since I began some forty years earlier. The big desk, which once was Caleb's, and the smaller desk, which had been mine at the beginning, as well as the old leather chairs, still remained. Different types of printing machinery had come and gone through the years. And at the end, we were using computers and laser printers. Although to keep with an old-fashioned tradition, we still printed the *First Day of Fishing Season Special Edition* on our old faithful printing press.

But I'm getting ahead of myself. My name is Ethel, Ethel Koontz O'Connor. I'm from Piney Bluffs, Maine, a small town not found on many maps. We're about fifty miles northwest of Portland, just the other side of Oxford. It's a close-knit community where the sky is blue, the water is pure, and most everyone loves to fish. And for the past thirty years, I have been the editor of *The Piney Bluffs Bugle* and

Fishing Weekly. *The Bugle* would still continue, but the *Weekly*, well that's why I was closing my doors. For most, *Fishing Weekly* had never been a blip on any literary guild's best of the best. But for me and the many faithful readers in New England and beyond, it was a lifetime of the best people you would ever want to know.

As I put the last of my files into my car, I heard a familiar voice say, "Hey, Ethel, be sure to stop by before you go." It was my old friend Jackie Farnsworth Frenetti. She and her family owned the Trout Inn. And her marriage to Andy of Andy's Diner provided the town with the two best dining options in town. "You'd better have our favorite bottle ready," I replied. The Trout Inn stocked the wines of Tyrell's Vineyard, our local winery. Jackie and I were particularly fond of their Calico Cabernet. Over the years, we had countless times said, "Just one more glass," as we had planned our lives sitting at our table at the inn. The inn's tavern had a breathtaking view of the lower end of Snowshoe Lake. And no matter the season, we always claimed the view on that particular day was *the* best ever.

My latest plan would take me away from Piney Bluffs just for a week. I had a fortieth class reunion from the University of Maine coming up. And I finally had told myself that this was the year I was going, or else everyone would be too old to remember who we were. And after that, I would return and start on life's next chapter. There had been many turns in the road; some U-turns and some that even though they had appeared to be the wrong way had always somehow ended up as the way it should have been.

The home where my husband Charlie and I had lived had been Daddy's. We moved closer to town and left our house on the outskirts to our son EC some ten years ago. The white cape with its black shutters and sunny yellow door was always a welcome sight at the end of any day. The flower gardens that surrounded the house and framed our backyard had gone through several generations of perennial plantings, just as this town had gone through a generation or two of life.

Growing up in Piney Bluffs was something I wouldn't have traded for anything in the world. One exception being the loss of my mother. Momma, her name was Stephanie, died when I was born, so it was just Daddy Koontz and me. Eddy, that was Daddy's name, didn't know much what to do with me. His brothers Earl, Ellsworth, Ernie, and Eubie all had sired girls, and I was the last hope for a male heir to carry on the family name and the family tradition—fishing. Sometimes his disappointment showed, but most times, I was told he was very proud of me.

Daddy and me did just fine early on. Each school day, Daddy and I got into the Chevy pickup, and off we would go. He would drop me off at Piney Bluffs High School and Elementary Complex and then continue on his way to the airstrip. Daddy had been an airplane mechanic during his time in the Air Force and now kept all of the local planes flying high. Piney Bluffs fishing tours and camp operators kept more than a dozen planes. If they weren't picking up clients at the larger airports, they were using their seaplanes to land on the larger lakes in and around our area. He doubled as the air traffic controller and ticket salesman as well. He also had his pilot's license, and every once in a while, we got the chance to take up a plane and look for the next best fishing spot. He loved to find a new fishing spot before my uncles did. And when he finally let them in on our new favorite spot, we would have our usual family contest. All of us certain that we would be the one winning one if not all of the big three—first fish, most fish, and biggest fish.

I was a happy girl; most folks said my looks favored my momma. I had gotten my dark brown hair from her and my height. When I was thirteen, I was five foot seven and could handle most things by myself. I had only a few pictures of her, mostly with Daddy, and they were well worn by my hands trying to feel her face and wonder what she would have smelled like or what her voice would have sounded like.

My aunts tried to help Daddy with me when some topics of growing up were beyond his talents. My favorite aunt was my Aunt Eleanor. She and Uncle Ellsworth lived next door with my cousin Ellen. Aunt Eleanor was a sturdy woman with snow-white hair. She smelled of fresh eggs and home cooking, always wore a housedress, and could tell when I needed a hug. She taught me all the non-fishing things a girl needed to know. By the time I was fifteen, I could cook, sew, grow vegetables, keep a house, skin fish, and dress and cook any other game that came through the door.

Aunts Edna and Earlene were sisters, skinny things with dyed blonde hair and clattering heels. They were the ones who took me on excursions out of Piney Bluffs to the shopping centers for my school clothes and for Christmas shopping. They always had the latest magazines and used all the new hair products, most of which was lost on my straight-as-pin brown hair. Aunt Alice was a mousey little woman with dull blue eyes and suffered from some malady or another. She was only seen during holiday dinners when we were given strict orders to keep the liquor cabinet locked.

I had four cousins—Eunice, Edy, Esther, and Ellen. I was the eldest with two to three years difference in between all five of us. I was closest to Eunice as we were only two years apart. She was the daughter of Uncle Eubie and Aunt Alice. Because of Aunt Alice's constant ill health, Eunice was frequently a visitor. We could always talk Daddy into taking us fishing and then stopping at Andy's Diner for a root beer float on the way home if we had been good. Life was good back then, and I can see how it had set my course to my destination of today.

Out of the corner of my eye, I saw a reflection on the wall. What was that? Oh my, how could I have forgotten this? It was my trophy from NESN, New England Sports Network, dated 1994 with the inscription, *New England Emmy Award, 1st Woman Fishing Reporter, Ethel Koontz O'Connor*. Now this brought back memories. What a wonderful reception in Boston at Anthony's Pier 4. I took it off the wall and wiped the rim of dust from its edges.

Nevertheless, as I said, I am getting ahead of myself. The changes that had come to Piney Bluffs had always been on the horizon. But with the strength of the community, we had held it off for forty years. There were several times when that strength was tested. The following pages will tell the story of one of those times.

One last look around. The latest *Boston Herald* and *New York Times* were on the table with the news beyond the town line. Caleb had once said that we needed to keep things in perspective, but we needed to keep our eyes open to the world. Because the only surprises we ever needed in life were birthday parties.

I pulled the door and tugged to hear the catch of the lock. I looked out over the town green as people were making their way through their day. Comforting faces and souls that had the sense of loyalty to one another and the community. They had allowed me to share their wonderful stories. Who would ever have thought those stories would have taken me this far, and for that matter, this close?

2

My talents were in writing. Ever since I was a young girl, I had written poems, short stories, and funny riddles. Some of my teachers were very encouraging, sending home notes on my essays and letting Daddy know what a fine writer I was. Daddy would read the notes, look at me, and shake his head. Sometimes he would comment on them.

"What are you writing this for?" he'd question. "I hope you're learning something else in school besides this." As an adolescent girl, this would send me into my room to sulk and hug my stuffed animals. I'd fall asleep dreaming about what my mother would have said. I knew it was hard for him without Momma, but it was hard for me too. I had never known her. I would close my eyes really tight and imagine her voice.

"Why, Ethel, that is so funny, or Ethel that was very good, that's my girl." But these were only dreams. And that was where my stories came from.

My stories were about people and places nowhere like Piney Bluffs. Sometimes my stories were mysteries, starting out with the typical "It was a dark and stormy night" during my phase of reading every Nancy Drew book that I could get my hands on. My heroine Nelle, unlike Nancy, had a dog, Sam, as her sidekick in her sleuthing.

I wrote late in the evening when I heard the low drone of the TV and the equally low drone of Daddy's snoring. I sat at my desk in my bedroom with my old Royal typewriter, hoping he wouldn't hear the bell of the typewriter as I hit the carriage return. I stood my flashlight up on its end at the edge of my desk, and it gave my room an eerie feel. It was just the right lighting to set the mood for writing my latest mystery. Sometimes, on nights like that, I could almost feel my mother's presence, that she was there reading over my shoulder.

I would continue until I heard my daddy clear his throat and let out a yawn. This was the signal that he was coming to bed, and I stashed the light under my pillow and lunged under the covers. As Daddy turned the corner to his bedroom, he would call out to me, "G'night Ethel," and I would try to fake my normal voice into sounding like I was being roused from a very deep sleep, "'Night, Daddy."

Miss MacGregor was especially supportive of my writing efforts. She started teaching in our school at the beginning of the fifth grade, and she was everything a ten-year-old girl could want. She was tall, young, and vibrant. Her teaching style made girls want to be like her. The boys behaved so she would let them clap the erasers, wash the black boards, or stack the books. She lived past my house in Knowles Corners and would give me a ride home when I stayed after school for extra projects.

One Monday morning, she made an announcement to the class. "Class," she began, tapping the chalk from one hand to another, "I have an exciting opportunity for you."

We started to buzz about what the opportunity could be. Could it be a class trip, or was someone famous going to visit us?

"The Young Writers of Maine Elementary School contest has just been announced for this school year. This contest is only open to fifth graders, and first prize will be to have your story published in the *Daily Bugle*. The local winners will have their stories sent to the *Maine Monthly Magazine*, and one grand prizewinning story will appear in the *Magazine*." She then passed out a paper, giving details. "For those who would like my help, you will need to have your story on my desk by this Friday," she finished. "The winner will be chosen by myself and our principal Mr. Anderson."

Excitement it seemed had different definitions to different people. The majority of the class started to talk about what they would write. But Big Bobby Baldwin and Tubby Carponowski slumped back into their seats and stared out the window. From our classroom window, you could just make out the playground, and Bob and Tubby were already planning for the baseball game at recess. They were nudging each other and rolling their eyes at me.

I decided right then and there to write about fishing. My story was about a young girl and her father who went on a fishing adventure up to Allagash, the largest town in Maine. Having just finished studying about the Lewis and Clark expedition and how others traveled across America to settle the new lands, I set the story in the pioneer days. I would describe the wonders of the Allagash with its beautiful lakes and streams, the fish, moose, and all of the other elements that made it one of the best towns in the state then and now.

That night, I told Daddy about the contest and what I was going to write about. He looked at me and wrinkled his brow as I continued, "What do you think they used to fish with, Daddy?" I asked.

"Well, it's a cinch. They didn't have Penn reels back then." He chuckled. His Penn reels were his pride and joy. He continued, "Let's see. They either used hand lines, nets, or started to work with a pole with a line on the end." Although he never gave me much encouragement in my writing, this topic had him a little more interested.

After dinner, I sat at my typewriter and began my story. I asked Daddy every day for his help on the story and how he thought my characters would have lived. While he still wasn't enthusiastic, he did ask if he could read what I had written each day. Since we had never been to Allagash, I had to use my social studies book and the 1953 edition of the Encyclopedia Britannica, which in my mind was almost of the same era that I was writing about. Friday came, and my story was finished.

"Miss MacGregor, I have my story. Can you help me with it?" I said as I handed it to her.

"Of course, Ethel. I should have known that yours would be one of the first," she said as she placed it in her leather briefcase. "I'll have some work to do this weekend."

On Monday, she handed back the stories that she had reviewed over the weekend and reminded us the winner would be announced on Friday. It seemed like that was a lifetime away. But on Friday, at the end of our English class, Miss MacGregor stood tall in the front of the room and made her announcement.

"I am very proud to see that all of you have written stories for this contest. You have done a wonderful job," she said. "And now to read the top three." She peered over her glasses at us. "I'll read the winner's story last."

My friend Jackie Farnsworth and I looked at each other and crossed our fingers. The first story read was Jackie's. She was disappointed, but gave me a thumbs-up. As Miss MacGregor took the next story, I recognized the paper. She read my paper. Jackie and I looked at each other with looks that told our disillusionment with the contest. The winner was Sally Frenetti, but by the time her paper was being read, my eyes were staring out the window looking for something to focus on so my tears would be held back.

When I got home that day, I told Daddy that I didn't win.

"I'm sorry you didn't win. But now, maybe you'll settle down to regular studies and stop this stuff." He stated that with enough conviction that he believed it.

I ran out of the house down to Aunt Eleanor's. The screen door banged, announcing my arrival. I took my usual seat at the kitchen table, and she came over and plopped down one of her chocolate cupcakes in front of me. This was Aunt Eleanor's cure-all for anything from to a bee sting to the world coming to an end. We talked for a while about everyday nothings, and then I finally started to cry. She held me in her arms and let me cry myself out. She gave me a kiss and then sent me back home "like a good girl." It was enough to keep me going.

When I entered high school and boys began to call, Daddy began to worry. I was maturing. He was losing his fishing buddy, and he wasn't sure just how he was going to handle this. His worry usually showed up as an angry response to any request I had. Daddy seemed to worry most when there was any sniff of an indication that a boy was involved. If they came to the house, he never remembered their name, and if they called on the phone, I was never at home.

In my senior year of high school, the decision on what to do next was at hand. Employment opportunities were not plentiful, and if I wanted to be more than the "glaze application specialist" at Miss Ruthie's Bakery, then I needed a plan. Most of the boys in town were told that they needed a trade so that they would always have work. They would continue on to Salmon River Technical College to study automotive or electrical engineering or some type of construction trades. The girls who were their girlfriends were happy to have graduated suma-not-pregnant and spent most of their time helping their boyfriends with their homework and planning their weddings. A couple of my friends were going to college in Boston, and I suspected our friendships would fade over time.

I had been the editor of the high school newspaper and also the roving reporter at the football games and other school functions, and I had organized our yearbook. At our graduation ceremonies, I received a five-hundred-dollar award for all of my work on the school publications.

Armed with all of these accolades from my small-town life, I entered University of Maine with a major in journalism and communication. My father was still not sure what I was going to do with this writing thing once I got out of school. "How are you going to get a job writing in this town?" he would continue to say in a frustrated manner. His glasses were perched at the end of his nose, and his Chesterfield cigarette sent up plumes of smoke from the ashtray. That eternal question hung in the air like the smoke from his cigarette.

Days flew by. I asked myself. Where was I going to get a job in this town? Don't think I hadn't thought about that more than once. We had a local paper written, edited and published by one man, Caleb Johnson. His wife Sadie helped some, but her gift was in her cooking, so most of the papers had a bit of her weekly epicurean experiment. I had asked him during the summers if I could intern with him, but he was never too receptive about this. He always appeared very busy, cigar puffing away, typewriter tap, tap, tapping out a story. The largest the *Piney Bluffs Bugle* ever got was during graduation time when he would do a biography on each student who was graduating from high school. Then it ballooned from four pages to six. Sometimes he even included a picture of each senior.

So as graduation from UM neared, I was formulating a plan. Move, go someplace, anyplace, just not back to Piney Bluffs to wait to be asked on a date by one of the few remaining bachelors in town, or to settle for a job at the Trout Inn or, worse yet, the Bowl-o-rama.

3

On spring break before graduation, I went home to start to prepare Daddy for my future. I had two interviews the next week—one in Boston with the *Herald* and one in Providence at the *Journal*. They were interning positions, and most likely, if I got one of them, I would certainly be in need of other jobs to supplement the meager salary. I was convinced though that one of them would take me to the next step in my life, which clearly was out of Piney Bluffs.

I had rehearsed my lines for my conversation with Daddy. And I was ready to defend myself against any of his arguments as to why I should be staying. I could see the Chevy pickup turning into the driveway as I did my last minute touch-ups on the table. Momma's blue vase was centered on the table and held a few of the first daffodils that had made their way to springtime. I had made Daddy his favorite dinner—pan fried calico bass with a side of fiddleheads and fresh cut fries. To round out the meal, I had stopped at Miss Ruthie's Bakery and picked up a hearty wheat bread.

He came through the door and went through his ritual of hanging up his jacket and hat and putting his lunchbox on the counter. After that, he turned and was ready to greet me.

"Smells pretty good in here," he said and smiled at me. "Good to have you home." He gave me a hug and started for his seat at the table.

I took a deep breath, turned to look at him, and just as I was about to start, he announced, "Caleb's looking for some help, you know."

16

"Really," I said, "did he place an ad in his paper?" I didn't mean for it to be snippy, but that was what came out.

"Don't get so smart with me, young lady," Daddy replied.

Almost twenty-one and I instantly became ten again.

"Sorry, Daddy," I said. *Take your time*, I reminded myself. *Don't get his back up before you begin.*

"You might think about going and chatting with him," he said without looking up at me.

Oh, why did this happen now? With the two interviews coming up, I was going to get Piney Bluffs out of my mind. This would be where later on in my life I would bring my children. They would visit with their Granddaddy, and he would show them the beauty of life here. He would teach then to fish and all those wonderful things that grandparents do for their grandchildren. But that would be after my new wonderful life wherever the hell it was going to be. But that would not happen if I stayed here. I had to leave, and it had to be now.

My mind raced to imagine what *The Bugle* could hold for me. Whatever could Caleb pay, or what could the job be? Collating two pieces of paper a hundred times? Making sure that Sadie didn't handle the papers in the middle of one of her adventures in cooking? No, this was not going to work; this was not going to be the anchor that was thrown out of my ship that was just beginning to fill its sails with a new wind. I was packed and ready for this solo journey, my ticket paid for, I was just about to put my foot onboard.

"I told him you'd be down tomorrow morning, 9:00 sharp," Daddy continued.

"You what? Daddy, I have some plans. I want to tell you all about them," I started.

"What kind of plans? I get a job all lined up for you, and you, you...you're not leaving, are you?" he questioned. He seemed hurt. For him that was the only path that I should take.

"Actually, I have interviews in Boston and Providence," I replied

"Boston and Providence, now that's just grand, ain't it? You can't do any fishing in those towns, you know.," He was hurt now.

"Daddy, you know I always wanted to write, and I don't think it can happen here," I said, trying to make him remember. From grammar school to now, that had always been my desires. Whether he saw them or chose to ignore them, they were never far away from the surface.

"Well, where the hell was I when that conversation happened? And just what's wrong with here?" His cigarette bobbed up and down in his mouth as the ashes fell like snowflakes onto the dinner table. As he stared at me, he looked like a man who momentarily had no recollection of who I was. I could see that his memory of the past twenty-one years held no highlights of my writing abilities.

"Okay, I'll go talk to Caleb tomorrow morning, but I'm not promising anything," not wanting to make this evening into a total fiasco, I gave in, as any good daughter would do.

"That's my girl. You'll see, something good will be waiting for you." Daddy had decided it was all going to be good, so in his mind, this topic was closed. "Now let's eat," and that was the end of the conversation for now. Dinner tasted good, albeit a tad cool. Daddy talked to me about who was doing what around town and how everyone had made it through another winter. Outside of ice fishing derbies and tournaments, Piney Bluffs saw little activity during those months. Spring and the opening day of fishing season was only a month away, and the town was beginning to prepare for its annual rebirth.

The next morning, I got up early, dressed in my favorite jeans, threw on a turtleneck, and pulled my Bean jacket from its peg. It was Saturday, and Daddy always slept in a bit on the weekends. So I made Daddy my special fish breakfast sandwich with a side of potatoes and onions and put it in the oven on warm. I left him a note to tell him I loved him and was out of the house by 7:00 a.m. I now had two hours to prepare for my conversation with Caleb. What was I going to say? It would come to me. I was a writer, and I just needed to speak as well as I wrote. The morning chill hit my face, and I knew that one stop before seeing Caleb was going to be at Miss Ruthie's Bakery. Her coffee would warm me up and settle things in place for me, and then I would be ready.

We lived next to Lewis' General Store, and Pappy Lewis was setting out the displays on the porch as I walked by. Pappy was a tall thin man. His wisps of gray hair sprouted from the left side of his head, and he was still attempting to fashion a comb over. His white apron was fresh and starched every day thanks to Ma Lewis, and he wore that over his favorite faded Beans canvas shirt. He also wore their boots. Rumor had it that he first bought that pair when he was thirty and had them resoled every so often just to keep them honest with their lifetime guarantee.

Pappy called out to me, "Good to see you back in town, Ethel. Your daddy has been missing you something fierce. Hear you're going to be working with Caleb."

What had Daddy done? How was it that everyone had decided my fate without me being a part of the equation?

"Hi, Pappy," I responded. "You just never know what might happen with me. Don't be too quick to count on me as a member of the Chamber of Commerce quite yet." Not wanting to discuss my future with Pappy, I continued down the street to the main circle of downtown. Even this conversation would take on a life of its own. By 8:00 a.m., when the store opened, there was no telling what folks would spin out of my reply. Probably that I was going to take over the Chamber of Commerce.

As I continued toward the bakery, my walk took me past the church. The crocuses around the front steps were the only things that were present to greet me or any other passerby. The quiet gave me a bit more time to collect my thoughts about how I would politely listen to Caleb. I had it figured that this interview should take about a half hour. After that, I could be on my way to visit with my friend Jackie and tell her about my plans for my interviews and my life away from here.

I was startled by the sound of a lone crow. He was sitting on the wrought iron fence at the entrance to the church cemetery. His gaze seemed to be directly at me. He continued to caw as I continued to walk. While I wasn't superstitious, this crow was making me feel like he had an opinion about my thoughts. It seemed that everyone in town had an opinion about my life.

4

I crossed over the town green and walked into Miss Ruthie's Bakery. The blue-and-white gingham checked tables were almost full. The familiar aromas told me that the morning coffee was brewing and the latest of sweet something fresh from the ovens were about to be placed in the glass cases and on dessert pedestals.

She opened daily at 6:00 a.m. and closed at 3:00 p.m. or whenever the day's baking had sold out. I had worked for Miss Ruthie ever since seventh grade, first starting out just sweeping and washing the pots and pans. My senior year in high school was my last year working with her. She had affectionately promoted me to glaze application specialist, certain that with that on my resume, I would always be able to find a job. She made the best of everything from breads to pastries and even wedding cakes. My youngest cousin Ellen had taken my place when I entered college and now worked for Miss Ruthie after school and on the weekends. She gave me a nod of her head as she poured coffee for folks that had just come in.

Miss Ruthie came from behind the counter to give me a big hug and kiss. She was a sizable woman—a by-product of her baking talents—with bright blue eyes and once blonde now graying hair done up in a bun. A pencil through the bun was always handy to make out your slip or take a special order for the next day. She always smelled like cinnamon and warm bread. She wiped her hands on her floury apron and stood back to look at me all the while trying to shoo the bakery cat, Sugar, from her feet.

"It is so good to see you, honey. Your daddy says you're going to be staying in town after graduation." She said, trying to read my face for the reaction to determine whether it was true or not.

The others in the shop, Big Bob and his sister Beulah, turned around to see too. They nodded my way and said their good mornins', and out the door they went. Ooh, small towns, what I wouldn't do to be anonymous right about now.

"That's what I hear too," I said, smiling and shaking my head.

After Beulah and Bob left, Miss Ruthie and I sat at the small table and chair set that was reserved for the help. She cleared away yesterday's paper and put her puffy hands on the table and said, "So let's talk."

Having known her for more than half of my life, she knew my dreams and the goals I had talked about for all those years working at her side.

"Daddy has this all figured out, or so he thinks. I have interviews lined up in Boston and Providence. And I can't make him understand that I need to leave. What can Caleb offer me? If I don't leave now, what will happen? I have some real talent, but Daddy can't see it." I spilled out my fears, and she took my hands in hers.

"Your daddy is scared he'll lose you, honey. He wants you safe and near him. You can't blame a daddy for that. Since your momma passed, you've been the one bright spot in his life. I can't offer you the right decision. You need to make that yourself." She looked at me with those blue eyes, searching for an acknowledgment of understanding.

"But here is his life. *My* life is just beginning out there. I can't have it begin and end in the same spot. It's just not the way it's supposed to happen." I was close to tears but held them back.

"Let me get you a coffee, honey," she said as she got up.

I drank my black coffee, and we were silent for a moment.

"I just know there is something special that I'm supposed to do. I can feel it. Like when we're fishing and you know that trout is just hiding under that overhang and bang you get him." I slapped my hands on the table to emphasize my frustration. "Why is this so difficult for him to see that this is just not right for me? I have to get out of here, or this feeling is going to die." The loudness of my voice attracted the attention of some of the other folks who took their time looking at me and then went back to their breakfast.

"Ethel, I have watched you grow into a very smart woman. You will find a way to have your something special." She reached out to give me a reassuring pat on my hands. And with that, we changed our conversation to talk about what was going on around town.

It was almost opening day of fishing season, and folks were getting anxious for what that meant to the town. With some of the best fishing waters in the state, the town looked forward, no, it depended on the extra revenue that outsiders brought in to our little town. With just over six hundred residents in town, our numbers swelled during each new fishing season. The spring meant the trout season began, and then as we eased into summer, the professional bass circuit started up. And then we finished the year with ice fishing. Miss Ruthie said the Trout Inn was booked for the opening weekend; and Big Bob's fishing camp was just about full. Tyrell's Vineyard was thinking of trying a new venture in room renting called "bed and breakfast." Folks stayed in one of the farmhouse rooms and were served a nice breakfast in the morning. Yes, the town was waking from its long winter's nap.

Dottie Brown, the postmistress, and Charlotte Lawrence, the town clerk, came in for their usual morning coffee and muffin special.

"What's the special today, Ruthie?" asked Dottie.

"Why it's a nut and berry surprise," Miss Ruthie said. "The surprise is that I was able to find the berries in the freezer at all!"

We all had a good laugh, and I said I must be going.

Dottie asked me, "So I imagine your mail will be staying with your daddy's address, Ethel?"

"Not so sure about that, Dottie. Why don't we wait a bit," I replied. Jeez, people were so ready for me to stay put.

"Take Caleb a muffin. Sadie still can't turn out a muffin that suits him." Miss Ruthie put a muffin in a bag for Caleb. I reached in my purse to pay her, and she shooed me away.

"Your money's no good here today, honey," she said. I gave her another hug; waved bye to Dottie, Charlotte, and my cousin Ellen;

and out the door I went, leaving the women to speculate about my next stop at *The Bugle* with Caleb.

From the street, I looked through the window. I could see Caleb already at his typewriter starting the day's stories. The paper was published for the afternoon, so there was always lots of time for things to happen before the final draft went to press at noontime. The old printing press that Caleb used printed two hundred copies daily. The paper was for sale at all of the local establishments. No one had ever asked for home delivery, as it seemed most folks came to town on a daily basis. If you missed coming to town, Caleb always had a few in reserve at the office and sold them for half price.

As I entered, Caleb glanced at his watch and looked at me over the top of his glasses.

"Well," he said, "I was wondering if you were going to show up."

I looked at my watch. It read 8:45.

"I was told my appointment was 9:00 a.m. Was I misinformed?" I wasn't going to let him get the best of me at the start. Although I didn't want to seem disrespectful, I wanted him to understand that I had a brain in my head.

"Your daddy said you were feisty." He smiled and then went back to his typing.

His cigar was lit and occupying an ashtray from the White Mountains. A man looking his late forties, Caleb was tall and thin, about six foot two with dark brown hair cut high and tight, making you wonder if there was military history in his background. He was dressed in a white dress shirt, cuffs rolled up twice, and a pair of tan chinos. His belt had a silver buckle with an inset of a fishhook. Deck shoes with no socks completed his look.

I continued to stand and looked around the office. Caleb sat at his desk that was an antique roll top with the pigeonholes stuffed with a range of items from more cigars to fishing lure packets and anything imaginable in-between. His chair was a wooden one on wheels. The padded leather seat seemed worn from years of sitting.

Over his desk was his diploma from Maine Maritime in a simple wood frame. Well, that would explain the haircut. The rest of the office was framed with pictures from various events around the town, office equipment, and a smaller desk with a typewriter, and lamp. To round out the office, a couple of old stuffed leather chairs flanked a coffee table. The table held a variety of past *Bugle* editions, as well as the *New York Times* and the *Boston Herald*. As I looked down at these, I saw that interestingly enough they were yesterday's editions. The smell of coffee came from somewhere in a back room off the main office.

I set the muffin on his desk. He acknowledged it and spoke again, "Get yourself a cup of coffee if you'd like."

"Thanks," I replied. "But I just finished one down at Miss Ruthie's."

"Have a seat," he said and motioned for me to sit. I chose the leather chair closest to his desk.

Then I waited for Caleb to finish his typing. He slid back in his chair and put his hands behind his neck.

"Ever have a vision, Ethel?" he started. This start threw me a bit; I wasn't expecting a philosophical conversation from him.

"A vision? For me?" I responded. I didn't know if this was part of the interview or if he really wanted to know my thoughts.

"I'm going to tell you a story, Ethel, if you'll indulge me a bit," Caleb said. I nodded to agree, and he began.

His story started with his graduation from Maine Maritime. His class was the first to graduate from the academy. It was 1945 and near the end of World War II. He and all of his classmates felt the pride of a country coming out victorious from this war. He had his mind set on being a captain of a commercial vessel doing trans-Atlantic runs. As he began the process for finding a ship, he was summoned back home to Boston. There had been an accident. While crossing the street, his father had died after being struck by a Massachusetts Transit Authority bus. In addition to this misfortune, Caleb now had his mother to care for. She had been institutionalized with a stroke during his freshman year in college. While still alive, she remained in fragile condition and was at the end of her life as well. With the financial burden of his mother's care and funeral expenses, Caleb soon realized that his career at sea was about to be put on hold. And as an only child, he was now facing life alone.

His father had worked for the *Boston Herald* as a reporter. When Caleb was younger, he would tag along with his father as he searched for the latest news stories. His father had been nicknamed Hook because his stories always had a hook to get you to read them. One year for Christmas to celebrate his nickname, his friends at the paper had given him a silver belt buckle with a fishhook in it. His father had taken a lot pride in his work and was deeply touched by their gift.

His father's coworkers had been fond of Caleb. And during the wake and funeral, they shared their stories of his father with him. The editor of the *Herald* also remembered Caleb. He asked him to stop by his office once he had things in order. Recognizing that young Caleb was now alone, he wanted to help the son of one of his best reporters.

Caleb stopped by the *Herald* to see what the editor had wanted with him. As he walked into the building, old memories came back to life. He remembered how he would sit and wait while his father wrote his stories and how he had listened to the other reporters sharing their stories with each other to get the right spin on them. He fielded a few waves from some familiar faces. As he was about to knock on Harry Fielding's door, Harry motioned him in. And he got right to the point.

"Caleb, I know the situation with the funeral and your mother and the bills that you are facing. I also want to advise you on your father's accident. Caleb, that accident was the fault of the driver, and the MTA should be held libel for its driver's actions. So I'd like to help you, if you'll let me." As Harry continued, he explained about the legal process and how it would lead to suing the MTA. Young Caleb felt his dreams were slipping away as one more thing was standing at the head of the line of his career.

"As for employment, I know you have just graduated from college, and although your focus was on maritime activities, I have to be honest, I need a reporter to fill your father's shoes." Harry looked at Caleb to see how he was digesting all of this information

"I don't know, I'm not really cut out for reporting," Caleb started to say.

But Harry continued with his advice and the offer of a salary, "Caleb, this damn war is ending, and soon, thousands of GIs will be returning to their hometowns, and jobs will be scarce. They will also have the war experience aboard ships, and that would put you in competition with seasoned sailors if you continue with the maritime route."

Caleb was looking at Harry with earnest appreciation as he continued.

"And second, there's the case that should be brought against the MTA. Now I've already been in contact with a seasoned attorney who should be able to bring this case to court swiftly leaving you with the funding to care for your mother. What do you say? Will you work for me?"

Caleb recognized what Harry was offering and made the decision right then and there to accept this man's help, telling himself this was only a short-term detour and his maritime career would continue if only a little later than he had expected.

So Caleb began covering his father's territory, the other reporters helping him along the way. Caleb surprised himself how he took to this abrupt change in course, but then that's what he had learned in Maine; how to change course but to still keep the same objective. The case against the MTA was won after several months of discovery and motions and testimony. All in all, it left Caleb with sufficient funding to care for his mother, to pay the remainder the household bills that had been accumulating, and to start a nest egg for himself. Six months after his father's accident, his mother blessedly passed away, leaving Caleb alone but now free to continue with his maritime career.

But as Harry had predicted, jobs were scarce, and what jobs there were had fierce competition. So he settled into reporting. He met Sadie while doing a story at a local hospital on a building project that would be the foundation for a veteran's home. She was working in public relations and was a pretty young thing with curly red hair and green eyes that sparkled. They sparkled the most for Caleb as he found himself finding more ways to speak with her for his story. The feeling was mutual, and Sadie invited him to visit her parents for dinner one day. Well, after that it was all over, Caleb was smitten. A wedding was planned within the year, and as 1947 began, Caleb found himself married living in Boston and being a reporter. None of these things had been in his plans, but he found that they seemed to make perfect sense to him. He had lost so many things since his graduation, and the job and his new wife brought him much comfort.

Before he knew it, fifteen years had passed, and Caleb was now the assistant editor for the *Herald*. He and Sadie had been unable to have children, so their lives were their own. She volunteered for many activities with the hospitals and churches, teaching, reading, and cooking for those in need. They vacationed all over New England but always felt most at home in Maine, loving the beautiful waters and the quirky people in the little towns that they visited. Caleb had managed his money well and began to feel it was time for a change. While vacationing in a small town, Piney Bluffs, he saw a building for sale. He and Sadie had spent time there in the past and had a more than a passing relationship with some of the folks in town. He learned that they had no daily paper, and he thought this might just be the change he needed. So he and Sadie sold their brownstone in Back Bay and moved into a farmhouse on the edge of town, and the *Daily Bugle* was born. The folks in town were happy to have a daily paper and so Caleb and Sadie settled into their new lives.

As he finished his story, Caleb again asked me the question, "Ever have a vision?"

I took some time to answer. What he had just shared with me was in some way a parallel to my own life.

"Yes, I have." But how did I tell him that my vision did not begin in Piney Bluffs?

"So go on. I let you in on my life. What are your plans?" He was not the least bit intimidating as I had once thought and actually seemed interested in me.

"Well," I began, "I want to write. I want to write things that people will remember, and I want to like doing it, but I don't want to do it here. I mean, while my writing began here and may end here, the middle cannot be here. No disrespect intended to you and the life that you have made and the success that you have found." There, it was out. I felt some relief in saying it out loud. Although I was not certain that the only person who recognized my writing and was trying to give me a job doing just that was going to understand my need to remove myself from this town.

"Not here, eh? I know exactly what you mean. Do you have any leads on jobs outside of Piney Bluffs?" Again he seemed to remember what it had been like for him.

"I have two, one in Boston and one in Providence. Both are technical writing jobs. Not much for creativity, but nonetheless, a beginning," I said trying to make them sound better than what they actually were. "But eventually, I want to write something that will make a difference," I continued

"A difference to whom?" he questioned.

I thought for a moment. I had been so focused on being away from here that what I was to write about had taken a backseat. And now that someone had asked, and meant it, I was at a momentary loss.

"It needs to matter to me first," I began. "This country is in the middle of such an uproar. With Vietnam still going on and all of the political and civil unrest, why there are so many things that need to have a voice. And I mean to give a voice to those things that have taken a back to seat to the war and politics. We are such a powerful country, and we ignore the most precious things that are the future— our environment and our youth. Since I began college, I have said good-bye to classmates going off to war who have never returned. And you can't help but see how the greed to possess puts our natural resources at risk—land, sea, and animals. You name it, and we think everything is replaceable." I realized that Caleb was watching and listening to me the way no one had ever done. The more I thought about what I had just said, the more determined I was to leave this town. I couldn't do any of those things that I had just spoken of if I stayed here. How could I? And how could I tell Daddy that this was what had to happen? The question hung in the air in front of me like the smoke from Daddy's damn Chesterfield cigarette.

28

5

"Do you care about Piney Bluffs?" again, he was asking in earnest.

"Well, yes, I do," I answered honestly.

"If you will indulge me a second time," he asked.

"Of course."

"I have been following your writing all throughout school. And while you aren't at Pulitzer Prize level, you do have a unique style. And I like it." As he finished, he looked straight at me as he pulled a file from his desk and handed it to me. It was just about everything I had written—clippings and papers, college newspaper articles, and even some editorials.

I was stunned. To think that someone, someone in my town had followed me, had thought enough about my writing, had thought enough about me to know what I had written, I couldn't tell anyone what I felt at that moment.

"The day-to-day operations of *The Bugle* is one thing, and I would like some help with that, but I want you to be my partner," he stated.

"Caleb, what are you talking about?" I looked at him in disbelief, thinking, *Partner, partner in what?*

"I have an idea that will put Piney Bluffs on the map. Together, we can write something that no one will be able to resist. And we can have a circulation that will rival the *New York Times!*" He had a smile and a look in eyes that made me want to know more.

Again I asked, "Caleb, what are you talking about?"

And he began again. Since coming to Piney Bluffs, he had been involved in the town's activities, both economic and political. It was no secret that Piney Bluffs depended on fishing and all that it brought to the town for its livelihood. And the word of mouth that our annual visitors spread about us was wonderful, but it was simply not enough. The business owners in town had tried to market themselves to their previous year's clients but had no luck in luring new folks.

Big Bob and Big Bertha had even gone to regional sporting events to pass out fliers and talk to potential fishermen about Piney Bluffs. But slicker outfits seemed to attract the customers more than this larger-than-life brother-and-sister duo. They usually came back with few new clients and feeling disillusioned.

"So how can something we write make us more well-known?" I questioned him. If the two of us writing something was going to help Piney Bluffs continue, then I was more than mildly interested. I could help write something and be on my way in a few months or however long it took. How long could something like this take anyway?

"Ethel, what I have in mind will take on a life of its own. What I have in mind is going to take the goodness of this town and the beauty around it. To that, we will add a dash of humor and be unstoppable." He was absolutely beaming as he finished.

"But what is it?" I asked.

He pushed himself back from his desk, opened the drawer, and from it he pulled out a folder. I could see from where I sat that the tab read *Fishing Weekly*. He opened the folder and sorted through the various papers until he finally withdrew a single sheet. He looked at it and smiled.

"Here, read this." As he handed it to me, I sat back in the chair and began to read. The page was on newsprint and had the title *Fishing Weekly*. The font style gave it an old-fashioned feel. It was about Piney Bluffs, but the reporting was written by someone I had never heard of. There was a column by Caleb as the editor, and as he said, there was a bit of humor in it. I chuckled to myself a couple of times as I read one of the fishing stories. As I finished, he looked at me for my reaction.

"Well? What do you think?" I said.

"I like it. There's a couple of spots that could be tightened up a bit, but it's funny. Still, I don't see how this is going to save the town, Caleb." Even more so, I wasn't sure this was going to be worth my giving up on the chances in Boston or Providence.

"As we go along, we'll expand on our story and build circulation." He was smiling and looking for my agreement.

"I appreciate the offer, but—" I started to explain my way out of this.

"But you don't think this is for you?" Caleb finished for me.

Here was my first actual job offer from someone who had taken the time to know what I wrote and what I wanted from a career, and I was turning it down.

"Again, I don't want you to think that I'm ungrateful, but I need to know if I have what it takes to make it outside of Piney Bluffs. And if I don't take this chance now, I don't think there will ever be another." As I finished, I looked at him with mixed emotion. But he knew.

"Ethel, you know by now I was exactly where you were at your age. But I didn't have the chance to make the decision. Life made it for me. I'll be here. Piney Bluffs will be here too. But don't wait too long," as Caleb was finishing, the look in his eyes was all-knowing. I wasn't sure if he was somehow wishing that I would take that chance to leave, taking it almost for him as well as for myself.

We talked for a little while more about Boston and Providence. He gave me the name of some contacts that still might be at the *Herald* and told me to keep in touch. He let me know he would be watching, and he would wait.

I stood up to go and realized we had been talking for two hours. I apologized for taking so much of his time, realizing that he would need to put *The Bugle* to print within the hour.

"Well, if you'd like to stay and help me with the printing, then I will almost be on time with today's edition," saying this, he let me know he truly would like me to know *The Bugle's* business.

I took off my jacket and put on the apron, and we walked to the backroom that held the printing press. I had become familiar with presses in college, and while this was an older model, its operation was basic. We set things up, filled the ink-and-paper areas, and the *Daily Bugle* was going to press on time. As the papers finished, I helped bundle them for the general store and the diner. Besides *The Bugle* office, those were the two biggest outlets for the paper.

"Good luck to you, Ethel," Caleb said as he shook my hand. "And thanks for the help."

"Thank you for the interview and your insight. My hardest part now is going to be telling my Daddy," I said as I was leaving.

Caleb nodded in agreement and waved good-bye as I left. I knew I was making the right decision; I just had to convince Daddy of that. Daddy had gone with uncle Eubie to check out some new fishing spots in Snowshoe Falls. So I had the afternoon to prepare my answers to what I knew were going to be the hardest questions I had ever been asked.

Once I got home, I passed the time making an apple pie. Aunt Eleanor had taught me how to make a tasty flaky crust and just the right amount of lemon, sugar, and cinnamon would hopefully take the edge off our conversation. While the pie was baking, I went from room to room straightening things here and there. I reminded myself that I needed to wash the curtains and air out the blankets when I returned after the semester was over. Daddy kept himself neat with very little out of place while I was gone. Most nights after dinner, he read *The Bugle* and then watched a little television and was in bed by nine. Weekends, he got together with my uncles for some fishing or conversation. A simple, quiet life but one that he found comfort in.

For dinner, I was going to make a fish chowder to take the chill off this March afternoon. I had stopped back at Miss Ruthie's and picked up some rolls to go along with the soup. She knew not to ask too many questions when she saw me. And I told her I would drop by before going back to school.

When the chowder was together and on a low simmer, I sat down in my favorite chair in the sun porch and looked out the to the back yard and beyond. The sound of Daddy's old Chevy truck startled me, and I realized I had fallen asleep while waiting. The bang of the door closing announced his arrival in the house.

"Ethel? You home?" he called out.

"In here, Daddy," I answered.

"Smells mighty good, girl. I see you haven't forgot how to cook." His comments were never really a compliment but more a reminder of what was important to him.

He came into the sun porch and took a seat across from me. Next to his chair, he had the table and lamp with his array of past *Bugle* editions as well as some favorite fishing magazines and catalogs. A pack of Chesterfields, a book of matches, and ashtray completed his area of the room. He set the mail on the table.

"So how did your interview go? When do you start? You know, you won't make that much to start with, but you can live here so you won't need to worry about a roof over your head. I know eventually you'll want your own place, but—" He was stating what he had decided in his own mind and was just making sure I understood.

"I turned it down, Daddy," I said quietly.

"You what?" he asked, a little astonished.

"I said I turned Caleb down." I tried to look him in the eye when I said this, but I had to look away and out the window. "I have two interviews, and I know one of them will take me and—"

He quickly cut me off, "What in the hell are you going to do in those cities? What do you know about working for some big newspaper? They're going chew you up and spit you out like a large mouth spitting out an unset hook. Good God, girl, have you lost your senses?" He started to go through the mail but then threw it down, scattering it all over the floor. He was mad, and his cheeks flushed red with anger.

"Daddy, I can do this. I've been preparing for it. I know it's going to be hard at first, but I have to go. Momma would have understood. She'd have been happy I was following a dream. You don't know what it's like. You chose to be here. I'm trapped in this small town with no way out unless I do this now!" I was getting louder as my emotions were mounting. I stood to go into the kitchen to get away from his anger. I didn't want to hurt him, but I knew he wasn't going to like it no matter how I spoke.

"You leave your Momma out of this. You have no idea about what she would have wanted for you. And trapped here, are you? Well, I guess I didn't notice how we had tied you up and put those lead sinkers around your ankles to make you stay. Go then. Get the hell out if that's the way you see it. You're going to find that family and life here is what's important in the end. Not that it seems very important to you. You're all set to throw that overboard." With that, he picked up his cigarettes and matches and went outside on the back porch to have a smoke.

That was his way of ending our conversation. Whatever else I was going to say would have no purpose now. I had lost my appetite, and I just needed to be out of the house. So I put on my jacket. Before I headed out, I went to the back door. Daddy had his back to me.

"I'm going to see Jackie. Dinner's on the stove," I said, not expecting him to respond. He grunted an acknowledgment and coughed a little.

As I closed the door behind me, tears were stinging my eyes. I couldn't remember when Daddy and I had ever had a conversation like that. But I knew I was right; I had to go.

Once I arrived at the inn, my best friend and I went into the tavern and took our seat by the window. I told her everything that had happened, and the tears started to fall as I ended with my conversation with Daddy. She took my hand and held it. We were such good friends; she knew how I felt about leaving and why it was so important. She then told me she had news that would cheer me up. She was going to get married to Andy Jr. of Andy's Diner. And the wedding was going to be in a month.

"A month! How wonderful! Oh, you're not, uh, are you?" I didn't want to say pregnant, never knowing who was within earshot.

"No, silly, we have been planning for months, and it just so happens it's going to be the night before opening day. So we'll have lots of friends and family returning to town for both events," she chided me for thinking otherwise. True to our town, the owners of the inn, her parents and the diner, Andy's parents, couldn't let one of the biggest events be outdone by the wedding.

"And I want you to be my maid of honor. Will you? I already have your dress." She looked at me with hopes I wouldn't say no.

"Of course, I will, I would be mad if you asked anyone else." We stood and hugged each other, and my tears of sadness turned to tears of joy for my friend. Because of her family's business, Jackie's future was set. Her two years at community college in business was all she needed to continue to operate the inn. And now with her marriage to Andy, both businesses would be able to continue for the next generation of fishermen, not to mention people in town.

I stayed for a while longer, and we continued to talk and make preparations. She had everything just about planned. Knowing that I was away at school, her mother had planned the shower for next week that would be here at the inn. The wedding as well would be here, 6:00 p.m. by candlelight. I went up to Jackie's room and tried on my dress. It was a simple long sheath of navy blue, and it fit perfectly. I joked, asking if I could wear my sneakers and then promised that I had a decent pair of pumps to go with the dress. About 8:30, I said my good-byes, put my coat on, and made the short walk home.

Daddy had already gone to bed. I finished cleaning up and then went to sit in the sun porch. Just as I was about to sit, I heard a noise at the door. I looked out and saw what looked like a rather skinny cat. I opened the door and went out to sit on the step. The orange tiger-striped cat shied away when I first came out, but once I was seated, it came right over to me. I put my hand out to pet it, and the sound of purring filled the stillness of the night. It was hard to tell just how old it was and why this sad creature had found its way to our step. I got up and went inside to get some leftover fish and a saucer of milk. The cat immediately devoured the food. When it was finished, it showed its appreciation by nuzzling my hand and purring more loudly. Knowing that Daddy would not take to a stray animal, I picked up the dishes and gave the cat one more stroke and went into the house. The cat curled up in the corner of the back step and settled into what looked like a long needed restful sleep.

As I went upstairs to my room, I was hoping that like that cat I could settle into a restful sleep. I hoped that tomorrow, Daddy and I would be able to talk more reasonably about my leaving. I watched the stars for what seemed like an eternity, and then finally, sleep came. Just before I fell asleep, I thought I heard Daddy say, "G'night, Ethel," as he always had, but I couldn't be sure.

6

The next morning, I woke to the smell of coffee and bacon. I dressed and hurried down the stairs to the kitchen. Daddy's back was to me, but he had heard me.

"Get yourself a coffee, if it's not *trapping* you into staying." He was hurt, and his tone told me so. But he was also gruff when he wanted to be, and today, I was seeing that too. "And you can figure out a way to get that cat the hell out of here." As he finished, he pointed with his spatula toward the sun porch, and there was the cat. It was sitting at the door as if this was its normal thing to do. As I walked toward the door, the cat lifted its front paw as if to say hello.

"Daddy, look at it. It's so sad, and I'm sure once we clean it up and have it checked out, it will be a great companion for us," I was trying to convince him. Plus it had been a long time since we'd had an animal in the house. Our last cat, Minnow, went out during a winter storm when I first started college and never came back.

"I'm not looking after no damn cat. And what's this companion for *us*? You have a change of heart overnight and see the error of you ways, girl?" He was not letting up on anything.

"Okay, Daddy, it would be a good companion for *you*," I said as I made my way to the door to let it in. Whether it was a good meal or a night in a secure spot, the cat looked 100 percent better than it had last night. I picked it up and cradled it in my arms. I wanted to check to see what's it name was going to be.

"Great, Daddy, it's a male. We can call him Mr. Striper after the striped bass. And he won't have kittens, so we won't have to worry."

Getting him checked out would be a while. The only veterinarian was in Oxford, and that was about ten miles away. I would have to get the number before I went back to school and make an appointment for next week. I would be home for Jackie's shower, so I would have time.

As I walked with him in my arms into the kitchen, Daddy glared at me. To the cat, however, Daddy reached his hand out and scratched him behind his ears. Mr. Striper reached his paw out and gave Daddy's hand a lick.

"See, he likes you," I tried again to sound convincing.

"Likes me my foot. I've been cooking a damn pound of bacon. He'd be stupid not to like me. Now get that thing away from the table. Breakfast is just about ready," he scolded me.

I put Mr. Striper down, and he twined himself around Daddy's legs. Daddy gave him a little kick to get him out of the way, but Mr. Striper was not to be discouraged. He followed Daddy to the table and sat next to his chair. Daddy looked down at him and shook his head. Sunday breakfast had always been Daddy's meal to make. Sometimes, it was pancakes and sausage, but today, it was bacon and eggs. The rolls for yesterday's chowder did well in place of toast. We ate in silence for a bit, both of us glancing down at the cat from time to time.

"Thanks, Daddy, that was good. I was hungry. I'll go down to Pappy's and get some litter after breakfast. I think we still have Minnow's things, so we won't need to get a lot of new things," I said, leaving no room for any more discussion. I had made Mr. Striper an official member of the family.

"Well, look at Miss Too Good for This Town. Making decisions like she was in charge of the world," he commented, more to Mr. Striper than to me. "So when are these interviews you been spouting about? How you going get there? Or is that something else I don't know about, you having a car?"

"The interviews are this Friday and next Friday. First one is Boston at the *Herald*. Caleb used to be the assistant editor there." I was trying, but Daddy's face was set on disapproval. "And I've got a ride to Boston from one of my friends at school who lives in

Cambridge. We going to her home on Thursday night, and my interview is at 10:00 a.m. Friday morning. I'll take the T in."

"And how you getting' back here for Saturday?" he asked. While I had taken the Greyhound that stopped at the diner for the past four years back and forth to college, Daddy seemed to forget that when it suited him.

"I got a ticket for the 2:15 Greyhound out of Back Bay. Should be home in time to make your dinner, if you haven't taught Mr. Striper to cook by then." I was trying to get Daddy to lighten up. It seemed to be working. I caught the edges of his mouth starting to curve upward.

"Maybe *I'll* cook a little striper for your dinner on Friday," he was trying to make a little joke. With that, Mr. Striper jumped up into Daddy's lap and settled himself down. We both started to laugh.

"I don't think he's going to let you, Daddy." There, we were all set again. "Oh, I didn't tell you the good news. Jackie is getting married," I continued as I got up to clear the table.

"Yep, already knew that. Invitation was in the mail a couple of weeks ago," Daddy said it like it was the Benny's circular that had come and not my best friend's wedding invitation.

"Where is it?" I asked him.

"Over near your things," he replied. Since I was little, we had made two spots in the house for our individual things. Daddy's was the sun porch on his table, and mine was at the kitchen table in a basket that had been Momma's. I hurried over and searched through all of the mail.

"You didn't even open it," I said as I ripped into it. It was a creamy white paper, simple with black lettering. The response card deadline was Monday. I quickly filled it in and sealed it.

"How many did you put down?" Daddy asked.

"Well, two, of course, you and me. I'm going to be the maid of honor, but it's still going to be two, unless you're going to bring the cat." I was wondering what was up with his comment.

"Well, I don't know if I'm going. The first day of fishing season is the next day, and I don't want to be out of sorts. I have my reputation to uphold, you know," Daddy said.

"Daddy, you have to go. Jackie's my best friend, and you'll be fine for fishing. You've never lost once, so what makes you think all of a sudden you'll lose?" I should have known he would try to get out of this. He was not comfortable in social settings that didn't have a rod and reel as part of his attire. And the annual contest between Daddy and my uncles was legendary. At least in our family it was. He had gotten the big three for as long as I could remember. First fish, biggest fish, and most fish. "You'll be fine, you'll know everyone there."

"I don't think I have anything to wear. Can't go looking like this. Don't want to embarrass Miss Too Good for This Town." He was not giving up.

"Daddy, cut the crap. We'll go today to Sears in Lewiston, and you'll be the handsomest man there." I was not letting him off the hook and that was that.

So off we went shopping for Daddy. He was easy to shop for. Had no idea what was appropriate, so between the saleslady Irma and myself, we outfitted him in less than a half hour.

"All that money for one night. I could use that money to buy a new rod and maybe some new lures," he said with a grin to Irma. She was an older woman who had been on her feet for longer than she should have in her life, and she chuckled at the two of us.

"You better watch out," she said to me. "He's quite the catch with that new suit. Won't be long for there's another wedding." And she impishly smiled at Daddy who immediately flushed as he ushered me out of the store.

On the way home, we did a quick stop at Pappy's for food and litter for the cat and a few more staples for us. By the time we got home, it was almost time for me to head to the diner to catch the bus. I went to look for Mr. Striper, and there he was curled up in Daddy's chair. It was like he had always been with us. I gave Daddy a quick kiss good-bye and headed out the door.

"I have something for you," he said and handed me an envelope with my name on it but in an unfamiliar handwriting. "I've been waiting for the right time to give this to you, and now seems to be it. Don't open it until you're on the bus."

I gathered my things and walked quickly across the green. I could see the bus coming down the road, but I knew it would wait. Over the four years of college, the various drivers came to know me, so I knew they wouldn't leave without me. I climbed the stairs to the bus and said hello to Jim. I found my seat and looked out the window at Piney Bluffs. The sun was starting to set as the bus took off. As Piney Bluffs became a spot in the distance, I turned my attention to the envelope. I opened it and read yet another envelope inside. I held my breath as I read the words, "To my daughter Ethel. Love from your momma."

7

I waited a moment to open the envelope. My fingers touched my name and her name. I held my breath for what seemed like an hour. And then as the light was beginning to dim, I opened the envelope.

April 20, 1950

To my dear daughter Ethel,

I don't know when you'll be reading this letter. I told your Daddy to wait until the time was right. So I can only imagine you must be at a time in your life for a decision that only you can make. I know a lot about that. My decision for you was made many months ago. Some people told me I was selfish. I wanted to have a baby, wanted to have you. The doctors told me no, that it wouldn't end well for me. But I had to take that chance. I told them it wouldn't happen to me. But as we both know, that was not true.

Your daddy was a good man, and we were so very much in love. I want to tell you how sorry I am for what I have done to the both of you. I know that his life and yours haven't been easy. I only hope the two of you have made your way the best that you can with family and friends. There are so many things that I will never be able to know. Have you graduated from high school or college? Have you ever been in love? Are you married? Do you have children? Are you happy?

As you lie here in my arms, I am so happy to hold you and kiss you. Your dark-brown eyes look into mine, and for this moment, nothing can come between us. I know in my heart of hearts that this was the right thing to do.

My wish and dream for you is to be the kind of woman that will make you proud of you. Life changes every day, and you will never be sure of your decisions until the end.

So, my dear sweet Ethel, whatever time in your life has come to pass, let your heart help you. I wish I could have been with you.

Love forever,

Momma

Tears streamed down my cheeks as I read the letter again and again until there was no longer any light to read by. I put my head back and closed my eyes and fell asleep.

8

The trip to Cambridge on Thursday went quickly. Betsy had given a ride to three other friends from school who were being dropped off just outside of Boston. All of us were seniors, and conversations ranged from job opportunities to marriage. One of the guys was in ROTC, but getting married before his actual enlistment. Thankfully, the Vietnam war was almost over, so the promise of peacetime duty meant a weight off our minds for him. When we arrived at Betsy's home, we found a note from her parents saying they had gone to the Cape for the weekend, but there was plenty of food in the fridge and to help ourselves. While we were feasting on non-college food, the phone rang. It was Betsy's boyfriend who was also home for the weekend. He was asking her out, and she motioned for me if I wanted to go too. I shooed her hand away. I had to be prepared for tomorrow morning and didn't want to jeopardize my chances by a late-night out. Besides, if the job came through, there would be many chances for a night out in Boston in my future.

By myself for the rest of the night, I opened my portfolio. I had sent a copy to both papers so they would be able to review my work ahead of time. I had carefully prepared some of my best writings along with recommendation letters from professors. I also had one from Caleb. In addition, he had provided me with a list of contacts that might still be at the *Herald*. After reviewing them I took out the letter from Momma and read it again. Her words that I had to be proud of myself echoed in my mind. I had always looked to others for approval, but now I realized I had to believe in myself first. I thought about what life would have been like for Daddy and me if she had still been with us. Her words seemed so wise to me.

I must have dozed off because the next thing I knew Betsy was shaking me awake. It was 7:00 a.m. and I had an interview in two hours. I showered, did a quick make-up and hair once over and then dressed in my suit and heels. I hurriedly packed. I was going to catch the bus after the interview and wouldn't have time to return to Betsy's house. Betsy went with me and we grabbed a coffee on the way. After several T changes we finally arrived at the *Herald*. Standing in the shadows of the Old State House I was overwhelmed by the history of Boston. Seeing me take in a deep breath and hesitate just slightly, Betsy gave me a hug and wished me good luck. I went in.

The guard at the desk gave me directions to the fourth floor. This was where I was to meet with Robert Hurley who was the assistant editor. I had thought that I would be meeting with someone from the technical writing department, but last week I had received a follow-up letter about the change. I hoped this change was a good sign.

I rode the elevator alone to the fourth floor rehearsing how I was going to present myself and the answers that I would give. The car stopped, and I stepped off toward the only door labeled Newsroom. I opened the door and paused a moment to take it all in. The clack of the typewriters, the ringing of the phones, and the din of low conversations had me looking wide-eyed at the workings of the newsroom. The papers I worked on in college didn't come close to what I was now seeing. I caught myself and tried not to stare as I found my way to an office and knocked on the open door.

"You must be Miss Koontz. Please have a seat." Not getting up, he motioned to a chair across from him in front of his desk. His office was somewhat like Caleb's. He had the roll top desk and the typewriter on an ell next to it. The cigar was replaced with cigarettes, and a roll of Tums completed his work area. Several stacks of copy lay waiting for the red marks of the final edit. The walls were framed with headline articles from the *Herald*, which I quickly noted had his name for the byline. He was a large balding man, sleeves rolled up, tie loosened around his neck, a red pencil behind his ear, and a cigarette in his hand. His suit jacket hung on a coat tree near his desk. On his feet, he wore stretched-out slippers. Seeing me glance at them, he responded with, "Bad feet, I give them a break every chance I get."

I nodded and said, "Please call me Ethel." I was a little nervous. This wasn't like my interview with Caleb where I hadn't wanted the job. This was for real, and I had to make this count. Over the next hour, Bob and I talked about journalism and newspapers. He inquired about all types of things that I had written when I was younger and what I thought was my most important piece to date. I told him I thought the article I written for my college paper on ecology and the respect for nature and our future was the one.

"I read that, and I've reviewed the rest of your portfolio. You have some nice work here, young lady. And I also noticed the note from Caleb. How is he doing?" He smiled at me as he mentioned Caleb's name. "I was a young reporter when Caleb was the assistant. I always admired him and his style."

"Well, he's doing just fine," I replied. "He brought a newspaper to our town. He offered me a job with him last week." I hadn't wanted to say this originally but thought it would be good for him to know I had another offer.

"But you came here anyway," he said.

"Yes, sir, I want to prove myself outside of my hometown. That is what I went to school for. Journalism is my life, and I know I can make you believe in my work." I hoped that he heard the commitment in what I had just said.

"Well, Ethel, I have to tell you that the job you applied for has already been filled. That's why you're talking to me. We do have another opening in our sports section. It's not reporting. It's just proofing, not quite copyediting. It's part-time. Thirty hours a week. Salary is nine thousand dollars a year. What do you think?" He looked at me, not sure of how I was taking this information.

"What exactly would that job entail?" I asked, thinking of the possibilities this could present. Proofing was very important; it made the reporter's piece a thing of excellence or something that would never make the cut.

"We have one sports reporter and one of our social reporters who gives him whatever help he can. So the job would be a huge help to him. The job would be all about the details of his writings," Mr. Hurley said and leaned forward a bit as he tried to get a read on my face.

I thought for a moment. It sounded better than technical writing, but it was only part-time. I hadn't even thought about where I was going to live. Would a part-time salary be enough? And sports, well, that wasn't such a stretch. I did know all the Boston teams, and I had played team sports, so it wasn't totally out of my realm of knowledge. But this was the *Boston Herald*, and who knew what could happen, look at what happened to Caleb. His dream was replaced by a sobering reality, a reality that had led him here and to the future that he had made. My mind raced. Were there other questions I should be asking, but I drew a blank.

"Do you need some time to think this over? I know this is not what you came for, but I think you would work in well." He could see I was wrestling with this change. "Most people your age have high hopes for that dream job, but I tell you, not many of those jobs exist. If you take this job, it can be your first step on your journey to that place.

Those words held more insight than I had expected would come from him. I had to take the chance, and I had to take it now.

"Mr. Hurley, I'll take it," I said with that nervous enthusiasm that only happens on your first job.

"Welcome to the *Herald*, Ethel, and call me Bob." And he extended his hand to me to confirm the decision. "Alice, will show you down to HR, and they can finalize all of your paperwork. Let's see, your graduation is on the twelfth, so we'll see you on the Monday morning of the fourteenth. We start at 7:00 a.m. You'll be working for Mike O'Brien. Stop by and see him before you leave to introduce yourself."

"Thank you, Mr. Hurley, uh, Bob. You won't be disappointed," I said and walked out of his office to find Alice and into the world of the *Herald*.

Alice was Bob's secretary and, as I would learn, was the treasure of the newsroom. Nothing happened at the *Herald* that she didn't know about. She put me at ease and welcomed me to the fold. As we walked through the newsroom, she let me stop to introduce myself to Mike.

The sports desk area was in the back corner of the main reporting area. Mike's desk was in the corner facing out, so he had a view of the entire newsroom. There were three other desks in the department, at the moment unoccupied, but piled with papers.

Mike had a Red Sox cap on with tufts of red hair sticking out from under it. He had an athletic build and looked in his midthirties. He was dressed in slacks and a dress shirt with a tie that had remnants of some recent meal. His coffee cup had the Celtics logo on it with many days' worth of coffee drips down the side. His desk was piled with stacks of papers held in place with various baseballs. He was on the phone and tapping his pencil. Whoever was on the other end of the line was irritating him.

"Yeah, yeah, just get the rest of the interview done by this afternoon. I don't care if Yaz is sick. This story has got to be ready for Sunday's edition. Opening day is only two weeks away, and I want full coverage on him," he said gruffly. As he hung up the phone, he looked up and noticed me. "Who are you?" he snapped.

"My name is Ethel Koontz, and Bob just hired me to do your proofing. I start on the fourteenth of May. I'm pleased to meet you, Mike." I hoped that by calling him Mike, he would lose his annoyance.

"You're who?" He looked past me at Alice. She gave him a nod that was to restore his memory as if to say, *You remember the job that was posted for a proofer?*

"Ethel, Bob just hired—" I tried to repeat myself to get the rest out, but he cut right in.

"Yeah, yeah, okay, Ethel you say. You know who Yaz is?" he asked me as if this question was the only one he would have asked at an interview. The pencil that had been tapping was now pointing at me.

"Ah, left fielder for the Sox?" I knew when I said it as a guess he wasn't going to like it.

"Well, yes or no, is he, or isn't he? You got to know this stuff, *Ethel.*" He was trying to get me to break at our first meeting. And the way he said *Ethel*, I knew eventually I'd have some kind of nickname if I were allowed to live past my first day with him as my boss.

"He is and is about to start his tenth year with the Sox," I answered this time with authority. I thanked God for those Saturday afternoons in the summer when Daddy and I watched the Sox in the coolness of the living room.

"Not bad for a kid. When are you starting?" He seemed to have some interest now that I had passed the first test. The pencil was back to tapping.

"Monday the fourteenth of May after I graduate," I told him, proud to tell someone I was going to be a graduate.

"Where from? Oh hell, never mind, I'll forget between now and then. Tell me when you come back." He was less annoyed and wanted to dismiss me to get on with his deadlines. "You got tickets for opening day?"

"No, I've never been to a live game, only watched them on channel 4," I said, somewhat embarrassed that I had never seen a professional ballgame.

"What the hell, never been to live game, and you're going to work for the sports desk at the *Herald*. Holy Mother Mary, what's this world coming to?" He was back to being annoyed.

"Well, I live in Maine, and we fish a lot more than we got to ball games," I said, trying to defend myself. I didn't even want to tell him that this was the first time I had been to Boston. That would have put him right over the edge.

"Well, here, take these." He had been rummaging through his desk drawer and pulled out two tickets. He shoved them toward me, and I took them.

"I can't accept—" I started to say.

"Turning down tickets to opening day? Holy Mother Mary, take the damn tickets, and I want you to write a two-hundred-word piece on what you saw. And when you come back, no suits. Makes us think you're out looking for another job. And you'll sit there." He looked at me again with a critical eye waiting for my response. The desk he pointed to seemed to have the highest piles of paper, no phone and one of the oldest Royal typewriters I had ever seen.

"Thanks, Mike. I'll see you then." I decided that the less said at this point, the better. I had my first assignment, and I wasn't even a reporter.

He picked up the phone and started to dial. His hand raised in what I hoped was a wave good-bye and not a wave to get out.

I turned and rejoined Alice who had been watching this exchange with some amusement.

"Don't worry, he's not always like that. Sometimes he's worse." She chuckled. "Come on, let's get you started."

With that, we went to HR where I signed all the appropriate forms and picked up my badge identifying me as PRESS. I was really overwhelmed by all of this. I had only walked in the door less than two hours ago, and now I was employed by the *Boston Herald*. Was this really what I should be doing? Should I have waited and gone to the interview in Providence? There really wasn't anyone to talk it over with. There was Daddy, but I knew what his opinion would be. He still didn't think I could make a *decent living*, as he was fond of saying. I was making my first major life decision, and the feeling of pride swelled within me. Momma's words were echoing in my head, *Let your heart help you*. I finally had a real job doing what I had always dreamed I would do.

"So what's your address here in Boston? You're not commuting from Maine, are you?" The girl in HR questioned me as she went through my papers. She looked about my age, had short blonde hair, and was dressed in a wool jumper and turtleneck.

"I don't know yet. This has all happened so suddenly. I guess I'll find something." I hadn't given much of a thought to where I was going to live. My head was still reeling from my meeting with Mike.

"Well, I have an extra room in my apartment, and an extra salary would help me out," she offered. "I'm Mary, Mary Kominski, happy to meet you." She held out her hand, and we shook hands.

"Thanks, Mary," I said. "I appreciate the offer, but can I get back to you?"

"Sure, the room's not going anyplace." She smiled. "And since you just met Mike, I bet you're still trying to figure out what you've signed up for." We both laughed at that. Now that paperwork was done, I said good-bye, and I was on my way out the door.

I took in a deep breath of Boston. Wow, this was amazing. Wait until I told my friends at school. I had a job at the *Boston Herald*! I was walking and thinking about how all of this was happening so fast when I realized that tomorrow was Jackie's shower. Oh shoot, I needed a present. I had just passed Filene's and so I ran back hoping that I would find something for her. I was ushered to the home appliance section by a helpful saleslady and started looking around. I had one hour to get to the bus station, so I had to be quick. Jackie liked to cook, so I settled on a fondue set and waited while it was wrapped. I felt bad that I hadn't put much thought into this and hoped this was the right thing for a maid of honor to give the bride.

As I waited, I looked around at all things a new bride would want or need and wondered if I would ever be married. Momma's letter had wondered that too. But I had plenty of time for that. Besides, I had my first job to start in a month and so many new things to experience. I would have time for all of those things that Momma had mentioned. And I was sure I was going to accomplish all of them.

Juggling the wrapped package, my suitcase, and my portfolio, I was quite the sight as I got to the bus station just in time. I bought my ticket and climbed up the stairs into the bus. I made my way to an empty seat and stowed all of my packages and luggage. I settled into my seat with a sigh of relief, and I turned my gaze to the window. I felt someone sit in the seat next to me and turned to look and said a cursory hello to a guy in a fatigue jacket and jeans. He was tall and had rather long brown hair. He had a handsome look in a dashing kind of way. He returned the hello while he stowed his duffle bag in the luggage rack.

"Where you headed?" he asked as he eased himself into his seat. He had a Boston or was it Irish accent.

"Home to Maine," I replied.

"I'm going to Maine myself. Some little town called Piney Bluffs. Ever hear of it? My buddy's getting married in a few weeks, and he told me to come and visit for a while. First time I'm a best man. I have no clue what that entails." He smiled, revealing beautiful white teeth and blue eyes that had an incredible sparkle.

"No kidding," I said. "That's where I'm going. Piney Bluffs is my hometown, and my friend is getting married too, and I' m the maid of honor." I was beginning to wonder if he couldn't be Andy's friend. I had to ask.

"You wouldn't be a friend of Andy Frenetti, would you?" I said.

"I am, Charlie O'Connor at your service," he replied. "And you must be Jackie's friend. Wait, I know your name. Begins with an E… uh, wait I got it. Ethel? Is that right?"

"You're right, and how is it that I've never heard of you?" I said, thinking back on all the conversations I had with Jackie. I couldn't remember her speaking of Andy's friends. Although Andy was a couple of years older than Jackie and so I suppose there was someone that I didn't know. And with me being away, we saw less of each other during the school year. I realized how much I needed to catch up on the details of her life.

"We were in 'Nam together, discharged last year. Andy told me he was going to come home and marry his sweetheart. And I guess he's a man of his word," he told me.

I remembered now. While I was at high school, Andy's number had come up, and he had been drafted. Jackie had been so scared. The evening news made it worse when it reported the weekly death toll. She held her breath hoping she would never hear Andy's name. She was so relieved when he finally came home in one piece.

Charlie started to ask questions about Piney Bluffs, and I was happy to oblige. From the folks in town to the businesses and last but not least the fishing, I provided a mini travelogue of my hometown. Our conversation was easy and went back and forth about the town, ourselves, and what we were going to do with our lives.

I was just bursting to tell someone about the job I just landed at the *Boston Herald* in the sports department and how I was going to opening day at Fenway. And how could life get any better that this?

He told me he was from Denisport out on the Cape and was going to community college for law enforcement when he got drafted. His mom was a librarian for the town library, and his dad was a carpenter. He worked with his Dad and his brother now that he was back from 'Nam. He was unsure of whether to go back to school or just what he would do. So he was happy to have the chance to visit a friend while he was putting his life back together. We were so caught up in talking that I was surprised to hear the bus driver announced Piney Bluffs.

As we left the bus, I was still trying to juggle all of my things.

"Here let me help you with your stuff," Charlie said.

"That would be great," I replied.

"How are you getting home? Is there a taxi?" he asked.

"No, no taxi here." I chuckled. "I don't live far, just a ten-minute walk."

"Well then, I guess a ten-minute walk would do just the trick to get the kinks out from that bus ride." And he pick up my suitcase and motioned, "Lead the way."

And with that, we walked through the twilight on that chilly March night to my home. On the way, I pointed out some of the places I had mentioned on the bus.

"This is a beautiful little town. No wonder Andy told me this was the best place to live." Charlie was looking around at those things people who live here take for granted.

I pointed out Andy's Diner as we came to it.

"There's Andy's place. I only live just a little bit further. I can take it from here if you want to check in with Andy." I was suddenly aware of me coming through the door with Charlie and what Daddy would think.

"No, I promised a full delivery, and I intend to keep my promise." He smiled. "I'll come back to see Andy once I see you home." His chivalry was very charming.

"Here we are," I announced. And we walked through the gate and down the path to the house. I opened the door and heard Daddy talking to someone. The smell of fried fish was in the air, and I heard Daddy telling someone about how well he cooked. I was curious as to who the visitor was as Daddy didn't usually have anyone over to visit. We set our things down in the entryway and continued down the hallway to the kitchen.

"Yes, indeed. This is the freshest fish and cooked the best way anyone in town could make it. You wait until Ethel gets here. She is going to be surprised I cooked for her," Daddy went on with his conversation.

As we walked into the kitchen, I saw that Daddy's conversation was with Mr. Striper. Daddy had the sleeves of his flannel shirt rolled back and his white apron folded over and tied at his waist. The ashtray was smoking his cigarette as his attention was to his cooking. Mr. Striper was sitting in a chair at the table, listening intently to what Daddy was saying, or maybe it was the smell of fish that had his attention. At any rate, Mr. Striper wasn't taking his eyes off Daddy. They both looked right at home.

"Hi, Daddy," I said. "Looks like you two have settled into things here." I gave him a kiss on the cheek.

"Ethel, I didn't hear you come in. That cat's going tomorrow," Daddy said with a smile. Then he caught sight of Charlie. "And who's this?" he asked, his smile fading.

I hadn't given Charlie much warning about Daddy as I had hoped there wouldn't be a conversation. So now here we were, and time for introductions.

"This is Charlie O'Connor, Andy's friend. He's going to be his best man at the wedding. We met on the bus from Boston, and he was kind enough to carry some of my things home for me," I said quickly, hoping that there wouldn't be much of an interrogation. However, in an instance, I was back to high school and about to go out on a date. And Daddy was starting with the questions. I saw him give Charlie a once-over.

"Going to get that haircut for the wedding? We have a fine barber out in Knowles Corner, fix you right up." And with that, Daddy had given his opinion of Charlie.

"Daddy, really, stop. This is Andy's friend that he was in Vietnam with." I was mortified. I felt my cheeks flushing.

"Mr. Koontz, nice to meet you. Ethel has told me a lot about you." And Charlie held his hand to shake Daddy's.

Daddy had no choice but to put his spatula down and shake it. Both Charlie and Daddy were about six feet tall and looked more like they were preparing for a hand-to-hand wrestling match than a handshake. There was more than a moment of eye-to-eye contact between the two of them, and then it was over. For whatever reason, Daddy turned off the interrogation lights, and he was back to normal.

"Well, now, I wasn't expecting Ethel to bring a guest, but I think we have enough. Would you care to join us?" Daddy amazed me with those words and the turnabout of attitude.

"I thank you for that, sir, but I should be going to see Andy. However, I will take a rain check on dinner, especially if it tastes as good as it smells." Charlie was good to recognize the situation when he saw it.

"Well, I really have to thank you for helping me with my things," I said as I ushered Charlie down the hallway.

"It was my pleasure. I'll see you tomorrow?" Charlie asked.

"The shower's tomorrow at the inn, so I don't know," I started to say.

"That's okay, I'm staying at the inn," Charlie said.

"Then I'll see you tomorrow." And with that, he gave my hand a squeeze, smiled, and out the door he went. With his duffle bag over his shoulder, he looked like a modern-day sailor. As he walked down the street toward the diner, he turned around once to wave. And then with his next few steps, he entered the diner. From the doorway, I could hear Andy yelling, "Charlie O" and saw the two men greeting each other.

At that, I closed the door and leaned back on it for a bit before going back to the kitchen to Daddy, Mr. Striper, and his Friday-night fish fry.

9

"Dinner's getting cold. I'll be giving yours to the cat if you don't get yourself back in here," Daddy said. I heard him putting the pans on the table and getting the plates out.

"Coming," I replied and made my way back down the hallway into the kitchen. "What kind of fish are you cooking?"

"Cod. Your Uncle Ellie went saltwater fishing yesterday with Big Bob out of Portland," Daddy replied, not looking up. He was making some fresh tartar sauce, and I could see he was missing something. He was still giving me a little cold shoulder over Charlie.

"What are you looking for?" I asked.

"Celery seed. I thought I told you to put it on the list when we run out of things." He fussed, now completely put out and apparently happy that I was going to be the blame for bad tartar sauce.

"It's right here," I said, reaching around in front of him and picking it off the shelf. I set it down on the counter near the dish.

"What the hell is it doing up there?" he sputtered. "I always put it down here next to the pepper."

Not wanting to continue this jousting, I sat down at the table next to Mr. Striper who now it seemed had his own chair. I turned my conversation and my attention to the cat, "Mr. Striper, why did you put the celery seed away on that shelf? You know better than that."

With a heavy sigh and a clearing of his throat, Daddy let me know his frustration. He finished the sauce and placed it on the table and sat down.

"Daddy, this is wonderful," I said as we ate. Daddy was a good cook especially when it came to fish. And this cod was no exception.

Ignoring my compliment, he went straight to what was on his mind.

"Well, girl, are you going tell me what happened in Boston? Or are you ashamed to tell me about it?" With that out, he put a forkful of fish in his mouth and looked straight at me.

"I took the job. I'm going to be the proofer in the sports department. I like the people there. And it's closer than Providence, so I'm not going for that interview. I start the Monday after graduation." I looked back at him with a smile and also took in a mouthful of fish.

With all that information out, I let it settle in while we both appeared to be lost to our chewing for a moment.

"Are they going to pay you enough? Where are you going to live? You're going to have to be careful in that city. It's not like here. You won't have everyone saying hi and asking, 'How're you doing today?'" My concerned father broke through his crusty pessimist exterior.

"Oh, Daddy, they'll be paying me enough. Twelve thousand dollars a year, and that's only part-time. And I might share an apartment with one of the girls I met at the paper. She's just out of college like me, and she has an extra room with furniture and everything. I wouldn't need a car, so I can walk to work or take the T. I'll be fine." I was telling a little white lie about the salary, but I knew I would find some part-time work. "And I have a surprise," I said as I got up from the table and went to my purse. Returning to my seat, I had the tickets to opening day in my hand. I slid them across to Daddy. He took his glasses from his pocket, put them on, read the tickets, and looked up at me over the top of his glasses.

"Opening day at Fenway. I've never seen a live game." He let out a low whistle to show his respectful appreciation. "They give these to all new employees?" He looked at me with a smile.

"Just to the ones from Maine. I do have to write a piece about opening day, so I'll actually be working. And I thought with you in the city, I can show you around. Will you be able to go?" I was excited and proud.

"I guess I'll have to see about that. Been saving most of my days for fishing this year. Could be a predicament for me making decisions like this." He was teasing me now, and his smile couldn't hide it.

Daddy's discontentment with my decision to move slowly dissolved over the remainder of dinner. By the time we were finished with dishes, our conversation was back to normal day-to-day topics. I reminded him that Jackie's shower was tomorrow, and I had best be going to check in with her. He told me to skedaddle and to say hello to Jackie and her parents. I took the keys to the truck, and out the door I went.

In no time, I was at the inn. I went in through the back door to the kitchen where Jackie and her mom were absorbed in plating desserts on beautiful silver platters. With a shush finger to my lips, I snuck up behind Mrs. Farnsworth and put my hands over her eyes and tried to disguise my voice.

"Guess who?" I said as I tried to talk in my lowest octave possible.

"Oh, Ethel, stop trying to scare an old woman. I heard that old pickup make the corner. So I knew it was you before you hit the step." She turned out of my blindfold and gave me a big hug. "Now get yourself busy. We have lots to do before tomorrow."

I gave Jackie a quick hug and, with that, helped to finish the desserts. Then we started making fillings for the finger rolls. After kitchen duty, we turned our attention to decorating the dining room. As we strung crepe paper flowers and wedding bell garlands, we talked about all the details for tomorrow and who was coming. Our friends from high school and their moms would be here, as well as cousins, aunts, and friends coming from out of town. Total responses for the wedding were now at one hundred fifty. This was going to be one of the biggest celebrations for Piney Bluffs, and coupled with it also being on opening day, the inn would be extremely busy.

"I'm not quite sure what I'm supposed to do tomorrow as your maid of honor. I asked some of my friends at school, and I got all kinds of answers," I said, hoping that Jackie's mom would have all the answers for me.

"Oh, Ethel, tomorrow will be easy. Just keep track of who gave what, how many ribbons are broken, and put all the ribbons together for the shower hat. And I'll take care of the rest," Mrs. Farnsworth recited. Thankfully, the inn, with the expertise of Mrs. F, had hosted most of the celebrations in town.

"What's a shower hat?" I asked, somewhat concerned with what was involved with this.

"My, my, girl. You put each ribbon and bow through a paper plate like a bouquet of flowers. And at the end of the shower, Jackie puts it on her head as her shower hat," Jackie's mom said through clenched teeth. She had pins in her mouth as she tried to pin the remainder of the flowers to the bride chair. ◆

"Jackie's going to wear a paper plate full of ribbons on her head," I said more to myself. "Remind me not to have a shower if I ever get married. I look terrible in paper plates." We started to laugh as I made a pantomime of what I supposed the wearing hat would look like.

"Okay, girls, we are done," Jackie's mom finally said. "Why don't you two relax and catch up. I've got some other things to attend to. Now remember, Ethel, I need you here at 1:00 p.m. sharp tomorrow."

"Yes, ma'am." I nodded, and Jackie's mom went back to the kitchen.

Jackie and I went into the bar area. It was vacant at this hour. We had been working for about four hours, and it was now almost eleven. Jackie took a couple of wine glasses down and brought a bottle of wine to a table by the window. She poured the wine, and we toasted.

"Ethel, it is so good to have you back here. I've missed you. And I can never seem to get through on that payphone in your dorm. Tell me about your interview," Jackie asked eagerly.

"I got the job at the *Herald*! Oh, Jackie, this is going to be so exciting. While it's not exactly what I wanted to do, it's a start." And we raised our glasses again to toast me this time.

"What do you mean not exactly?" Jackie asked.

"Well, the interning job turned into proofing for the Sports Department. And while sports is not where I really pictured myself, at least I've got my foot in the door," I answered and then went on to tell her about the people I had met at the paper. We talked about

living in Boston and how exciting that was going to be and how different it would be from Piney Bluffs.

"And I met Andy's best man today." I had almost forgotten to
mention that. "We were on the bus together. He's a very interesting
guy. Kind of cute too. Daddy met him, and was that awkward. He
said he was going to be staying here."

"I've only met him a couple of times. Andy said Charlie saved
his life in 'Nam. He never went into any detail about it, never does
when that subject comes up. What was your dad's problem with
him?" Jackie asked.

"I'm pretty sure it was his hair. He let Charlie know there was a
barber in Knowles Corner." We laughed at that. "But I can never be
sure with Daddy. He never liked any of the guys that I went with."

"Your daddy is going to give anyone a hard time when it comes
to you. You know that. I don't care if a guy was born with a silver fishing pole in his mouth," Jackie stated the obvious, and we laughed.

"I know, I just wish he'd be happy for me," I said as I looked out
to the moonlit lake.

"Oh, he is, Ethel. You should hear how he talks about you. He
is so proud that you are about to graduate from college, first one in
the family." She reached out to pat my hand. "Daddies just can't let
their little girls go no matter how old they are or what the reason is.
You should have heard my daddy when I told him Andy had pro-
posed. You would have thought I was leaving town and never coming
back again. We'll be living in a small house that belonged to Andy's
uncle out on the other side of the lake. And we'll both be working,
he at the diner and me still here."

We laughed and continued to chat about our families and finished our wine. About midnight, I said good night and made my way
home. When I got home, Daddy called out to me. He was sitting in
the sun porch with Mr. Striper on his lap.

"Everything all set for tomorrow?" he asked, stroking the cat.

"All set. Thank God for Mrs. F. She knows exactly what I need
to do for tomorrow," I responded. "You're up a little late, aren't you,
Daddy?"

"Well, I got a message for you. Caleb asked me to have you stop by tomorrow. He wanted to know how you made out." Daddy looked at me from over the top of his glasses with a noncommittal look. "I told him you had Jackie's shower, but I thought you'd be able to take a minute to let him know."

Always trying to maintain that possibility of me having a second thought about staying. I did have Caleb to thank, though. I know that his letter, along with the respect that the *Herald's* veteran reporters had for him, had helped me get the job.

"I'll stop by tomorrow morning. I want to thank him. And then I have to be at the inn at 1:00, so not much time to be idle tomorrow," I replied. I then went over and kissed him on the forehead. "Night, Daddy."

"G'night, Ethel." I turned and made my way up to bed. I stopped for a minute as I thought I heard Daddy talking again. I tiptoed back down the stairs, hoping to eavesdrop on his conversation with Mr. Striper.

"You say something, Daddy?" I called to him.

"No, just talking to the cat," he replied and lowered his voice a bit. "Yes, sir, Mr. Striper, that there is a smart young woman. Her momma would have been proud of her. She's going to be one helluva writer." And with that, I heard him take one last puff on his cigarette and noisily snuff it out. The chair scraped on the floor as he pushed the hassock and sat back in his chair. "Yes, sir, one helluva writer."

I sat on the steps like a child waiting for Santa, not believing what I had just heard. Those words were some of the most important that I had ever heard my daddy say. My heart swelled as I finally realized my father believed in me. I hugged my knees and held back the tears. I quietly backed myself up the stairs and up to my room.

"G'night, Ethel," Daddy called to me.

"G'night, Daddy." And the tears fell.

10

The next morning, I awoke early. I had heard Daddy snoring, so I let him be. As I left the house, the March air hit my face. It still had more of that hint of winter than spring. The town green was quiet this morning as I made my way across it. The sun was just rising over the lake and starting to cast its warmth on the town. With the light frost still clinging to the trees, houses, and shops, Piney Bluffs looked like a sugarcoated fairy-tale town. As I continued to walk, I realized that this was going to be one of those moments that I would keep with me forever. Boston was going to be very different. I doubted that there would be quiet moments like this. But then, that was why I was leaving now, wasn't it?

I stopped at Miss Ruthie's for coffee before I went to see Caleb. No one was at the counter or the tables at the moment. I could see she was in the back putting the finishing touches on what looked like a wedding cake. And judging by her sputtering, things were not going according to plan. I poked my head in to say hi.

"Ah, good, Ethel, get yourself back here. I need a second pair of hands. And I still have some teaching to do with your cousin before she can be of any use." It seemed she had seen me coming from across the green and had been waiting. And now Ruthie was looking at the cake and back at me with that expectant "well come on now, girl" look in her eyes. She was trying to get the third tier up onto the supports and not having much luck. I could see her left arm was in a sling. From the looks of her, my cousin Ellen had been trying to help, but there was more frosting on her than on the last tier of the cake.

I gave her a quick smile and a nod of my head, understanding what Ruthie was putting her through.

"What are you two up to?" I said as I took my jacket off and grabbed an apron from a hook.

"Oh, the damn thing was just a little bit warm and isn't stiff enough to toss around the way I like." Ruthie was shaking her head. When she tried to lift her left arm, I could see the hint of pain cross her face.

"What did you do to your arm?" I asked with most of my attention to the cake. I finally had the supports and the tier in place. I looked to see how level it was and then stepped back to let Ruthie continue.

"Thanks, girl, you came around at the right time like you always do." Ruthie now had her attention to the cake and its finishing touches.

"Ruthie, what did you do to your arm?" I asked again.

"Oh, just damn foolishness. I must be getting old. I was rushing around day before last getting this cake ready for Jackie's shower, and Sugar got under my feet and just didn't budge this time. Well, down I went and tried to grab onto the mixer with my left hand so I wouldn't whack my damn head on the floor. And next thing I knew, my apron got caught up in the on/off switch, and around the bowl my arm tried to go. Just a bad sprain, so Doc says. Hurts like hell, though." Ruthie never looked up. She was wrapped up in making the cake right.

"Shower's not till one o'clock. It's only 7:30. What's the rush? And why such a big cake? I thought you were making someone's wedding cake," I talked mostly to Ruthie's back as she worked her magic on the cake.

"Mrs. F is picking this up at 10:00 sharp. And they wanted this to be a miniature of the wedding cake, so that's why it's a little more than usual." Her sputtering was lessening, but she was still focused on making the cake right. "Going to be people from all over seeing this cake, got to be one of my best."

"Anything you do is always your best, you know that," I spoke over my shoulder as I went out to the shop and poured a coffee and looked at the case for my breakfast.

"What's the surprise muffin today?" I yelled back to Ruthie. The mixer had started for another batch of frosting, and the strain of the motor was letting us know its age.

"New one today, Ellen's Surprise. I came in this morning, and surprise, here she was, taking muffins out of the oven." Ruthie had a smile on her face and gave a glance to Ellen.

"They're banana chocolate chip," Ellen said, absolutely beaming.

"Damn, girl, these are good," I said as I took a second bite. "Ruthie never let me bake until I was a senior."

"You never got here early enough to bake. That's why you were the glaze application specialist. Only thing you were here in time for" Ruthie joked now with the both of us.

"Where you off to this morning? Shouldn't you be up at the inn getting ready for the shower?" Ruthie was coming back out to the front of the shop now.

"I'm stopping by to see Caleb. Daddy said Caleb wanted to know how I made out in Boston at the *Herald*," I answered.

"So out with it, girl. How did you do?" She now was turning her full attention to me.

"I got the job. I start the Monday after graduation," I said with a big smile.

"Oh my goodness, I am so happy for you." Ruthie came, gathered me up from my chair, and gave me a big floury one-armed hug. We gathered up Ellen and danced around the bakery for a mini celebration. "I'm going to miss you. You best be coming back to visit. So what are all the particulars? And what about your daddy? How's he taking this?" Her words flooded out as she tried to get all of her questions out at once. We sat back down, and I began my answers.

"Well, I'm going to work as a proofer for the sports desk. Just part-time to begin with, but I'll be fine. I think Daddy is going to be okay. I'm taking him to opening day of the Red Sox, writing a short column, part of my job. So I'll have time to show him around and let him see that I'm going to be all right. And I might be sharing an apartment with a girl I met at the paper. So everything's pretty well taken care of."

"Got everything nailed down. Good, good. I knew you would."
Ruthie was smiling but with what I thought was a bit of melancholy.

"What's the matter?" I looked across at my old friend. Ruthie
had been one of my surrogate mothers while I was growing up, and
I could see that motherly concern surfacing now. "I'm going to be all
right, and I'll be back every chance I get. It's less than a two-hour bus
ride. And when I get enough money, I'll buy a car, and then I can
come home when I want." I looked and saw her wiping her eye with
her floury hand, making a little paste from the tear rolling down her
face. I wiped it away with my hand.

"Oh, I'm an old fool, letting you get to me like this." She looked
away and started to straighten yesterday's *Bugle* and the other mail
on the table. We both knew that any additional conversation would
really turn on the waterworks. I stood up to leave.

"Well, I better get over to talk to Caleb. I don't want to be late
to the inn, or Mrs. F will have my head. I'll see you at the shower."
And with that, I gave Ruthie another hug, and out the door I went.

As I stepped outside, I saw a man running—no, jogging—
around the green headed my way. There was no urgency in the way
he ran, just a strong, steady gait. His hooded sweatshirt hid his face.
The man stopped in front of the bakery, and before I could speak, I
saw that it was Charlie.

"Mornin', Ethel. What a great place this is to run. Four miles
of peaceful roads and beautiful scenery. I can just imagine what this
place looks like when the leaves are out and the flowers are in bloom."
His breath swirled like smoke around his face, and steam was coming
off his head out the sides of his hood.

"Mornin' to you, Charlie. Not used to people running around
town. And four miles, where have you been?" I smiled and took a sip
of my coffee and waited for the rest of his travelogue.

"Let's see. I left the inn, took a right, and made a big circle to get
here, so you tell me where I went." He smiled back at me and waited
for my answer.

"Okay then, if you took a right at the inn, you went completely
around Snowshoe Lake to get back here to town. Find any good

places you'd like to come back to for fishing once the season opens?" I answered and asked.

"As a matter of fact, I did. Just about a mile out, a little protected area, looked like there would be potential for some nice ones," he replied.

"Oh, that's Daddy's favorite spot, Snowshoe Cove. He's gotten some of his biggest catches there. Other people fish the same spot and come away with nothing. I don't know how he does it. Not even my uncles can figure it out." I took another sip and looked back at him.

"Well then, I'd like to come back and try that out. Maybe I can figure out his secret." He winked at me and then finished, "So after the shower today, how about you and Jackie and Andy and I get together for a bit? I want to make sure that I don't make any mistakes on the big day. I know you girls always have all the answers."

"That sounds good. And as far as answers, I rely on Jackie's mom, Mrs. F. She plans all the events both at the inn and around town. Trust me, she'll let us know before we make a mistake," I replied.

"I doubt you make many mistakes," Charlie said.

"Is that what you think?" I asked. "Don't ask my daddy about me and mistakes. You might get a different opinion from him."

"Well, until I can have that conversation with him, I'll use my own judgment. See you tonight." And with that, our conversation ended. He gave me a wave, and off he started with that strong stride toward the edge of town in the direction of Knowles Corner.

As I watched him disappear around the corner of the green, I thought, *I can just imagine that conversation. Daddy and Charlie or Daddy and any guy for that matter. No, best I not think about that, not right now. There would be time enough for those kinds of conversations. Plenty of time.*

11

Walking up to *The Bugle*'s door, I saw Caleb give me a wave through the window. "Congratulations are in order from what I hear, Ethel." Caleb was getting up from his chair and came to shake my hand as I walked in. "I hoped you would stop, I know you have a busy day today. I appreciate that you came."

"Why, thanks, Caleb. Actually, I wanted to thank you and tell you how much I appreciated your letter. And how did you know?" I realized that Daddy, Jackie, and Charlie were the only ones who knew that I had gotten the job. And I had only told them last night.

"Bob gave me a call after your interview." He smiled more to himself than me. "He thanked me for sending you his way. I told him I didn't send you, but I thought you had the right stuff. Thinks you're going to do a great job for the sports desk."

"Well, I certainly intend to do my best. Sports wasn't where I thought I would be, but it beats interning in the Social column department," I said. "I even have tickets to the Sox for Opening Day. Mike gave them to me. I'm going to take Daddy. And I'll show him around so he'll know that everything will be fine."

"Opening day, that's quite the welcome." Caleb nodded with appreciation for the tickets. "What do you think of Mike?"

"He's a little crusty, like Daddy. So I don't think we'll have a problem," I said and added, "and as far as my knowledge of sports, well, I did cover games in college for our paper. Then there are all of the fishing events that we've had here in town that I have been a part of. So while being a girl in sports is something new, I'll be able to handle it. And it's just proofing to begin with, but Mike wants me to write a two-hundred-word piece on opening day. So who knows where it will lead."

Caleb was smiling as he listened to me. "Mike's a good man. I don't know of anyone who knows more about sports than he does. And he's used to girls. Has five daughters, and he doesn't cut them any slack either."

"I'm not looking for the easy way out, just a chance to show what I can do," I said.

"I'm sure he'll give you that. And now that you are a member of the press, how about a freelance article or two for me?" He looked over the top of his glasses at me with a smile.

"What do you mean freelance for you?" I asked.

"Well, you'll be at the game with your dad, so a roving reporter with local ties wouldn't be that much of a stretch. What do you think?" He looked at me waiting for what he knew I would say.

"I think I might be able to do that, might even get a picture of Daddy. Wouldn't he love that," I said and thought about what a great game this was going to be.

"But the first story that I want from you is on opening day of fishing season here." Him saying that made me look at him in astonishment.

"I can't cover opening day and be in Jackie's wedding too," I stated in disbelief.

"Ethel, the wedding's not until four. You'll be up before sunrise for the first cast. You'll have your story done by noontime." Caleb was looking back at his article on his typewriter with a sideways glance at me.

"I...I don't know what to say." Words were failing me. What was I getting myself into? Could I do this? And my best friend was counting on me to be there for her. Why did everything in my life come with complications? I sat back in the leather chair and enjoyed how small it made me feel, if only for a moment. In the past couple of weeks, I had made a lot of decisions. I had grown up, and suddenly, it wasn't all that it had been advertised. I continued to sit back and think. Caleb went on with his article and gave me the time I needed.

I looked around the office and thought about the future. I looked at the empty desk and thought how that might someday be mine. But not for a long time; there were so many things I needed to do. Finally, I looked back at Caleb. He took this as a sign that I was ready.

"Just say you will. And to give you something else to think about, I want you to write the story for *Fishing Weekly*, not for *The Bugle*." The twinkle in his eye confirmed that he had me.

"The what?" I asked.

"You remember the newsletter I showed you when you came in for your interview? The one you said you didn't want to be a part of. I'm asking you again. I want opening day to be our introductory issue. And I want you to put a bit of a different spin on it," he continued with the assumption I had bought into this. "I want you to create characters out of the real people that fish here. Locals or out-of-towners, make them a little larger than life. Why you can start on the story now. Build those characters with humor, poke a little fun at them, at yourself too."

"But what will people say? Won't they be upset that we're making fun of them?" Although concerned, I was already thinking of what characters I could make with Daddy and my uncles, but how would they take it?

"You leave that to me to worry about," Caleb said with confidence. "You'll see, this is really going to be something. Now what do you say? I'll pay you fifty dollars a column."

"Well, I do have a few weeks to play with this idea. My graduation is set. I have a job, so all I have is time. And I have to admit this seems like a fun challenge. Now all I have to do is break it to Jackie, worse yet, Mrs. F I'm not sure how she'll take this." I knew how she'd take it; my goose was cooked! But what a chance to take. I couldn't say no.

"Good then, we're agreed." Caleb held out his hand, and we shook with that handshake that was more binding than a written contract. Little did we know what this handshake contract would turn out to be. "To new partners?"

"To new partners," I agreed.

12

The rest of the day was a blur. I knew I needed to go straight to the inn from my visit with Caleb. But I had to stop at home first to ask Daddy if I could take the truck. He agreed and said he was only walking next door to Uncle Ellie's to plan their strategies for opening day. Andy's Diner was putting up a two-hundred-dollar prize and lunch for a month for the biggest catch of the day. Weigh in was at noon to tie into the "lunch for a month" theme. Needless to say, Daddy and my uncles were already sure that one of them would win, and why was anyone else bothering to enter? I chuckled to myself as I headed out the door. I was thinking about the article that I was to write for the *Fishing Weekly*. Making people into quirky characters was not going to be a big stretch with my family. Why, I could do an entire series just on Daddy and my uncles. Yes, that was it; I would stay with them on opening day from the first cast to the weigh in. I ought to explain to him though what this *Fishing Weekly* was going to be. But not right now, I needed to be at the inn before two o'clock, and I was just going to make it.

From the time I entered the inn to prepare for the shower, Mrs. F was like a drill sergeant. And so Jackie and I fell right into order like good little soldiers. It made no difference that it was Jackie's shower. We filled rolls, arranged trays, made punch, positioned plates and silverware, and then finally, the cake arrived.

Ruthie was in a huff. She had closed the bakery early to get ready for the shower and to get the cake into the car. The back of her station wagon looked like a torture chamber for the delicately decorated confection. The layers were held in place by a series of wooden vises, and she quickly set about to unlock them. Since her arm was in a sling, she ordered Jackie and I to help carry the layers in. She followed behind us into the kitchen with her litany of "Now be careful. Keep it level, or I'll have your hide!" Setting them down on the counter, we drew a sigh of relief. We went back and gathered the foundation plate and the frosting cloths. I mentioned that I could finish for her if she wanted, but her glare let me know the final construction was hers. We left the kitchen to see what else was left to do.

"Well, half an hour to go," Mrs. F said as she looked at her watch. "You two better go and get ready. I'll wait for Aunt Flo." Aunt Flo was Mr. F's older sister and was known for being the first to arrive and the last to leave. Not that she was nosey, but she just didn't want to miss a thing. And she always had her opinion on most anything whether you wanted it or not. She was an accountant and had never married. She lived in Paris Maine, although when meeting new people, she most times left off Maine just to see their reaction. Although almost sixty, she looked no more than fifty. Good living and no men on a regular basis was her answer when asked how she kept such a youthful look.

Jackie and I got to her room and started to change. She was talking about who was coming and where in their "new" old house everything was going to go. As she continued talking, I nodded. I knew I had to tell her about my first writing assignment and that it was going to be on her wedding day. And I knew that it was better now than later.

"Ah, Jacks, I have something to tell you." I looked down at my slacks and picked at a nonexistent piece of lint. "I'm going to write a story for Caleb about fishing."

"That will be great. The first story by the hometown girl." She was fixing her hair and smiled back in the mirror at me. "What's the story about?"

"Opening day." I didn't add any more as I saw her eyes grow to the size of silver dollars.

"Opening day, my wedding day?" her voice, while it wasn't shrill, could have gotten a couple of dogs to turn their heads. She turned to look at me. I had gotten her full attention now.

"The very same, but I can make this work, you'll see. I'll be up at 4:00 a.m. and have my story handed in by noon. The wedding's not until 4:00 p.m., so there's plenty of time for me to get back here. You have your mom to take care of all the details. Since I've never been in a wedding, I know my help wouldn't be much and—" I was rushing out with my words, hoping that she would see the logic in my thoughts, but she cut me off.

"Stop right there. Why do you think you're my best friend?" Her eyes had gone down to the size of nickels, and her voice had softened.

"Because I kicked Tubby Carpanowski when he pushed you down in third grade?" I was trying to figure out if she was mad or not and couldn't quite get a read.

"No, silly, because we know what's important to each other." She looked at me and shook her head. "You have got a great gift, Ethel, and nobody knows that more than me. And I know that you will be here when I need you. And that is going to be about 1:00 p.m., before the wedding. So there, I've given you one hour more than you thought you needed. You know, you could write about the wedding too."

You have got to be about the best friend that anyone could ever have." I was surprised at my friend's unselfishness. But then not that surprised. For growing up together, we did know what mattered to each other. "And it's not going to take me that long. Caleb and I are writing a different type of publication. I'm not sure about the wedding, but maybe it might work. This story is not for *The Bugle*." And so I told my friend about the *Fishing Weekly* and that I was still not sure how the town would receive this. Jackie gave me hug and wished me the best in my writing, whatever it was. Mrs. F's voice called us out of our conversation, and we hurried down to greet the guests.

The shower was well attended by the ladies in town as well as all of the friends and relations from elsewhere in Maine. I mastered the art of the shower hat all the while keeping an accurate accounting of the gifts, even if I did have to ask what things were from time to time. The highlight was the cake that everyone thought was a wonderful creation. Miss Ruthie absolutely beamed from the comments. It was quite the afternoon.

Those from out of town were making their overnight reservations before they left. Most were coming in the night before. Eavesdropping, I heard a good number of them say this was the first time their husbands were actually looking forward to a wedding. I chuckled to myself knowing that the most of the men would be here for the fishing. I thought that by the time the band was playing the second song, those same men would be "resting their eyes," and their wives would be scolding them to get up and dance.

As the last of the guests were leaving, Andy and Charlie walked in. Andy hugged the ladies and introduced Charlie as his best man. This sent the women out with their hushed conversations about Charlie and how good looking he was.

He came over to me, and we started to talk. He was asking about what our present to our best friends should be and other duties that were needed for the wedding. We seemed lost in conversation when I heard a voice. Of course, it was Aunt Flo who had to leave us with her parting thoughts.

"Well, it was nice to see you, young people. Ethel, come here a moment." Her look over the top of her glasses told me I was not to deny this request.

"Sure, Aunt Flo, what can I do for you?" I put my hand lightly on her shoulder, and she motioned me out of the hallway away from everyone.

"You and Charlie seem to be quite good together." She winked one eye at me and slowly nodded her head.

"Aunt Flo, where did you come up with that one? I barely know him," I asked, turning a bright shade of red.

"I'm not that old that I can't sense what's going to make things right. Don't wait, my dear. Life becomes short too quickly." With that, she walked into the hallway and out the door. "You'll see." That last comment trailed back in as she walked out to her car.

"What was that all about?" Jackie asked.

"Just another one of Aunt Flo's take on the day." I hope my blushing cheeks were fading.

Andy broke the brief silence. "Nice hat," Andy said to Jackie. She forgot she was still wearing her shower hat.

"I owe the creation to Ethel." Jackie's hand swept my way. We all laughed and then set about to clean up the dining room.

We were just about finished when Mrs. F came out and announced that Reverend Ezra was on his way over and that rehearsal was in five minutes. Right on time, Reverend Ezra came through the door and greeted us with handshakes and hugs. The ceremony was to be in the dining room with the view of the lake at our backs. Ezra went through the wedding vows. Jackie and Andy had added some of their own words to each other and for all who would be present. They were heartfelt, and I was sure the words would move some to tears. Mr. F came and escorted Jackie up and down the aisle while Mrs. F guided us through the entrance and exits. Charlie and I had our responsibilities, he the ring, and I the flowers. Then we were to stand to the side together until the ceremony had ended.

"They look right together, don't they?" Charlie whispered. His lips barely brushed my ear, but that closeness was unexpected. His touch made me take in a breath.

"Yes, they do," I replied, looking up but not wanting to look into his eyes. Aunt Flo's comment and now his nearness made me draw in a breath and hold on to it.

I quickly looked back at Jackie and Andy and tried to push this feeling out of my mind. I had no time in my life for anything complicated, and somehow, Charlie was starting to be a complication.

13

Back at school, I started to sort out everything that had happened in the past few weeks. Landing a job was one thing that I didn't need to worry about any longer, but living arrangements were. I had called Mary a couple of times to discuss the possibility of rooming with her. If I decided to, my portion of the rent would be two hundred dollars a month, and that included utilities. She knew I wasn't full time, and so she would pay the remaining four hundred dollars until I either went to full time or found a part-time job. Mary said there were lots of places from restaurants to bakeries and all sorts of other opportunities in between for extra work. It would all work out, she said. It seems like a lot at first, but we could manage. I planned to visit her the weekend after the wedding to see where the apartment was and maybe check out a few places for part-time work. In addition, that following Tuesday was going to be the Red Sox opening day, so I needed to familiarize myself with the area and how I was getting Daddy into the city.

The wedding rehearsals with Reverend Ezra had us all set for the big day. Jackie had explained to her mother that I would be arriving at one o'clock because of the story that I had to do. While not too pleased with me, Jackie had made Mrs. F understand what I was doing and how important it was for me and maybe even for the town. Before I had left for school, I had set out Daddy and my clothes for the wedding just in case my reporting of opening day ran a little over. And I knew that Daddy would be looking for any excuse not to go to the wedding. Leaving opening day at noontime was almost sacrilege for him. He had started to make some grumblings about it just before I left. But I reminded him that the handsomest man in Piney Bluffs would be missed by all of those single ladies at the wedding. He harrumphed at me in his usual way and said that would be the day when anyone in this town had any interest in him.

The only two things that were not resolved were the stories I needed to write. I had started to do some research at the library on the Red Sox and especially Carl Yastrzemski. I wondered what Mike O'Brien would expect from his new proofer who was not a reporter. Certainly, play-by-play action was not what he wanted. The game was in April, and I didn't start until May. No, I had to find an angle that would get his attention. As it was both Daddy and my first time at a live game I thought that might be just the aspect to write from—a father-and-daughter's perspective on their first live ballgame for their favorite team. The sights and the smells and the feeling of being at Fenway, yes, that's what I would write about. And even though I wasn't going to be at the *Herald* until May, I would send it to Mike, just in case it had enough interest to be put in the paper. But from my first encounter with him, more than likely, it would end up with a "Holy Mother Mary you call this reporting?" Or some other comment like that.

The last thing now was the article for *Fishing Weekly*, which at this point seemed the easiest thing I would be doing that day. I first outlined the events of the day based on all those years that I had fished alongside of Daddy. The start of the day would be breakfast at Reverend Ezra's church. We would have a prayer, and then off we would go to our respective secret spots. All of my uncles would take up positions in just about the same area. We could just about see each other through the undergrowth by the shore of the lake and still within earshot. And then once we were settled in, we would wait. The waiting was sometimes the best part. Since I usually squirmed like a worm, as Daddy put it, he would tell me stories to pass the time. These stories could be about when he went fishing as a young boy or remembering the fish we had caught last year. We would always have bought a couple of pieces of Miss Ruthie's blueberry cake at the church breakfast. This was saved until the first fish was caught. The victorious bite of blueberry cake and the fish's first bite just couldn't be compared to anything if you asked my daddy and me.

Amid all of these memories, I now started to think of how I would poke a little fun at everyone in the story. First, I would start with myself. People usually wouldn't fault you if the humor started at home. And Caleb had said that he would take care of this aspect of our new publication. I chuckled to myself as I listed all of the people that would be in that article and how I would make them a little larger than life. I also was thinking of writing a social article about Jackie's wedding. My mind was racing with all the funny things that could be made out of a wedding that was on opening day of fishing season. From Mr. and Mrs. F to the relatives from out of town and the husbands who were really here for the fishing, now this was going to be fun.

With all of those ideas in my mind, I was ready to start my first article for *Fishing Weekly*. The details would come on that day, but most of the story was a given. Daddy had always been the first to catch a fish. My uncles never knew how he did it; he just did. And hopefully, the winner of the contest would be in the family. Then there would be all those out-of-towners with their "more tackle and outfits are better" attitude to write about as well. Daddy had been a guide for Big Bob, and I had seen the more tackle attitude numerous times. They spent most of their time fishing trying to decide what bait to put on or what hat was best with their outfit. The fish were pretty safe with these folks. Why they could be an entire story to themselves, especially thinking that most of them were going to be at Jackie and Andy's wedding at four o'clock. Yes, this was going to be fun.

14

A Fishing Weekly edition

Opening Day
by Ethel Koontz, sporting events editor

I'm Ethel Koontz here on location for opening day. I am the head of the Sporting Events Department of *Fishing Weekly*, guess that would be by default since I'm the only one in the department. But pay that no mind. It is just going to be a grand day of fishing. To keep with tradition here in Piney Bluffs, we have all just heard the official fishing prayer by the right Reverend Ezra Baldwin. It's 5:30 a.m., and fishing season has now officially begun. Before the prayer, the ladies of Reverend Ezra's church served up a fine breakfast for the fishermen and women, or should I say woman. I appeared to be the only female going fishing today. I might just get lucky. Anyway, tip of our fishing hats to the church ladies. To make today's fishing a total experience, Andy's Diner has a put out a contest. The biggest fish caught in these here waters of Snowshoe Lake in Piney Bluffs will be awarded a two-hundred-dollar prize and lunch for a month at the diner. Weigh in will be at high noon in the parking lot of Andy's. As I survey the fishermen who have gathered today, well, it's quite a sight. On one side are the local folks I grew up with from my daddy and my uncles to all the guys in town. They got their favorite pole in hand, fishing pole that is, and a no-nonsense attitude just focusing on fishing. The other side of the gathering area is a colorful array of our fine visitors and everything that could be purchased from those fancy fishing catalogs. Some of these fellas got tackle with them I've never seen before. Thank God they got Big Bob to ride herd over them, 'cause most of them wouldn't be able to find the water, never mind catch a fish. However, this is a fishing contest and not a fashion show.

So today, my reporting will be with one fishing group in particular, and that would be the Koontz family. Being that most of the fishing spots are sworn to secrecy within our family, I was *the* selected reporter for this here job. It didn't hurt that I am the only reporter for *Fishing Weekly*, but that is beside the point.

We have now arrived at the first spot, and click, kerplunk! Yes, sir, that's there's the very first cast of opening day right here in Piney Bluffs with my daddy, Eddy Koontz an' all of my uncles, Ellsworth, Eubie, Earl, and Ernie. It's a beautiful morning about 5:45 now an', that sun is just about to come up over the...oh, wait a minute...now I can't divulge where we are, but as you know by the rules of the contest, we must stay at Snowshoe Lake in Piney Bluffs, an' we are. Wait a minute, I think someone's got themselves a bite. Ooh, this one looks real good. About a nine-inch brook trout. Well, sir, in my family, that makes Daddy the winner of one of the big three. He got the first. Now who's going to take biggest and most? Real careful now, I see Daddy releasing his first catch back into the water. This one won't be the biggest, and as long as the family knows, it was Daddy who got the first one; that's all that matters. Time for that bite of blueberry cake. *Mmmm,* um, is that good! Wait now, I see my uncle Ellie about to slip a little something on his line. I'll make my way over to him real quiet like so as not to disturb the fish. Uncle Ellie tells me this is special bait that he and my daddy been working on. Kind of a combination worm and bug bait. And if that doesn't work, they have the Koontz Kicker. Now this is special little lure that is shaped kind of like a boot with a single hook at the toe. Them there trout are looking at this flashy thing just a zipping through the water and trying to catch it. Well, that's just their undoing, and before they know it, *bang* they're hooked. A hush has fallen over my family, seems Tubby Carpanowski is walking by and almost come upon us. Thank God he's a big guy and can't go too quiet in this low brush area. Also the fact that Tubby must have had some baked beans last night at the diner has been some assistance in notifying us of his arrival. Coast is clear now. Tubby's gone and just in time cause Uncle Eubie's line is just singing, taking a lot of line out. This might be the big one! Careful bringing that in, unk, got to play it like you were playing a real sad song on a fiddle. Wow! What a beauty! Got another brookie. On the hand scale, she weighs in at near six pounds. That one's going into the live well.

The fishing is going well for my family. Poles pulling up quick to set the hook and then deciding if that one's good enough to keep. Will you look at the time? The morning has just flown by. It's almost 11:30 a.m., and we got to be getting back to the diner for weigh in. As Daddy and I ride back to the diner, I do a one on one in-depth interview.

Q: Mr. Koontz, what was the best part of your opening day?

A: Well, I guess it would be that my family and me were all together for this wonderful occasion. Also the fact that I beat my brothers for first one caught just added a little icing to my cake.

Q: Do you think you are going to win Andy's Diner contest?

A: Well, we'll see now, won't we? But I got a feeling' that one of mine could be in contention.

Q: Well, thank you, Daddy, ah I mean, Mr. Koontz for letting me ride along with you and your brothers.

A: Ethel, what are you talking about? You're my daughter, and you always go with me on opening day.

Q: Thank you, Daddy.

We are now pulling up to Andy's Diner, and my, what a crowd has gathered for the weigh in. Well, that was as far as I could go. I would have to wait for opening day to put the final details to it. I hoped that this was what Caleb had wanted. As I had started to write, I realized how much I liked doing this. It had been fun to write about the people and twist their characters just a little. Caleb had told me that he was working on a couple of columns himself. One was an editorial, and the other was an advice column for fisherman. And if he had time, there might be a column by Sadie on her favorite recipes. I still didn't know what influence this could have on our town. This was probably something that we would do just this once.

1 5

"Program! Get your program here," the vendor shouted. In his wooden enclosure, he looked like a policeman in the middle of an intersection elevated above the crowd. Daddy held up his money, and it was quickly exchanged for the glossy covered program for opening day. Yaz's picture was on the cover—bat raised, jaw set, the unmistakable number *8* on his uniform. Today's game was to be against their lifelong rivals, the Yankees. It would be the first of many games this year to attempt to dispel the curse of the Bambino, the longtime grudge of Babe Ruth leaving Boston for the Yankees.

And oh, what wonderful aromas! My nose quivered like a bloodhound that's taken the scent of the trail. The grilling hot dogs, the sausages with their accompaniments of onions and peppers mixed with the hot popcorn and peanuts, and an underlying stale beer smell thrown in as well. Already hungry game goers were forming long lines in search of their favorite baseball food.

America's national pastime was about to begin for another season with fans waiting for the cry of "Play Ball!" We were caught in the noisy stream of fans, feeling like fish swimming upstream. With ball caps emblazoned with the signature *B*, satiny jackets with Boston embroidered on the backs and red pennants with the white letters of Red Sox, there was no mistaking that the fans loved their Sox. They shouted to one another in greetings or that they had found their seats. They were excited about what Yaz would do today against Stottlmyre. And what about Tiant's pitching? Would he be able to take the Yanks on? And did Fisk, Petrocelli, and Aparicio bring their

82

bats? As people found their sections, an eddy in the crowd gave us a chance for escape. On an entrance ramp and away from them, we watched the river of baseball fans flow by.

It was a chilly but sunny day, not unlike most opening days in Boston. Or at least that was what I was overhearing as fans walked by. I was looking for the press section signs, and Daddy had his nose buried in the program. Pulling the sleeve of Daddy's jacket, I motioned for him to follow me up the entrance ramp. I couldn't wait any longer; I just wanted to see what Fenway was all about. We walked up the stairs and left behind the din and the darkness of food joints and vendors hawking their souvenirs.

Stepping out into the open, I held my breath. The sunlit field was nothing as I had expected. Fenway was absolutely huge and one of the most unbelievable sights I had ever seen. The sun warmed my face, and my smile grew. Daddy elbowed me and nodded his head in agreement. There were so many things that our twenty-inch TV had not captured in all those years of faithful watching. The green of the grass was in stark contrast to the white foul lines. I scanned a panoramic view from the stands, to the outfield, and around to the diamond. There was the endless height of the Green Monster with the CITGO sign rising behind it. And the players were right there. They wore their vivid white home uniforms with their namesake red socks. You could hear the ball smack the leather of their gloves as they warmed up in the outfield. There was the chatter back and forth between the players and their answers to the fans who yelled out the question, "Are you going to win today?" Yes, this was going to be some day.

We made our way back down the stairs and followed the signs to the press box. A group of little leaguers in their Red Sox team uniforms fell in step in front of us. Their ball caps looked almost too big for their little heads. They were an excited group acting up as boys do, elbowing and pushing and loud. They carried their gloves slapping their fists into them, getting ready for their big chance and taunting each other with who was going to catch the first ball and be the hero of the team. Like a school of young fry rapidly swimming, they made their way toward their section entrance ramp, their coaches trying to keep the boys together until they made it to their seats.

Finally, we saw the sign for the press box and made our way up the stairs. We opened the door to see a three-tiered room. The smell of stale smoke and hot dogs met my nose. Years of both had permeated every counter and chair of the box. The entire front was glass with some sliding windows at the bottom. The location was right behind home plate above the spectator seating with a view of the entire stadium. The top row had microphones set up for radio and television announcers, most of whom were already in place testing their connections. The bottom two rows were for the various newspaper and magazine reporters. Payphones were on the walls for each level with reporters already getting their demands in for placement in their publications. I heard the "Come on, this is going to be big. Sox and Yankees, opening day, don't you dare bury me below the fold!" While I had never written a piece for a major paper, I knew the consequences of the fold. Above the fold was what sold the paper on the newsstands. It got the bigger print, and your byline was bigger. The fold was the make or break of a reporter's worth.

Following Alice's directions, we found our way to the *Herald*'s spot, three metal chairs at a long counter with the name Herald taped to the food-stained counter. Two ashtrays finished the sparse décor. I set my notebook down on the counter and put my jacket on the chair and took my seat. Daddy did the same and took out his cigarettes and lit one. Around me, conversations between newscasters continued with them giving me only a momentary glance.

I tried not to read too much into those glances. I knew when I started that journalism had few women of notable reputation. Newspaper reporting was still mostly a man's area. Women had the society and advice columns. Television enforced that as well. Women were the "weather girls," not the anchors on our evening news. And the morning news shows had women reporting only light stories, sipping tea with whomever they were interviewing. Having been surrounded by the men in my family and being in the sport of fishing for my life made the glances roll like water off a duck's back.

As I surveyed the gallery, most of the press corps here were men as well. The few women present were assisting the broadcasters. I appeared to be the only woman reporting. The men wore dress shirts with ties already loosened, sleeves rolled up, and hats pushed back on their heads. The women were in slacks with sweaters or suit jackets busying themselves with papers and glasses of water. The low conversations were starting to quicken like a buzz in a beehive. First pitch was only minutes away.

The day's programs were being handed out, and most reporters had started their writings. The broadcasters were busy jotting notes. I had enlightened Daddy on our way to the game about etiquette in a press box area. In one of my journalism classes, I had learned that while the talk among newscasters was normal conversation level, there was to be no emotional reaction to a play on the field. You were there to report on the entire story with no biases. Any cheering or booing would be frowned upon and would really show my novice status. Daddy had promised he would control himself and not make me embarrassed.

"Looks like you're in the minority here, Ethel. You going to be okay with this men's club?" Daddy had never been one to mince words, and his observations were correct.

"I can handle myself, Daddy. I'll show them all. I know it's not going to be easy, but they won't forget me once they've seen what I can do," I said and looked Daddy square in the eye.

"That's my girl." And Daddy was all smiles.

The box was almost full now with most reporters taking their places. The empty spaces next to me had now become occupied, and one of them turned to speak to us.

"Hi, I'm Jimmy from the Globe, and over there's Walter and Sonny. Where's Mike?" He held out his hand to greet me. The other two men raised a hand to wave.

"Hi, I'm Ethel. I'm new at the *Herald*. I don't know if Mike is going to be here or not," I answered, shaking his hand and wondering if Mike was going to appear. I hadn't prepared Daddy for that. I added, "This is my dad, Eddy."

Jimmy nodded. Just then, the PA system came to life, and we were instructed to rise for the singing of the National Anthem. As the song was ending, the door to the press box opened, and in rushed Mike, a to-go cup of coffee in his hand. He slipped into the empty chair between Jimmy and I.

"Good, good you're here. Well, that's a good sign that you can follow directions," Mike said as he dropped his briefcase on the counter. Papers were sticking out from every opening.

"Mike, I'd like you to meet my father, Eddy." Daddy extended his hand, and both men shook. I held my breath for a Holy Mother Mary moment or some other type of annoyed response.

"Thanks for the tickets, Mike. This is a real treat," my father said in appreciation.

"Yeah, yeah, don't mention it. I have to get to know people, and the best way I know how is at a game. Besides, I have to put you to work, so don't think you're just going to sit back and have a dog and a beer," he said as he continued taking out his notebook and blank score sheets. He passed one to me and started to explain.

"You've seen one of these before, I hope. Okay, now here's how this works. Bear, our photographer, is down on the field trying for that AP photo of the year. Good luck with that. We might see him but probably not. So up here, we always have three in the booth, two doing the play by play, and the other is the lookout. That's in case we are both looking down and a play happens. It's all live, and we only have one chance to get it right. So, Eddy, you're going to be the lookout while Ethel and I do the scores." Mike was all business and looked up as Daddy and I both nodded in agreement to our assignments.

Mayor Kevin White threw out the ceremonial first pitch, and then we heard those famous words, "Play ball." The game began. The conversations in the room changed. The broadcasters with headsets on now started their commentaries that would last more than two hours. As the game continued, I marveled at these men and the knowledge they had about baseball. When there was a lull in the action, they filled in the time with anecdotes or facts about the players. Most had no notes with them at all. Sports casting was truly the dream job for people who loved sports.

Mike had decided that I would score the Sox, and he would take the Yanks. I had helped call some baseball games in college, so the score sheets were familiar to me. And so we penciled each hit for each player—balls, hits, and strikes around the diamond, inning after inning. My sheet was filling in nicely as the Sox were ahead.

During the change of sides and in between innings, Mike, Daddy, and I talked back and forth about the Red Sox, baseball, and life in general. Daddy and I spoke about Piney Bluffs and our love for fishing. And Mike talked about his for baseball. In his senior year in college, he had been scouted by the Sox but wound up playing double-A ball for Baltimore. And that was as far as baseball had taken him, at least on the playing side. In his last year with the Orioles, he met Katie, got married, and they moved back to the Boston area for his job with the *Herald*. That was fifteen years ago, and he couldn't imagine doing anything else unless it was TV or radio. Although he said he wasn't "pretty" enough for TV. We chuckled at that and went back to the game. It was a terrific game, and in the end, the Sox put the Yankees in their place—fifteen to five with Tiant going the full nine innings and Yaz scoring four of the fifteen runs.

"I've got to tell you, I'm impressed. You did well with the scores. And I don't impress easily." Mike was shaking his head as if he had wanted to be able to find something wrong. Daddy sat there and smiled. I hoped he was feeling proud of me on my first assignment.

"And don't forget, two hundred words on today's game, and no help from your dad." Mike smiled with his last piece of sarcasm as he pointed at Daddy.

Mike had been right. A ballgame was a good way to get to know someone. As the day had gone by, Mike's hard edge had dissolved a bit. I learned that he was hard when he had to be. Getting the best stories or the interviews for the paper was not a task for the introvert. If you didn't go after it, it certainly wasn't coming to you.

As we walked out of the ballpark, Daddy invited Mike to come out to Piney Bluffs for a little fishing and to see that fishing was also a way to get to know someone. I was surprised that Mike was a bit hesitant.

"Not sure that fishing is for me. I never quite had the patience for it. Always seemed that there were better things to do with my time," he said, shrugging his shoulders.

"Well, in case you change your mind, we'd welcome you out to Piney Bluffs for a day of nothing better to do than fish." Daddy hadn't liked that comment, I could tell. He was smiling, but it had an edge to it. "You might find your patience along with a few other things."

Although he didn't say anything, I could tell Mike didn't like Daddy's comment either. He waved good-bye and took off in the opposite direction.

"I'm not so sure I like him, Ethel. I know he's your boss and all, but just something there that's not to my liking." Daddy had squinted one eye down and shook his head. "Better things to do than fish, nope, man's got to understand how sometimes it's not about the fishing but being there, out there with nature surrounding you."

I weighed and compared the comments that both men had just shared. I thought to myself how baseball and fishing had many similarities. Most of the time, they were calm, relaxing sports interspersed with brief spots of excitement. Getting a fish on the line and connecting the bat with the pitch were energy-charged moments. Setting the hook was like the crack of the bat. Was the fish on? Was the ball fair? Would the fish slip off? Would the runner be thrown out? Landing the fish and scoring a run were what it was all about. It was like a cycle. Until you played at either sport, you would never know the satisfaction that it brings.

Daddy had explained that playing and working were part of that cycle of life. You had to find the balance of each. Satisfaction in either one depended on you and how much of yourself you put into it. Sit back and let the world flow by, and you only see one spot in the river. Jump in and work the current, and your visions are ever changing and exciting. You only had to put your hand out to let the current take you.

Trapped in the exiting crowd, I saw the same group of little leaguers who were in front of us on the way in. While the coaches looked a bit tired, the kids were charged up. One in particular was very excited. Edging nearer, I heard him tell all who would listen, "Did you see me? I caught Yaz's foul ball. I just put my glove up, and there it was."

Like I said, you only have to put your hand out, and life changes forever.

16

"Hurry, Daddy," I yelled up the stairs. "We have to be at the inn in ten minutes!" We had been rushing for the past half hour. The fishing tournament had gotten us behind in our schedule, and now we were scrambling throwing off fishing gear and jumping in to our wedding-day attire.

Daddy hurried down the stairs tying his tie. He stopped in the hallway to check in the mirror. He paused as he always did for a moment at Momma's picture. Her smiling face and her trim figure wearing Daddy's plaid shirt had been taken by Snowshoe Lake in the spring so many years ago. She held a stringer of three trout. Daddy had said they were the best-tasting trout he had ever eaten. That old Souvenir of Maine wooden frame had been on the hallway table ever since I could remember, and this pause was always the last thing he did before he left each morning.

"Daddy, you're handsome. Now let's get going. There are lots of Jackie's aunts who are dying to meet you." I was already out the door walking toward the truck.

Daddy closed the door and hurried into the truck, and off we went. While it was a short ride, we had a moment of silence, and both of us seemed to let out a sigh. Finally, I spoke up, "Hell of a contest today, Daddy. Sorry you didn't win. I think this is the first time a Koontz hasn't won a fishing contest in town since I can remember." I knew he had been disappointed when even Uncle Eubie hadn't won.

"Well, it's time for some of those young ones that we taught to step up. Shows we were good teachers if they win," Daddy said with firm nod of his head. He always had a way turning things around to show the goodness. That was something that he had taught me early on.

I remember back to when I was in grammar school, Daddy had taken a couple of the boys in my school fishing. Their mother was raising them on her own and didn't have much time for discipline, never mind an afternoon of fishing. So of course, they were the ones staying after school because they were always acting up. I had told Daddy about them, and one day, when he picked me up at school, he had asked them if they wanted to go fishing. Their mother was thankful that someone had reached out to help her try to set her boys straight if only for an afternoon. After that, those boys fished off and on with my daddy for several years. And through that time, their behavior improved, and they came to know that they should be helping their mother and not burdening her with their antics. They moved away when I was in seventh grade. But before they left, they came to say good-bye to Daddy and to thank him for taking the time to be with them. They still send a card at Christmas letting us know how they are and how they will never forget their fishing afternoons.

"How did your story come out, or whatever it was you were writing," he asked.

"Oh, I think you'll enjoy it. I put the finishing touches on it and gave it to Caleb at the ceremony." I thought of *Fishing Weekly* and hoped that Caleb was right about what it was going to do for the town. I had told him I would stop by tomorrow before I went back to school.

"You going to be all right being the maid of honor," Daddy asked. It surprised me that he had thought of how and if I was going to be able to deal with my duties.

"I think I can handle it. Besides, Mrs. F has this thing all set. She should write a book of the how-tos of weddings and the like." I wasn't nervous, but I was hoping that I didn't make a mistake.

"You'll have to make sure that she helps you when it's your time," Daddy said softly. He was looking out at the road ahead. I could see him straighten his shoulders a bit. He did this when he was trying to keep his emotions in check.

"Oh, I'm sure she'll be happy to help us, Daddy. But that won't happen for a good long while. Not too many prospects here in town now, are there?" I was trying to make light of my comment. There really was no one here. And besides, getting married was the farthest thing from my mind.

"You'll make sure he likes to fish," Daddy said with his jaw set. We were getting out of the truck and heading for the back door of the inn.

"Oh, Daddy, how could I ever have anyone in my life who didn't?" I slipped my arm into his as we walked.

"You look pretty, Ethel." He patted my hand. "Just like your momma."

"Oh, Daddy," I said softly, holding back the lump in my throat that was in the way of my tears.

As I put out my hand to open the door to the kitchen, Daddy put his hand on my shoulder. I turned, and he lightly tapped his finger on my nose, something he had done since I was a little girl. This had been his way to tell me he loved me. Then he winked and shooed me in the door.

The kitchen was a flurry of activity, and the air was full of wonderful aromas. From lobster canapés to blueberry crumble and everything in between, the menu by Chef Rocky was not going to disappoint. He was in full control directing his small kitchen staff in their steps of preparation. Trays and pots were sounding like cymbals and drums as they were readied for use. Everything had to be perfect for Jackie.

"Perfection," Rocky said in his French Canadian accent. "No, no like these, little Ellen." He hurried to Ellen's side to make sure she had the correct grip on her pastry tube.

My cousin Ellen's head popped up, and she waved at me. Her eager face let me know she was eating this up. Under the watchful eye of Rocky and with all the concentration of a diamond cutter, she piped the lobster filling into bite-size pastry shells.

"Ethel, is that you? Come on up," Jackie's voice yelled down the back stairs from the second floor.

I left Daddy to talk to Mr. F who looked a little nervous.

"Come on, Jack, let me buy you a beer," Daddy said as he steered Jackie's dad out of the kitchen and into the inn's tap room.

I ran up the stairs to Jackie's room to find Mrs. F trying to get the bride to stand still while she helped her into the underskirt of her wedding gown.

"Will you hold still for just one minute." Mrs. F had pins in her mouth, and she sounded like a bad ventriloquist as she tried to talk without moving her mouth.

"Ethel, will you please tell my mother that there is no need for whatever the hell this thing is that she's trying to pin on me. I just want to put the damn dress on." Jackie was showing her last-minute bridal jitters, and I could tell Mrs. F had had just about enough of it.

"Jackie, I swear if you make one more move, these pins will draw enough blood to supply the blood bank at Portland General." Mrs. F was tugging trying to get the underskirt to lay even, and something was holding it back.

"Mother, please, stop. The damn thing just isn't going on." Jackie was now tapping her stocking foot on the bare wood floor to show her continued impatience. As Mrs. F continued to work behind her back, Jackie stuck out her tongue over her shoulder at her mother.

"I can see that in the mirror, young lady. Are you twelve, or are you twenty?" The boiling point was coming, and I wasn't sure if Mrs. F was going to hold out or not.

"Come on, Jackie. Stand still like you used to when we were trying to sneak out and you thought your dad was coming." I was trying to lighten the moment before the wrong words were said.

"Ethel, now is not the time for reminiscing about silly things." Jackie glared and turned her attention toward me, now allowing her mother to put the last of the stitches in place. "Oww! Mother, will you stop!" Mrs. F had gone just that one stitch too far.

"Okay then, you two figure it out. I have other things to attend to." And with that, she threw up her hands and started to walk out of Jackie's bedroom. She paused and looked at herself in the mirror. She was outfitted perfectly in a light-blue dress and matching shoes. A striking woman, her platinum blonde signature bun had a silver pin to hold it in place. Still she frowned at herself as she left the mirror and headed out of the room.

"Ethel, don't ever get married in a stupid gown," Jackie said as she plopped herself on her bed and let out a heavy sigh.

"You know you could have saved yourself a lot of aggravation and had the wedding at the weigh in. Heck, most of the men were already there." As I finished saying that, Jackie threw her pillow at me. I caught it and threw it back, hitting and bouncing off the top of her head.

"Hey, don't mess up the hair." We laughed at that. Jackie had always kept her hair short, so there wasn't much to mess up. As we talked, we worked, and finally, the underskirt went on, and then we were ready for the gown. The creamy white fabric whispered as it floated over her head and came to rest perfectly in place. We both stopped talking and looked in the mirror—two friends standing side by side.

"Wow, Jacks, you look beautiful," I said as we continued to look in the mirror.

"Aw, it's the dress." And she elbowed me in the ribs. We laughed again.

"Are you ready for this?" I asked her

"Oh, Ethel, yes, I am. I love Andy, and he is all I want. And I love this town and everyone in it. We'll be good together here." She turned to me, and I gave her a hug.

"Well, let's see about finishing up." We both had tears in our eyes, about ready to tumble out. So getting busy was helping us not give in to our emotions.

In a way, I envied Jackie. Her life was what most girls would dream of. The great guy, family businesses in a wonderful town, how could you not help but consider yourself lucky with all of that? If I had known someone like Andy, would I be doing the same thing right now? I couldn't truthfully say yes. As I had told Caleb, there was something that I needed to do, and it wasn't here.

Jackie brushed her hair and reached for her flowers. Instead of a veil, a simple headpiece of miniature white roses and baby's breath with pastel ribbons completed her wedding ensemble. The bouquet was a single white rose tied with pastel ribbons. When we were finished, I looked at the clock. Three o'clock, only another hour till the wedding.

We began to hear voices downstairs. Looking out the window to the front lawn below, some of the guests were arriving. They carried boxes in a variety of sizes all covered in different styles of white-and-silver paper, tied in shiny white ribbons.

As I looked out, I wondered what my wedding day would be like. Would I be standing in a window here at the inn waiting for my guests to arrive? Or would the location be somewhere else? No, most definitely, I would come back to Piney Bluffs, back to my home and friends and family. I would show my husband's family all around and introduce them to the people and places that were woven into the cloth that I was made of.

I told Jackie I was going to scoot downstairs to check on her mom and let her know everything was all right. Going down the stairs, I met Mr. F on his way up. I straightened his tie for him and gave him a kiss on the cheek.

"How's she doing?" he asked me. He still looked a little worried.

"I think she's ready for her father now," I replied. He nodded and kept on going up to Jackie's room.

Downstairs, I found Mrs. F and gave her a hug. She looked up at me and said, "You're a good friend to her, Ethel. Don't forget her and the rest of us here at home." At that, Rocky called out her name, and she was back to her role of the event planner instead of the one she would rather have been for today—mother of the bride.

I moved through the guests giving hugs and good wishes to Jackie's family and friends from town. Aunt Flo was doing her best to introduce me to everyone else I didn't know. As I looked around at the people gathering in the lobby area, I saw Andy and Charlie talking to Daddy in one of the side rooms. They seemed at ease with each other, a respect shared between them. Dressed in their suits and ties, they were a contrast to the way they had been dressed in fishing attire this morning for the derby. Clean-shaven faces and the aroma of Old Spice filled the air around them. Charlie even had his hair tied back in a ponytail, which I'm sure made Daddy a little happier. I hadn't heard any more comments about the barber in Knowles Corner that he had directed at Charlie when they first met.

"Well, I've never seen three more handsome men in my life." I smiled at them as I walked into the room.

"And look at you. You clean up rather well yourself." Charlie was returning my smile. "Let me see, turn around." He held out his hand, and he spun me around. I felt like the ballerina dancer in my music box from so very long ago.

"Anybody for a little fishing," Daddy asked and chuckled.

"I don't think that Jackie would be too pleased with that, never mind Mrs. F," Andy said, and we all agreed to that.

The inn's dining room was almost full now as the guests had taken their seats. Aunt Flo was in the front row, ready to absorb every detail of the wedding. Reverend Ezra had arrived, shook hands with Andy and Charlie, and the three made their way to the front of the dining room. Off to the side, Caleb stood ready with his camera. As his wedding present, he had offered to take pictures of the wedding. He gave me a smile as Mrs. F signaled to me from the stairs that it was time. I started up the stairs and met Jackie and her dad, hand in hand on their way down.

The happy chatter of the guests quieted as guitar music began to fill the air. I hadn't thought to ask Jackie about music. I had assumed that there would be a record playing "Here Comes the Bride" or one of the ladies from the church singing an assortment of off-key hymns. I handed Jackie her flower, gave a quick check to her head-piece, and proceeded to take my place in front of Jackie and her dad. Mrs. F went to the doorway of the dining room and signaled to someone. The guitar and singer now started the "Wedding Song" by Peter, Paul, and Mary.

As we began our slow entry to the room, I saw that it was Charlie standing and playing this simple but beautiful song. His voice was full and rich and enhanced the simplicity of the music. He smiled at me as he paused for a breath and continued with the song. It was as if he was singing only to me. For a moment, I held his gaze and felt the exchange of emotions between us. These past few weeks had held a mix of sensations whenever I was near him. I swallowed and held my breath for a moment. I wasn't sure how I had arrived, but as he ended the song, we were all standing in front of Reverend Ezra.

The ceremony was brief but meaningful. Jackie and Andy had written some vows to each other and to their families. Reverend Ezra had just pronounced them man and wife, and hankies were out as they kissed their first kiss of married life. Charlie had picked up his guitar to begin to play again.

In that moment of silence before the music began, there was a loud slamming and clattering from the main doorway and front desk of the inn. Heads turned, and necks were craned to see what the commotion was all about. A man's voice was heard to be cursing.

"Holy Mother Mary, where the hell is anyone? Cars all over the place, and no one here. What the hell kind of place is this?" The voice of Mike O'Brien made me stiffen.

17

Charlie began to play "How Sweet It Is (to Be Loved by You)" for the recessional song. This focused everyone's attention back to congratulating the newly married couple. Still some tried to look through to the main desk to see what the boisterous conversation was all about.

I quickly left the dining room to see about Mike. When I arrived at the front desk, I saw Mrs. F was already present and speaking to him. As I came into his eyesight, he nodded his head toward me.

"There she is," he was speaking at Mrs. F. "Why didn't you tell me you lived on the outskirts of civilization?" He stood there with one hand on the desk impatiently drumming his fingers and the other hand on his hip. It was the look of someone obviously irritated.

I looked at Mike and shook my head. He looked like he should have been with Big Bob's fishing expedition along with the rest of the overly outfitted fishermen. He was laden with a fishing creel, saltwater plugs, flies for fly-fishing, a freshwater rod with a fly-fishing reel, and a gaff for what could have taken in a swordfish. His clothing was no better. A large brimmed hat with mini beer cans glued to the sides, a T-shirt with a large mouth bass jumping from his chest, and a bright-blue fly-fishing vest. His jeans were about the only normal item he had on. On his feet were knee-high white boots usually worn by saltwater boat hands. I wasn't sure if he had tried to look as ridiculous as possible, or someone had actually let him buy all of this gear without questioning the type of fishing he was going to pursue.

Mrs. F was looking at me, eyebrows raised with that "you really know this nincompoop" gaze.

"Well, and here you are. Mrs. F, I'd like you to meet my future boss at the *Boston Herald,* Mike O'Brien. Daddy and I had invited Mike for a visit to discover fishing here in Piney Bluffs. We're glad you came, Mike, but as you can see, we're in the midst of a wedding, it's my best friend and Mrs. F's daughter." I was trying not to laugh at the sight of him as I explained the circumstances at hand.

"Your dad said come anytime, so this weekend, my wife and the girls went to visit her mother, and I thought this was the perfect time to come. So I'll meet you and your dad by the water, wherever the hell that is, in about half hour? I'll just get a room here for the night and be ready to go." Mike was just not getting the fact that fishing was not in my game plan for the day. He began to search in his wallet for money to pay for the room.

"I'm sorry, sir, but we have no rooms. We are full due to the wedding. Big Bob may have a fishing cabin available. Let me call him for you," Mrs. F, gracious as always, was trying to be helpful and get Mike someplace else and quickly so the wedding festivities could resume.

"Ah Jesus, no room here? A fishing cabin? Does it have running water? What kind of town is this anyway?" Mike, without realizing it, had annoyed Mrs. F, and as we all knew, that was not a good thing to do. Just as she was about to speak, Daddy appeared at the desk. He looked very distinguished in his new suit, which made Mike look all the more clown-like in his appearance. Daddy had overheard the conversations and was none too pleased either with Mike's comments.

"What do you mean a place like this?" Daddy was looking at Mike with a bit of disgust at those statements. "Can't you see what's going on here? And who the hell sold you all that getup?" Daddy was eyeing Mike up and down and shaking his head at what he saw.

"What's wrong with what I got? Some guy at the Outpost tried to tell me about some of this fishing crap, but he was just trying to sucker me into stuff I knew I didn't need. I figured this out all by myself." Mike was actually proud of what he had purchased and stood a little taller as he finished his statement.

Mrs. F had been dialing the phone, and I could now hear her talking to someone at Big Bob's. It sounded like there was a room. She hung up the phone and came back to the front desk.

"Big Bob has a cabin, forty-two dollars and fifty cents for the night, and that comes with breakfast at the diner. And, yes, it does have running water. Just take a right out our driveway, and follow the signs at the town green, about a five-minute ride." Mrs. F was a bit short with her remarks. And if that didn't convey her annoyance with him, her cold stare added more than her words.

"Tell you what," Daddy said, he was trying to diffuse the situation a bit, although I could see he would go at it if provoked any further. Daddy or anyone for that matter did not take insults about anything or anyone in Piney Bluffs lightly. "I'll come get you for a little early fishing tomorrow morning. Meet me at the diner at 5:00 a.m. We'll have a little breakfast, and I'll show you what fishing is all about."

"You mean I wasted my time driving all the way out here today? What a crock. Oh well, all right. What the hell is there to do in this town anyway?" Mike, red faced and cocky, was perturbed things weren't going his way. Giving in, as it appeared, was not something he was used to.

"Well, there is Fancy Franks Hum & Strum. It's a local watering hole with the band playing nightly at 7:00 p.m." Mrs. F had all she could do to control herself at this point. In a matter of twenty minutes, Mike had managed to piss off the two people who mattered the most to me. And his continued remarks about Piney Bluffs were beginning to draw the interest of another townsfolk who was in attendance at the wedding. Caleb took in the comments as he stood by the doorway waiting for the newlyweds to have their pictures taken outside.

Mike gathered up his things, and back out the door, he went muttering about what kind of town this was and other things we couldn't make out. I could see him as he loaded his gear into his old Volvo station wagon. As his car left the inn's driveway, I let out a sigh of relief.

"A little short on manners at the *Herald* these days," Caleb said as he looked at me.

"Yes, it is going to be quite the challenge to work for him," I replied. I was mortified that Mike had behaved the way he did.

During the interview and at the game, I had realized that he was going to be a bit difficult, but he had been downright rude. Daddy looked at me and shook his head.

"Well, let's see what kind of fisherman he turns out to be tomorrow. I've got my work cut out for me, I can tell you that. But right now, I think we have a wedding to enjoy." Daddy smiled at me and put his arm around my shoulder.

"Picture time," Caleb reminded me. Jackie and Andy had finally come through the well-wishers and stood waiting for our pictures. Charlie was coming along, having just packed up his guitar.

"I didn't know you played the guitar," I said as we fell into step going out the door. "And your voice is wonderful. I couldn't have imagined a more perfect song for the wedding."

"Lots of things you don't know about me," he replied. I found myself wondering just what those things were. I'd had so little time to get to know this man. And it was getting harder for me to push thoughts of him from my mind.

We all gathered outside by the forsythia that was in full bloom. With the lake in background, the pictures were going to be breathtaking. We took turns with both the families and then the separate shots. Caleb was very professional at the way he moved us in for just the right shots. He shared that he had worked for a photographer in college and that it had come in handy once he started working for the *Herald*. In those times, most pictures weren't usually of life's happy events. They were more the ones that had told the story of the latest crime or murder. The old adage "If it bleeds, it leads" sold more papers if the picture captured that gruesome moment of that headline.

"Ethel, go get your dad, and I'll take your picture too," Caleb said. I looked up at the inn, and Daddy was on the outside patio having a drink with Aunt Flo. I waved at him and motioned for him to come down. Caleb took a few pictures of Daddy and I together and then had Charlie in with us too. For whatever reason, it just seemed right to have the three of us in the picture together.

After the pictures, we all went back inside for the reception. As we settled in to begin the meal, Charlie stood to give the traditional best man's toast.

"I'd like to make a toast to Jackie and Andy for health and happiness and the best that life can give them together. I came here a few weeks ago to be the best man for my best friend. He had told me about Jackie and Piney Bluffs during the time that we were stationed together during the war. I would never have believed that this town was exactly as he had told me and that it was so much more. The spirit and the love that you all have for each other and this town are amazing. To Jackie and Andy, I wish the very best for prosperity and sustained happiness and a little Andy the Third to keep up the diner's legacy." And as he finished, there was a resounding chorus of, "Here, here," and then the clinking of silverware on glasses encouraging the kiss from the newlyweds.

The remainder of the reception went quickly as if on fast-forward. After the meal, music was cued up from the inn's reel-to-reel system, and dancing began. When the customary dances by the bride and groom and daddy's girl were over, all guests were invited to dance. I felt a hand on my arm and saw that it was Charlie motioning me to come and dance with him. I let him lead me to the dance floor. It was a waltz, and all the couples were out on the floor. He took me in his arms, and we started to dance. While I didn't know the name of the song, I did know how it felt to dance with him. If was effortless. This wasn't stiff-armed high school stuff. This was natural and unencumbered. As we moved across the floor, I looked up into his eyes. They were smiling back at me.

"You look incredible," he whispered in my ear. His lips touched my ear and sent an electric shock-like wave through me. He pulled me closer to him. I could feel his hand on the small of my back and his thumb rubbing my spine. I hoped the dance would never end. And then I felt a tap on my shoulder that woke me up from mini dream world. It was Daddy.

"Can I have the next dance?" he asked.

Charlie released me, and Daddy began his dance with me. In the middle of the song, he looked down at me and said, "You know Ethel, your momma used to look at me the same way you're looking at Charlie."

"Oh, Daddy," I said, trying to dismiss his thoughts of any connection between Charlie and me.

"I'm just saying, some things you can't hide," and then Daddy added, "and he does like to fish."

We laughed and shook our heads. I gave Daddy a push on the shoulder. He then feigned back the attack and then gave me a hug at the end of the dance. After that, it seemed that Charlie and I danced every dance. That is except for the times when some of Jackie's aunts were tugging at his sleeve for their turns. But each time he took me in his arms, I found myself aching to stay that way for more than just the length of the dance.

The guests dwindled away, and by eleven, there were just the newlyweds, the parents, Daddy, Charlie, and I. We had gravitated to the comfy chairs and couches of the tap room.

"I'd like to propose a toast," Andy Sr. said, his words just a little slurred. He tried to hoist his largess from the leather club chair. Years of his good cooking was holding him back just a bit now, but he finally managed to prop himself on the generous arm of the chair. With the glow from our drinks showing on our faces, we all raised our glasses and waited for Andy.

"To Jackie and Andy, may you remember the love from the people that are in this room right now. This love and these people will be what you can depend on for the rest of your lives." The words were from his heart, and he smiled as he looked at his son and new bride. With his glass to his lips and head back, he slowly fell back into the chair. We all laughed, and then there were several more toasts and I believe several more drinks. I seemed to remember Jackie and Andy kissing me good night, the clocking chiming twelve, and then that was all.

18

The next morning, I woke to the sound of Daddy in the bathroom. I looked at the clock, 4:30 a.m. Ugh. Why did I feel like this? The last thing I remembered was having shots at the bar with Jackie, Andy, Charlie, and Daddy. I put the pillow over my head to drown out the noise.

As I lay there, I tried to recall the events of the night before. We were dancing. There was the limbo with the mop handle, then the Alley Cat, and then there was a twist contest. At some point, I remember Daddy dancing with Aunt Flo and then him walking her out to her car. Hmmm. It was all starting to return. I was dancing with Charlie wishing it would never end. Then I danced with Daddy. And then we had a few more drinks and more dancing. I could still smell the aftershave Charlie had been wearing. That scent made me almost feel his arms around me. Inhaling, I closed my eyes and smiled.

I turned over and tried to go back to sleep. The harder I tried, the more wide awake I became. Mr. Striper was curled up at the foot of my bed and put his paws up to cover his eyes at my tossing and turning. I heard Daddy coming down the hallway toward my room.

"You up in there, Ethel?" he said. Early rising was the custom in our home, so now, at 4:45 a.m., why it was almost noon to him.

"Yeh, kinda," I murmured back to him.

"Can I come in?" he asked and waited for my response.

I quickly did a one-eyed survey of the room to see how badly I had left it, given the way I felt. Not too bad, nothing hanging from the curtains. Actually my dress was on its hanger, and my shoes placed neatly below them. I knew I couldn't have done that. So who? Better not to ask. I looked to see what I was dressed in, and I had my soon-to-be alma mater sleep shirt on. But oddly, I realized I still had my underwear on. As I said, better not to ask.

"Okay in here, come on in," I said and tried to sit up.

"Well, young lady, you had yourself quite the night." He had a cup of coffee in his hand, and he sipped it as he looked at me. The aroma of the fresh coffee filled my room, and my eyes were fluttering open. He had taken a seat in the red gingham ruffled chair by my bed. The chair had been Momma's. Daddy said she had loved to sit and do needlework by the window.

"Yes, I'm starting to remember," I said as I tried to sit up. This movement caused Mr. Striper to look up at the two of us with what could only be labeled as annoyance. He repositioned his body curl toward the wall and squeezed his eyes shut. His indifference to us spoke volumes of his opinion of our human lives.

"Damn cat," Daddy said and continued sipping his coffee.

"Could've brought me a cup, waking a person up this early," I nagged at him. Sitting wasn't working, so I propped myself up on one elbow and yawned.

"Some down on the stove when you get yourself up." Never one to cut me any slack, he continued sipping.

I could hear him thinking as he sat and sipped. Something was on his mind. What was it? Had I said something last night that I would be regretting? Or was it Charlie? I remember Daddy's words on how Momma had the same look in her eye when she looked at him as I had for Charlie. Or was it Mike? Yes, that was it. The more I thought of just how badly Mike had acted when he barged into the inn yesterday. I mean I could get that fact that he was a hard-nosed reporter, but he was way out of line yesterday. And did he not have any concept of the types of fishing? It was almost that he tried to be as ridiculous as he could. But why? For what reason? I was still thinking about it when Daddy interrupted my thoughts.

"Care to join us for breakfast? You got ten minutes," Daddy said as he got up and headed for the door. He offered his coffee, which

I eagerly took. "Could be, you'd find out a little more about him. Breakfast tells you a lot, you know."

"And how's that? I didn't realize you took up psychoanalysis while I was away." I cupped the coffee in my hands and grinned at him.

"You don't have to do no fancy studying to figure out human nature," Daddy replied as he stood in the doorway. "A man who takes his time at breakfast has a plan for his day and beyond. If you rush off out the door with half a cup of coffee left behind, then you're always playing catch up for the day and most likely until life catches up with you. And sometimes, life doesn't give you what you thought when the two of you finally collide."

"Why, Daddy, I'm impressed." I couldn't believe what I was hearing, but he was right.

"Well, if you want to find out what he has for breakfast, you'd best be getting out of that bed, young lady." Daddy was heading down the hallway now. "Oh, and by the way. Charlie gave me a little help getting you home last night."

"He what? What do you mean he gave you a little help with me?" I hollered to Daddy as he was on his way down the stairs. My thoughts had quickly turned from trying to figure Mike out to wondering what kind of help Charlie had been to Daddy. What happened to me last night? And what kind of help? I blushed thinking how the two of them had gone about getting me undressed and into bed.

"I'm just saying he was very helpful, and you should thank him when you see him next," Daddy called up the stairs. "You only got five minutes now, missy."

I jumped out of bed, sending Mr. Striper off the end of it. Twitching his tail, he looked back at me and jumped into Momma's chair. His tail curled around his nose, and he almost seemed to sigh in disgust.

I pulled on my jeans and a sweater and found some moccasins. I hurried down the hall to the bathroom and quickly washed my face and brushed my teeth. I ran the brush through my hair, and I was ready. Grabbing my jacket, I headed down the stairs to find that Daddy was already out in the truck and just about to leave.

"I could of bet money on it," Daddy said as he looked in the mirror to back up as I climbed in. "I knew you couldn't stand the not knowing."

"Well, I just think that I need to see what is what with my soon-to-be boss. Besides, I need to know a few more things about last night." We only had a few minutes to get to the diner, so I had to make good use of my time. "So tell me, what were you and Aunt Flo talking about last night?"

"Oh she's a good old gal, and I do mean old." Daddy was looking straight out the window.

"Daddy, she's only sixty, you're fifty-two. You make her seem ancient." I was trying to get him to open up a little. I was going to ask about him walking her out to her car but thought better of that.

"Well, it was just good to talk to someone from out of town, even if it's only Paris," he said. "Well, here we are. Now let's see if he shows up." And that ended any further discussion of Aunt Flo. But he did seem to have a little smile, and that was good to see.

We parked in the front of the diner and went inside. We were the only customers so far this morning. Andy Sr. was at the griddle, turning home fries over to show that golden brown crust that the diner was famous for. The aroma of bacon was making me realize how hungry I was.

"Morning, you two. Didn't expect to see you up this early, Ethel. You had quite the time," Andy greeted us but made me wonder again just what had happened.

"It was a wonderful evening, Andy. Best time I had in a long time," Daddy said as we took a seat at the counter. Andy set a couple of coffees in front of us.

"Yes, it was quite the day. Starting with the derby and ending with the wedding. Your fishing derby had quite the draw. How many entries did you have?" I asked.

"One hundred and two if you count me. Although I had to come back in early. Wife was wanting me to be ready for the wedding, I swear at ten o'clock in the morning. Next year, like I said, we'll add some more prizes and maybe have a little more news coverage." Andy nodded my way. I decided not to notice that Andy was referring to me working for *The Bugle*.

As we sat and waited, Daddy was stirring his coffee and looking my way. He had been doing this for several minutes now.

"What is it, Daddy?" I implored of him. "What do you want me to ask you?"

"Oh, nothing much. I just want to know what I'm supposed to do with that ass of an almost boss of yours. I mean, do I piss him off and get him lost? Or do I make him out to be the next best thing to this year's winner of Maine's best fisherman." He had a smile on his face. I knew that more than likely, he would love to lose Mike in the thickest part of Snowshoe Lake's undergrowth.

"Well, I guess that all depends on how he acts this morning, now, doesn't it,"

Just then, the door opened, and in walked Mike. Gone was most of the excess gear from yesterday, but the big bass T-shirt still remained. He also looked like he had a bit of a hangover.

"Morning, Mike, how goes it?" Daddy asked, surveying his new best fishing buddy.

"Yeh," Mike replied. "Can I get a coffee?" He grabbed a copy of the *Fishing Weekly* on the counter and took a seat next to Daddy.

"How was your night in town?" I asked.

"Well, I'll tell you, they're out of Johnny Walker Black at Frank's," Mike said and hunched over his coffee.

"How about three Sunday-morning specials, Andy," Daddy said, and we moved from the counter to a booth by the window.

"What's a Sunday-morning special?" Mike asked. "I'm not up for praying before my meal or any nonsense like that. Just coffee for me."

"Andy makes us what he thinks we need, never missed yet," Daddy replied. "So tell me, Mike, what kind of fishing do you want to do today?" Daddy was waiting to see what Mike had to say.

Mike had started to read the *Weekly* and ignored Daddy's question. Then he started, "What the hell is this? This a joke right? Do you let the grade-school kids publish now? Hey, your name's on this.

You do this? Really?" He put the paper down and looked at his watch and looked around the diner.

"I have a confession to make," Mike said, talking mostly to his coffee. "I really don't want to go fishing. I came out here to see what you were all about. You, this town, people who liked to fish. Just sounded like a bunch of crap to me. I wanted to see what you would do, how you would handle yourselves."

"Are you saying that that whole thing yesterday was just some cockamamie stunt to see how we would react? What kind of person does that?" I was incredulous. I couldn't believe what I had just heard.

"Who do you think you are to come here and try to embarrass us into acting like fools? Is that what you were after? Well, let me tell you something, Mr. Mike 'Sports Department' O'Brien, my daughter will never work for you, ever. Do you understand that?" Daddy was mad. His face was red, and he had stood at the side of the table, gripping its edge. I had never seen him this angry.

"Hold on, this was just a joke, nothing to go getting this upset about. Holy jeez, calm down," Mike was trying to make light of what he had just unveiled to us and was now realizing just how serious we were about Piney Bluffs. "And besides, I think Ethel might want to say whether she is going to work for me or not."

"I've got to tell you, Mike, in this instance, my Daddy is speaking for me. I would never work for a person as mean-spirited as you. Maybe you've never lived in a town like this, a town who cares for you and your family, but I do. And you are not going to come here and make fun of us. And then to think you can say it was just a joke and we'd forget about it, well, you're the joke," I was just getting started. My pride was hurt, and I was not going to let him forget what he had done here. "My dream was to work for a good paper like the *Herald* and to begin my journalism career with people who I could learn from and perfect my craft. But if you are an example of what kind of people are there, I want none of it. I'll spend my life writing for the people of this town. These are good, honest people, and how dare you to come here with your stupidity? I quit!"

I was shaking inside and out as I spat out the last words to Mike. I looked across the table in disgust at this man who had meant to make a mockery of my town. Daddy had taken a seat back at the counter with his arms folded while he listened to me. His face was set and stern. Mike got up and headed for the door.

"You change your mind, you let me know. I think you're making a big mistake." And with that, Mike and my dreams of life in Boston walked out the door.

I looked down at the table and over at Mike's cup of coffee. I picked it up and looked in. He'd left a half a cup.

19

"Well, would you two like your breakfast now?" Andy said, speaking more to the grill than to us. "Shame to waste these eggs, just about the most perfect Sunday-morning special I've made in a long time. But I'm glad he's gone. Wouldn't want the likes of him eating my special."

I was still sitting at the booth with my eyes closed and clenching and unclenching my hands. I had never been this mad or disappointed in my life. Daddy came over to the booth and put his arm around my shoulder. I turned my head into his chest. I wanted to bury my head in his plaid shirt and cry until there was nothing left to cry about.

"I think breakfast is just what we need. Come on, Ethel, let's sit at the counter," Daddy said as he pulled my elbow, forcing me to get up.

"Great, hate to see good food go to waste. Eggs over easy, slab bacon from Mcreery's Smokehouse and Mountain Farm, and Miss Ruthie's blueberry muffins." Andy set the plates in front of us and wiped his hands on the towel hanging from his apron strings. He and Daddy exchanged looks, not really knowing what to say next.

"Thanks," was about all I could manage looking up at Daddy, holding back my tears, and trying to swallow the lump in my throat. I lost myself for a moment in the golden yolks of my eggs, drawing my fork through them.

The bell jingled announcing that someone had just come in the diner, but I didn't care to know who. I felt someone sit next to me, and then a hand reached across my plate and grabbed my bacon. Startled, I looked up and saw it was Charlie, smiling and thoroughly enjoying the bacon.

"Well, I didn't expect to see you up this early," Charlie said and continued chewing. "Your Dad tell you we put you to bed last night?" His smile turned to concern as he saw the look on our faces. "Hey, what's going on?"

"Oh, nothing, just I quit my job at the *Herald* as my almost boss turned out to be one of the biggest asses this side of Portland." I was pulling my lips tight to keep other words from tumbling out. "Guess I'll be coming home now to figure out what to do when I graduate." And with that, I told him what had happened just moments before he had walked through the door. He remembered the story about Mike I had told him last night and how he had appeared at the wedding. He had been inside playing and had missed the bizarre combination of attitude, clothing, and equipment that Mike had presented with.

"Too bad I wasn't here," Charlie said. "He would have gotten a little lesson in respect that would have stayed with him for a while." Sitting between Daddy and Charlie was helping me have a restored sense of wellbeing.

"Well, the less time spent thinking about him now, the better," I said. "Andy, can you please get Charlie his own breakfast so I can enjoy mine now?" I had started to stab at Charlie's hand as he reached for yet another piece of my bacon.

"Just so happens I have an extra Sunday-morning special all set to go." Andy smiled and set the breakfast in front of Charlie. I snatched a piece of bacon back from his plate.

"So now do you two mind telling me just what happened last night?" I said. Daddy and Charlie smiled at each other and just continued on with their breakfasts.

"Oh, let's not spoil a good meal. Maybe later," Daddy said, and though I tried several times to get more information, we settled into Sunday morning small talk as if this was the most natural thing to do.

After breakfast, we went back home. Charlie said good-bye and headed back to the inn. At home, I went to sit in the sunroom for a while with Mr. Striper. He was very content to have a lap to settle into. Stroking his soft fur and hearing his purr put a calming to my jangle of feelings from this morning's events. I needed to sit to reflect on what I was going to do with my life now.

Less than twenty-four hours ago, my life had been set. I had known where everything was. It was like looking into a tackle box where I knew where all of my plugs and hooks were. And now the contents of that box were strewn out on the floor, leaving me to look for those special ones that were no longer there. So now what was I going to do? Did I change my style of fishing or give up fishing altogether?

I had turned down the interview in Providence saying I had taken another position. Maybe I should try there citing difference of opinions for my reconsideration. No, one disappointment like Mike made me realize that I needed something different. And I also made me realize what Piney Bluffs meant to me.

I gently pushed Mr. Striper from my lap and brushed his fur from my jeans as I stood. I grabbed my jacket, and out the door I went. The morning sun was now past the tree line from the lake and shone warm and bright on my face as I found myself walking toward *The Bugle's* office. I waved and said good morning as I passed a few folks hurrying to church. While services were advertised to begin at ten, Reverend Ezra didn't usually get going until ten fifteen as folks silently slipped into their pews during the first stanza of the opening hymn.

As I approached *The Bugle's* office, I saw Caleb sitting at his typewriter, intently working. The Sunday's paper came out later in the afternoon. He looked up and motioned me in.

"Glad to see you," he said and pulled up the other office chair to his desk without letting me say yes or no. "I'm writing about Jackie and Andy's wedding, and I know I don't have it quite the way it should be or which of the pictures to choose. Which one do you think should go in?" I looked at both the story and pictures and was thankful that he didn't ask anything about Mike.

"I really like this one," I said as I came to a picture with Jackie and Andy smiling at each other. I took the seat beside him.

"You're right, does have just that right feeling," Caleb replied and put the picture to one side. "So do I have this right?" And he turned his typewriter for me to read the copy he was writing. I read through the piece and started making suggestions. He gave up his seat, and I moved over and started with my additions to the story. Before I knew it, I had been there a half hour and had finished the piece. Caleb read it through and gave me a thumbs-up. We looked at the pictures and finally agreed on two—one of the newlyweds and then one of the entire families.

As that had been the last story, the paper was now ready to print. We took the copy into the print room and got set for the day's printing. We printed extras for distribution to the folks who had come into town for the diner derby and the wedding. In addition, copies of the *Fishing Weekly* were inside. Caleb had written a small piece in *The Bugle* describing the *Fishing Weekly* and how he would like to know what folks thought about it. He asked that folks stop by *The Bugle* and let him know. Knowing folks in town the way we did, I knew that he wouldn't have to wait too long.

"If you're not busy, I could use a hand with delivery," he asked. "I need some to go out to the inn and Big Bob's.

"Sure, I'd love to." And I went to pick up the piles.

"Would you rather have the jeep or the bike?" Caleb asked, giving me the choice. It was such a nice day that I chose the bike. It was outfitted with a big basket to accommodate the papers.

"Funny a paper route isn't quite how I had imagined my career in journalism would begin," I joked with Caleb.

"Well, if you want, we can talk about that when you get back," Caleb said with a more serious note in his tone.

"Sure, I'd like that." And I headed out the door with my papers.

As I rode along, I composed a letter that I would send to Bob Hurley, the editor of the *Herald*. I mulled over my desire to tell him exactly what I thought of Mike and how he had acted. But I thought better of that and decided to just leave it as "I have reconsidered my options and have made a different choice," or something like that.

Mike had made that choice for me, and I would never forget that feeling of mistrust and humiliation that he had brought to me. And living in Boston on my own would never be, or at least not now. Yes, there was an entire part of my life that I would never know, thanks to Mr. O'Brien and his little test. I was still deep in thought when I found that I was already at Big Bob's.

As I entered the main registration area, I saw that some derby contestants were checking out and getting ready to return home. Gone were the sporting catalog outfits and the great fisherman bravado. In their place were clothes that provided a glimpse of who they might be in their day-to-day lives. The two redheaded men who had been bickering at the weigh-in were continuing to squabble, and this time, it was about who was paying the bill. They were now dressed in sport coats and slacks, but the civility of their clothes didn't make them any less confrontational with their struggle about the bill. Big Bob had left them and had turned his attention to the man who had lost the fight with the briar patch. He had on jeans and a Sox jacket and was amused at the spectacle that the other two were making. He took a paper and shoved it into his duffle bag.

"Good morning, gentlemen," I said, hoping that a new voice might stop the two from bickering. They looked up at me and stopped their conversation in midstream. It had worked, and so I continued, "Would you care for a copy of our Sunday paper? And inside, there's a special edition of our new publication with coverage of the fishing derby." I offered each of them a paper. Momentarily, they were quieted, absorbed with their reading. Big Bob looked up at me and mouthed, *Thank you*, and smiled. I placed the other papers on the desk.

One of the men had opened his paper to the *Fishing Weekly* and was chuckling. The other, not to be outdone, quickly dropped *The Bugle* to find out what the other had found so humorous.

"Say, this is quite good. Who writes this?" the one said.

"Caleb Johnson, *The Bugle's* editor and myself," I replied and pulled my shoulders back and hoped I looked more like a reporter. "Do you like it?"

"Yes, yes, I do. And you would be?" he asked as he looked at me over the top of his horned-rimmed glasses, but quickly, his eyes went back to the *Weekly.*

"I'm Ethel Koontz, and I freelance for *The Bugle* and the *Weekly*." *What the heck*, I thought, *the fact was Caleb had asked me to freelance for him.* And I did just finish the article on Jackie's wedding. With my resume building with each passing second, I was surprised I didn't say I was the distribution manager as well. But I knew they wouldn't be fooled when they saw the distribution vehicle was a bicycle with an oversized basket.

"Allow me to introduce ourselves to you," he continued. "I am Russell, and this is my brother Robert. We are Brown and Brown, a small publishing house from New York City. We come to Piney Bluffs several times a year. Big Bob has been good enough to share his knowledge of fishing with us. And I must say we are improving quite nicely. Don't you think so, Big Bob?" Big Bob nodded and cleared his throat, seemingly happy he had another customer and couldn't join this conversation.

"A pleasure to meet you, gentlemen," I said and tried to calm myself as the possibilities were beginning to course through my brain. I tried to find something more sophisticated to say but could only manage, "Glad you like our paper."

"Oh, I love it, don't you, Robert?" Russell said, looking for his brother to concur.

"It does seem quite humorous. You must excuse me. We are preparing for the annual book show next week, and my mind is running through the countless list of last-minute details. Do you have a card, dear?" Robert folded his copy and placed it in his briefcase.

"No, I'm sorry, I don't, but the address to *The Bugle* is in the paper." I really felt like a small-town girl now.

"Oh, we'll be in touch. Now come along, Russell, the car is waiting. We've a plane to catch in Portland." Robert was all business and ushering his brother out the door and to the cab that had arrived. The driver was quickly packing gear and luggage into the trunk while Russell was still reading the *Fishing Weekly.*

"Bye, bye, my dear," said Russell and waved out the window as the two sped off in the cab toward Portland.

I waved at Russell as he and his brother rode out of sight. What had just happened? I couldn't believe they were publishers from New York City. And did they really like what they were reading? I couldn't wait to tell Caleb. Waving to Big Bob, I hurried out the door to deliver the rest of the papers to the inn. For a day that had started out with my hopes and dreams being sunk like an old rowboat, I felt now like everything was about to resurface.

20

"Up so soon," Mr. F said as I came through the door to the inn. He was just finishing up with a guest who was checking out when I plunked the papers on the counter.

"Well, it is afternoon, and I didn't want to miss the day," I replied, facing the fact that everyone always had his or her opinion as to when someone should rise. "Did the newlyweds get on their way?" I asked, trying to divert any further questions away from me.

"Oh yes, took off for Portland bright and early this morning. Had to catch a ten o'clock flight to Philadelphia and then a drive to the Pocono Mountains," he finished. I remembered Jackie had said they had found a honeymoon spot where each room had a red heart-shaped tub. These honeymoon retreats had been heavily advertized in her *Modern Bride* magazine as a *must* for honeymooners.

I left the papers as another guest came to the desk to check out. I recognized her from the wedding, so I nodded and spoke my pleasantries. My hand was on the latch to close the door when I heard a familiar voice come from the kitchen area.

"Thanks so much for your hospitality, Mrs. F. And I'll be back." Charlie had his duffle bag over his shoulder and guitar case in hand. As he came through the door, our eyes met. Our expressions showed that neither of us had expected what we were now seeing—me seeing him about to leave, and he running into me on his way out.

"Well, I guess you were going to be writing to me at some point. I can see it now, 'Dear Ethel, if you ever get to the Cape, be sure to give a call,'" I said, hurt clearly evident in my tone. I could feel the color rising in my cheeks, the tears stinging my eyes. I jammed my hands into the pockets of my jeans and looked at him for a response.

"Hey, Ethel, wait, you have this all wrong. I was headed over to see you." His voice was earnest, and his eyes were honest. "Come on, let's go back to your house and talk." He had come toward me and was putting his arm around my shoulders, moving us out the door of the inn.

"I'm not sure I want to know what you have to say, Charlie. And I'm almost willing to bet that you weren't going to my house to see me," I continued with my upset feelings and folded my arms across my chest, although I hadn't pushed his arm away. "Besides, I have to get back to *The Bugle*. I have a meeting with Caleb. Now that I had no job, I have to swallow my pride and see if he is still willing to give me a job."

"Ethel, please, we have a lot to talk about. Things have happened here in the last few weeks. And I want to make sure that what I'm feeling is the same thing that you're feeling." The sincere way that he spoke to me made me snap out of my momentary juvenile attitude.

"Well, okay, let's hear what you have to say." I was not giving in that easily, but why was I acting this way. Was I feeling the same thing he was feeling? I really didn't think that we had a relationship, but I knew that with the events of yesterday, I had certainly come to recognize that something was happening. I was uncertain about these emotions. I had never had any steady boyfriends in high school. And at college, it had been friends going out for the night to see a group or hanging out at a coffee house or bar. We lived for the fun of the moment. No one in those times had ever caused any of these emotions that I was feeling now. Seeing Charlie about to leave, thinking he wasn't even going to say good-bye, made me panic.

"Boy, you are your father's daughter," Charlie said with a little laugh and released me as I wriggled out of his one-armed hug.

"And what's that supposed to mean?" I shot back at him but showed a bit of smile now.

"Just saying that you're a tough one, and no one is going to get involved with you without realizing the consequences," he finished as I stopped to get the bike. "Nice ride."

"Part of my job interview. If I can handle a paper route, Caleb might give me a chance," I said and started to push the bike toward home. He fell in step beside me as we walked in silence for a while.

"So did you want to know about last night?" he broke the silence that we had fallen into on our short walk. "I mean how I helped your father put you to bed."

"Now that you mention it, I would like to know what happened since it seems to be a big secret between the two of you." I put his abrupt leaving to one side for a moment. I really did want to know. We had arrived at the gate. I put the kickstand down on the bike, and we walked up the path into the house. The daffodils along the path seemed to be a brighter yellow with the sun today. We entered the house. Charlie put his things down, and we went to the sunroom where we sat on the couch. Mr. Striper was in his chair and yawned to let us know that we had been recognized. I sat back against the end of the couch, grabbed a pillow, and hugged it. I turned toward Charlie and sat cross-legged. He draped an arm over the back of the couch. The conversation could begin.

"Well, after the toast from Andy's dad, there were several more as we had decided that each of us should give one. We drank a shot after your dad's and then another after yours." He looked to me for some type of acceptance.

"Continue," I said, still not knowing why I was being so bitchy.

"Your toast, I assume you don't remember, but it was made to your dad and me." He half smiled as he looked at me. "You said you hoped that the two of us would find respect for each other as this was going to be a long relationship. And then you asked him when was he going to take me fishing."

I vaguely remembered saying something like that. I wanted to ask what kind of a reaction that had gotten, but that wasn't what had me worried.

"Who helped me get undressed? I can't believe it was Daddy," I said and swallowed hard, waiting for the answer.

"Is that what you're so worried about?" He chuckled and kept on with the story. "We called it a night after your toast. Andy and Jackie said their good-byes and went up to their suite. Your dad asked me to help him get you into the truck, which I did. And might I say you didn't make it easy. You were trying to be very independent and kept pushing us away. Anyway, we got you into the truck, and then your dad asked if I wanted to ride along to make sure you didn't try anything. By the time we got home, you were asleep. I picked you up and carried you to your bed. As soon as you were on your bed, you started to kick your shoes off and take off your dress. At that point, your dad and I stepped out of your room. When you got quiet, your dad peeked in. We went in saw that you had found your nightshirt and put it on and had gotten into bed. I hung your dress up and put your shoes together. Your daddy kissed you good night, shut the light off, and that was the end of that." As he finished, I could see that it was the truth.

"Well then, thank you. That was very gallant of you," I said. With that out of the way, I got to the heart of the new issue, "But now what did you want to talk about, and why are you leaving?"

"Let's see where do I start. When we met on the bus that day, I couldn't believe you. You were so different from other girls I had met. You're beautiful in so many ways. A small-town girl, graduating from college, job lined up in Boston, an honest attitude, not afraid to say how she loved her family and her town. You were unlike the girls in my town. Oh, our town is small and all, but because you say you're from the Cape, things just get different somehow. Everybody's got their nose up in the air with a inflated set of values. It's just not like here." I nodded for him to continue.

"This town is a whole, and each person has their part to be in that whole. And since I've been here, I've felt like I've been part of that, with my own purpose. The longer I was here, the more I got to know you, and well, I can't explain it. I know it's only been a little over a month, but my life has changed. What I want to do and who I want to do it with all changed. My dad is expecting me to continue with him in his carpentry business back home. The last thing I want to do now is leave you. But I have to go talk with my folks, you know, sort things out, and make my decisions. I've never felt this way about anyone. I know this may be a lot to take in, but I had to tell you how I feel." He looked at me, and before I had a chance to answer, he leaned forward and pulled me close to him. My arms went to circle around his neck. His arms slid down around my waist. As he lay back on the couch, gravity took over, and I was on top of him, looking into those serious eyes. Our lips lightly touched in a soft kiss that sent astonishing feelings through me. Then his hands pulled me into him, and our kisses became deeper and more intense. A slow heat started to rise in me.

I pulled back for a moment to look at him and to think of what was happening. Charlie had been the first guy in my life who had made me feel like this. Had Daddy really meant it when he'd said Momma had looked at him the same way I looked at Charlie? My head was swimming. His hands reached up and cupped my face. He kissed me again tenderly.

"Hey, where did you go?" he asked me. He tilted his head to one side as if to see the road my thoughts had taken. He kissed me again, and his hands were now gliding over my body, pausing to caress and stroke. His touch burned through my clothes, lighting my skin on fire.

All the reasons for no flashed through my head. But I felt only yes. I hungrily kissed him back, took his hand, and led him upstairs to my bedroom. We undressed each other in the rays of the early afternoon sunlight, clothes falling in slow motion. We lay down and entwined our limbs, our torsos fitting together in perfect lines. Our kisses were long and wet. We explored each other with our lips and trailing fingertips. Unable to wait any longer, the urgency of our desires overcame us, and we burst with the celebration of our newly discovered love.

I pedaled across the Green to *The Bugle*. It was three o'clock. I hoped that Caleb would still be there so that we could talk about his previous offer and if it was still available. I also couldn't wait to share the news about the Brown brothers and the prospect of a New York publisher liking the *Weekly*.

Although I knew I should be preparing myself for the interview, my thoughts were still on Charlie. He'd left to go back to Dennisport on the afternoon bus. He'd kissed me good-bye and said he would see me after my graduation. We decided not to dwell on the consequences of what had just happened. Strains from Stephen Stills' "Love the One You're With" came to mind as I watched the bus disappear around the corner until it was out of sight. Even though the free love ways of the sixties had spilled over into the seventies, I knew this wasn't the case. There was a lot more here than just a conversation on a bus and an afternoon of desire, but I had to keep things in perspective.

Charlie, like me, really didn't have a job. While his father wanted him to join his carpentry business, he wasn't sure he was still meant to be there. He'd almost finished his criminal justice course before being drafted, but again, where was he going with that? State or local police? Probably not. The last thing he wanted to do was be involved with any violent situations. Vietnam had changed many things for him. The men and women who had served came back changed in how they viewed life. Also people were not welcoming home their soldiers. Criticism and bad feelings were still hot topics for many. And as much as he loved Piney Bluffs, jobs were scarce. There were places where he might be able to help out, but nothing that would be a steady source of income. If he stayed at home, that meant a long-distance romance, and that could be hard to maintain considering all that was needed to nourish a relationship.

Caleb's voice woke me from daydream dilemma.

"I thought you'd run away with *The Bugle*'s only paid off asset," Caleb said as he came from the side of *The Bugle*'s office. He had a shovel in his hand. "If we had a police force, I would have filed a stolen vehicle report and told them the suspect would be a pretty but devious young journalist."

"This town's too small to hide from grand theft auto. That's why I brought her back," I joked back with him. It was good to put the thoughts of Charlie aside for a bit and concentrate on trying to become gainfully employed. Our teasing continued as I said, "What were you doing out back? Preparing the shallow grave for my body once I was convicted and put to death by hanging?"

"Oh, since we spend more time here than home, Sadie's going to put in a garden, and I was checking to see what kind of a stonewall I was going to build with all of the stones I'd be digging up." He was wiping the dirt from his hands on his shirt.

"Sadie won't be pleased with that dirt on your shirt," I scolded him. "What's she going to plant?" We all knew Sadie was known more for the failure of her culinary ventures than her successes.

"She's not entirely sure, but hopefully, it won't be something that has to be cooked." Caleb winked at me. He truly loved Sadie but realized that for all the amazing things she did, cooking was not one of them. Most of their meals were taken at Andy's, Miss Ruthie's, or the inn. "She did say something about medicinal herbs and how they can cure all kinds of things. Something she read in an article in *Yankee*. She's been hell-bent ever since to start. Well, enough of that, come on in, and let's sit down and talk."

It was now time to get down to business. We went into the office and took seats, he at his desk and I in one of the side chairs. I had been preparing an apology, and I was just about to start when Caleb cut me off.

"Ethel, I'm not going to drag this out," Caleb said as he looked straight at me. "My offer still stands. I need someone here. I need you. I like what you've done with the first *Weekly* and the articles you've done for *The Bugle*. I can't pay you a lot, but I can give you five thousand dollars a year. And as we go along and we grow, that salary will grow with it. Besides, you have full use of the company vehicle." He ended with a smile.

The money was more than I thought it would be. In fact, as I thought, where did the money come from? Doing some quick math, I calculated at a quarter a paper for the weekly and a dollar on Sunday, which was only fifteen thousand dollars a year with one hundred papers printed a day. And that didn't include the cost of materials. There was no way he could afford to give me that kind of money.

"Caleb, I accept, but how can you afford that much?" I wanted to let him know that I was well aware of costs and how my salary might possibly affect his lifestyle.

"Well, nice to see someone whose concern is not just for themselves. Don't you worry about where the money comes from. I do a few other things than put this paper together. There's the small print business from our local merchants. And my photography is bringing me some jobs from time to time," he said in a way that assured me things would be all right.

"Oh, I almost forgot. While I was delivering the papers to Big Bob's, two of his clients started reading the *Weekly* and were very excited about it. They are from New York City, and they own a small publishing house." I was excited to tell him, and my words came tumbling out.

"What do you mean they're excited about the *Weekly*? We've only done one edition." He looked at me, quite puzzled.

I explained how they've been coming to Piney Bluffs to Big Bob's camp several times a year. And that after reading the *Weekly*, they were chuckling and said they would be in touch. They had some big book show coming up, and they needed to concentrate on that.

Caleb was listening intently as I finished my chronicle of the afternoon event.

"Well, that's a good omen, don't you think?" he said. "I'm going to check into Brown and Brown. Seems that name is vaguely familiar."

"I don't know about omens," I said. "I just hope they make good on their word." I realized I sounded like a child who was not about to wait too long for a toy that had been promised.

"Well, Ethel, sometimes the waiting is the toughest part," he said in a contemplative way. "And if fortune smiles our way, then the wait was worth it."

After that, we settled into a conversation about what I would be doing at the paper—schedules, coverage of events, and so on. Caleb shared some of his visions for *The Bugle*, the *Weekly*, and life here in general. He in turn asked me about my own visions. He had asked me that at my first interview and although only weeks ago, it had now changed. I still wanted to be a journalist, but how I would accomplish that was going to take a different path. Mike's exploits had been the first time someone had let me down. I would never again place that much trust in someone. I would be cautious as to how high the pedestal was for my heroes. I had learned a hard lesson. It seemed even though college was ending, my education was just beginning.

21

It was a beautiful day for our commencement, and the town of Orono had swelled to capacity. University of Maine students were responsible for about a third of the town's population, and we were always reminded of how much the town embraced us. Merchants had put out their welcome signs with our blue-and-white colors. Diners and coffee shops had breakfast and lunch specials. Even places like Sarah's Second Hand store were advertising special cash deals for those moving out of their apartments. I had lived in Cumberland Hall dorm for my four years and was leaving with the same trunk I had moved in with, give or take a few items on hangers. Recent bus trips home had been good for taking items like my records and books. The rest of the trappings of college life were left to the undergrads.

Underclassmen had crowded the dorm hallways eager for all the extras that seniors were leaving behind. From posters and Indian print bedspreads to incense burners and hot pots, they left our rooms laden with a wonderful bounty. Our new lives wouldn't need the incense or the hot pots. Most of us would be trying on our new role as adults with interesting careers. While my career was still in journalism, I was going to have to work at improving the interesting part of my hometown. However, I considered myself lucky as some of my classmates would be working as educated bartenders and shop clerks while they waited for that long studied career.

Friends and relatives were gathering now for noontime commencement and beginning to file into the football stadium. The last-minute hugs, kisses, and congratulations jostled around me as

I looked around for Daddy. Graduates had been given two tickets a month before, and I told him he could bring whomever he wanted. He had kidded me that he was going to bring Mr. Striper. At last, I saw him waving as he walked through the parking lot. He had a big smile and looked handsome in his suit that he had worn for Jackie's wedding. And to my surprise, he had Caleb with him. He too was all smiles as they walked toward me.

"There's my college graduate," Daddy said as he gave me a big hug and a kiss. "The first Koontz to get a college degree. This is really something, Ethel. I only wish your momma had lived to see this day." He took me by the shoulders and looked at me with a tear in his eye. His put his finger on my nose, our sign of I love you.

"Hold that for a minute," Caleb said. He had brought his camera and was expertly moving around us to position our picture. "I'll get some more when you receive your diploma. The whole damn town is so proud of you, Ethel. This will make front page of the *Bugle* tomorrow. Then you can follow up in a day or two with your own story for our readers. That's your first assignment."

"Boy, such a taskmaster." I smiled at Caleb. "I might have to reconsider my options.

Just then, the announcement was made for the ceremonies to begin. Daddy and Caleb gave me a hug once more and then went to find their seats. We found our places in line and helped each other to make sure our white tassels were on the right side of our blue mortarboards. Not long after that, the marching band began the "Stein Song." It was a peppy number about filling our steins and thinking with fond memories of happy hours and careless days with our school being the college of our hearts. A lot had happened during our college years. Peace, love, and war had converged on our lives. Some chose only one of those; others had one chosen for them. Our hometowns and our world would never be the same again. Some of us had gained four years of knowledge, but we had lost the lives of those who would never have a fond memory of the college of their hearts.

Our speaker was Governor Kenneth Curtis, an alumnus of Maine Maritime Academy as well as Colby. His speech, though filled with what I assumed was standard fare for a college commencement presenter, had one part that will stay with me forever.

> The world is run by those who show up, not by those who wait to be asked. When a job opens, whether it's in the chorus line or on the assembly line, it goes to the person standing there. It goes to the eager beaver the boss sees when he looks up from his work, the pint-sized kid standing at the basketball court on the playground waiting for one of the older boys to head home. "Hey, kid, wanna play?" You want to be that kid.
>
> And there's a false assumption out there that talent will surely be recognized. Just get good at something, and the world will beat a path to your door.
>
> Don't believe it. The world is not checking in with us to see what skills we've picked up, what idea we've concocted, or what dreams we carry in our hearts. You have to be there and have the courage to transport those dreams and ideas through to the next level of life.
>
> Most important, don't let the noise of others' opinions drown out your own inner voice. You must have the courage to follow your heart and intuition.

These words made me think of some of my classmates who had been handpicked by corporations to join their ranks. Sure, they were good at what they did, and as long as they kept with that corporation's belief, they would live well. But at what price? For them, the inner voice from their hearts would be silenced. I made a silent vow that I would always remain true to heart and my intuitions. Whether I stayed in Piney Bluffs or life took me elsewhere, I would not compromise. My inner voice had started as a whisper, a conversation with myself. And now it was time for that conversation to be heard loud and clear.

Diplomas were presented next. I waited while our row was called and then paused at the podium to have Caleb take my picture as our college president shook my hand and said his congratulations. Finally, we were done. The marching band struck up the "Stein Song" again, and we almost ran from the stadium, eager for our friends and families and new lives.

Daddy and Caleb met me, and Daddy placed a small present in my hands.

"What's this?" I asked. I had worked part-time in a coffee shop here and at home when Miss Ruthie had needed a hand. But that just paid for some of my books. Daddy had paid for my four years of school from overtime and guiding tourists in the pursuit of their dreams of the fishing excellence. He had told me I was not to worry about the money but to do a good job. So I wasn't expecting anything for completing my education.

"Just go on and open it," Daddy said as he motioned with his hand for me to continue.

I ripped open the package and found a small black box. I shook it and then looked at him quizzically. There was one thing in it, and it clunked on the top of the box.

"Jewelry?" I questioned. I had forever tried to guess what was in a package before actually looking inside. This always drove him crazy, and he stopped me as I was about to guess again.

"Nope, open it," Daddy pleaded with me. He looked very excited, which was so unlike him to break that usually stoic façade.

I obliged and opened the box. I gasped. It was a key to a car. For four years, I had taken a bus back and forth to school, dreaming that someday, when I got a job, I would buy a car. I looked at him with a smile and flung my arms around his neck.

"Oh, Daddy, thank you, thank you." I was crying, and I thought I saw his eyes tearing up as well.

"Don't you even want to know what kind it is?" Caleb was chuckling, at the same time, taking pictures of our little celebration.

"Come on, let's go see it then." Daddy put his arm around my shoulders, and we walked out to the parking lot. Finally, he told me to close my eyes. He guided me for a few more steps and then told me to open my eyes. There in front of me was a shiny red VW bug with a little white bow on its windshield wiper.

"Oh, Daddy, she's beautiful," I said as I rushed to the car and unlocked the door. I jumped in behind the wheel. It had white interior and looked brand new. "How did you ever have enough—"

"Don't you worry about how much. Had a customer at the airport who wanted to leave a little car here for when he went fishing. Last trip through, he decided he didn't want it anymore and so I bought it for you." Daddy was very matter-of-fact about the entire transaction, but I could see that he was just about as happy as I was.

"Well, let's get your stuff loaded into the truck, and then you can ride home in your new car," Daddy said. "And don't dillydally 'cause Miss Ruthie is expecting us back home for five o'clock. Opening up the shop afterhours for a little celebration dinner, and I don't want to miss her cooking."

I waved at Daddy and Caleb as Daddy's old Chevy truck was leaving the lot. I looked around the campus for one last time. I had grown up here and learned many lessons, least of which was to believe in what was good and right. *Memories of these people and places will fade over time,* I thought. I was now going to make new memories and find my place in the world. I started the engine of my little bug and pulled out of the driveway of college. Even though my world was going to be what others would consider only a sleepy little fishing town, I promised myself to make the world know Piney Bluffs.

22

From the dim light of dawn peeping through my window, I guessed the time to be about 5:30 a.m. The morning doves cooing in the trees outside my window and I looked over, and the luminous hands of the clock showed 5:45. I had it set for 6:30. The cardinal clicked to his mate to tell her it was safe to go to the feeder. It was my first official day at *The Bugle*. Caleb had said starting time was 7:30, but I wanted to be up early and have some breakfast with Daddy. I pressed the knob in to stop the alarm. Even though I was working in my hometown, I had a reputation to live up to. All I had ever told people that I wanted to do was write. And now they would be waiting. What would I write about? Caleb had said to write about my graduation.

I showered and dressed in casual slacks and a shirt. Reporting could lead you anywhere, so a skirt and heels wouldn't be a wise choice. Caleb wore slacks and a dress shirt most days. He had a wardrobe of ties in the back room. He said you never knew when one might be needed, but most days, they hung in quiet expectation, gathering dust.

I went downstairs to start coffee and feed Mr. Striper. To my surprise, coffee was just starting to perk on the stove, but Daddy was nowhere in sight. Then I saw he had left a note on the table.

I smiled as I read it, "Dear Ethel, had to go in for an early arrival. Have a great first day. Daddy."

I fed Mr. Striper as I waited for the coffee to perk. He purred and wound himself around my legs to show his appreciation. I, however, did not appreciate the fur that was now on my pants' legs. I sighed and looked outside as the sun was just starting to show on through the trees. Those first rays of sun caught the drops of dew on the daffodils by the back step and made them almost sparkle like yellow crystals.

I poured my coffee and was about to put some toast in the toaster when the phone rang.

"Hello," I said. Not many people called early in the morning, maybe it was Daddy.

"Mornin', is this the best journalist in Piney Bluffs?"

Hearing Charlie's voice was a definite surprise. "It is, and you would be?" I responded, not wanting him to be too comfortable with our familiarity.

"This would be the guy who didn't show up at your graduation party," he said a little sheepishly. "I'm sorry, I tried to call your dorm and your room, but the phones had been disconnected, so I called your dad and told him what had happened and that I couldn't come up. I do have a present for you." His tone brightened a little to sweeten me up.

Daddy had explained to me that Charlie's mother had fallen and broken her foot last week and was having trouble getting around. His dad was working on a house out at Martha's Vineyard, and Charlie had told him to stay and finish with his crew, and he would take care of his mom.

"Well, what makes you so sure I want a present?" I was just teasing to see how he would react.

"Oh, stop it, Ethel. Everyone likes presents. Speaking of that, how do you like your car?" He was taking no more of my taunting.

We talked for a bit, and I told him about the car and about the party at Miss Ruthie's. Family and friends had crammed into the bakery with warm wishes for me that night. Miss Ruthie did not disappoint with the food either. With help from Rocky, Mrs. F's chef at the inn, she had made a great buffet for us. The cake was the front page of *The Bugle*. White fluffy frosting held the headlines written in black chocolate, Local Woman Becomes First Female Reporter in Piney Bluffs. No one walked away hungry that night.

He told me he would like to come to see me this weekend if I wasn't busy. I let him know that while I might get a chance to cover a big story, I would most likely be free. He said he would be there Friday night and then we could make plans from there. Looking up at that clock I said I had to go. It was 7:15, and I didn't want to be late. We joked if I was going to ride to work or walk. I said at this point if he talked any longer, I was going to rediscover my long-lost talent for the two-hundred-meter race. I hung up and patted Mr. Striper on the head and bolted out the door. I jogged through the town green to the office and saw Caleb was just turning on his desk light.

"I was wondering if you'd beat me in, first day and all." Caleb looked over his glasses at me with a wink.

"I would have, but the phone rang at the last minute. It was Charlie." I had to let him know that I wasn't going to start my days rushing in as if from the playground like an adolescent boy.

"And how is Charlie? We missed him at your party, although you dad did tell us what had happened to his mother. He's coming back soon I hope. You two make a good couple. That is if he doesn't keep you from your writing." Again, the look over the top of the glasses was filled with a little mischief.

"Yes, he's coming up Friday, unless there's a big story to cover," I dished it back to him.

"Well, you just never know now, do you. Oh, by the way, got a letter from those two brothers from New York. What were there names now," he was baiting me to see how I would respond. I took the bait and swallowed the hook.

"Russell and Robert Brown. They sent a letter? Well, what does it say?" I could hardly contain myself. Caleb handed the letter to me, and I started to read half out loud but mostly to myself.

> Dear Mr. Johnson and Miss Koontz,
> My brother and I have read the *Fishing Weekly* with great delight. We have shared it with some of our literary friends who were equally as amused with your tales. This is a wonderful piece

of Americana and has great potential for a larger market than your beloved Piney Bluffs.

We would like you to send us the next editions as they become available. Our next trip to Piney Bluffs will be in July for the Big Bob's Basstile Day contest. At that time, we would like to make an appointment to meet with the two of you to discuss the future plans of the *Weekly*.

Until then, we remain,

Russell and Robert Brown
Brown & Brown Publishing
1045 E. 41st Street
New York, New York

"Whoohoo! What a chance." I grabbed Caleb's arm and shook it. "You told me this was going to put Piney Bluffs on the map. But I never imagined this." I couldn't believe it.

"Well, as they say, things happen for a reason. You being there to deliver the papers, but no, let's go back to you refusing the job in Boston. If you hadn't been there to show them the article about the fishing derby, they would have tossed the paper and gone back to New York none the wiser about the *Weekly*. Ethel, you are going to find that life is a funny thing. You may think it's normal and sometimes mundane and that it doesn't seem to matter. But that's where you're wrong. Every day counts to someone. You just have to find out who that someone is."

23

That first week, things were bustling at *The Bugle*. I wrote my introductory article about my graduation and returning to my hometown. I wanted to let people know how much I had appreciated their support to myself and to Daddy throughout my college years. I hoped that my article would inspire other young people in town to continue their education beyond Piney Bluffs High and reach for that dream. I also reached back to what the governor had told us at my commencement.

One of the best things about going away to college was that I had Piney Bluffs to come home to. My family and friends and the support that I found here were the foundation that built my values. These people always remembered my dreams and were content to listen to my progress throughout my college times. And now to be able to return and apply that knowledge and share it with those who sustained me is truly wonderful and a chance that I accept wholeheartedly.

There are forty-five colleges, universities, and community colleges in our state, offering degrees from medicine to mechanics, teaching to stock trading. As well, our state offers opportunities to support the abundance of the environment and the natural resources of our mountains and lakes. The chance of a college education or any path to bettering your life is something to embrace.

To further support that belief of higher education, we decided *The Bugle* would now have a career corner. Each month, I would highlight a particular vocation and the possibilities for either employment or its education in and around Piney Bluffs. Caleb and I had struck on that idea that first morning. Discussing our daily schedule, we made the decision that we would devote the beginning of each day to new ideas. They would be written down, and as time allowed, we would develop that idea into some part of either *The Bugle* or the *Weekly*.

While it should have been my first article for the *Herald*, Caleb ran the story of Daddy and I going to Fenway on my second day. This story got folks talking about how they loved the Sox. So that prompted Charlotte, the town clerk, to get a Boston bus trip together for all who were interested. With help from Phil Wheeler at the Gas'n Go, a bus was chartered, and plans were made for the Saturday following the elementary graduation. By the end of the week, all the seats were filled, and Charlotte had started a waiting list for cancellations. The town was finding new life. Caleb said, "Young minds with young thoughts were alarm clocks for the older folks whose thoughts had been napping."

In addition to our early-morning brainstorming, Caleb started a storyboard for *The Weekly*. The board was hung in the backroom with a stack of three by five cards, pens and thumbtacks next to it. With Basstile Day and the arrival of the Brown brothers only two months away, we needed to develop a plan for the next several issues. Within several days, cards with holidays real or invented, fishing derbies, town events, and even a cuisine column featuring Sadie, littered the board like a ticker tape parade. The next edition was to be themed for Memorial Day but with a patriotic twist of remembering the "Ones That Got Away."

Sadie was thrilled to be able to contribute to the *Weekly*. She told me she was already working on revising Caleb's favorite dishes to have them become appropriately inappropriate. To this, Caleb had said, "I have favorites of your cooking?" Undaunted by his comments, her wit shone through as she substituted some ingredients with fish parts or even accented the dish with herbs from the latest endeavors in the herb garden. She hadn't stopped there as she created whimsical recipes for things such as Fish Fin Chips and Crawfish Cookies. We thought of reviews of the local eateries and future cooking events with the accent on fish recipes to round out the Cuisine Column. She had yet another idea of mail-order catalogs for Sadie's Country Concoctions and other hard to find culinary delicacies. Yes, the cobwebs were being swept away, and the clear view of what could be was coming into sight.

The first month flew by as Caleb and I settled on my routine. In by seven, idea time and working on the days stories by seven thirty or eight. We would break for coffee about nine and check in at Miss Ruthie's to see how everyone's day was going. More than likely, I would get a hint of a human-interest story from one of the regulars who had heard something from a neighbor of a friend. This would set my wheels in motion. Quite literally, they were *The Bugle's* bicycle wheels. That is if the story was within a mile or so of the area surrounding the green. If I had to visit outside of town, I would head home and get my car, and off I would go. For lunch, I would go home and check on Mr. Striper or make a couple of sandwiches and pay a visit to Daddy out at the airport.

Knowing today was forecast for sunny skies, I had packed a lunch and went to visit Daddy, where I ran into one of Big Bob's fishing camp regulars. He was a man of about forty. He wore gold wire-rim glasses, and his hair was brown and short-cropped. He was almost as tall as Daddy and was dressed in comfortable but high-priced fishing pants and shirt. He and Daddy were talking about his flight in from Blue Hill, Maine. When he saw me, he said hello and reminded me the last time he had been here was the day of the Diner Derby, and he had overheard me talking to the Brown brothers as he was checking out. He further jogged my memory by describing his misfortune of getting up close and personal with the finest of our bramble bushes. We chuckled as I did recall him and had thought that he was just another one of Big Bob's beginners, never to be seen again. From the looks of his gear, I saw that first opinion was quite the opposite. He had fly-fishing gear with him this time, and I couldn't help but comment on his Hawes pole. These handmade poles were coveted in the world of fly-fishing.

"That's a beauty of a rod, a Hawes, isn't it?" I said, hoping the conversation could continue and I would be able to store the information for a later story.

"Yes, it is. You've got quite the eye, young lady," he said, nodding in approval at me. "My boss let me borrow it today. Said he went to visit Hawes in Canterbury, Connecticut, to have that rod made just for him. Best fly rod he ever used."

"You must have a great boss," I said, admiring his boss's trust for the rod's use. Daddy had explained about the Hawes rods as fly-fishing was one of his specialties in fishing. Only about one thousand rods had ever been produced by the father and then later on by his son between the late 1800s and ending as supplies to World War II were in demand. The rods prices were now said to be between one and two thousand dollars.

"So how's that *Fishing Weekly* coming along," he said as Daddy helped him with the rest of his gear. "That was quite an interesting take on your little town. I shared it with some of my friends, and they want to know when you publish it again. Gave us quite a chuckle it did."

"I'm glad you liked it. I'll tell Caleb. The next one should be out by the end of the month in time for Memorial Day. We will be remembering the one's that got away. Maybe a title of the Red, White, and Bluegill. What do you think?" I was happy to recruit yet another person to the slowly growing list of *Weekly* readers outside of Piney Bluffs.

"Sounds like a winner. I think Norman would like it. Say if I gave you my address, would you send a few copies to us? We'll pay you for the *Weekly* and for postage. I'm Bill, Bill Rushford." He was looking in his wallet now for a business card. Locating it, he handed it to me. As I read it, my eyes widened. His name was William Rushford. The card announced that he was a publishing assistant for Norman Williams. The Norman he referred to was Norman the New England Fisherman himself. I should have put that together. Blue Hill was where Williams had a home. He was the pioneer of television fishing programs in New England. Throughout the 1960s, he had motored into our homes each Friday night showing us yet another wonderful spot for fishing. It had been one of Daddy's favorite television programs, and he always said he wanted to fly to those spots just like Norman. To think that he had read our *Weekly* was another feather in our cap.

"Why, I certainly will do just that. My boss will be pleased to hear Mr. Williams liked our first edition," I replied, but my reporter's wheels were turning. "Say does he do interviews? It just seems like a natural thing for me to highlight him in one of our upcoming editions." Never was shy Daddy said.

"Oh, please call him Norman. I think he would be tickled to do a story for you. I tell him about Piney Bluffs all the time, but he's never taken the time to come with me." He was enjoying our conversation. Daddy too was watching us and smiling. "Tell you what, Ethel, if your dad agrees to be my guide this trip, I'll make sure to arrange an appointment for you with him."

I was speechless as I looked at Daddy with a pleading grin. He looked back with a contemplative teasing nod.

"Well, it is Friday, and I don't have any other flights on the schedule for today. But you never know when someone might just fly in, and then where would they be if I wasn't here to help," he continued to tease me, but he was relenting as I was just about jumping out of my shoes. "However, there's a little spot that I haven't been to in a while that would be just the place for the action on that rod. I guess maybe just this once." Daddy's fishing expertise was well known, and he only offered his time to those who truly appreciated it.

"How about you, Ethel? Would your boss let you off for the afternoon? Good way to set up plans for the interview with Norman." Bill's invite was hard to turn down.

"I don't think I've worked long enough to ask for an afternoon off to go fishing. But I'd like to ask you to join us for dinner tonight.

Whatever the two of you catch, I'll cook," I replied. I hoped he would accept the invitation.

"And if we don't catch anything," Bill questioned.

"I guess you never *have* fished with Daddy. But just in case, I'll have a plan B. Now you two better take off." I was in such a hurry to get back to the office to tell Caleb. I hoped I didn't appear to be short with him.

"Well, if your dad can give me a lift to the inn, we can go right now," Bill said to Daddy.

"I'll close up, and we'll be on our way," Daddy said. "I'll stop by the house and pick up my rod and flies on the way to the inn."

As they took off, I waved good-bye and pedaled back to *The Bugle*. I could hardly wait to tell Caleb the good news. An interview with Norman the New England Fisherman! I couldn't believe my luck! Why of all days to go visit Daddy today. I just couldn't imagine if I hadn't gone.

As I peddled along, I was lost in thoughts of what I would ask during the interview. Should it be how he got started? No, that was known from his shows. Favorite fishing spots? No again, that's what the show had been about. What had he been doing since the show? Yes, that was a good way to begin and then on to his future plans and the future of fishing. It was well known that he was a supporter of our natural habitats and resources. I could ask him what he had been doing with conservation now that he had settled in Maine. Yes, this would be a great piece. Daddy could fly us up to Blue Hill, and we could see his fishing world. I could just imagine the pictures of him and all the places and fish that had happened in his life.

"Not making enough money to buy gas for your car," I heard a familiar voice call out to me.

I looked to my right to where the voice was coming from, and there sat Charlie. I hadn't seen him since the day he left after Jackie's wedding. We had sent letters and talked on the phone. He had tried to come out to Piney Bluffs, but his mom's broken foot had turned into a bone infection, and she had been hospitalized for several weeks. At one point, it was touch and go as to whether or not she would even survive. His last letter explained that the doctors had operated to remove some infection on one of the bones, and that led to the removal of two of her toes. She was now in a rehab center going through countless hours of therapy to learn how to walk again. His father had been beside himself with worry and had spent most of his days at the hospital by her side. Charlie had kept the carpentry business going, so that meant working with the crew seven days a week, which left no time for trips to Maine. Having never met his folks, I had been hesitant to go to Dennisport to visit under the circumstances. So seeing his smiling face and his handsome form sitting on a bench outside Miss Ruthie's was a wonderful surprise.

I turned my bike around and went back to him. Wordlessly, he came to meet me and wrapped his arms around me and gave me a long and tender kiss. It felt so good to have him close to me. I drew in a breath as the smell of his aftershave brought me back to that afternoon before he had left. When I opened my eyes, I looked over his shoulder, and I could see my cousin Ellen peeking through the window and giggling. I shooed her away with a wave of my hand. But she just smiled and waved back at me. I could see Ruthie grab her by the shirt and steer her back to work. Then the door to the bakery flew open, and Ruthie came out and stood with her floured hands on her broad hips.

"Well, it's about time you got around to coming back here. Leaving this poor girl pining away for you, it's not right," Ruthie said, shaking her head. Even though I had told her why Charlie hadn't been here to visit, she just couldn't help letting him know her point of view.

"Now, Ruthie, you know why he hasn't been around," I said in his defense.

"Well, you best be staying for a bit and coming back on a regular basis. Just not right," she continued to sputter as she turned and went back into the shop. "Got one whoopie pie left, seems to have your name on it," she called over her shoulder just before she closed the door.

"She is something." Charlie chuckled as he shook his head. "I tried calling this morning to let you know I was coming up, but you'd already left for work, and I don't know *The Bugle's* number.

"I am so happy to see you. Is everything okay with your mom?" I asked hopefully.

"Mom's doing fine now. She's finally out of the woods. And dad's back to work," he replied.

"That's good to hear, I know how worried you've been." I put my arm around him with a hug.

"She's pretty feisty, so I knew she wouldn't be down too long." Charlie kissed the top of my head. "And what have you been up to?"

"I can't wait to tell you. So many things have happened here. Where are you staying?" I asked.

"I'm staying with Andy and Jackie. They want me to look at putting an addition on their house, so they offered to put me up while I'm in town for a few days."

"Good, then you can come for dinner tonight. Daddy is fishing with Bill Rushmore who is the publishing assistant for Norman Williams. And I'm making dinner out of whatever they catch," I said, but then the look on his face puzzled me. "What you don't think I can cook?"

"No, it's not that, but who is Norman Williams? Should I know this?" The look on his face told me he truly did not know.

"What am I to do with you? He is only the father of sports fishing on television in New England. His show in the 1960s was the best thing for fishermen everywhere," I said almost incredulous that he had never heard of the man. "Look, I have to go back to work. Come to the house about six, and you'll learn about the man whose interview will give *The Bugle* and the *Weekly* just what is needed. And don't forget to get your whoopie pie. Miss Ruthie will have your head if you don't go and visit with her." And with that, I headed back to *The Bugle*.

I ran up the steps of *The Bugle* and burst through the door like I was on fire. I looked at the clock. It was 1:30 p.m., and I had left at noon. Caleb looked over the top of his glasses at me and then at the clock.

"Caleb, I can explain. Wait until you hear who I met and who I'm going to have an interview with." I was just gushing with excitement. And so for the next half hour, I detailed my meeting with Bill

Rushmore and how he and Norman had liked the *Weekly* and wanted us to send copies of the next one. And the best part of all was the interview with Norman himself. As I ended, Caleb was smiling.

"See, Ethel, that's what I was trying to tell you. The *Weekly* and stories about fishing is just the ticket. I'm just delighted that you're going to interview Williams. He might be able to help us with the *Weekly* even more than the Brownings. You've got to admit, he has the right connections for anything fishing," Caleb said as he sat back in his chair and crossed his arms putting his hand on his chin. This I had learned was his thinking posture.

"Well, what's next?" I asked as Caleb continued to sit and think.

"First, we need to rough out what the next *Weekly* is going to look like. We don't have much time, and we should seize your energy for the flow of thoughts. Let's spend the rest of the afternoon at the board." And with that, he got up, and I followed him to the back room.

For the Memorial Day issue, we started with interviews of fishermen in the area to tell us about the ones that got away and those memorable almost catches. There would have to be a Koontz with a bass fishing story and then probably Tubby Carponowski who was renowned for bullheads, and, last but not least, Jackie's dad Jack with his fly-fishing for trout escapades. Then there would be Sadie's Cuisine Corner and Recipes. She surprised Caleb by stopping by with a little late lunch and sat right down with us and cooked up her own ideas. We chuckled as she threw out a list of ideas—red snapper, white perch and blue gill casserole, Yankee Doodle dandelion salad, and catfish cake. The inspirations kept coming as we added an advice column by Caleb. Each edition would have a poor misguided fisherman with a tale of woe that only the famous Caleb "Hook" Johnson could provide the professional assistance to solve the unfortunate man's plight. We were so engrossed that time flew by, and before we knew it, it was five o'clock.

"Holy cow, I've got to get going. Daddy, Bill, and Charlie are coming for supper," I said as I put my jacket on and turned off my desk light.

"I could give you some suggestions, why just the other day, I tried this new way to make a good coleslaw with pineapples and peppers," Sadie offered.

"Honey, that's okay. She wants to keep all those men alive," Caleb kidded her.

"Oh you. Ethel, I really can cook. You know that, don't you?" She elbowed Caleb who feigned an injury to the ribcage.

"Well, yes, I do, Sadie. I know Caleb just wants to keep all that good cooking to himself," I said, trying to keep peace with my boss's wife. "I'm thinking some oven-baked potatoes, corn fritters, slaw, and then broiled whatever kind of fish walks through the door. I've got to go before Pappy closes the doors."

"I want to go with Ethel. You don't mind, do you, Sadie dear?" Caleb was just not letting up.

"You can go, but don't think you have a home to come back to." Sadie dished it right back at him.

"Okay, you two, that's enough. Kiss and make up, and have a good weekend," I said as I waved at the two of them as I headed out the door. They really were a great couple. They stood there smiling, Caleb with his arm around her, giving her a peck on cheek.

*****

I came through the door of the house so quickly that I scared Mr. Striper. He had been curled up on the stairs catching the last rays of the spring sun, and started to run up the stairs. He recovered when he realized it was me and that the crinkling of the bags meant that there was food and he might just get some of it. He followed me down the hallway tail straight up in the air and hopped up on his chair and watched while I put the bags down and started to get ready. I got out the deep cast-iron pan, filled it with oil, and turned on the gas to get it hot enough for the fritters. Next, I turned the oven on for the potatoes. I was slicing cabbage when I heard footsteps coming through the door.

"I don't smell anything," Daddy's voice came down the hallway.

"Well, I don't see anything worthwhile in this kitchen to cook yet," I yelled back at him.

"She's not shy," Bill commented to Daddy on my sassing.

145

"You got that right," Charlie's voice was chiming in with the other two.

"Is this going to be three against one, and where are all of you?" I questioned. "Somebody best show me some type of fish, or I'm shutting off the oven, and you'll all be taking me to the inn for dinner."

In they filed and took a seat at the table. They had big grins on their faces, but I still saw no signs of any fish.

"Daddy, I can't believe you got skunked," I said and stopped slicing cabbage. I wiped my hands on the towel and took a seat at the table. "What is up with all of you?"

"I can't keep up the joke. Let me get the fish." Daddy was up and back down the hallway. He came back with a brown paper bag. I reached in, unwrapped the butcher's paper, and found eight trout fillets.

"Now that's more like it," I said. "These are beauties. How'd the rod work, Bill?"

"Anyone who considers themselves a fisherman should have the chance to use one of those rods at least once in a lifetime. It has just the best action on any rod I've ever used. And the place where Eddy took me was perfect. It was truly a beautiful afternoon for fishing," Bill said quite sincerely. "Your dad is one of the best guides I've ever fished with. I have to thank you for making time for me this afternoon."

"You're welcome, Bill. It's not often I get to go with someone who knows what he's doing," Daddy replied.

"And now, Bill, will you please explain to Charlie who Norman Williams is? And I'll get this supper started," I said.

With that, Bill began the story of Norman who had been a sales representative for fishing equipment. He had a love for travel and fishing and was somewhat of an amateur filmmaker. He began filming his fishing exploits as he traveled. And then he hooked up with a producer in the beginning of the 1960s and the New England Fisherman was born. Bill had teamed up with him during the last televised episodes. His love for fishing had endeared him to Norman more than others who worked for him. And so their special working/ fishing relationship had evolved. Williams had retired to Blue Hill,

Maine, and continued to fish. By the time Bill was finished with Norman's exploits, dinner was ready. We sat, ate, and enjoyed an evening of good conversation. Charlie was being initiated into our fishing way of life. And by all estimates, he seemed to take pleasure in his education.

Daddy took Bill back to the inn about ten o'clock but not before he promised to contact me Monday with possible dates for my interview. Charlie had helped me clean up, and I gave him a ride out to Andy and Jackie's. On our way, I stopped the car at the bridge most town folks called our wishing bridge. It was a full moon, and the reflection was almost perfect on the still water. We walked to the middle of the bridge and looked out over the water.

"I have missed you," Charlie said as he put his arm around me.

"Me too," I said. "I was thinking that the letters and the calls would probably stop soon."

"What are you talking about?" Charlie said as he took me by the shoulders and turned me to face him. He took my chin and lifted it up and kissed me. My arms circled around him, and we held each other as we stared out at the moonlit water.

"What are you wishing for?" I asked.

"I'm wishing I knew how to be here with you," he said.

"But you are," I replied.

"No, I mean for more than just a night or a few days." He looked into my eyes with the deepest look anyone could ever give someone.

"We have a lot of time, Charlie. And now that you'll be building the addition, you'll be around for a little longer," I reasoned. "Who knows maybe if you're here longer, you might not like me that much."

"Why? Do you plan on changing yourself?" Charlie chuckled.

"Nope, pretty much what you see is what you get. But I do have my job, and I am serious about it," I said.

"Ethel, I have no doubt in my mind that you are one of the most serious people I have ever met when it comes to your convictions and the plans you have for your life. I only hope that you have a little place for me in it," as he said this, he kissed me again and hugged me. "Now let's get me to Andy and Jackie's before we get too serious tonight."

But for the AM station fading in and out on the radio, we drove along in silence, but he held and stroked my hand. When we got to their house, the lights were out. Charlie gave me a quick kiss and got out of the car with promises to see me tomorrow. In the moonlight, I saw him wave good night. He opened the door, and then he was gone.

I looked at my friend's home and thought that someday, I would have a house of my own. And instead of a man walking in to stay in the guest bedroom, he would be walking into our home. The radio faded in with strains from Carole King, "I feel my heart start trembling whenever you're around." I turned the radio off and hummed the rest of the song to myself on the way home. "I feel the earth move under my feet / I feel the sky tumbling down, a tumbling down."

24

Fishing Weekly Memorial Day Edition
May 1972

Remembering the One That Got Away

Big Beautiful Bullhead
By Ethel Koontz, Sporting Events Editor

An interview with Tubby Carponowski, bullhead fisherman

Tubbie Carponowski has been fishing since he could walk, so he says. His daddy, God rest his soul, took him fishing every chance he had. So it was just natural that when his daddy passed, Tubby and his Ma, Tiny, took the insurance premium and opened Tubby's Tackle Shop on the banks of the Salmon River. Tubby gets to fish every day, even though he tells me he is just demonstrating the merchandise for the customers. And as an added treat, Tiny fixes box lunches for the customers. But we caution folks to ask for the lunch first before she gets your bait, as Tiny sometimes forgets her handwashing routine.

One afternoon, I sat with Tubby at the tackle shop on the back deck looking out as the river slowly flowed by. And I asked him what was the one fish he remembered that got away. Without hesitation, he uttered, "Bullhead." He leaned back in his oversized wooden chair, put his muddy boots on the railing, and started his story.

It was just about dusk in July. I'd had my dinner. Ma's cleaning up the dishes, and I'm ready. I've been thinking about this all day. No, not the dishes, fishing. That's right it's bullhead season. I'd gotten in new rods that were sure to catch one with ease. But that night, I went back to the old ways that my daddy had shown me— Cane poles, bobbers, three-ounce weights, and cheap canned cat food. Bullhead have a keen sense of smell, and they are bottom feeders, so the weights would keep the smelly bait on the bottom. When the red-and-white bobber popped in the water, I knew I had a bite.

As I said, it was a perfect summer night, and Big Bob had come along with me for a night of it. We walked in down river from the shop where the water gets a little swamp-like. We had our lantern and the cooler for the bait and the beers. We set up our chairs and our rod holders, cast our lines out, and just about cracked our first beer when Bob said, "Tubby, I think there's a little movement at the end of your line." I looked, and the pole was taking a slow dip. Kind of like what Fred Astaire used to do with Ginger Rogers. I put down my beer and grabbed my pole and started to play it. The thing is with a bamboo pole, there's no reel, so you need to be patient and have a net nearby, and I'm not talking about Annette Funicello neither. From the way my pole was bending, it was a big one. Bob had the net, and we watched in the dim lantern light as the fish slowly played back and forth, dorsal fin just cresting, making a ripple in the black water. From what I could see, he was a beauty. I finally got him in close enough, Bob had the net ready to scoop, and I lifted my pole to get him out of the water. I put my hand out to guide him into the net. From the size of him in my hand, I believe he would have weighed in at about eight or nine pounds. It was if my touch made him realize his fate. We saw him give a quick jerk, and he was gone, leaving the bait swinging like a piece of dental floss in the breeze.

I asked if he had tried to get him again, and Tubby said no. That was a once-in-a-lifetime sighting. That fish is still living in that bottom and will for a long time to come. He's just waiting to be another man's memory of the one that got away.

Subscription News

Remember, if you want to keep on receiving this fine testimony to the life of fishing, just send in $19.95 to me, Caleb Johnson, c/o FW, Rural Route, Piney Bluffs, Maine. This will insure that you don't miss a moment of FW, and it will also insure that Ethel has a job to come to as we know how she loves to stray off. But that's a story for another time.

Sadie's Recipe of the Month

Red, White, and Bluegill Fish Fry

This is one of my favorite recipes for the beginning of the patriotic summer cooking season. To start, you will need about three fish and one six pack per person. The six packs are needed if you have each guest go fishing for their dinner. If you happen to have a number of bluegill in stock as I usually do, then you can cross the beer off your shopping list. Or you can leave them on the list and enjoy a beverage or two whilst preparing this meal. Because depending on the number of guests, you may be frying a while. Fillet your fish, leaving one scaled skin side, and prepare an egg wash and seasoned cracker dip. Heat your skillet till smoking with your best lard. Your fillets will only take about three to four minutes. So before cooking, it's time to prepare the red and white portion of this fish fry. For the red, we will use red onions hollowed out and steamed, seasoned with a little fresh thyme. If you are fresh out of thyme, then you should find some time as fresh is best. Next, cook and puree a head of cauliflower seasoned with salt, pepper, and a tablespoon or two of horseradish. If you are digging your horseradish, be careful bending over. In the spring/summer season, it is rutting time for many species of large animals. While most are afraid of humans, they sometimes are overcome by natural instinct. So just a word to the wise and keep you rear near to those who might mistake you for a deer. Or it could be no use if you live near moose. Serve your meal with red and white wine or a selection of blueberry beer. And enjoy, my friends, enjoy!

Letters to the Fishing Creel

Dear Fishing Weekly,
    I have loved fishing all of my life. But for some reason this year, I cannot find my way to my pick up my pole. I have always loved the way it feels in my hand and responds when I am just about to dip my line in. My wife is concerned

and thinks I should take up square dancing with her. Please help as I hate square dancing.

Signed,
The Thrill is gone in Tunbridge

Dear Thrill,

It seems that what you might need is some good old-fashioned faith healing or church going. I would advise against any square dancing as this may cause more physical disability if you cannot master the allemande left or right. Could ruin your casting hand for life. After several weeks of attending these services and being with these righteous folks, I believe you will welcome the chance to fish and be able to take things into your own hands once more. Your pole should feel right at home, and you will definitely enjoy your time alone with the peace and quiet of the outdoors. Good luck! FW

Fishing Report
by Frosty Perch

Snow Shoe Creek—Reports in for this May from fishermen say they are getting their limit on trout within about three hours. Staying away from where Snow Shoe Lake feeds in as there is too much water runoff to have a trout be comfortable in that spot. Although in that area, you may find a bass or two that have gone over the falls. I have been trying a new spinner bait but find that those little red garden worms work the best. We remind folks that fishing with corn is illegal as is fishing with TNT, although this was mostly the bait of choice for the lazy lake fishermen. A couple of guys came up from down South and thought they'd bring their lazy red neck ways with them. See, they'd light a stick, throw it in the water, it explodes, and the fish come floating to the top, dead. Well, the Fish and Game wardens made a quick arrest, with a hefty fine and a promise that they won't come back to Maine.

Snow Shoe Lake—Smallmouth bass are coming in around the three- and four-pound range just as we're getting into the height of the season. Folks are still trying to break the record of old George Dyer. In 1970, he caught an eight pounder in Thompson Lake, just south of here. Largemouth folks, that is to say folks fishing for large mouths, are doing about the same. Although that saying rings true from time to time how people look like the fish they are fishing for. Anyway, they're using plastic worms or live bait. Just as long as there's some action, the bass will hit on it. Record breaker in 1968, Robert Kamp used a minnow to catch his eleven-pound twelve ounce at Moose Pond. Keep fishing, and remember, "You shouldn't let a week go by without dipping your line."

Wanted - Woman who likes to fish and will share my life. A boat with motor is a plus. Please send picture of boat c/o Post Office Box 15, Piney Bluffs, Maine.

25

When I arrived at the airstrip, I saw Daddy performing his final inspection of the Cessna. He looked up at the sound of the car and waved. I waved back and pulled into a parking spot. I grabbed my bag from the backseat and headed for the red-and-white plane. I had a pad of paper and my favorite pen that Caleb had given me for graduation. I had also brought a tape recorder just in case. Sometimes it was just nice to chat with people and not be so intent on writing their every word. This let people relax more, often forgetting that they were being interviewed, and their story just flowed like a natural conversation. I opened the passenger door and threw my things in. I climbed in next to Daddy. He pushed the ignition switch, and we were off.

Daddy had arranged to borrow one of Big Beulah's planes for the day. She was Big Bob's twin sister, and as folks knew, she would never be a beauty queen. But she had the heart and soul that had made her one of the best businesswomen in town. She knew flying, fishing, and people. And that had turned her small fishing guide business into a well-known and respected little company both in Maine and throughout New England. She had started out by joining the Civil Air Patrol in grammar school, and that interest had led her to take flying lessons during high school. Along the way, her brother Bob had taught her all about fishing, and she had combined both interests into a business. Beulah had two planes now, the Cessna and a de Havilland Otter float plane. She frequently contracted with Daddy to be a guide and pilot to fly folks to remote fishing areas. So when Daddy needed a plane, like today, Beulah was happy to oblige him.

In confirming our times for today's meeting, Bill had arranged for us all to have lunch together. After that, Bill had promised to show Daddy around their compound's fishing areas while I had my interview with Norman. Our flying time would put us into Blue Hill just about lunchtime.

It was a beautiful day in late June. There was just a little wind out of the southwest that set the leaves to fluttering. This would be a good tailwind for our flight up. The trees were fully leaved out now providing a rich green canopy that would soon be our carpet as we made our way north.

"So, your first big interview," Daddy said, more of a statement than something that required an answer. There was a lot of pride in the way he spoke. I knew he would have wanted to add "for my little girl," but he knew that he couldn't say that anymore. He had faced the fact that his little girl was a young woman now. "What are you going to ask him, Ethel?"

"That question seems to be on everyone's mind," I said, reflecting back to the folks in town who had pulled me aside once they knew I was going to this interview. All of the "Make sure you ask him about that time he fell in," or "I always wanted to know about those lures," and most common on all their tongues was, "Make sure you ask him to come and visit us."

Caleb and I had discussed the interview for a week. We were excited at the possibilities this could mean for us. We had sent several copies of the latest *Fishing Weekly* to Norman. He in turn had sent a thank-you note and a review of it. He was happy to see that while it was a humorist's take on our town, the information that we cited was factual. He had written, "The details are what people look for. They want that special thing that makes your story different from all the rest. That's what hooks them. Never lose sight of that."

So with that and our ideas, I was ready for my story. For those who didn't know him, I would introduce and provide the background on Maine's adopted New England's Fisherman. Most people who had followed his show would want to know why he had stopped. And then the typical what are you doing now would be the next logical conversation. What Caleb and I, and most of the town, ultimately wanted was for him to come to Piney Bluffs for a fishing derby. An event like this had so much potential for exposure for the town and in turn for the *Weekly*.

As Daddy prepared for the landing, Bill's voice came through the headset announcing that the airstrip was ready for us. Daddy put us down as gentle as a dragonfly lighting on a lily pad. Once down, Bill drove over in the jeep, loaded our gear in, and we were off. Just a short drive from the airstrip brought us to our destination.

Bill had told us Norman had loved flying, but he never had taken the time to learn. So when he was looking for a retirement home, he found this one with a private airstrip and a single-engine plane thrown in to seal the deal. Still hadn't take lessons, but Bill had his license, so that was just fine with Norman. The compound was on the banks of a sparkling river. As we got out, I looked up and down the vista. The water shone clean and clear in the sunlight as it tripped its way over the rocks and into small pools that looked like the best spots to find prize trout. There were a couple of other cabins in view with the smoke of the morning fire still evident as it curled from their chimneys. Located on a large bend in the river and spanning a good three hundred feet of riverfront, the main building, Norman's residence, took center stage. It was a sprawling log cabin with a wraparound porch. Several cushioned rocking chairs waited for someone to begin relaxing. The docks led from the lawn down to the water's edge and to the boathouse. A canoe was tied up at the end of the dock, gently rocking and beckoning you to find a paddle. Behind the main house were two smaller cabins, most likely for guests. Maple trees and balsam firs provided the finishing touch to this attractive home.

A hello turned our attention back to the house. Norman was unmistakable—a tall man wearing that signature long blue billed hat and wire-rimmed glasses framing that smiling face. He walked down two of the several wide stone steps. An aging black lab followed by his side, wagging for all he was worth.

"Hello, Mr. Williams. So very happy to meet you," I said as I climbed the steps to meet him. "I'm Ethel Koontz, and this is my dad, Eddy."

"Oh, please call me Norman. I am so glad to finally meet you. I think we have a lot to talk about. And this is Ducky," he said, indicating the dog with a nod of his head as he extended his hand to Daddy and me. "Well, come on in. Set your things down. Georgia has made a great lunch for us. I hope you like fish!"

The interior of the log cabin was everything you would expect from the home of a sport-fishing celebrity. The walls spoke of a life that was enjoyed in the great outdoors. Framed photos hung in groups showing Norman at various freshwater and saltwater venues either alone or shaking the hands of other smiling fishermen with their catch. Trophy fish hung in graceful arcs. Trophies and awards were displayed on the thick wooden mantel of the large stone fireplace, and a variety of rods were stored like a spray of cat o' nine tails nearby in a cozy den area.

The center of the main floor was the kitchen and dining area. A loft overlooked it and held an office with overstuffed desk cubbies, bookcases, and filing cabinets. Navy and forest green braided rugs on the wide planked floor gave a homey feel. The picture windows had crisp beige linen curtains framing the peaceful panorama of the river. The furniture outside of the camp-like style of the dining table and kitchen area was overstuffed leather chairs and sofas with rough-hewn end tables holding laced lamp-shaded lighting. The kitchen was filled with wonderful aromas and the aforementioned Georgia was already showing the merits of a gracious hostess.

"Now come right in and make yourself at home," she said. A woman of perhaps sixty, she was about as tall as I and wore relaxed khakis and cream-colored linen shirt protected by an apron made of blue ticking that tied around her slim waist. Wire-rimmed glasses framed warm brown eyes, and a gray braid lay halfway down her back. If you were to have a sporting-life cabin, she would be whom you would picture as your personal chef and housekeeper. "If you'd like to freshen up, the bathroom is the first right down the hallway."

As she extended her arm to point the way, a symphony of sterling silver bracelets helped to guide me.

"Georgia's been with me since I moved here. Started with a chance meeting in the market. Her grocery basket looked a hell of a lot better than mine, so I asked her if she could cook like that for me. She came by that next day, and as they say, the rest is history." Norman smiled at Georgia.

"I felt bad for him. All he had was a can of coffee and a loaf of white bread. I couldn't let him loose in our waters without some type of meal under his scrawny built," she joked back to him. Norman had never married, so it seemed that at this point of his life, Georgia was doing her best to take care of this aging adventurer. Her status was undetermined as a large silver ring adorned her ring finger. Whatever the arrangement, it seemed to suit them both.

The table was set with hand-thrown pottery plates. Each had a different fish painted into its glaze. We sat down to a wonderful lunch of fresh vegetable soup served in small crocks. Then followed grilled trout with pan-fried potatoes. The wheat bread was freshly baked with strawberry jam and butter to accompany it. All was washed down with homemade lemonade. Conversation around the table flowed from one fishing story to the next as we truly enjoyed each other's stories. There was plenty of good-natured one-upmanship. I made mental notes of some of the stories. They would be great material for future articles.

"What a wonderful lunch, Georgia. Everything was delicious," I said, smiling across the table at her. Daddy nodded in agreement, still savoring the last bite of bread and jam.

"Yes, indeed, that was a mighty fine meal, Georgia. Thank you," Daddy said as he wiped his mouth with the linen napkin.

"Anyone care for more?" Georgia asked as she rose from her seat. A chorus of nos and thank yous were the answers.

"Well then, let me show you around, Eddy, so Ethel and Norman can start talking," Bill said.

"Lead the way," Daddy replied. And with that, the two of them headed out the front door.

"Georgia, let me help you with the dishes," I said as I started to stack plates.

"Oh, you go on now. That's why Norman pays me so much money." She chuckled as she shooed me away from the table.

"So now, Ethel, where would you like to sit?" Norman asked.

"I'd love to sit on your porch, if you don't mind," I answered.

"One of my favorite spots, Ducky's too," and with that, the three of us made our way back outside to the rocking chairs. The afternoon sun was beginning to warm the porch. Ducky curled up next to Norman's chair into a large patch of that warmth. I took out my pad and pen, set them on my lap, turned on my recorder, and we began, rocking and talking.

"This is truly a beautiful spot, Norman. Its' much like Piney Bluffs, clean and fresh," I said, not wanting to jump right to a line of questioning as if he were a suspect in a crime.

"We are fortunate you know, Ethel. Some people will never see places like this, or even if they come near here, they will pass right by and not take the time to stop and appreciate what Mother Nature has allowed us to share with her," he said reflectively as he looked out over the river.

I knew that Norman was an advocate of enhancing people's awareness of the out of doors and our natural resources, so this comment came as no surprise.

"I know, I consider myself very lucky in where I have grown up and will continue to live. Several classmates of mine in college who had come from the cities were in awe of just how peaceful and amazing our state is," I added.

"It's up to your generation to help people realize what we have here in our country. I have fished all over and was always amazed at how each spot was more beautiful then the next. But I also saw signs of people disregarding what they had," he spoke with an intense passion, and my ideas for our interview were quickly changing course. "Sorry, Ethel, I'll get down from my soapbox now. You ask away."

"I've read a lot about how you started out, Norman, with your work in radio and TV. Is there anything that you can add that would provide additional insight into who Norman Williams is?" I hoped that I wasn't sounding too standard in the way I began.

"Well now, one of things that most folks might not know is how I actually got started fishing. I owe it all to my aunt. Yes, sir, she was the one who showed me how to fish those many years ago out in Ohio. And I think that's important 'cause most folks want to think that fishing is a man's sport. But you and I know that's just not so." His smile crinkled his eyes as he spoke with the soft Midwestern drawl. "Just look at you, Ethel, a woman, reporting on fishing. Now in most papers or magazines, they'd still have you relegated to the society or fashion columns."

"Oh, don't I know it. Thankfully, growing up in Piney Bluffs, it wasn't so uncommon for women to enjoy fishing. But breaking the barriers in reporting is proving to be a larger hurdle. I hope to overcome that. You're my first step along that pathway." I found that I was sharing more of my story than his story.

"I want to help you, Ethel. Bill and I like what we've read of yours already. And I still have contacts both in radio and TV who would love to get a hold of something fresh in our realm of reporting." I could see in his eyes that he meant what he was saying. "Fishing, hunting, and the nontraditional outdoor sports are untapped segments that are just waiting to bust out into TV. The shows I did back then were the just the tip of the iceberg of what is to come along. You wait and see."

As I looked into the face of this man, I saw the passion that he had for not only the fishing life but for the promise of things that could be. And so the interview became a conversation between two new friends. I let my tape recorder do its job while the time rolled by. Georgia came out and provided more of that refreshing lemonade.

"Helps to have something to quench your thirst when you're listening to those fish stories of his," she chided.

"Why did you stop?" I asked as we sipped.

"Just getting a little too old, I guess," Norman said a little wistfully. "People's interests change and so you must be truthful with yourself. You need to know when the time has come for something different. So I left while I was on top. I miss it, though."

As we were finishing up, I asked about what he thought had made his television show so popular and what he would like his fans to know.

"I'm no expert, never have been, and never will be. I was just an average fisherman that made pictures for all the other average fishermen. I only went where the typical fisherman could go and only used tackle that he could afford. Nothing I ever used cost more than fifty dollars. If I didn't catch a fish, I showed that. If I fell in the water or my line got hung up in the trees, I showed that too. With elements like that, the fisherman that watched my show saw his own reflection in the TV. That's what they enjoyed and appreciated—that I was only human," his eyes were intent while he spoke. "I also believed and still do that there is goodness in all folks. You just have to give people the opportunity to show that. I can see that in you too, Ethel."

"Well, thanks, Norman, I appreciate that," I said, shaking my head in agreement, looking into those knowledgeable eyes.

"You have heart, Ethel, and don't be afraid to let people see that," he continued. "Whether it's TV or books or papers, people like to read something that makes them smile or brings a tear to their eye. Sure, the headlines of something horrible will catch their attention. And once they're through the grizzly details, they quickly turn the page or the dial on the TV, looking for something better. Something that makes them feel good. But one of the most important things to tell people about is our great outdoors. I've seen too many people not caring about what they are doing to our beautiful land and waterways. Once something is used up, it doesn't come back. When we fill in a swamp to build stores, the wildlife that called that swamp home moves on, or if they can't, they die. I tried to help spread that message, but most times, people told me what was I worried about. There will be plenty of everything forever. As I said, it's going to be up to people like you to remind them that it's just not so."

"I believe that too. We see folks that come into Piney Bluffs from big cities and they are careless with how they act around nature and our resources." I sighed as I thought what an enormous project it will be to keep things in balance. "We want to grow, but at the same time, we want to keep the beauty that we have around us."

"Don't ever lose sight of that, Ethel," Norman said as he leaned forward and patted my hand. "You're the next generation, and you will have to be the voice of nature. She can't speak for herself."

Daddy and Bill were coming back up the driveway in the jeep, so I knew my time was coming to an end.

"Norman, I want to thank you for taking the time for me today. I can't tell you what this has meant to me. But I would like to ask you one last thing," I said with a smile of hope on my face. "Originally, I was to ask you to come to Piney Bluffs for a fishing derby. However, in light of your powerful commitment to the preservation of the outdoors and wildlife, I'd like to propose we do more than that. Along with our catch-and-release derby, we can showcase the conservation of water, land, and our nonaquatic wildlife. With your help, I think we can wake people up a bit and get them to start thinking now before it's too late. What do you think?"

"Well, I think that we have just started a very interesting partnership," he said and reached over to shake my hand. "You have no idea of how happy I am to see someone your age 'get it.' When Bill gets back up here, we'll make some plans."

Ducky's head came up, and his dusty black tail started thumping as he saw Bill and Daddy coming up the walkway. He got up and came to sit by me.

"Good boy," I said and reached down to scratch behind his ears. "Why do you call him Ducky, Norman?"

"Oh, quite simple. When he was a pup, we had some mallard chicks that we were raising. He was a runt and a quiet thing and just got to following along with the rest of the chicks. Slept right with them. The hen never seemed to mind him much, except when they went in the water. He splashed just a little too much for her liking," Norman was shaking his head as he explained. "Anyway, Ducky just seemed to be a natural name for him. Never could get him to fetch a duck during season, so he's just always been a good fishing buddy."

"You two seem to be getting along," Bill said as he and Daddy walked up the steps and leaned against the railing.

"You've got a great gal for a daughter, Eddy," Norman said to Daddy.

"Thank you, I'm pretty proud of her," Daddy said as he smiled at me.

"We got some plans to make Bill for the end of the summer. You're going to take me down to Piney Bluffs for the 1st Annual Fishing and Conservation Tournament. How does that sound to you, Ethel?" Norman was glowing at me with the sound of the event rolling out of his mouth.

"I like the sounds of that just fine," I said excitedly. My mind was racing with what this would mean for us. I couldn't wait to get back and tell Caleb and the whole town. End of the summer, wow we would have to get our publicity going and fast.

"We'll get some media coverage of this too, if you don't mind, Ethel. I'll get down to see you and Caleb within the week to get the ball rolling. Summer goes quick, and we don't want people to miss this one of a kind event," Bill said, and I could see him thinking through the steps as he talked.

"Sure, come on down. We're in the office every day," I said as I packed my things in my bag. Turning to Norman, I said, "I can't thank you enough for this interview and your wonderful hospitality."

"Happy to meet you, and I want you to know that you and your dad are always welcome here," Norman said as we stood to leave.

We all shook hands and said our good-byes. The screen door slammed as Georgia came out.

"What, not even saying good-bye to me? Hell of a thing. And here I was going to give your dad a little snack for the way home." Georgia had that look of a false disappointment that was dissolving into a smile. In her hand, she had a brown paper lunch bag that she handed to Daddy. "Don't get that jam on your shirt. It's a bugger to get out."

"Well, where are my manners," Daddy said a little sheepishly. "Georgia, thank you for a wonderful lunch and for this. We have thoroughly enjoyed ourselves here today."

With that, we got into the jeep, waved our good-byes once more, and Bill drove us back to the airstrip. As we packed ourselves back into the plane, I turned to Bill.

"This has been just about the best, Bill. Norman is such a wonderful man," I said.

"Yes, this is a one-of-a-kind job, working for a one-of-a kind man. He is what you see. A man very passionate about fishing, but conservation is his big thing, and he just can't seem to make people understand how important this is. I'm glad you do," Bill replied.

As we lifted up and banked, Bill waved one last time and then got back in the jeep. Daddy and I flew in silence for a while as I looked at scenery disappearing below. I "got it" as Norman said. I couldn't imagine that someday there wouldn't be enough trees and brooks and ponds to fish in, that people would be so ignorant not to realize what they were doing. So that's what we in Piney Bluffs could take on. We would begin to educate them to the extent that they were hooked on it.

"What you thinking, Ethel?" Daddy asked.

"I'm thinking about all the work there is to do to help Norman but to help us all," I replied thoughtfully, my brow furrowed.

"Well, if there's one thing I know, it's that you'll find a way to do it," Daddy said as he glanced sideways at me. "You always have been a stubborn one that way."

"What do you mean stubborn?" I asked him. "I'm just persistent," I said emphatically in my defense.

"However you want to say it, but you'll get this done," Daddy said and shook his head. "Just remember at the end of the day, you look at yourself in the mirror, and you have to like what you see. If you don't, then either break the mirror or change. But I don't think, with you, we'll worry about breaking or changing anything. You are the best just as you are. The only thing that will happen to you is that you will improve with the wisdom you'll gain every day. Ethel, you're like your momma was. She was smart and knew why she was put on this earth. But she left us too soon. So now it's up to you to do what you need to do. You have the time, and you have the intelligence. You also have a handsome father who loves you very much." As he ended, he chuckled and reached to pat my hand.

I let out a low chuckle too. With my head on the window, I let gravity pull the tears from my eyes. Daddy didn't speak of Momma very often, but when he did, it was always of her aptitude and abilities to do the things she set out to do. I swallowed hard and pulled in my lips trying not to cry. I just wish she were here, just once. I had so much to tell her, so much to ask her. I drew a breath in holding back the tears.

Daddy's hand reached out and patted me on the shoulder. My tears fell like rain beginning on a spring day—slowly, softly at first and then the downpour. When my storm was over, I wiped my eyes with my sleeve and my nose with the back of my hand. Daddy reached in his pocket and pulled out his handkerchief and held it out for me.

"Thanks," I said as I sniffed and took it. "I'm sorry, must be the altitude."

"Must be," Daddy said and cleared his throat. As I looked up at him, I saw the thin wet trickle on his cheek. "Must be."

26

"I think you need to move that star a little to the left," I said as I stood back from the Christmas tree. We were gathered in the taproom at the inn. I was giving instructions to Daddy who had been helping Jack Farnsworth with the finishing touches for our annual Christmas Eve get-together.

Ever since Jackie and I were little, our families had spent Christmas Eve together. We'd dress in our sweaters, plaid shirts, and jeans and have a relaxing evening of stories of fishing or past Christmases, good food supplied by Mrs. F, and, of course, numerous toasts with eggnog.

While we decorated the tree throughout the week, the last thing to go on was the shining silver star that had been handed down in Mrs. F's family. Jackie and I had made most of the decorations for the tree throughout the years. And it was a reunion of sorts when we decorated it, remembering what we had used to make the snow on the little house or the beard on Santa. This year, we made two more. Jackie found a little Mr. and Mrs. Santa to remember her wedding. I found a miniature typewriter that I decorated with little greens and a red ribbon for my job as a writer.

The inn's doorways were decorated with fresh laurel and fir garlands. The tables held vases of holly and poinsettias placed on each step of the staircase. The fire burned brightly in the stone fireplace of the taproom, and the tree stood proudly in the center of the room with a plaid tree skirt covered by presents. If you were looking for that Currier & Ives Christmas picture, then surely, it was right here right now.

"How's that?" Daddy asked. Never one to have been fond of heights, Jack held the ladder steady for Daddy as he deftly positioned the star atop the ten-foot balsam fir.

"Fine, fine, perfect. Now come on down so we can have some eggnog," Mr. F replied. "Even holding this ladder, I get the heebie-jeebies." Jack wiped his upper lip glowing with sweat and forehead with his handkerchief.

"Who's going to propose the first toast?" Jackie asked as she was ladling the eggnog into the silver cups. The ornate cups and bowl had been Mr. F's grandparents and took center stage during holiday parties. Somehow, beverages just seemed to taste better when you drank from them.

"You're not having any, are you, Jacks?" I said, my eyebrows arched as I questioned my friend.

"Definitely not. Little Andy's going to be a perfect baby, and besides, I have some eggnog that doesn't have Mom's special additives," Jackie said as she rubbed her hands over her protruding belly. She was five months pregnant now and glowed with happiness.

"Is this enough wood?" Andy and Charlie were coming through the door, arms laden with logs for the fire, stomping the snow from their boots. They dumped their load of wood into the box next to fireplace and brushed the dirt from their clothes.

"That should hold us for a while," Mrs. F said as she came from the kitchen wheeling a cart with trays of appetizers. Lobster puffs, a fondue pot with crisp bread for dunking, apples and pears with a maple cream dip, and skewers of venison tenderloin. Stopping the cart near the fireplace, she turned to the stereo and clicked on the radio. The FM station out of Portland was playing Christmas music till the end of Christmas day. Music now rounded out the scene.

"Wow, Mrs. F," Charlie said as he turned his attention toward the cart. "Ethel said you always made wonderful food for this night, but this is something else." His eyes went from item to item showing an inner struggle of what he would eat first.

"Are your mom and dad coming tonight, Andy?" Mrs. F asked as she started to set the napkins and plates out for us.

"Maybe, my Aunt Lucy, mom's sister, is in the hospital in Portland, and they went out there this afternoon to see her," Andy said. "She fell off a ladder while she was decorating the tree outside her church and broke her leg in a few places. She's doing okay but won't be out for a week or two."

"See, I told you this decorating stuff was dangerous business," Jack said as he took a long sip of his eggnog.

"Oh, Dad, you are such a chicken," Jackie said as she tried to give her dad a hug, her tummy leaving her with only the option of a one-armed pat on the back.

"Charlie, what about your parents? Did you convince them to join us?" Mrs. F asked.

"No, not this time, but they will be out for dinner tomorrow," he replied. We had discussed this with his parents, and while I had now met them a few times, they didn't want to impose and stay overnight at the inn. Charlie was building a house on the lot next to the inn, and though it wasn't done to a parent's way of thinking, he had told them they could stay with him as well. They were coming out tomorrow to join Daddy, Charlie, and I for dinner. I was hoping for the best with my culinary skills, having taken some last-minute tips from Aunt Ellie. She had advised me to stick with ham, mashed potatoes, a couple of vegetables, and an apple pie. And I knew she would stop by in the morning just to make sure I was all set. As always, she would bring a few extras for me that I had forgotten like some homemade relish or pickles and fresh rolls. She made some potato rolls that even made Miss Ruthie swoon.

"Okay, I have the first toast," I said as I raised my glass. "Everybody ready?" We all stood by the Christmas tree, Andy with his arm around Jackie, Daddy and Charlie next to me, and Mr. and Mrs. F filling out the circle. "All the best to Jackie and Andy as they embark on parenthood." Here, here's were said.

"Mine next," said Jackie. "I wish for the Christmas feelings that we have tonight to last forever."

"Oh that's sappy," Andy said as he playfully mocked her "lasts forever."

"It is not," Jackie said and elbowed him in the ribs.

"Ow, boy, I won't have to worry about little Andy getting out of line. You're going to be tough," Andy said as he rubbed the spot she had jabbed.

"I have one," Charlie said. "I first want to say that never in my wildest dreams would I have thought I would be where I am today, standing here with friends old and new getting ready to say something I've never said before in my life." We all looked at each other quizzically as he reached in his pocket and put something in his hand. He turned to me and took my left hand. He slipped a ring on my ring finger and looked into my eyes. "Ethel, will you marry me?"

"Oh my," Mrs. F said and put her hand to her mouth.

My eyes widened as I looked at Charlie and then at Daddy. I saw a slow smile start to spread across his face as he returned the look.

"I don't know what to say." My mind was racing, I think my breathing had stopped. I looked at my hand and the ring he had placed on it. It was beautiful, a sparkling emerald-cut diamond in a silver setting. I looked back at Charlie who was searching my eyes for a hint, a clue, anything that spoke of a yes answer.

While those around us must have thought that this proposal was sudden, to us, it wasn't. In the past six months, we had discovered a love that filled that empty part in both of us. For me, it was the emptiness of wondering about my mother and my need for a career in journalism. He understood why I had chosen life here in Piney Bluffs.

Since returning from Vietnam, he had been trying to find his way and started wandering. His wandering had led him to find a new life in Piney Bluffs. While the Cape had been his home, it didn't have the thing that hooked his heart, he told me. We had spent many hours talking about what a life together would mean to both of us. He was starting a carpentry business and already feeling part of life here. My smile started to grow, just like Daddy's.

"Well, Daddy, what do you think?" I looked at him, his smile now wide across his face.

"He already asked my permission. I told him you're not easy, and you're a strong-willed son of gun." Daddy's smile gone now, and a serious look came across his face. "And that he's going to have to learn how to fish a hell of a lot better than he does now if he's going to be in this family." This brought a round of laughter that lightened the moment. All eyes were now on me.

"Well then, I guess, if it's all right with Daddy, oh hell, of course, I'll marry you, Charlie," I said and threw my arms around him and kissed him. The comfort of his arms, the warmth of him, as Jackie said the Christmas feeling that I felt now, I wanted it to last forever.

"Congratulations, my friend," Jackie said as she hugged me next. "This is the best Christmas ever."

"To Ethel and Charlie," Andy said as he raised his glass and slapped his friend on the back.

"Should I get the calendar now? I think we have an opening in June." Mrs. F was smiling.

"Oh, I think we can wait a bit to schedule the wedding in," I said and looked at Daddy.

"My girl," Daddy said as he hugged and held me tight. "Merry Christmas. How I wish your momma could see just how happy you are right now."

"Oh, I think she can, Daddy." And the tears in both our eyes glistened in the light of the Christmas tree.

"Damn!" I sputtered as I pulled back my hand. I thought my fingers could handle the edge of the plate and hadn't used the pot-holder when I was trying to turn my apple pie. Aunt Ellie had told me to always turn it halfway round as you baked it, as the part toward oven door was a little cooler, so this evened out the baking. The pie needed to be out soon as the ham was waiting its turn in the oven so it could eventually become the *ooh* and *ahhh* of the meal.

"You all right in there?" Daddy called to me. He was in the sun porch with Mr. Striper, putting the finishing touches on our tree. It seemed Mr. Striper had not had previous experience with a Christmas tree. And while most of the time he spent lounging beneath the boughs, he occasionally tried to climb up the tree in a quest for an unknown prey. Daddy had the tree tied to chair railing and had threatened to nail it to the floor if he had too. He too was sputtering at the cat with his disdain. Mr. Striper, on the other hand, just switched his fluffy tail back and forth to show his annoyance at the interference of his indoor accommodations.

"I'm okay, just need this pie to hurry itself up, or it's going to be vegetables and rolls for dinner," I replied. Reciting the "watched pot never boils" mantra, I turned my attention to the dining room table. On top of the white linen cloth, I set Momma's china, a cream-colored background with tiny multicolored flowers and a gold rim on the edge. Being worried about my first formal dinner, I'd been to the library to see how to set a formal table. And while the white linen napkins could hold enough silverware to keep everyone guessing, I decided against that as I would have needed to hand out instructions of which to use first.

I just wanted the dinner to be special for all of us. Charlie was going to break the news of our engagement to his parents on the way over, and hopefully, that would go well. My visits out to Dennisport during the summer and fall with them had been very warm and welcoming.

His mom had now recovered from her fracture and was quite the little spitfire around their home and in the town. The fact that she was the town's librarian was no way indicative of her character. From reading programs at the schools to hosting local authors and creative writing workshops at the library, she was an advocate for readers young and old alike. She was interested in my career in journalism, and we shared a great connection to all things written. Every week or two, a new book would find its way to Piney Bluffs with a note from her discussing the books merits. I in turn, would give her a call to either agree or disagree. All in all, a fondness had grown.

His dad was a little more reserved, and I could see a trace of sadness in his eyes when Charlie spoke of starting his own business in Piney Bluffs. Charlie's older brother John worked with his father, and it had just been assumed that Charlie would join them. Charlie explained to his dad that he was just branching out the business to Maine and that they could still have the sign say O'Connor and Sons.

Just then, the phone rang.

"I'll get it," I said as I turned to grab the phone. The pie was now out, and I was just putting the ham in. I grabbed the receiver and said, "Hold on a second," and slammed the oven door with my foot. "There. Hello and Merry Christmas," and I stopped to take a breath.

"Well, hello and Merry Christmas to you too," Caleb's voice sounded full of spirit of the day. "What's this I hear congratulations are in order for you and Charlie?"

"Boy, never underestimate a small-town grapevine," I replied. "But thank you very much. It was a very beautiful surprise."

"Great, great, and I have another surprise of sorts for you too." Now his voice held a little mystery.

"What? Tell me! What's going on?" I was never good at waiting.

"We got a Christmas card in the mail yesterday from the Browning brothers." He was letting this play out now.

"Get to the point!" I was just about jumping out of my sneakers.

"They're going to publish the *Weekly* in a quarterly New England country store magazine, and they're coming out after the first of the year to plan it out." He sounded excited finally.

"Oh my, I knew it, I knew it!" I almost shouted. "The comments that they had for us after the Basstile Day edition were terrific. They seemed more excited than us."

"I just thought you would like a little present and to know that our hard work hasn't gone unnoticed," Caleb said.

"I don't think I could stand much more in the way of presents like this. This is amazing. Say, what are you and Sadie doing for dinner today?" I asked.

"Oh, we're relaxing by the fire and having a little something," he said, trying to make it sound a little more than what I knew it was.

"Why don't you come over and join us? I have plenty. At least that's what Aunt Ellie said. And if you stop at the Gas n' Go and pick up some vanilla ice cream for the apple pie, that would be super. What do you say?" I was hoping they would come. It would be great conversation with new people meeting each other.

I could hear Caleb shout to Sadie and heard her respond something back.

"Okay, she said yes. And she'll bring over a little something extra. She's been experimenting again," Caleb said the last part very softly. "Try not to make a face if it's what I think."

"Oh, it will be fine. See you at one o'clock sharp," I said and hung up after our good-byes.

"There'll be two more for dinner," I yelled out to Daddy.

"Okay," was all I heard and thought it came from upstairs.

"You all done with the tree?" I continued as I put two more place settings on the table.

"Yep," man of few words today and he *was* upstairs. "I'm busy," was the response.

Oh well, I thought, *busy means busy.* No time to dwell on that, I had to finish getting out the serving dishes and finding the Christmas albums for the record player. My friends all had eight tracks that were popular now, but I still liked my LPs. And besides, we didn't have an eight-track player. So rummaging in the cabinet, I found our favorites—Andy Williams, Bing Crosby, Tony Bennett, and a few festive instrumental albums. I stacked them up on the spindle, and in the time it took for the needle to touch down, the air was filled with the rich voices of holiday spirit.

With everything set now, I went up to change out of my jeans and sweatshirt. I had had selected black pants and a white cable turtleneck sweater, hoping that my cooking adventures wouldn't end up on me. But then again, that's what they made aprons for. Aunt Ellie had taken care of that and had quilted one for me for my Christmas present this year. She had always handcrafted something for me each year; ornaments for the tree and stuffed animals when I was a younger and now more practical things. As I left my room, I passed Daddy's door that was closed.

"Almost ready?" I asked on my way down the stairs.

"For the love of Pete, what is the need for me to be ready?" he answered back in an irritated tone still from the other side of his door.

"Easy, Daddy, I was just asking. No need to get annoyed. It's Christmas day," I yelled up from bottom of the stairs. But what was the man doing? Oh well, time would tell.

I went back into the kitchen and put on my new apron. Aunt Ellie had done a beautiful job as always using a log cabin style of quilting and patching together colors so that the squares looked like a Christmas tree. I started to look for her signature. Whenever she had made something, she always had her signature in a heart hidden on that item. As I looked at myself in the mirror, I saw that the top block on the tree was a heart and her *EK* embroidered at the bottom. I smiled as I fingered the heart hidden in plain sight. I walked back into the kitchen and started to do last-minute preparation, humming along with "White Christmas."

I heard Daddy coming downstairs. After his last comment, I didn't say anything to him for fear of another cranky retort. I was at the counter with my back toward him as he walked through the kitchen and into the sunroom. I heard him say a little, "Good kitty," to Mr. Striper, and then he came into the kitchen.

"Smells mighty good, Ethel." And I turned to see him smiling at me and rubbing his hands together as if he could hardly wait to eat.

"Excuse me, but did you happen to pass a crabby man on your way through? I could have sworn there was one in here just a bit ago." I looked at him with questioning smile.

"Oh, I was just having a...," and he stopped in midsentence as there was a knock on the door. "I'll get it," he said and left me to answer the knock.

"Merry Christmas," I heard him say. "Come on in. I'm Ed. nice to meet you."

"Hi, Ed, I'd like you to meet my parents John and Peggy O'Connor." I heard Charlie's voice and hurried down the hall to greet them.

"Congratulations are in order so Charlie tells us," I heard John say to Daddy, and the two fathers shook hands. Charlie's mom came and gave me a big hug.

"I am so happy for the two of you," she said as she took my hands in hers and looked into my eyes. Tears glistened at the edges of her blue-gray eyes.

"Peggy, you don't know how happy Charlie makes me," I said and hugged her. I looked at Daddy, and he was smiling. Whatever had made him a little disgruntled earlier had disappeared, and I was happy of that. With this the first time that they were meeting, I wanted the in-laws to at least start off on the right foot. Daddy ushered everyone into the kitchen and was taking requests for cocktails. As I was hanging the coats in the hall closet, there came another knock at the door.

"Merry Christmas," I said as I opened it.

"And Happy New Year. Smells good in here. Did you hire Miss Ruthie?" Caleb and Sadie said as they both hugged me. Caleb held up the ice cream I had asked for, and Sadie was carrying a pie basket with a foil-covered dish.

"A little something else for dessert, peppermint sugar cookies," Sadie said, beaming at the fact she was bringing a dish that someone other than Caleb could weigh in on. Caleb's eyes rolled, and I gave him a little nudge to stop it.

"And here's the ice cream, just in case," Caleb said, and it was now Sadie's turn to give him a nudge, no more like a jab in the ribs.

"Why, thank you. I'm so glad you came. Come on in and meet Charlie's folks." And I led them into the kitchen. Charlie took their coats and went to hang them up. Daddy was taking care of the introductions.

Eventually, all had drinks in hand and were in the sunroom, settled for the moment. Mr. Striper was trying for as much attention as he could muster, going from chair arm to lap. While most shooed him away, Sadie cooed and petted him, rendering her his now favorite person of the moment. Daddy, Charlie, Caleb, and John were looking at a picture of Daddy's squad during his time in the Air Force. One of their planes was behind them, and they all looked dashing and young dressed in their flight jackets and holding helmets under their arms. Choosing the wing chairs by the fireplace, Sadie and Peggy seated themselves and were talking about Christmas and how nice it was to meet new people. I checked on dinner one more time and went over to join them taking a seat on the stool.

"I'd like to propose a toast," Daddy said, and we turned to face him with our glasses raised. "To Ethel and Charlie, may life always be good to them." Charlie came to my side and pulled me up and put his arm around my waist. Standing side by side, we smiled as we drank our toast knowing that this would be the beginning of many new wonderful memories. A chorus of good luck was said, and hugs were given.

"Thank you," we said together.

"And now if you'd like to take a seat, dinner is served," I said, and we all started toward the table.

The next sound we heard was glass shattering on the floor. As we turned to look, Caleb's glass had fallen from his hand, and we watched in what seemed like slow motion as he collapsed to the floor in front of the fireplace.

Sadie hurried to his side and screamed, "Someone call Doc McAllister!"

Daddy ran to the phone and hurriedly dialed the phone as Charlie knelt over Caleb, checking for breathing and started CPR. In an instance, Sadie's terrified sobs had replaced the joyful conversation. And Daddy's words of "life being good to us" felt heavy on my shoulders. The wood crackled, and the scene unfolding in front of us looked like a picture slowly burning into nothing.

27

"Ethel, not much more time left. Everyone will be here in little bit," Charlie called up to me. We were having Christmas dinner at our house this year. Jackie and I had started to take turns with holiday meals after Charlie and I had married. I had spent most of the morning getting the meal ready, putting the finishing touches on the table, and had just finished calling Daddy and Jackie to make sure everyone was coming. Charlie's parents were coming up later in the day after spending Christmas morning with the grandchildren at his brother John's house. He and Julie had a boy and a girl, Sarah was two, and John III was just turning five.

I looked at my watch, 11:00 a.m. I had just enough time to lie down for moment. I drew the quilt around my shoulders. It was a yellow-and-white pinwheel design, and it gave the room a sunny feeling even on the gloomiest of winter days. Aunt Ellie had made it for Charlie and I for our first Christmas as husband and wife.

Charlie, as always, had been a big help this morning in getting the house and the meal ready, but I was a little tired. I had gone into Portland last week to see my gynecologist. I'd had a funny feeling and had found out that it wasn't so funny after all. He announced that I was about eight weeks pregnant and started handing me pamphlets and discussing on how to develop a plan for my pregnancy. My mind started to work overtime as everything he said after that seemed like a conversation being held with someone else, and I was just eavesdropping.

A baby. A smile started to grow across my face. What a wonderful Christmas present. Oh, how happy Charlie will be. Not to mention Daddy. I could see their faces now when they opened their presents. I had framed the words "Merry Christmas, Daddy" and "Merry Christmas, Grandpa," for them. I could hardly wait.

But a baby? How was I going to keep everything going? My days were so full of juggling the operations of *The Bugle* and the *Weekly*. How would I find the time? It seemed like I had just gotten everything under control after what had happened on that Christmas Day six years ago when Caleb had collapsed.

It had seemed impossible at first. I was totally alone. My days flew by as I reported and printed and did it all over again the next day. In the past, Sadie had helped me with the presses when Caleb had gone out of town. But she had taken a hotel room near the hospital in Portland when he was transferred. After that, he was transferred again to a cardiac rehab facility for an additional month. And so she didn't come back until she brought him home.

Thankfully, the late winter, early-spring season was a bit slower, so I was able to keep up with the day-to-day running of the paper. Folks in town knew what I was going through and stopped by to pick up their stack of papers for their businesses. After the first couple of weeks, I had hired my cousin Edie to replace me as the distribution coordinator. She was in eighth grade, and after school, she would stop by, park her bike, and take the company wheels to deliver the day's papers.

I had even gone back to Piney Bluffs High School and checked in with the guidance counselor. With Mr. Winslow's help, I found Jeremy Johnson, who like me was a journalism student and had been accepted at Central Maine. He came each day after school and helped with the presses. I had also encouraged him to write a weekly column that would highlight an interesting program or student. These stories had helped to create new readers to see if their student was the weekly highlight. Jeremy was a true asset and came in a half day on Saturday and Sunday to help out as well. Jeremy had such a positive experience with this that the school asked if I would continue to promote this program as part of the high school's intern sites and mentor the junior and senior students.

Photos of events and people were missing from the paper those first few weeks, so with Charlie's help, I was able to learn to take pictures with Caleb's 35 mm SLR and develop the film. *The Bugle* had a small darkroom, and I had helped Caleb from time to time, never thinking that I would need to know how to do all of this. While my first attempts were either too dark or too light, I finally had been able to produce a photo that looked good in print.

And so it went that way for three months—myself and my two assistants bringing the news to our customers. I called to check and see how Caleb was doing, and each time, Sadie told me he was getting stronger. Sometimes I was able to talk with Caleb, but he sounded very weak and only spoke for a moment or two. Sadie was very grateful and amazed that I was able to handle the day-to-day operations of the paper. She apologized that she couldn't be there to help me, but it was Caleb who needed her most now. Once he came home, Sadie stopped in each day to check on things and provide me with his daily reminders of don't forget this and that.

When Caleb was finally able to come back, he was a little different. He was tired, and at first, he was trying just to absorb what had happened since he had gone. I hadn't really changed things; I had just worked differently being only one person. He was amazed and grateful for the work I had done, my ingenuity to continue without missing one day of *The Bugle*. And he was thrilled with our high school intern program that had been created.

His nose for news quickly came back but with a new kind of attitude. His angle for local stories went to the heart of the matter and not just reporting what the surface told him. When he went to follow a lead on a story, it took him most of the morning. He said he was taking time to really get to know folks and to understand the fibers that made up the cloth of this town.

When we had the chance, our conversations were much like those we had when we first met. He again went back to asking what my vision was. While his was still the same, he felt his time was growing shorter. He had experienced a great scare, and he had been reevaluating what was truly important to him. After being back about two months, he decided that he would let himself be part-time. He would come in for the morning, but lunchtime was now the end of his day. We talked about what I had done and how my job would now change to have more responsibilities. And as a result of this, he was happy that he was able to double my salary. As I had in the beginning, I asked where the money came from. While circulation was increasing a bit, it in no way was enough to supplement a doubling of my salary. He said as he had then: life had been good to him, and he was happy to be a part of something that never seemed like work.

He was thrilled with the editions of the *Weekly* that I had created. And as the subsequent editions were due, he let me compose them and added his personal touches here and there. But by and large, *The Bugle* and the *Weekly* were my designs now. I had less than a year's worth of working for my hometown paper, and for all intents and purposes, I was the editor. My vision of succeeding in journalism had materialized sooner than I had ever expected.

We had continued on this way for the past six years. Each year, we had grown our circulation of *The Bugle* little by little. As the cities seemed to close in on them, people were relocating to the quiet welcoming ways of Piney Bluffs. The *Weekly* was gaining in popularity, and although it was a spoof of sorts, it brought more and more people through town to see if we really did exist. And it was as Caleb has said. The *Fishing Weekly* was finally putting Piney Bluffs on the map.

As an engagement present, Daddy had given us a piece of property that bordered the edge of Tyrell's Vineyard and Snowshoe Creek. Charlie had begun to work on the house as soon as the weather started to break that spring. It was a cape with a wraparound porch to the back overlooking the creek. Inside, the floor plan was open, and a river-stone fireplace was built that took up the entire north end wall in our living room. Daddy joked that the kitchen didn't need to be too fancy for me with my limited cooking skills. Aunt Ellie and Miss Ruthie took exception to that as I had learned at apron's length from the both of them, and so they ignored him and helped me to design the kitchen. There was a big office on the south side of the house where I placed my books, my typewriter, and a comfy chair for reading. Upstairs, our master bedroom had a smaller river-stone fireplace, and then there were two other bedrooms. One for each of the children, we joked, but by the look in our eyes, everyone knew what children would mean to us.

Charlie and I had married in June of that next year. Our ceremony was held in our backyard by the banks of the creek with Mrs. F taking command of everything from catering to decorating and anything in between. Jackie had been by my side as my maid of honor. My cousin Ellen was taking care of Jackie's twin boys. Yes, she had thought she was only having one, but Andy Jr. and Jack had been born three minutes apart. And at one-year-and-half old had been quite the handful that day.

Charlie had sung to me during my entrance to the makeshift altar of stone and birch saplings that was centered between two spruce trees. I can still hear him singing John Denver's "Annie's Song." Daddy had my arm escorting me to Charlie waiting by the banks of the creek. Reverend Ezra performed a simple ceremony, and that was that.

Daddy never said a word about Momma that day. The look in his eyes told the story. They had that faraway look from time to time, and I knew he was missing her.

I wore her necklace of white gold. An oval locket hung from it. The locket held their pictures on their wedding day. Daddy had given it to me that Christmas when Caleb had his heart attack. I remember him being crabby that morning as he said he had misplaced it and had finally found it. It was Christmas night when we were finally alone, just the three of us, Daddy, me, and Mr. Striper. I cried, and he had held me as we sat in front of the fire. We talked for a while, and then he asked about the plans for my future with Charlie.

I knew just what to say as Charlie, and I had spent those first summer nights lying in each other's arms, under the stars, planning our life. He was going to build a home for us. And then eventually, there would be our family, at least a boy and a girl. And then we would see after that. I had told him that while my work and family were here, I still felt that there were other things that I was going to do. Charlie had told me that he knew there were many great things that I was going to do, and he wanted to be there for me every step of the way.

Daddy had been happy that Charlie realized my potential and knew that I was going to lead the dance every now and then.

With the construction of our house, Charlie's skills as a carpenter became well known. From time to time, his father and brother came up to help when he was involved in brand-new construction. He had taken a cue from me and contacted the tech school for students who were interested in hands-on experience. This had proven to be a mutually successful venture for both he and the school as now only the most skilled students were allowed to do site work with Charlie.

Charlie had told me that he felt complete now being married to me and being successful in carpentry that he had learned from his father. After his tour of duty in Vietnam, he had been empty and wondered what would ever fill that void. He confessed that he almost never returned the call when Andy first contacted him. He was turning a cold shoulder to any emotion and had thought that a wedding was not the place for him. But Andy had called again, and this time, his friend convinced him that a change of scenery would do him good. And if he didn't come, he was going to the Cape and kick his butt all the way back to Piney Bluffs!

And so we had settled into our new lives together. And the past few years had just flown by. Our fifth anniversary would be coming in June, just about the time for our baby.

The Browning Brothers had been very understanding while Caleb was recovering, but they were in the publishing business. And that meant that their new publication *New England Country Roads* had deadlines. Thankfully, it was going to be published quarterly, and the Christmas edition was their kickoff issue. I had submitted *The Weekly* on time with the required four pages. It had been easier to create than I had first thought. Being the holiday edition, I created the framework that I could build on each year. There would be an ice-fishing derby, holiday recipes with a twist from Sadie, and stories about how the townspeople were preparing for Christmas and New Year's Eve. This would be updated each year to bring the reader back to the special time of the year and renew their acquaintances with our lovable characters.

They were very receptive as usual, gushing over the phone on the work I had submitted. They had big plans they told me. Their love affair with New England had spawned the idea for their new *Roads* venture. Reacquainting their readers with the charm of the towns along the roads of New England was their goal. And the *Weekly* was an integral part of that as its comic relief. The next phase they said was to be a catalog. We discussed product lines for the items that Sadie used and other items that I had created within the pages of the *Weekly*. The fact that we had Pappy's general store was a plus as they would include items from there as well. They even had thought of approaching Miss Ruthie for a special line of fish-shaped cookies. The towns, along the highlighted routes in each issue of *Roads,* reported spikes in sales and visitors wandering through their lovely towns. Certain areas were featured during just the right season in order to bring the reader the best experience when visiting.

For the next several years, Piney Bluffs enjoyed the boom. Mr. and Mrs. F had contracted with Charlie and his dad to build an addition to the inn. Our fishing camps were filled for each season. Big Bob and Beulah had increased the number of cabins to handle all those who had rediscovered the fishing wonders of Maine. Events like Basstile Day and the Annual Fishing and Conservation Derby grew in popularity. Our town council held more meetings on zoning as more companies were evaluating the area to see if we fit the market for their products. From spas and supermarkets to sporting goods superstores, we were now on the commercial radar.

Most folks thought that these speculators were wasting their time. It was only just a momentary thing. The extra rooms were good for the fishing trade, but what was the big deal with all these other stores and services? Still, others thought this was our big chance. The slow trickle of new people moving into our area brought with them some very specific needs and wants. Sure, they appreciated the peace and quiet, but why were the malls so far away? The council meetings increased attendance as public opinion had found a voice. There had never been too much of a plan for our sleepy little town. It was just assumed that the ebb and flow of our population would continue in a way that would be comfortable for generations to come. But now it looked like a wave was about to disrupt that calm ebb and flow. And we had to discover how well we would ride this wave.

"Ethel, honey, time to get up. Your Dad's downstairs wondering where you are." Charlie had nuzzled my ear, and his words sounded like they had on fuzzy coats.

"Uh-uh, just another minute," I murmured, my eyes still shut. He had put his arms around me, and the warmth of the quilt and his body made me feel like I never wanted to leave this very spot. He kissed my ear again and started to tug at the quilt.

"I'm just going to give your present away if you don't come down. And never mind when the twins get here. I'll just send them up to get Aunt Ethel out of bed." His threats were waking me now.

"All right, I'm up. Boy, you lay down for two minutes," I said.

"Two minutes, it's almost noon, Mrs. O'Connor," Charlie said in a fake horrified voice.

"Noontime, oh my God! Why didn't you come and get me? I have so many things still to do." I whipped the quilt off and started slipping into my shoes and running my hands through my hair as I leaned to take a look in the mirror. "I look absolutely—"

"Beautiful. Period. I have never seen any woman who can take a nap and look like you've been primping yourself all day like a high-priced pooch." Charlie's compliments always had something that made me retort back to him.

"Are you calling me a dog? Yes, you are, you're calling me a dog." I was smirking at him now as he came up behind me and slipped his arms around my waist and began kissing my neck. "Careful now, the family show is about to begin. We don't want to yell down and tell them this is a self-serve Christmas dinner." And I wiggled out of his arms to stand to face him.

"Merry Christmas, Mrs. C," he said as he cupped my chin and kissed me tenderly on the lips.

"Merry Christmas to you, Mr. C." And I hugged him for all I was worth.

"Hey, you two, it's time to eat. Where's the cook in this joint anyway?" As we walked from the bedroom, Daddy was looking up the stairs at us and smiling. "I got another invite, if I don't see some food on the table pretty quick."

"Oh, Daddy, I know Mr. Striper can't cook, so who's your invite? Diner's closed. You going out to the interstate for Howard Johnson's?" I smiled at him as I came down the stairs. "Damn, a girl can't take a little nap."

I gave Daddy a hug and a kiss on the cheek and then said to the two of them, "Come on before everyone else gets here. I have a surprise for you two." I linked my arms through theirs and pulled them to the Christmas tree. The looks on their faces were priceless, and I thought, *Just wait!* I reached into the tree and took their presents from inside the branches and handed the packages to them.

"It's not time yet to open presents," Daddy said. "Mine are still in the truck."

"It's okay, these special presents are just for you two," I said as I watched them open their frames. They turned them over, and I saw them each read the words and then repeat them.

"Eddy, I think I have yours. This says Merry Christmas, Daddy. Ethel, you must have gotten these mixed up." And Charlie looked a little puzzled.

"No, there's no mistake," I said. "I've got the right words for the right person."

And in a flash, they both understood. They started to whoop and then came to hug me and then stopped to check if that was too hard.

"Oh, you two. I am not going to break," I said. "Now come on and help me. I've got dinner to put on the table, and you two had better take lessons because I'll be a little busy next year."

28

Fishing Weekly Christmas Edition, 1979

New Year's Eve Fishing Derby
By Ethel Koontz, Sporting Events Editor

Some of you may have your sights set on New York City for New Year's Eve as we say good-bye to the seventies and jump headfirst into the eighties. And still others of you may be taking the missus to the big bash at the Moose Lodge in Knowles Corner. But before you rent that monkey suit or buy that train ticket, I am here to offer you your salvation. The Piney Bluffs Annual New Year's Eve Fishing Derby and Celebration Extravaganza. (We started calling it an extravaganza the year Channel 22, KARP started their own derby. Extravaganza just sets us apart from the rest.) You should be calling and making your reservations right now as here's all that's included. The excitement begins at 2:00 p.m. with a warm-up derby in Snowshoe Creek. It doesn't matter what you catch, the biggest wins a year's supply of worms from Tubby's Bait n' Tackle shop and a meal a month made by Tubby's mom, Tiny. Her culinary talents have improved a lot in the past year. Not nearly as many folks have shown up at Doc McAllister's for stomach pumping. After the warm-up derby ends, there's a winter buffet at the Trout Inn. Mrs. F knows how to entertain and will have nothing but the finest from our local cooking celebrities. Now most of the meats on the buffet are courtesy of Little Earl Watson. He may not be a great fisherman, but he sure has a way with roadkill.

So you may want to shy away from anything that's labeled chicken. And Tyrell and Muffie Newman will be uncorking some of this year's Calico Cabernet. It's named for the calico bass that Muffie found in the very first vat of grapes they were processing.

Sadie will be trying new recipes for side dishes. Her most requested is fish fin chips. You just can't walk away after having just one dipped in pollywog dip. Delicious! Fancy Frank always sets up his Karaoke machine from 9:00 p.m. until Big Bob can't sing anymore. By then, you will need to get your rest. At 5:00 a.m., breakfast is served at Andy's Diner. And after that, the Derby begins. At noon on New Year's Day, there will be prizes awarded for the first, the biggest, and the most. Winners will receive one-day bush trips with Big Beulah and an oil change from Phil's Gas n' Go. Life doesn't get much better than this. Price for this day and half of fishing fun is yours for just $29.95 per person. Only $19.95 if you're not fishing. Overnight accommodations are available at The Trout Inn starting at $35.00 per person. But Big Bob's got a great special going. A roomful for $20.00! And he's rented a bus to bring the guests back from the inn after an evening of fun and karaoke. So don't miss out! Write to us for reservations soon.

Subscription News Special

What better gift for your favorite fisherman than a year's subscription to *Fishing Weekly*. And for a special Christmas treat, we'll send along our limited edition Piney Bluffs's fishing lure. This was designed by our resident bass pro Tubby Carpinowski. Tubby guarantees that if you don't catch a fish within the first ten minutes of that lure hitting the water, well then, you must be fishing in your bathtub! We will also include one of Sadie's favorite holiday appetizer recipes, salamander snackies. You get all of this for only $19.95. So wrap up your shopping, and mail in your request to Caleb Johnson, c/o FW,

Rural Route, Piney Bluffs, Maine. This will ensure that your favorite fisherman won't miss a moment of FW, and it will continue to insure that Ethel has a day job. I hear tell that she's been frequenting Fancy Frank's Hum & Strum on the Wednesday's Karaoke & Wet Tee Shirt night and thinks she's bringing the house down with her singing. But that's a story for another time.

Exclusive Christmas Album

If you've been looking for that one-of-a-kind holiday album, then look no further. For the month of December only, FW has available *A Piney Bluffs Christmas*. The church ladies at Reverend Ezra's church have put their beautiful voices together for this year's exclusive arrangements. Unfortunately, Tubby's mom was not able to be at the recording as her throat warts were acting up again, and well, it just wouldn't have been a pretty sight when she starts coughing and her warts start leaking. Anyway, here's just a sample of the songs you will hear. "Cod Rest Ye Merry Gentlemen," "A Wave in a Manger," "We Fish You a Merry Christmas," and "I'm Dreaming of a Whitefish Christmas" to name just a few. There's also a special collaboration by Ethel and the rest of the Koontz family singing their favorite, "Oh Fish All Ye Faithful" with a fine instrumental by her Daddy on the spoon lures. So send your money in as quickly as you can as follows: $19.95 for a cassette, $10.95 for an eight track, and $5.00 for an album in case you haven't caught up quite yet.

Sadie's Recipe of the Month

The holiday season is just the time to bring out those family favorite recipes. And I would be remiss if I didn't share one with you. Marinated baked mussels is going to be a new favorite of your clan when you serve them this. Now I suggest that you do yourself a favor and get some PEI mussels, none better. Oh I've tried the mussels on the bottom of the fishing boats and the ones that the muskrats find. Outside of the inconvenience of having to put your bathing suit on and then the snorkel mask, the cost does not outweigh the quality. You will need about three to five pounds of these black beauties and place them in a kettle and pour in a bottle of the wine of your choice. Either a nice chardonnay or Chianti will do fine. Please don't try Night Train, Mad Dog 2020, or Bali Hai. While excellent beverages for your parties, they don't impart quite the right taste. Next thing you'll need is some garlic. Go ahead and put about four or five chopped cloves in with your wine. A little salt in the pot, and a pinch over your shoulder (or you could pinch someone as they walk by, it's all for good luck!), and a glass of wine for yourself. By the time you have finished your wine, those little suckers will be ready for some heat. Put your kettle over medium heat until they start to open. Any that didn't open should be tossed.

Unless you have a guest that you don't like and you could save those for that person, but it's the time of goodwill toward men, so knock it off for a day. Now mix a pound of butter with some flavored breadcrumbs. Take the mussels out of the broth and put a thumb full of the mix on each one and place on a baking sheet. Place them in a hot oven, and cook until the breadcrumbs brown. This will take about the time it takes you to drink a half glass of wine. Serve these immediately, and tell your friends they need to suck on their mussel! If they have already had a glass or two, they should find this comment hilarious. If they haven't, what are you doing making food for these people anyway? Merry Christmas and enjoy, my friends, enjoy!

Letters to the Fishing Creel

Dear Fishing Weekly,

I have tried to find the best way to talk to a new lady. She works at our local diner and is quite a looker. I know she must like me a little 'cause she is always giving me a little extra piece of pie or putting an extra scoop of soups stuff in my bowl. She smiles at me and tells me to have good day and come back and see her tomorrow. And I always do. But every time I try to talk to her, I feel like my mouth is full of worms! And I all I can do is wave good-bye and tip my good Bass Pro cap at her. Can you help? Sign me Silent in Sebago.

Dear Silent,

Well, I can certainly sympathize with you. A real looker can take your breath away. But first thing you must do is check your mouth. Being a great fisherman, are you sure that you still don't have worms in there? I know how you can get caught up in the moment and forget. Second, I would write down what you would like to tell her and then practice. Now don't trying anything fancy like saying, "Would you like to see my pole?" as she might get the wrong idea. And last, just relax, and be yourself. Don't relax too much; I wouldn't pass gas or anything. And hopefully, she will see that you're a great guy and give you an extra piece of something else if you get my drift! Good Luck! FW

29

After dinner, we took seats by the fireplace. Daddy made sure everyone had either coffee or an after dinner cocktail. Snow had started to fall as the sun was setting, and we made our predictions about the snowfall. Andy and Jack, now five and usually quite rambunctious, were thankfully busy with their new trucks loading and unloading discarded wrappings and bows. Charlie's parents, John and Peggy, had joined us as we were finishing dinner and were now regaling us with stories of their grandchildren and how John III was now dragging around hammers and T-squares "helping" his dad.

"It won't be long before Charlie has a helper too," I quietly said to Peggy. All conversations stopped as Peggy clutched John's arm.

"What are you saying?" Peggy was looking from Charlie to me with the look of expectation.

"I'm hiring a neighbor's kid to help out," Charlie replied. "Business is getting better, you know. I could use the help." Then he started to chuckle and shake his head.

"Charles Patrick O'Connor, I swear if you're..." Peggy's eyes narrowed as her gaze demanded the truth from her son.

"Ethel?" Jackie said in surprise as she turned to me and started to smile.

"Yes, we're going to have a baby," I confirmed to end the suspense.

Tears glistened in the corners of eyes as hugs and congratulations abounded. Toasts to the addition to the family and to everyone's health in the New Year were made. Then Jackie and Peggy took me aside and needed to know the gamut of details from when was I due to how was I going to manage the paper.

"Everything will work out," I reassured them. But my inner voice was not sounding all that reassured. The announcement to Caleb would need more than just a few words. Monday at work would be time enough. As we always had, we would put a plan together for the time that I would be out. The baby would be due in July, which would hit our semiannual seasonal lull. The *Weekly* for the fall *Roads* edition would need to be finished prior to June 15, so that was doable. The day-to-day operation of the paper would be where help was needed. Caleb was spending more of his time doing investigative journalism as he called it. Thankfully, Bobby, our high school junior, was working out well and would be that extra hand that was going to be needed.

Caleb had been slightly guarded when I questioned him about what he was investigating. With the quiet overnight success that the *Weekly* had brought to our town, also came those little feelings that made you not seem to accept that it was all for the common good. He had told me that soon, he would share all his findings, and then we could decide how to go about publishing them.

But enough of what would happen in the next several months. Conversations were now all about being grandparents and what had we picked out for names. The tugging of my arm quickly brought me back into the thick of it.

"Auntie Ethel, Mommy said you're going to have a baby. Can you make sure it's a boy, 'cause Andy and me need someone to throw the ball in when we play baseball," Jack said with such a serious tone that I had to hold my laughter in.

"Well, Jack, I'll see what I can do about that. But wouldn't it be okay if the baby turned out to be a girl? She could still play ball with you two," I said and watched Jack as he mulled that over.

"I guess that would be okay, but I really think you should have a boy just 'cause it would be easier for us to play with him." Jack was pretty matter-of-fact with the possibility of a girl and with a five-year-old's logic had found the only thing that mattered to him and that was playing. As long as you could play together, things were fine. Didn't we all wish that playing were all that was needed in life?

"I noticed a few Sold signs on the for-sale properties coming into town. Nice pieces, got any inside information on who might be coming in?" John asked me.

"No one saying anything yet. Town zoning meetings are the place where all the action is happening. Caleb goes to the meetings to keep on top of things. But so far, they're just LLCs with no definite plans. Just fishing as Caleb says," I replied. "Of course, when they actually apply for a specific type of zoning, then there'll be some speculations."

"It would be nice to have a few things closer than Auburn or Lewiston," Jackie joined in.

"Like what?" Andy questioned. "I thought you said everything you'd ever need was right here in Piney Bluffs." He smirked at her as he pointed to himself.

"Oh, Andy, you know what I mean," she replied. "Women like shopping, and sorry, but Lewis's General Store and mail order from catalogs doesn't fill that need. Even Jolene at the Sewing Box has to go into Portland for the fabrics that people are asking for."

"Pappy said some of the new folks are asking him for special orders. And I also noticed that UPS has put on a bigger truck. Changes are coming," I mused.

"Let's just hope those changes are for the best," Daddy said. "Now who wants some of Jackie's pecan pie?"

"Boy or girl?" Caleb said as I walked in the door. He was there earlier than usual. Since his heart attack, he had been coming in about eight or nine, but it was just seven, and by the looks of things, he had been in for some time.

"And good morning to you," I said, shaking my head. I put my things down on my desk and went to hang up my coat. "You know just because I'm pregnant doesn't mean I can't work. I have this all figured out. Now if we can just go over the plan, you'll see that there won't be any problems. And who told you I was pregnant?" I had moved to the side of his desk, my hands on my hips, my head inclined toward him.

"Beware the woman with arms akimbo," he said as he peered over his glasses at me. "And it was Miss Ruthie. Charlie told her this morning when he stopped in the bakery."

"Oh, but what does that mean?" I asked, still in my akimbo position.

"I don't quite recall. Our family physician used to say that about his nurse, rough thing she was, didn't take anybody's guff. Kind of like you." The corners of his mouth curled up into a smile. "Oh, just sit, will you. I know we'll be fine. I have bigger fish to fry than you having a baby. You will name him after me, now won't you?" He shied away from me as if expecting a fierce blow.

"Oh you," I shook my head and took a seat at my desk and turned my chair to face him. Over the past few years, we had replaced the small junior reporter desk with a queen-size roll-top desk. Our chair backs faced each other now. The junior desk was currently used for our intern. "So now, what are we frying?"

"Remember I told you I thought that there was more to your friend Norman the New England Fisherman than met the eye? Well, I think I may have figured out what's going on," Caleb said as he flipped the pages of his steno pad and tapped his pen on it. "Here's what I was after."

"Why is it he was always my friend?" I questioned. "Norman's done a great deal for the town what with sponsoring the annual derby and starting a fishing scholarship for kids. He could have said no the first time we met him."

"Yes, yes, that's just so noble of him. We should carve his likeness into the White Mountains. Now are you going to listen for a minute?" Caleb was just bit edgy this morning, so I gave in and stopped defending Norman.

"All right, what is this mystery that you have unraveled?" I said as I sipped my coffee.

"Well, he's been buying land in and around town and on the other side of Snow Shoe Lake," he said and laid his pen down.

"That's it?" I said incredulously. "The man is buying land in town and on the other side of the lake, and this is solving the mystery of the sphinx? I'm calling Charlie and telling him we're moving. Caleb, I don't get it. Why is this so horrible?"

"It's the way he's going about it, Ethel," Caleb said. "He's visiting people in their homes and asking if they were thinking about selling any of their land. They've seen him around town now for a few years, and they think all that same goody-goody stuff like you. Been telling folks he wants to preserve the land and not let those out-of-towners come in and destroy this wonderful town. Some of the folks have been struggling, and his offer is making them not think twice."

"But really how much land is out there to buy?" I said, half believing what he was saying.

"He's bought fifty acres from folks, and a mile and a half of water frontage of the lake is in the works," he said, tapping his pad again. "And I did a little digging, and this is not the first time he's done something like this. Seems like he goes about buying property in sleepy little towns that are coming into a boom and then waits for developers. The old 'buy low sell high.'"

"Oh," was all I could say as I let this new information sink in. "So even though folks did get money for their land, they could have made much more from the developers directly."

"Exactly. And they think that he's just going to use it as land preserve so they don't ask for a big price. And then when the developers come along and buy the land, they end up forcing the folks out since they don't have that much of their original land left, and they get less than what they sold it to Norman in the first place," Caleb finished and put his pen down.

"How is it that you're the only one who's got this figured out? Surely, other towns must have noticed this pattern." I was slowing shaking my head, thinking of what had happened to our good honest folks.

"There are folks in these towns who get a little extra in their Christmas card, if you know what I mean. From zoning board members to town clerks, seems his charm works well. And if not the charm, then the money seals the deal." And he finished with, "And I am not going to let that happen to this town."

"Where did you go to get this information?" I still wanted to know more of how this could come about.

"Andy Sr. is on the zoning board, and he came to me in October after one of the meetings. He said outside of the meetings Norman had been calling around and asking folks how things were going. He even stopped in the diner a couple of times. Said he was just looking for other sites for the derby and things like that. But Andy's pretty shrewd and wasn't buying it. So he acted all small town–like and played up to his ego and asked him about other places he's been and helped out. Norman was happy to expound to a certain point. Andy gave me the names, and I went to work." Caleb stopped and looked to see if I had taken this all in.

"I can't believe this. This makes me very angry," I said. "How could someone do this to these wonderful people, people that believe in him."

"Because that's the kind of person he is. We wanted to see someone else, someone who was here to help when we needed it. His notoriety coupled with the success we were having with the *Weekly* being in the *Roads* publication was just the perfect combination for him," Caleb said summing it up. "Don't feel bad. I thought he was okay in the beginning too, but there was just that feeling, the old reporter's notion of there's something not quite right here."

"So now, what are you going to do with this information? Surely, we can't just call him up and say, 'Oh, Norman, by the way, we know what you're doing, so please stop and give our nice folks their money back.'" I was mulling over how we were going to end this ruse of his.

"Oh, I've got a little plan brewing, but I need to find the right bait, a nice shiny lure. One that our big fish Norman won't be able to resist," Caleb said and closed his notebook. With that, the door opened, and there stood Norman himself.

"Well, looks like you two are working on the story of the century," Norman said. Care to let me in on it?"

30

I tried to control myself and hoped my face didn't give me away. Caleb had turned his chair and made his way to shake Norman's hand. That movement allowed him to regain his composure, if he had given any sign at all that it had been lost. He motioned for Norman to have a seat.

"Well, Norman, good morning. What brings you to town? Sit down, won't you." Caleb had never missed a beat. Norman sat down, putting his hat on the end table.

"Good morning to you both," Norman said. "Hope I'm not interrupting anything."

"No, no, really. First thing in the morning is our planning session for the day's edition," I chimed in with a smile on my face. Looking at him now, the littlest of things rang of insincerity. His smile made my stomach turn, or was that the pregnancy? Either way, our guard was up, and now we had the upper hand. "What can we do for you?"

"Well, I'm in need of some advertising in both of your publications," Norman said as he pulled some notes from his shirt pocket. "I'm planning on having an ice-fishing derby in February. I've drafted a story about it, but I'm sure the two of you will be able to make this a great deal more appealing." And he handed his notes to Caleb.

"Looks like another winner for you, Norman," Caleb said as he read through them, jotting down some notes on his pad. "President's Day Derby, going to be cutting it close for the *Weekly* in the *Roads*, but I think we can get a special edition in. And even if it doesn't make it in there, we have a good following now and can distribute ourselves."

"I was hoping to have some of the folks in town donate toward prizes for the winners," Norman said. "Do you think they could help out?"

"Well, I think you could find some," I said as I now read through his notes. "A few folks are still having a tough go of it even though most are doing better now."

"I'm sorry to hear that. I certainly wouldn't want to put a hardship on anyone," and he looked at us in earnest. I was having a hard time containing myself but knew I needed to remain calm, if we were to let out a little more line.

"I see that you didn't put down what the prize would be. What did you have in mind?" Caleb asked.

"I was hoping we'd be able to raise five thousand dollars for the grand prize and then maybe some runner up prizes of fishing gear and related equipment," he replied.

"Wow, that's quite a prize," Caleb said as he let out a low whistle. "Haven't ever had a prize like that in this town that I can recall."

"And that's why the big prize. This will put Piney Bluffs on the fishing circuit radar. It gets better as this will almost pay for itself. The entry fee is going to be a little higher, one hundred dollars. That will bring in your bigger fisherman, ones that fish the circuits for a living. And then I am looking for some major sponsors to pay for the advertising on television and radio and fund the prizes too," he continued. "I'll get coverage the day of the event as well. Ethel, I think you'd be great doing some reporting that day, with all you know about fishing, and it doesn't hurt that you have pretty face."

"Well, I'm not so sure about reporting on television," I responded. "I don't have any experience."

"Ethel, you'd be such a natural for it," Norman said. "I saw that from the moment I met you. And there's not a woman fishing reporter in New England, never mind that you actually know what you're talking about. I can have some of my contacts do some preliminary training with you before the derby."

"Why so much coverage for an ice-fishing derby in our town?" Caleb asked.

"It's time for people to get to know Piney Bluffs and what it has to offer. Sure you're getting people to stop as they're driving through on the way to New Hampshire for apples and maple syrup or out to Portland for lobster. But you need to make this be their destination," Norman sounded very convincing.

And he had no idea how this very event was going to play into his undoing. As I listened to him, I realized his real reason for bringing the media to this town. The land that he had been purchasing was going to skyrocket in price. My anger was growing. I had never really despised anyone in my life as much as I did Norman.

"Well, I'll be going now. I'm going into Boston to check with the station that used to cover my show," he said as he stood and put his hat on. "There's still a few folks in the business that remember me and will be able to see what a great new adventure for New England sports television this is. I'll take care of getting posters back to you. Maybe you could have a school kid put them up. And then I'll make sure the surrounding towns get some too. We'll also have to work out the details of where the weigh in will be. TV crews will be out to scout out the locations. I'll be in touch with some of the businesses for a little contribution."

"Take care, and we'll get this story into print soon. Do you want to see the copy before it goes out?" Caleb asked.

"I trust you'll do a great job, but fax one up to the office when you're done." And with that, Norman was out the door.

"Well now," I said and let out the breath that I had been holding in. "Wasn't that just the perfect timing? Do you think he heard anything before he came in?"

"People like Norman could care less what you and I were talking about," Caleb explained. "It's all about him. And knowing what we know now, he's really banking on a big payday, and he doesn't have to do a thing. You heard him. Sponsors will pay the bill. Piney Bluffs gets exposure, and the payday for him just gets better."

"Then we'd better get to work to make sure that payday never happens," I said. With that, the phone rang, and we were back to the business of the daily paper. But I couldn't stop thinking of what was happening. I really needed to speak to Daddy and Charlie. I knew that they could help set the trap for Norman. It would have to wait until tonight. I'd stop by Daddy's house on my way home and have him come for dinner, and we could talk. There were lots of details to be worked out in the two months before the derby.

"Smells good. Charlie must be cooking," Daddy said as he came through the door. Mutt and Jeff, our two golden retrievers, happily wagged their tails and escorted Daddy into the kitchen.

"Any more talk like that, and I'll just turn the boys loose on you," I said. The dogs were waiting patiently at the counter near their treat container. Daddy always fed them when he arrived.

"I can just see that now." Daddy chuckled as he reached for their treats. "They are always on the verge of biting me." And with that, he gave them a treat for which they sloppily licked his hand in thanks.

"Did I hear comments about my dinner?" Charlie said as he was coming down the hallway. "Eddy, you'll like this, an old family recipe for Irish stew."

"Just as I suspected, the girl still can't cook," Daddy said and gave me a hug as I raised my wooded spoon in mock defense.

"Okay, you two, sit, and I'm not talking to the dogs," I said curtly as I filled the bowls and set them on the table.

"We're all business tonight, aren't we?" Daddy asked, his focus on me narrowing. "What's going on? You feeling okay? Baby's all right, isn't it?"

"Daddy, I'm fine," I said, a bit softer to reassure him. "But I do have something to tell you two."

"What's up, Ethel?" Charlie asked as he looked at me with concern.

"Well, I have something to tell you about Norman," I replied and then proceeded to tell them the entire story as Caleb had explained it to me. For a moment, neither one said a thing.

"Why that no good son of a bitch," Daddy said, shaking his head. "I should've seen that. I can't believe he's doing this and thinking he's going to get away with it."

"He hides that evil side pretty well," Charlie said. "Why didn't we see this before?"

"He's fooled us all," I said. "We wanted to see what we got. Somebody to help us, seemingly for nothing in return. That's where we made the mistake. As they say, ain't nothing for free. And never mind us, there's folks in other places that went through the same thing."

"Why didn't anyone catch him before?" Charlie asked.

"As Caleb said, the folks didn't have enough money to hire lawyers to bring him to court. And the town officials looked the other way to keep their private pockets full," I said and shook my head. "It's absolutely disgusting."

"So what's the bait that Caleb's going to use?" Daddy asked.

"I don't know. We've got to find just the right person with that piece of land that he won't be able to resist," I answered. "And then get him to fall for it without a thought to it. He's so arrogant he has no idea that we're on to him. So in a way, it will be easy to set the trap. I just wish we could make him give back the land and the money to all those folks he's swindled."

"If we work this thing right, we could get that back, but we've got a way to go," Charlie said. "We need this to be very public so when he bites, everyone will know that we've caught a big fish."

"He's getting us television coverage for the ice-fishing derby," I replied. "Seems like that might be just the place to reveal him for what he is. And he did say he wanted me to do some reporting. I can just see it now, doing a thank-you interview on him and turning it into expose."

"We're going to need some legal help," Charlie said. "We've got to make sure this works, or we could have the rug pulled out from under us."

"Caleb's going to check in with the Browning brothers' ad and see if they can point us to someone who can help," I said. "With the way they love Piney Bluffs, there's no way they're going to let anything happen to us."

"I hope they can help," Daddy said. "'Cause we're going to be fighting a big fish with a light line. One false move, the line will break, and the big one gets away."

31

From the window, I could barely see Miss Ruthie as she rolled dough for the daily treats. The windows were streaked from condensation of the heat of the ovens and the cold of the day. Beginning of January always seemed a little colder once the warmth of the holidays had faded. It also didn't help that it was cloudy and just six thirty in the morning. It felt like more snow was on the way. I pulled my hood off and stamped my feet of snow as I opened the door.

"So what's the little mother having today with her tea?" she said as she turned away from her work as I entered. Stopping each morning had been a part of my daily routine on my way to *The Bugle*. But now coffee somehow didn't agree with my pregnancy, so Ruthie had switched me to tea. Wiping her hands on her apron, she came over to give me a quick hug. It was just the two of us in the shop, and she grabbed her coffee cup and took a sip.

"Have you got a diet muffin? I think I gain five pounds even thinking about food," I lamented to her. I went to the counter and poured hot water into a cup, choosing a chamomile tea.

"Oh, Ethel, you are one of the prettiest pregnant girls I've ever seen. Why you're still wearing your jeans, at what is it now, ten or twelve weeks?" She shook her head at me. "However, I have been experimenting with bananas and applesauce to see if I can cut a few calories out. Have a piece of this banana bread, and tell me what you think." She cut me a thick piece of dark bread and handed it to me on a napkin. The aroma of cinnamon and bananas filled the air.

"It's twelve weeks now, and I may have my jeans on, but I'm not showing you how high the zipper goes," I confessed and took a bite of the bread. "Oh, Ruthie, this is heaven, so moist and rich tasting. This can't be low in calories." And I continued to savor the treat.

"Well, let's see. I cut out some of the oil and the eggs and made applesauce to make up for it. Added a few other things like some wheat flour and oats and flax seed to keep you healthy." She was looking up, making a mental list to make sure she remembered everything. "Some of my new customers have been asking for lighter items. Imagine coming to a bakery and asking for such things. Doesn't bakery equal calories?" And she chuckled heartily.

"It's kind of nice having new folks around, isn't it? Keeps us on our toes," I said. I was baiting her now to see where her conversation would go.

"It is, and it isn't in some respects," she said. "I've been doing some special orders for folks and then trying them out as a regular item. Some things are catching on, and some aren't. Like that banana bread you're having. That's a good seller, but it takes a little more time, and to do it right, I make my own applesauce. Most of them don't know from homemade applesauce to the stuff you buy in the grocery store. And I also hear them say things like 'I wish the donut shop in Portland wasn't so far away.' Or 'Maybe this town will finally get with it and have something with a little faster service.' With all these developers putting down claims, speculating on property, well, it just worries me, that's all. I could be put out of business with a fast-food bakery."

"I'm sorry, Miss Ruthie, I had no idea," I said. "I had thought that everyone was enjoying a little more prosperity now that more people were coming into the area. But then there's always some price to pay, and it depends on how much it's worth to you whether you pay it or not."

"Oh, don't worry about me. I've got a little reserve to pay the price," she said, patting my hand. "Besides, the Browning brothers came to see me right before Christmas. Not only do they want me to have an ad in *Roads* to sell my fish-shaped cookies, they want me to write a cookbook. What do you think of that?"

"Why, that's wonderful! Why didn't you tell me?" I hugged her. "I can help you with editing if you like."

"It seems that Russell is quite taken with everything that I make here. From the beginning, he'd come in every day for a treat when they were here fishing and then take home a box when they were leaving. He's asked me to come up with about thirty recipes for everyday baked goods and then also a section on special things like wedding cakes. He's got all kinds of ideas." She was in a better mood now talking about her new venture. "Robert too. He wants to have pictures of me baking and the cases and close-ups of the pastries. I tell you, it's just turned my head to think that I could have a cookbook."

"I am so happy for you," I said. "They're more honest than some of the new folks around here lately."

"Ethel, why don't you just ask me what's on your mind, girl. I've known you too long for you to treat me like some type of in-depth interviewee." She looked at me square and waited.

"That's what I love about you, Ruthie, never takes you long to size someone up," I said as I took another sip of my tea. "So I have a question for you. What do you think of Norman?"

"Well, now he's an interesting fellow," she said and returned back to the dough. She started to cut out biscuits and began placing them on a baking sheet. "He always stops by when he's in town, which seems to be a bit more frequent now than when he first came here. I'm not sure he's all that he seems. But then you already know that if you're asking the questions." She looked around at me as she placed the biscuits in the oven. "I do know that he's been asking questions about various things, like how's business and if we're getting along all right. But the way he goes about it, you almost don't think he's interested in the answer. More like he's just passing time by making small talk. So are you going to tell me why you're so interested?" Ruthie was just this side of impatient, and I either had to tell her or risk having her ask more than I wanted to tell.

"Do you have any property other than the bakery and your home?" I asked. I knew she had a home on the other side of Snowshoe Lake. I also knew that her father had been a doctor in Fryeburg and, story goes, was well off when he passed. I was hoping that the "well off" part of the story equated to land and that she might have inherited a piece somewhere.

"I do have a good portion on the Salmon River just past Tubby's," she said, and her eyes narrowed. "Why do you ask?"

I hesitated now. Caleb and Andy had been discussing how to lure Norman out. But they needed just the right piece of property. Her piece might just be the right one.

"Tell me more about the land," I said. "How much is there?"

"Well, it runs along the river for about a mile or so. Just before it joins up in Gray before the springs. The old Poland Springs hotel is still there just past where my land stops. Someone's been trying to fix it up, but I don't think it'll do any good," she said, opening the oven door, talking more to the biscuits in the oven than she was talking to me. "Good fishing along those banks, they say. Why are you asking about my land? Are you going to tell me what this is all about or not?"

This property sounded like just what might catch his interest. But I needed to check with Caleb first to make sure this was what we were looking for. I loved Miss Ruthie to death, but I didn't want to involve her just yet until we were sure.

"Oh, will you look at the time, almost seven. Caleb is going to think I quit. Honest, Ruthie, when I can tell you, I will, you know that," I said and came to give her a hug. "I want to make sure." And she shook her head at me as I made a quick exit out the door.

"Banker's hours for you?" Caleb asked as he peered over his glasses at me.

"I've been on the job since six thirty," I said as I hung my coat on the peg and took my seat. I swiveled around toward his desk. "I think I have the bait we've been looking for."

"Really. And just where were you shopping for bait so early in the morning," and Caleb turned to face me.

"Miss Ruthie's. She has a piece that Norman won't be able to resist." And I began to explain how much there was and where it ran to.

"Gray, huh," Caleb started nodding his head. "That's interesting. I've been looking at towns around us to see what's developing, and I've heard that piece is on more that a few radars. Seems that their water business is taking off, and they're going to be distributing it outside of Maine. The old inn is just about to have a rebirth as some type of health spa. People appear to be interested in the so-called healing qualities of the waters. Same type of story that Atlantic City was built on, "healing waters and peaceful surroundings." But I think you're right. This could be the piece that Norman won't be able to resist. And with Ruthie being a female, he'll think he can waltz right in and convince her to sell that worthless piece. I'll call Andy and let him know that we've stocked the pool. And now we just need to let Norman know that fishing season is open."

32

I thumbed through the worn parent's magazine for what seemed like the tenth time. The articles about the care of newborns for the first-time mothers were just a little too matter-of-fact for me. While the information seemed logical, it was a lot to comprehend. Charlie and I talked about what kind of parents we were going to be and how we would do things. Our hopes and dreams for our baby were everything from when he or she would be president to when Daddy would be able to take his grandchild fishing for the first time. Today, we were going to learn the sex of our baby, and then we could think about names. Charlie had dropped me off to check at the lumberyard for a special order he had made last week, and then he would be back. Dr. Simon always liked to have the father in at the end of the visit to explain how the pregnancy was progressing.

"Ethel, you can come in now," his nurse called to me from the doorway. "You're looking great. Now let's just weigh you, and then you can go right in to the exam room."

"Can I use the ladies' room first? It's been a long ride, and I will pee right here if I have to wait any longer," I pleaded with her.

"Of course," she said and chuckled. "Use this room right here, and give us a sample in the cup."

"Wonderful, thank you," I acknowledged and quickly slipped into the rest room. Relief at last! I swear, men have no idea what women go through. With Jackie as my only resource for my pregnancy, she agreed that Charlie had no clue about any of the day-today changes that I was going through, never mind the need to pee every two minutes.

"There you are. Now just step up on the scale," she said and busily wrote down my weight. "You're doing well, twelve weeks and right on track. Okay, right in here and the doctor will be right in. Everything off below the waist. And here's this year's fashion statement." She held out the aqua-colored paper drape, laid it on the exam table, and before I could turn around, she was gone.

I struggled to pull my pants off as they had become snug over the past few weeks. I shuddered to think about buying those pants with the stretchy panels. Maybe I would just wear the flowing Indian print dresses and long corduroy jumpers and bypass the pants issue altogether. I pulled the paper drape around me and sat on the cold plastic exam table to wait.

Looking around the room, the walls were filled with photographs of mothers and babies in those intimate moments where it was just the two of them—the hand of the baby wrapped around her mother's pinky finger, a baby nuzzling at his mother's neck with his eyes closed and the peaceful look of sheer bliss, the mother cradling her baby's head in her palms while the body stretches out on her forearms and the mother smiling down. I hoped I was ready for those moments.

I thought back to the letter that Momma had written to me. She never had a chance for a moment like those displayed. Her moments were dreams of a healthy child who would have a long and loving life. My emotions got the best of me, and Dr. Simon walked in as I was hunting for a tissue in my purse.

"Ethel, what's the matter?" he asked me, placing a hand on my shoulder.

"Oh, it's just those pictures make me think back to my mother and how she never had the chance for anything like that," I confessed to him and let out a deep sigh. "And I hope that my baby and I will be able to have those kind of moments."

"Well, don't you worry, you'll be just fine. All of your blood work looks great. Your test values are right where they need to be," he reassured me. "And today, we find out what name you'll need to be thinking about." He finished his exam and announced that everything was fine and asked if I had any questions about the procedure. Having none, he opened the door signaling to his nurse and Charlie that we were ready for the ultrasound. With Charlie by my side, holding my hand, the scanning began.

"Well, there you are," Dr. Simon announced. "Let me be the first to introduce you to little Mr. O'Connor."

Charlie and I watched as the doctor pointed out hands and head and the most important appendage of the hour. We giggled, and tears of joy fell down my cheeks. He continued to move the probe over my swollen belly pointing out other features of our soon-to-be son.

"So are we having a Charlie Jr.?" Dr. Simon asked as he put things away.

"We don't know," Charlie said excitedly. "But now that we know what we're having, you can bet that we'll know by the next appointment."

"Are there any questions that I can answer?" Dr Simon asked again.

"I do," I exhaled with a "here goes" heaviness. "I know we have talked about what happened to my mother and what she could have had. My father only knows that it was something that happened in the last few weeks. And the doctor that delivered me is gone now. The small hospital burned, the records were lost in that fire, so there's no place to check. How can we be sure that something won't happened to me?" The tears started a slow trickle down my face, and Charlie brushed them softly away with his thumb.

"Ethel," Dr Simon began, "I have tested you for all the known complications of early pregnancy and even more in the area of genetic factors. All have come back negative." His smile was comforting and reassuring. "But," he added, "as you go along with the pregnancy, there will be things we need to watch for. And I will be there with you and checking and testing for all of them. I know it's easy for me to say, but I want you to enjoy this time of your life and not worry. Charlie, do you have any questions?"

"I just want Ethel to be safe," Charlie said as he looked into my eyes and back at the doctor. "I don't know what I would do if something were to happen to her."

"Medicine has made many advancements in the past two decades since you two were born. Technology has lead to the discovery of how we can prevent things that twenty years ago were just assumed would lead to a bad outcome," Dr Simon said. "Please you two, relax. Okay?"

"Okay." I exhaled and nodded my head. "I'll see you in a few weeks." Dr Simon gave me a hug and shook Charlie's hand and walked us to the reception area. I made my next appointment, and we walked out into the bright sun of a winter day.

As we made our way to the car, we held hands tighter than ever before. It seemed that we were more careful walking, driving, or just doing anything now that I was pregnant.

"Charlie," I started as we made our way home. "What if something were to go wrong?"

"Ethel, I would never want to lose you, if I had to choose." He held my hand tighter. "What we have is very special, and a child will only make it more so. But if your life were in danger, we would have to choose you. Do you see that? You have made such a difference in my life, in the lives of everyone who know you. Now stop talking like this. Everything will be fine. I love you. I love you more than you will ever know. And nothing on earth is going to take you away from me."

"And I love you too," I said. We rode in silence for a while letting the enormity of our conversation sink in. I felt a sense of relief having had this conversation. It had to be discussed, and it had to be in the back of both our minds that something could happen.

"How about E. Charles O'Connor?" Charlie broke the silence with his first name choice. "The E is for your dad, and it doesn't carry that junior category that most kids hate. What do you think?"

"You know, I kind of like that." I smiled, and the pall of the previous conversation lifted from the air. "I think we hit it right the first time."

And with that, Charlie took my hand and kissed it. The smile on his face broadened. We passed the remainder of the ride talking about all of those things that soon-to-be parents think of—nursery colors, toys, and college. And then there would be his first day of fishing with Daddy, going to Miss Ruthie's for a treat, and all of the wonderful things that would be part of his life.

Between Jack, Andy, and now EC, the next generation had begun. As parents, we would continue to build our community where we valued the loyalty of each other. In turn, our children would continue to insure the quality of the life that hooked each of us every day when we greeted one another on the street. Only one thing stood in our way—Norman. And soon, he would understand how that loyalty was the one thing he could never possess.

33

The tiny bells jingled as I opened the door to the post office. They hung from a piece of red velvet ribbon now faded from many Christmases past. It looked like each day would be the last day for that ribbon, but it continued in its supporting role to assist the bells in announcing the customers to Dottie, who came from the back sorting room and ambled slowly to the counter, shaking her head. The radio announcer was just finishing the weather report. Through the static on the AM station, we heard more snow predicted for this evening.

"I tell you, Ethel, I'm not sure how many more of these winters I can take," Dottie remarked. "My cousin lives in Florida now and is always after me to come and stay with her. One of these years, I just may take her up on it." She pulled her dark-gray sweater closer over her government-issue uniform shirt. Even though she had been told she could dress in warmer clothes if she needed to, she stuck to her US Postal Service garb. She was proud to be our postmistress, and her appearance always let you know just that. She gave a little shiver and then adjusted her glasses signaling that she was ready for business.

"Why, Dottie, what would you do in Florida?" I teased her. "Charlotte and Ruthie would never be able to find another partner like you for the bowling team. And besides, who would take the time to call me when there was something special in my mail?" While some people might have thought Dottie to be a bit of a busybody, she really did have our best interests at heart. She smiled, pleased with herself as I said this.

"Oh, I know, but it would be nice to get away for a bit. Sometimes, the Christmas mail season gets the best of me." She busied herself straightening the counter as she talked. "And all these new folks want things faster. It's always 'How fast can this get to Boston?' or 'Are you sure the UPS guy can't come again today?' They say they came here to enjoy the change of pace, but they don't seem to want to slow down at all. And then there's Mr. Norman and all of his things for the derby. I've got almost a pallet full of things waiting for him."

"Really," I tried to hide my interest. "I suppose there's lots of flyers and things like that."

"Oh, that would be too easy. Its tons of trophies and all kinds of boxes from different fishing companies, sponsors I suppose," she said as she held her hands up in bewilderment. "And he dropped by the other day to let me know that there would be things coming in. He didn't even take what there is in there! I can hardly move. I swear there's more for this event than I have at Christmas. Just when is that derby?"

"February, just around President's Day," I answered. "So it won't be too much longer." I gave her a sympathetic nod.

"So then, here for *The Bugle*'s mail or home?" she asked, poised to turn in either direction depending on my answer.

"Just *The Bugle* for now unless there's something interesting for home," I replied.

"No, just the usual bills, being the first of the month and all. There's something from Charlie's mother, probably a thank you from Christmas," she answered with her observations of my home mail. She had turned to get *The Bugle*'s mail from our large box. "Looks like the Brownings have sent something from New York." She was reading the envelope as she handed it to me. "Haven't seen them around for a while. Too cold for them I guess."

"Well, the publishing business does get busy at the beginning of the year as they start to prepare for spring shows, and as far as I know, they're not much for ice fishing," I said as I flipped through the envelopes and packages on the counter.

I heard the stamp of heavy feet, and the door opened, letting more cold air in.

"Hi, Dottie. Hey, Ethel. Sorry I have to bring things in through the front today. Got the old truck, and I don't think she can make the turnaround in the back yard, what with all the snow piled up." It was Willie, the UPS driver. His large frame filled the doorway as he wheeled in a load of packages. "Got some more for the derby again. They're all for Norman Williams." He swiftly unloaded them onto the counter, and then he wheeled the hand truck, clanking out the door for more.

"More? I swear I may just give that man a storage bill." Dottie sputtered as she made her way to the sorting room carrying the first of Norman's packages.

I turned my attention back to our mail and opened an envelope postmarked from Blue Hill. It was from Norman.

> Dear Caleb and Ethel,
>
> I hope all is going well as your town prepares for the biggest derby yet. I know you will agree with me, it's just the shot in the arm you need. I wanted to make sure that I expressed appreciation to everyone and would like you to print this ad in the paper the day before the derby. Thanks, Norman.
>
> To All Good Folks of Piney Bluffs,
>
> I wish to express my heartfelt thanks in helping make this Ice-Fishing Derby possible. Your open hearts and homes have made me feel a welcome that has been unforgettable. This couldn't have happened without your support.
>
> Your friend,
> Norman Williams

I wanted to gag, and it wasn't because of my pregnancy. How could he believe that no one saw through him? Had he lived this lie for so long that this was his truth? Enclosed was a check for more than enough to cover the cost of the ad. Did he think that he could throw a few dollars at us, and somehow we would be grateful? I would make sure he got every penny back. Open hearts and homes indeed. The day of the derby couldn't come soon enough so we could slam that door of our homes in his face. I clenched my fists and hit the counter without thinking where I was.

"Ethel, what's the matter, your face is so red, and what was the thump I just heard?" Dottie had come back for the next load. "Honey, do you need to sit down? You don't look so good." And she started to come around the counter, dragging an old desk chair with her. "Here you sit." And with that she gently pushed me into the creaky chair and stood looking at me. "What's that you're reading? Is it bad news? Is it Charlie's mom?"

"No, no, Dottie, I'm fine, and so is everyone," I said. "I didn't expect the note I just read, that's all. I'm good you go back to what you were doing."

All right, you're sure I shouldn't call Charlie or Caleb? I'd never forgive myself if something were to happen to you." And Dottie was grabbing another armful for the back.

"I'm okay really," I said and motioned for her to go back to her sorting. I was so mad I just wouldn't consider that the man had that much gall to think we were so stupid not to think something was up. That was what made me the maddest, that he thought we were country bumpkins, easy pickings for the likes of him. Our plan had to work; it just had to.

Left alone to gather myself up and get back to *The Bugle*, I glanced at the return addresses for the packages on the counter and all looked like just that. Names were familiar for the lure-and-line companies boxes with what I was sure would make up the contents of giveaways bags for the contestants. However, one large envelope caught my eye. It was from Anderson & Anderson *Esquires* of Boston, and it was marked URGENT. *Oh, how I'd love to see what was in there,* I thought. And then the idea came to me. A little mail mix-up, that's all it would be. Could I do this? Don't think about it, Ethel, just do it! So with Dottie in the back and Willie outside, I quickly grabbed the envelope and put it with the rest of my office mail.

"Dottie, I got to be going," I called out to her as I turned quickly toward the door, lest she see the mix up. "I'll be back for the home mail after we close up today."

"You're sure you're okay? You watch yourself on those snowy streets. Wouldn't want you and that baby to get hurt if you fall," she yelled back to me.

"I'll be careful, thanks," I hurried on my way back to the office. My thoughts, however, were on how I had just committed a felony by stealing someone's mail and wondering if they had maternity wards in prison.

"Ethel, you look like you're scared to death. What's the matter?" Caleb asked as I hurried through the door. I quickly crossed the room to my desk and deposited the stolen package along with our mail.

"Is Bobby here?" I whispered.

"No, he's out on an errand. What is going on, and why are you whispering?" Caleb had turned his chair toward me. His face showed his growing concern.

"I just stole mail," I confessed in a hushed tone.

"You stole what? Mail? Whose mail?" I nervously nodded to his questions.

"Norman's," I answered.

"How in the hell did that happen?" Caleb was running his hands through his hair and had now stood to look at the mail.

"I just saw it, and it was on the counter near our mail, and I knew that there had to be something in it that we could use to trip him up, and I just took it." I had never talked so fast in my life. And then I let out a heavy sigh. "What have I done? I hate to think I'll end up having my baby in prison." I slumped in my chair letting out another sigh and looked up at Caleb.

"Well, let's just see what it is, and as long as we don't open it, it's just a mistake. And I don't think we have to worry about delivering the baby in prison. Although I will tell your son when he's old enough just what kind of a mother he has." His voice of reason and twinkle in his eyes made me feel a little better, but I was still worried.

"I just know there's got to be something in here like bogus legal paperwork for all those poor folks he's planning on cheating." I was shaking my head.

"Well, first, we're not going to open anything. Just let me do a little digging. You go make a cup of tea while I make a call." And with that, Caleb picked up the receiver and began dialing.

I went to the back room and put the kettle on the stove to heat the water for my tea. I picked out a tea bag and put it in my cup as I heard Caleb's voice.

"Frank, how the hell are ya? Caleb here. Yes, yes, I know it's been too long. Say, I need a little help, ever hear of Anderson & Anderson Esquires? Address I have is Tremont Street," I could tell by the creak, he had leaned back in his chair.

I heard one of the side drawers slide open. He used this one as a footrest when he was going to have long conversation. I heard his voice lower, and then there was silence while I assumed there was a response. This exchange continued long enough for the water to come to a boil and my tea to steep. As I walked back out to my desk, he was finishing.

"Thanks, and I promise, the next Sunday we have without snow, Sadie and I will come down for dinner. You take care, and say hi to Joanie." And with that, he hung up.

"Well? Who was that?" I questioned as I sat back down at my desk. I sipped my tea and began to open our mail, leaving Norman's package to one side, not wanting to even touch it.

"That was Frank O'Malley. Whenever I need to know who's who, he's my man. He used to be one of Boston's finest and then went back to school, got his law degree, and works for city hall now," Caleb said, smiling, as he became wistful for a moment seeming to remember good times gone by. "Hell of hitter. We had a baseball team, and no one could stop us for years."

"And," I urged, not wanting to be too impolite about this stroll down memory lane. "What does he know about Anderson & Anderson?"

"Seems they operate on the shady side of the street," Caleb said.

"What does that mean?" I questioned.

"Well, if you have enough money to pay enough people, most times, you get to do whatever you'd like, doesn't matter if it's wrong," Caleb replied. "And it seems Norman pays them well. Anderson & Anderson advertise their practice listing as just a father and daughter. However, both are licensed in all New England states and New York too."

"The two of them must be pretty busy with all their clients," I thought out loud.

"Frank said it's hard to tell. He wasn't able to find too much today. He promised he'd do a little digging and see if he could discover more," Caleb said. "He did say that Anderson and his daughter have never had anything stick to the point of embarrassment, but they're not winning many humanitarian awards either. They do real estate law mostly with elderly clients who end up having to sell their properties to pay their fees. Folks get enough money to rent an apartment or go into an old-age home, but Anderson & Anderson's profit margin just seems to increase. The properties are then put up for sale at a price below market. Firms like this have their list of investors who salivate at the notion of these kinds of deals. And Norman's at the head of this list, if not the only one on the list. His name's on the mortgage too."

"Really? His name," I shook my head as I was unable to conceive of someone so calculatingly bad.

"Yes, well, not his entire name, but Williams Entertainment Corporation is registered to Norman Williams of Blue Hill, Maine. Unless there's more than one Norman Williams in Blue Hill, then I'd say it's him." And Caleb continued, "Now there's nothing to say a person can't own property. And what with his fishing show, television rights, and all, I'm sure he incorporated to accommodate his personal appearances and endorsements."

"I wonder about Bill," I said as I thought back to how genuine he was when we had met and how he'd gotten along with Daddy. "Surely, he can't be tainted by this greedy man, could he?"

"I had Frank check on him too, and he didn't find anything on him," Caleb said. "But if he's been with Norman long enough, he's got to be in deep too. He's got the type of personality that makes you trust quickly. Not good for us but plays into their plan very well. Oh, I suspect that when they started out, it was just for the fishing. Then somewhere along the line, you get hooked on those extras. You only have to look the other way for a moment. First couple of times, it may make you squirm, and you may question yourself. And then after the next time, it just becomes your way of life. And keep in mind, this is not illegal what they're doing."

"I know, I know, but it's just not right. I cringe to think what he could be doing here," I said emphatically and shook my head. "I will be very pleased if we can put a gaff into his plans."

"We need to be careful going about this. So no going off on your own with some notion." He pointed a scolding finger at me as he got up to put his coat on.

"Where are you going?" I asked.

"Not me, us. If I want to keep you working, I've got to keep you out of jail. And the only way to do that is to return the package to the post office," he said and gave me a look and shook his head.

"But don't we even get to shake it or anything?" I pleaded, knowing it was futile.

"No, no shaking. Good thing you're pregnant. It's going to come in handy as an excuse." And with that, he picked up the package and waited for me to put my coat back on. And we were out the door before I could object.

I sighed and thought how actually relieved I was that we were bringing the package back. If Norman had lawyers preparing his paperwork, then it hardly seemed possible that there would be something we would be able to catch him at. And as we had discussed, he wasn't doing anything really illegal. Highly unethical and without remorse, that was a fact, but still, it would be hard to try in a court of law.

"Dottie, I've got a return for you," I said as we came through the door.

"What's that?" Dottie replied as she got up from her desk. "A return? Did I put the wrong mail in your box?" Her face showed true concern that she had made an error as she looked at us.

"Now don't you worry, not your fault. It's our little mother here." Caleb smiled and nodded his head in my direction. "She wasn't paying attention and gathered up a package that Willie had put on the counter. I hope this baby comes soon. Her mind just doesn't seem to be with it." He placed the package on the counter and pushed it toward her.

"Oh, now the girl's got a lot on her mind, haven't you, hon? I know you don't say it, but you've got to be worried about that baby given your momma and all." Dottie came to the counter and took the package. She glanced at it and said, "Another for Mr. Norman. Hmmm, urgent. Well, that goes on the pile with the rest of the stuff, urgent or not."

"Does he come by often?" Caleb asked.

"Like I was telling Ethel, he gets in here about once a week, usually a Tuesday. Says he likes Andy's meatloaf special," Dottie replied. "He takes an inventory of what's come in. I've asked him when he's going to take it. And he says he's sorry, but he says he doesn't have a place to put this stuff until the day of the derby. I ought to charge him rent."

"You should," Caleb agreed. "He should at least offer, seems he has enough to pay a little something." Caleb glanced at me to indicate we were going to see how much Dottie's hand was on the pulse of things. We were throwing out a little bait to see if there was anything worth catching.

"I suspect you're right," Dottie said and looked over the top of her glasses and from side to side as if someone might hear her. "I hear he's trying to buy a few pieces of land in town. And if that's the case, he's got to have some kind of money."

"Really," I said. "What land is that?" We had been right; it did seem to be a good day for fishing.

"Well, there's that piece the Blaney sisters have out on route 2, out past Fancy Frank's. It's right there on the corner before the state highway," Dottie said and pointed toward that end of town. "They say their taxes are just getting the best of them. And now that Susie needs more care since her stroke, Nancy has no choice but to sell it. They had always planned to have a little bookshop in their retirement. Sad when something you've dreamed all your life just disappears when fate deals you a new hand."

I thought how that piece of land would be perfect for developers—on a corner lot by the state highway, why that would be a prime site. But I knew if Norman got to talking with the sisters, he'd get them to believe it was worthless, as it was so far out of town. Ethel knew they would have to be prepared to take action on the day of the derby, or more of Piney Bluffs' folks would become victim to Norman.

"You said there was a couple? Where's the other?" Caleb asked.

"Well, Ruthie has that piece that runs down toward Gray right before the springs. Good size piece all along the Salmon River," she replied. "Said she was talking to Norman last week when he was in town. She told him she was thinking of selling 'cause she had no use for it and could use a little money to make some improvements on the bakery and to put some away for retirement."

"Well, I hope that means Ruthie is going to add to her menu. You know Sadie tries to expand her culinary horizons, but I thank the Lord for Ruthie." Caleb chuckled.

"Oh, Caleb, stop it. Sadie's a fine cook." I shook my head to show my dismay.

"Oh, you know me, I just love to see her get fired up when I say things like this. Seems it makes you the same way too." Caleb chuckled. "Just the same, this is why it's home here, with you standing up for my wife when I joke about her."

"You know it's true. As much as we talk about moving south when we retire, we'd never really be happy." She looked at us with a smile. "We have everything we need here—a good life, good friends and family. Not too many people can say that. Take those new folks that have been moving in for the past few years. They like what they see, but how long will they last? I hope they stay, most won't, I suspect. Sad that some folks just never seem to find what they're looking for. Kind of like Dorothy in the *Wizard of Oz*, she was searching for something that was right under her nose."

"You're right about that, Dottie." Caleb nodded in agreement. "Since the day Sadie and I moved here, we knew this was what we had been looking for—a home and being part of a community that values each other. Well, we best be getting back to *The Bugle* for any late breaking stories. You take care."

"You too," Dottie said.

And with that, Caleb and I were out the door and hurrying back to *The Bugle*.

"Well, it seems Ruthie has already put the worm on the hook for that big fish Norman," Caleb was the first to talk.

"Yes, it does," I agreed. "Now we just have to make sure we set the hook before we reel in the catch. This may be the first of many derbies for Piney Bluffs, but we've got make sure it's Norman's last."

34

Fishing Weekly, Derby Edition
January 1980, President's Day

Ice-Fishing Derby
By Ethel Koontz, Sporting Events Editor

What would you do with five thousand dollars? Well, if you win the Piney Bluffs President's Day Derby, that would be your "problem"! See New England's top fishermen compete against Piney Bluffs' finest on Snowshoe Lake. It will be the first of the four-season derby says promoter Norman Williams. This reporter interviewed him recently, and here's what he had to say. "These derbies will put Piney Bluffs on the map for fishermen. You have an extraordinary fishing paradise here, and it's time that everyone knows it. Ice fishing will begin our season, followed by opening day of regular fishing in the spring. Summertime will bring us the fly-fishing derby, and we'll finish in the fall with a bass tournament. The ice-fishing derby's program will begin the night before with a welcome dinner for all entrants. Derby morning, there will be a breakfast at 5:30 a.m. with 7:00 a.m. starting time. Finish and weigh-in is at 2:00 p.m. Total highest weight wins the five thousand dollars. There will be a second and third prizes of five hundred dollars and one hundred dollars respectively. Each entrant will receive a package from lure-and-line companies as well as other fishing accessory retailers. New England Sports Network will broadcast live the day of the derby to bring all of the action to those of you who can't make it to the event. But trust me, this is one event you won't want to miss!" When asked what he expected for a turnout, he replied that no less than one hundred entrants from outside of Piney Bluffs have already expressed their interest.

Yes, it will certainly be a revealing day to all participants and spectators who will be discovering Piney Bluffs and all it has to offer. The entry fee is one hundred dollars. Now I know that's a little higher than most of you have had to pay for a vacation let alone a fishing tournament, but then you haven't been in too many contest where the purse is five thousand neither. So sharpen those augers and find your hand warmers. There's some ice fishing to do!

Fishing Derby Frenzy
by Frosty Perch

As derby day nears, the town of Piney Bluffs is caught up in a whirlwind of activity. Business owners are preparing specials for the influx of visitor. Here's just a few. Tubby's Bait Shop will feature a dozen shiners and meatloaf sandwich for four dollars. Tiny has been working on her recipe, and no one has reported stomach problems in a week. Or you can go the safe route and just get the shiners. Fishing tip ups will be on sale three for ten dollars. Miss Ruthie's Bakery is making a fish-shaped cookie sampler, featuring trout, perch, and bass shapes. Pappy at Lewis General Store has laid in a supply of hand warmers, felt liners, and ice fishing sleds. Big Beulah and her brother Bob have decided to be our goodwill ambassadors. They will help folks find their way around the twenty square miles of Snowshoe Lake. And the FW will run the following fun contests: Neatest Tackle Box, Most Layers of Outerwear, and Fanciest Pair of Fishing Boots. Winners will receive a subscription to FW. Andy's Diner and the inn are having breakfast and dinner specials for those spectators in town. Hearty stews and brews will be featured at The Inn and Andy's corned beef hash and poached eggs are not to be missed. See you at the derby!

Sadie's Recipe of the Month

What better way to end your day at the derby than with a little brandy and a hearty bowl of Losers Stew? It gets its name from the fact that if you didn't win, you are thinking, "What am I going to do with all this fish?" Now it doesn't matter what kind of fish you caught. Just cut, gut, and fillet your losing bounty. Hopefully, you've got at least two pounds of fillets. If you were that bad of a fisherman, then I suggest you join forces with another friend or two to pool your fish. I'd also suggest if it takes three of you to make up two or three pounds of fish, then you should hire a fishing guide or find another hobby! Take your fillets and put them in a cheesecloth bag. Fill a pot with about eight cups of salted water. Add to that a cup each of chopped onions and celery. Cube up about three pounds of potatoes and add them in. When the potatoes are nearly cooked, insert your bag of fillets into the water. You want to keep your eye on the fish, so make sure you don't have too much brandy; otherwise, your fish will turn to mush, and you'll have to go to Andy's Diner for dinner. The fish should only take about ten to fifteen minutes depending on how good you are at filleting. Take out the bag, go through it, and remove any remaining bones. If you have big ones, you can keep them as tooth picks. Add enough flour to thicken to your liking, and then add about a pint of heavy cream. Season with salt and pepper and a tablespoon or two of brandy if you haven't already finished the bottle. Heat to almost a boil, and add the fish. Serve this with a loaf of crusty bread and a little more brandy. So you see, losing isn't so bad when you can share it with other losers. Next time, make sure you're the winner, and I'll tell you where to make dinner reservations! As always, enjoy, my friends, enjoy!

Letters to the Fishing Creel

Dear Fishing Weekly,

 I have been wondering about this for a good long time now, and I got to ask it. How come this is called *Fishing Weekly*, but it only comes out monthly? At first, I thought I hadn't paid for a full subscription. And then I thought someone was sneaking it off to the outhouse when we'd run out of real wiping paper. But no, the stories carried right along, so I knew I wasn't missing anything at all. I sure would appreciate an answer as I got a bet with my buddies down at Cindy's Bait Shop up here neat Ellis Pond. I say it's one of them kind of marketing stunts. It makes you think you're going to be getting something, but you don't. Not that I don't like what I'm reading here, but I just like more of it. And while I'm at it, do you go on location for your stories, 'cause we got some real good fishing up here. Why, one of the boys took a three-pound trout out of Willy's leap before the season ended. We sure like to see Ethel come on up here. She sounds like a hell of a gal. Well, I guess that's enough from me.

Signed,
Eager in East Andover.

Dear Eager,

Well, there's certainly no flies on you. You have put to paper what I'm sure most of you are wondering about. The *Fishing Weekly* is a monthly publication, pure and simple. Oh, when we started out, we thought we could do this weekly, but there's so much good fishing to do. Well, we just didn't have the time to work that hard. And besides, if it came out weekly, you wouldn't have no time to fish neither! Now as far as going out on location, we'd be tickled more than a dog in tick season to come out and see your fine fishing area. We try to visit with folks who love fishing like we do, and you sound like just the kind of people we'd love to meet. I've passed your letter on to Ethel. She's always looking for a good time, especially with folks who got the same interests going as you do. She's mighty handy with a rod, least that what the boys here say. Thanks for writing, and look for us next month! FW

35

It felt good to be back in Daddy's kitchen, if only for the afternoon. It brought back memories of how he and Aunt Eleanor had taught me the basics of home cooking. Fried eggs and toast, fish fillets, biscuits and stews, all had been made in the simplest of ways. Things were uncomplicated then. Everything you needed was here, and everyone had a sense to take care of his or her neighbor. My, how things had changed.

It was Sunday afternoon, and the late January sun was setting with a bright glint on the crusted snow. The red apple clock whirred softly as the second hand marked time for my baking. Daddy had asked me to make a few things for our meeting. His favorite had always been oatmeal cookies, so I had doubled the recipe today. The cookies were cooling, and the pumpkin bread was almost done. From the smell, the coffee was just about ready as it perked its wet *plop, plop* on the stove.

The fire in the fireplace was fading as I passed by. Mr. Striper wound around my legs, purring as I walked. I took a seat in my favorite overstuffed chair in the sunroom. The afternoon sun always warmed that chair last, and I could almost see the edge of Snowshoe Lake through the leafless trees. The cat jumped up into my ever-vanishing lap and managed to find a way to settle in. I stroked his pale golden fur as his purring grew louder. Was it for themselves that they purred? I never could remember. But it was comforting to me. As I sat still, I felt something in my belly, was it indigestion, or could it be? Was it? No, it couldn't be. I was only three months pregnant. I think it was just the stew I had made for lunch. Onions weren't settling well with me now. So then, yes, that was it, just a little heartburn from the onions. Next time, just onion powder, no chopped onions.

I was waiting for everyone to arrive. We were meeting to discuss our sting plans for Norman. It felt strange to be plotting against someone. It wasn't our nature to think about doing bad things to people, but in his case, we were making an exception. Frank had gotten back to Caleb with some more details about our supposed benefactor. Even though it had been years since his show had gone off the air, *The New England Fisherman* still had a following. He did everything from endorsements to personal appearances. It was during those appearances that his country charm had greased the way for his scheme. While in those cozy little towns, he'd cast his net to see what he could catch in the way of folks down on their luck and being land poor. In the fifteen years or so that he had been doing this scam, he had amassed between five and ten million dollars depending on whose books you reviewed. And he'd been nervy enough to ask for the townspeople to help put up the purse money for the derby! I was so angry. I had never felt this way about another human. Well, maybe Mike from the *Herald*. But he, I had decided, was just an ass. Norman was despicable. I wanted everyone, not just the folks in this town, to know what he was doing.

The back door opened, and Daddy stomped the snow from his feet on the old braided rug. His arms were loaded with wood for the fireplace. He noisily dumped the wood into the box and then went to close the door.

"It's about time you got in here with some wood," I kidded Daddy. "I was about to make a muff out of Mr. Striper."

"You could have come out and helped, you know. Exercise is okay for pregnant women these days," Daddy said as he loaded the fireplace with more wood. The fire caught, and a blaze started again. There was something about the comfort of the fire and looking at the flames as it burned. He stood in front of the fire for a moment and rubbed his hands to warm them. Mr. Striper jumped from my lap and onto the stool near the hearth and reached out for Daddy with his paw. Daddy gave him a quick pat on the head then shooed him off and took a seat.

"That's why I married Charlie so you could have someone to help with the wood." I chuckled back at him. I got up from my chair and went into the kitchen to check on the bread. Using a toothpick, it tested done. I took it out of the oven and set it on a rack to cool. The spicy warm aroma was making my stomach growl again. My pregnancy made just about every food irresistible. I promised myself I would wait until everyone was here before I had a piece.

"Did I hear my name taken in vain?" Charlie came through the back door with another armload of wood. He gave me a kiss on the way by and dumped the wood into the box.

"Not really, I was explaining to Daddy the sole reason I married you was so I didn't have to carry wood into the house anymore." I smiled at him as he walked back toward the door. He didn't get to close it when Andy Sr. appeared in the doorway.

"The Koontz family must have a lot of money. Do you always leave the door open in the middle of winter?" Andy chuckled heartily as he walked into the kitchen shutting the door behind him. "Oh, is it nice in here. Just that little walk from the diner, and I'm cold already. And what are you baking, Ethel? It smells wonderful!" And he went to the fireplace to stand with Daddy.

"Oatmeal cookies and pumpkin bread," I replied as I slipped the bread out of the pan to cool.

"What do you say, a little brandy to chase that chill?" Daddy asked Andy.

"No, you go ahead. I'll have a cup of that coffee I smell along with a cookie or two. I still have supper to manage tonight, and I don't want to mix up the meatloaf with the meatball special. Although with this weather, not too many folks coming out," Andy replied.

"Oh, it's just the after-holiday diet time Andy. You know how everybody starts the first of the year," I said and patted his husky shoulder. "I've been helping out though, haven't I?"

"Yes, you have, Ethel, with your chicken rice soup, BLT, light on the mayo and grape nut custard." Andy smiled as he ticked off my daily lunch menu on his imaginary order pad.

"No wonder you're starting to ah...fill out a little," Charlie said, trying to choose his words carefully.

"Really?" I said in mock annoyance.

"Careful, son, tread lightly in this area," Daddy advised Charlie. "How about you join me?" Daddy offered and went to get the glasses and bottle from the cabinet.

"I will if it gets me out of her line of fire," Charlie replied. And Daddy poured two snifters of brandy. They both took a long sip.

"Now an oatmeal cookie with this, and I'm all set," said Daddy as he let out a quick breath catching from the brandy.

"That just not right," I replied. "Cookies and brandy, not for me."

"As it should be, no alcohol for the little mother," Charlie said and came to give me a quick hug and a pat to my belly.

A knock at the front door brought our conversation to a slight pause. I went to the door and, through the etched pane, could see that it was Caleb and Ruthie.

"Come on in," I said as I opened the door for them. "Let me take your coats, and go warm up by the fire." And with that, I ushered them down the hall and into the kitchen. "Coffee or brandy? What's your choice? Daddy says cookies go well with the brandy, but I'm not buying that."

"I'll get some coffee in a bit. Right now, I'd like to warm these old bones," Ruthie said as she pulled her coarse-knit sweater closer around her and gave a little shudder. "I swear, January is the coldest month."

"Eddy, you got a little brandy left?" Caleb asked. "That sounds more my speed."

Daddy grabbed another snifter and poured some for Caleb.

"Thanks. Now this warms the heart." And Caleb smiled a tight smile after his sip.

Ruthie went to the stove and poured a coffee and started to stir her sugar in with a faint musical clink on the mug.

We settled in around the kitchen table, everyone silent for a moment. As I looked from face-to-face, their eyes showed a mix of determination and disbelief. Gone were the smiles from moments ago when we first greeted as friends. These looks gave the indication of the importance that was weighing heavy on all of us. It was sobering to think how this could be happening to the beautiful people of Piney Bluffs.

"Well," I said as I looked from person to person. "Let's begin, shall we?"

"I sure hate this," Ruthie said as she sipped her coffee.

"Me too," said Daddy, "but that son of a bitch is going to remember that it was Piney Bluffs where he met his waterloo."

"You should have seen him that day when he was in my shop," Ruthie said as she shook her head. "He thought he was playing me like a well-tuned fiddle."

"How did you know what he was up to?" I asked.

"Well, the way you *weren't* asking me about him and then started hinting about that piece of land I had kind of tipped me off. I may be an old woman, but not much gets past me, you know." And her blue eyes flashed that smile of deep knowing. "On top of that, Martha and Bill Carlson had dropped by one day for a coffee and were talking about how grateful they were to Norman for bailing them out. Seems he offered them a fair price for their land out on the other side of Snowshoe Lake. They said he told them he didn't want them to go to the bother and expense of involving a lawyer. Sure, no lawyer and no one looking out for the fairness of the deal. So he just had them sign a paper. They said it looked legal enough, and that was that. They had a cashier's check, and he had the land."

I thought back to the "urgent" parcel from his lawyers that had almost started my life of crime. I was certain now that it must have contained some type of fill-in-the-blank contracts that would enable him to carry out his dealings swiftly before folks had a chance to question what they were doing.

"Isn't the Carlson's piece of land that butts up against the state forest?" Andy questioned.

"Yes, it is," replied Daddy. "Some of the best little streams in there. And if I remember, the state had filed for rights to access the lake through Carlson's property."

"You're right," Ruthie said, nodding her head in agreement. "And wasn't there a payment to them for those rights? So not only did he get the property, but also, he got the state payments too. And I'm sure the state compensates at a damned good rate."

"I'm sure that his lawyers will get him that and then some," said Caleb.

"So how are we going to do this?" asked Charlie. "It can't be as simple as saying, 'Hey, Norman, we know what you're doing, give the money back.' Is it?"

"We could, but he'd just laugh his ass off all the way to the bank, after he'd sued us for slander," Caleb said. "No, we have to script this almost like it was a play. And we have to count on two very important things. One is the media coverage. He has been telling us that after this derby, with all the coverage we'll get, we'll be turning people away for years 'cause we'll be so sought after. The second thing is that he can't resist what we have on the end of the line for him. And that's more land."

"The only thing that I want 'away for years' is him," Ruthie said with a slap of her hand on the table.

"He's told me that I'd be a natural in front of the camera," I reminded them. "Maybe I'll have an interview with him that takes a very bad turn. I could go from a Barbara Walters to a Geraldo Rivera, and he wouldn't know what hit him."

"You'll need every journalist's instinct to catch him off guard, if that's how we'll play it," Caleb said. "You've got to be at the right place at the right time with a microphone and a camera."

"You're going to need an ally with the media. Do we know who's going to be here?" Charlie asked.

"He did mention the Boston station WBZ," Caleb said. "I can check with Frank and see if there's anyone who would be our connection. Or maybe you could check with Mike back at the *Herald*, Ethel. What do you think about that?"

"I had promised myself that I would never want to cross paths with that man again," I said, shaking my head remembering back to my brief attachment to the *Boston Herald*. "But if talking to him could in some way help, I would do it."

"Timing is going to be everything. We're going to need Ruthie to be desperate for her money from the land sale on the same day as the derby," Caleb said, his eyebrows almost knitted together as he began to outline our plan. "And we've got to hope that he won't be able to resist it, and that's when we get him to reveal his true colors on national TV."

"That's a big hope," said Andy.

"Amen to that," replied Daddy.

After we'd left Daddy's, Charlie and I went home. Mutt and Jeff wagged their entire furry bodies to show their delight in our return. They continued to be insistent while we hung up our coats and finally sat down on the couch where we were obliged to pet and scratch ears until they felt well greeted. I pulled my legs up around me as I snuggled into my husband's strong arms. We looked through the picture window at the night sky and were silent for a while, both of us lost in our own thoughts.

"Going to be a tough thing for you to do, isn't it?" Charlie said and kissed the top of my head.

"Yes, it is," I murmured. "But I'll find a way somehow to show him for what he is. I think back to that day when Daddy and I flew up to do that interview. There wasn't a thing in what we talked about to give a hint of anything underhanded. Unless I just didn't want to see it. That was my first exposure to a somewhat celebrity figure. I might have been a bit starstruck, but I don't think so. He was so genuine about his love for the land and being good stewards of our natural resources. I understand what his love of land was all about. Even his housekeeper Georgia was such a sweetheart, and now I was wondering about her."

"She might not know," Charlie offered. "It would seem sad that he has infected everyone around him with his disease."

"I know, part of me really hopes that's so," I replied. "Now I'm more determined than ever. To think I fell for that 'aw shucks' routine. No, I'm going to find a way. And while we might not be able to help those folks who have lost in the past, I'll make sure that it won't happen to anyone else."

"That's my take-charge wife." Charlie smiled proudly. "Norman has no idea just what he's got himself into coming up against you."

"Come on to bed," I said as I uncurled myself from his arms and pulled his hand to stand up. "Your take-charge wife is a little tired. And I need all the sleep I can get if I'm going to lead the charge in this battle."

And with that, we went to bed. I lay awake for a while listening to Charlie's soft snoring and the rhythmic breathing of Mutt and Jeff who slept in our room by the bay window. Why was it that men or, for that matter, all male species, just simply fell asleep so easily? How could they clear their minds that quickly? I always had those last minute "did I remember to" things to check off as I drifted off to sleep. Eventually, my list was done with the one thought still undone. How would I get him? Just out and out ask him to come clean on the air? Or should I let his own greed do it for me? The scales tipped back and forth, and eventually, I let go of both thoughts and let the sleep come.

36

Monday morning brought a light snow cover to the already foot and half that was on the ground. Charlie was driving me to work in his 4x4 truck. I had told him that I could take care of myself, and it was just a little snow, but he insisted.

"Really, I'm fine," I pleaded. "I've been driving since I was twelve. This is just a little snow."

"Oh relax, Ethel," Charlie chided me. "You deserve to be pampered a little. And besides, when you were twelve, you weren't married to me, nor were you pregnant. Were you?" And he gave me a sideways glance.

"What? Oh you," I sputtered and managed to poke my mittened hand into his ribs.

"Besides, I like spending time with you." And my husband reached out for my hand and squeezed it. "And also the fact that I don't have any local work today. I have one developer in Bar Harbor that I'm going to see later this morning. He's heard of my work and has a project. But I'll be back in time to pick you up by the end of the day."

"What kind of a project?" I asked. While most of Charlie's work had been new home construction or repairs, lately, he had been receiving calls for larger projects. This had brought the need for his brother and dad to come out. The O'Connor family's reputation was spreading from the Cape all the way up the coast to Maine. Charlie was enjoying this renewed relationship with them.

"Not sure exactly," he answered. "Although he did say the building wasn't to be in Bar Harbor. So we'll see what it's all about."

"Hmmm, the unknown is very interesting," I mused. "Well, we're here. Okay, my handsome father-to-be. You keep yourself safe on these snowy roads."

"Ethel, really," Charlie said, giving me the same look I had given him earlier. "Okay, yes, I will be careful. Now give me a kiss, and get into work. Caleb's waving from the window. You must be late." And with that, he pulled me toward him and gave me a long kiss. "You're sexy for a mother-to-be. Love you."

"Love you too," I said as I held on for a dreamy moment longer. Time for work, and I stepped out of the truck, waved good-bye, and went up the steps to *The Bugle*.

"Morning, Caleb," I said as I came thought the door.

"Good morning to you," Caleb said as he peered over the top of his glasses. He was already tapping away at his typewriter. "Some service, door to door, must be nice."

"Oh, Charlie's worried about the snow and me driving. I'll be glad when I finally have the baby, then I can go back to normal. Although with a baby, I don't think *normal* is a word that we'll ever use again," I said, smiling. As I peered over his shoulder, I added, "What's got you at work so early?"

"I'm keeping a log of what we did and when we did it, just in case," Caleb kept on tapping away at the keys.

"Just in case of what?" I questioned. I took my seat and turned my chair and waited for him to stop. He continued for a moment more then took his glasses off and turned his chair to me.

"In case we get sued," he stated and looked me square in the eye.

"Sued?" I replied. "Why would we get sued? He's the one who got this horrible scam going." I was stupefied. How would anyone think that we did anything wrong?

"I know we have truth and justice on our side, but"—he sat back and sighed—"if things don't go the way we planned, we could be in for more trouble than you've ever seen in your life. He'll turn those lawyers loose on us, and the dust won't settle for years."

"I never thought that we wouldn't win." I slumped a little in my chair as the gravity of this was sinking in.

"Even if we win, I can't guarantee that he won't make a run at it," Caleb said with a shake of his head. "He didn't get where he is today by giving up and slinking off to the next waterhole. But this will be his first time that he's had somebody who knows what he's up to. And with an entire media circus, I imagine that's more than he's had to handle in a long time. He might get a little distracted trying to keep all the balls in the air at one time, and that's what we have to count on."

"Who are we going to find?" I was racking my brain for attorneys in our area. The closest one I'd heard of was in Fryeburg, and his practice was mostly wills and divorces. Also he was almost a hundred. So that didn't seem to be what we needed.

"Frank gave me a couple of names and cautioned that some might not want to tackle this when they hear our story," Caleb said and shook his head. "I'm going into Portland tomorrow to meet with one Samuel J. Cantaro. He's advertised as concentration in tort and property liability. And he's licensed in both Maine and Massachusetts. Hopefully, he'll take the case."

"Sounds like it would be his area. Maybe he'll be attracted by the notoriety this could bring." I tried to sound optimistic. "Can't you just imagine what will happen when this does hit the rest of the media? Norman's name will be mud. They will have a field day with him. Not to mention all the folks that he's deceived in the past. Anderson and Anderson will be very busy trying to keep people at bay."

"I was also going to give Russell a call and see what kind of help they could give us," Caleb added. "You never know who they might have on their literary and entertainment legal staff."

"Of course, they would have attorneys at their beck and call," I agreed. "And if they knew what was going on, they would stop at nothing to help us. How about I give them a call too?"

"Wouldn't hurt to have them in the loop," Caleb said. We're going to need all the help we can get. Now let's get back to the day's news."

And with that, we settled back into the news stories of the day. Some things seemed incidental. Caleb worked on letters to the editor and headlines; I worked on town committee announcements. Andy Sr. had dropped off the agenda for the Planning and Zoning Committee meeting for next week. Town bylaws dictated that the agenda must be published in some sort of freely available way, either in a print or posted in a public place. The agenda usually carried notice of one neighbor wanting to access some of his land that was too close to the other neighbor's property line. Most times, this was settled in one meeting, and everyone was happy.

However, this agenda had two items, however, that could cause attendance to increase considerably. My gaze rested on these two items as my brain was processing the information. Ruthie had asked to change the zoning of our bait property from residential to commercial. Why didn't she mention this to me? The second item was from Norman on the former Carlson's property. He was asking to change that zoning to light industrial. What did that mean? I was about to turn to Caleb to show him this when the door opened. Norman was making his way through the door, and another man was with him.

"Good morning," said Norman. "I was wondering if today was a good time to plan some media for the derby? I've brought my site coordinator with me."

"Holy Mother Mary! Ethel, I can't believe you're still here." And with that, the face of Mike O'Brien came into view as Norman stepped aside.

37

Standing in front of me in *The Bugle*'s office were the two men who were vying for the title of the most despicable man in my world. It took all I had to compose myself. I wanted to both vomit and run screaming from the building. However, in almost the instance after Mike's condescending greeting, I managed to find my voice.

"Why, Mike, good to see you too," I replied and handed it back to him. "*Herald* had enough of you? Or was it your great love of fishing and the lure of Piney Bluffs that you couldn't resist?" And I stood to cross and shake his hand, motioning for them to take a seat.

"Oh? What's this? Family on the way?" he remarked on the visible outline of little EC. "First one?" And his face, while showing some interest, floated back to documents in his hand.

"Yes, first one, a boy, due in July," I replied and sat back down and turned to face these two. "But you didn't come all the way from... where is it now...still Boston to ask me how I'm doing?"

"Dorchester. Always been home, no changing now. And yes, still with the *Herald*. Doing this derby as an extension of the sports department in association with some freelancing for the New England Sports Network," he said with that cocky air of his. God, how I cherish the day that I made the decision to stay in Piney Bluffs!

"You remember Caleb, don't you? *The Bugle*'s editor." Caleb reached out to shake Mike's hand.

"Mike. How's Bob doing? Still at the desk?" Caleb said, inquiring about his friend who was the assistant editor when I had interviewed.

"He's good, stepping up to the big desk as editor in chief next month," Mike answered. "He deserves it. And he's taking us into the age of computers, so he says. Damn things, they'll never replace my old Royal." Mike shook his head and rolled his eyes to show his distaste.

"Well, seems that everyone knows each other, so let's get down to business, shall we? I'm sure the two of you have a paper to put out, so we don't want to take up too much of your time." Norman seemed to be just a bit put out that we three knew each other somewhat. His folksy edge had a slight hardness that I'd not seen before.

"Few things we need to confirm so that when the trucks start rolling in, we know where everyone's going to be. For stage placement, we've got two spots that have the feel for the town. One is the general store, and the others would be Tubby's Tackle Shop. What do you two think of that?" Mike asked.

"I think Tubby's would be your best bet," Caleb said. "You've got a nice backdrop of the river with the big deck wrapping around the shop. The boat launch is right there. Good open spaces for people to gather in. Be good for his business too. I'm sure he'd be very helpful."

"Good point," replied Norman. "Glad to help out a business in town as well. We could even have him fielding some entry questions for us."

"The general store would give you that New England town feel, but I think it would get crowded but depends on how many entrants and spectators you think will be here," I added. "And then there's your power needs. How will you manage that?"

"So far, we have almost one hundred entries received in our main office. And we'll take walk-ins too. I expect to have about two hundred by day of. With that many entrants and the association with WBZ, expect several hundred more spectators. And the stage unit is self-contained with its own generator. We just open the sides, and it's all set, with sound and lights," Norman explained. "The perfect spot for you to do your interviews from."

"You still think someone would want to see me?" I didn't want to sound too put off by the thought of me up on stage. Having the ability to be on stage with access to the media was going to be crucial if our sting to expose Norman was going to work.

"Ethel, I keep telling you, the camera will love you," Norman said back to his soft-spoken ways. "Don't you think so, Mike?" And Norman looked to Mike for his approval.

"You'll be great, kid," said Mike as he nodded his head. "Your interviews with the contestants will be natural conversations, what with all you know about fishing."

"All right then, I'll do it," I agreed and smiled my best at these two.

"With all those folks coming, just to protect property and such, you do have insurance policies for the event?" Caleb questioned.

"Sure, we do," Norman replied. "Lloyds of London been carrying my policies since I started doing these events. We cover your property, theft—you name it, and it's covered. I have a crew that will set up the grounds and take things down as well. Here's a few things I'd like you to run. These pieces usually get a little more excitement in the air for local folks. I'll settle up with you after the derby, just keep adding these to my tab." Norman handed the papers to Caleb who placed it on his desk with just a slight glance.

"Will do," Caleb said, not offering much but being ever the observer.

"Will Bill be down for the derby?" I asked Norman. "My dad was asking as he had a good time fishing with him that time when we first met."

"Ah, no. Bill left for a job out in San Diego with a TV station. Trying some saltwater fishing venue. He's young enough to start a second career and try out what I've taught him," Norman said, and his eyes widened just a bit showing he hadn't expected that question. Mike shifted in his chair, and his eyes went back and forth from his paperwork to some spot on the wall between Caleb and I.

"Going to miss him, but I'm trying to sway Mike away from the *Herald* as Bill's replacement." And he grinned as he slapped Mike on the shoulder. Mike gave what I thought was a forced smile, but maybe, I was reading too much into things. I found I was suspicious of anything that came from the two of them.

"Really, well good for him," I said and thinking about just what kind of things Norman had taught him.

"Yes, he found a spot out in San Diego, had an old Navy buddy out there who got into TV. Who knows, someday he might have a show like I did." Norman looked away and, in that instance, showed a glimpse of the man I thought I had interviewed a few years ago. "Well, I'd like to go have a chat with Tubby and explain what will happen and look around a bit more for the placement of things," Norman said, returning to the man we knew today.

"And we've got to get today's paper out before it's tomorrow's news, so if there's nothing more that you need," Caleb was turning back to his typewriter.

"Good to talk to you," Norman ended quickly. He and Mike got up from their chairs and headed out the door.

"Nice to see you found what you were looking for," Mike said, and he almost looked earnest as he closed the door behind him without giving me a chance for a response.

"Well, what do you make of all that?" I said to Caleb. "Seems like a match made in hell if you ask me. Can you imagine what the two of them could do? I wouldn't put it past Mike to have had something to do with Bill's exodus to the west coast." My emotions were getting the best of me I was blurting out my thoughts.

"Interesting match indeed. Bill's leaving was not what I expected to hear. I've got to call Frank and see if he can find out anything on Bill," Caleb said.

"Maybe we were wrong about him. Maybe he finally figured out what was going on and left. I'd like to think so. But Mike with Norman, both are despicable," I said and shuddered. "I can see where Mike would be attracted to the benefits of knowing Norman once he figured out the angles. Mike's five girls are high school and college age by now and, with tuition payments knocking on the door, must be a bit tempting."

"Let's hope that somewhere along the line, if Mike is truly involved with this, he sees what Norman is all about and gets out. As they say, the truth will set you free but usually not before you've paid the price," Caleb said with a reflective look and shook his head. "I always feel bad when folks do things for the wrong reasons. But back to business, we've got a paper to get out."

"Before they came in, I was going to tell you about the zoning agenda that Andy handed in," I said and reviewed the weekly notations. "What I can't figure out is why Ruthie is putting her property on the agenda to change it before she 'sells' it to Norman."

"Less he has to pay," Caleb noted. "Remember, you have to pay to file the application first and then pay the fees to have the changes recorded. And if there are boundaries that need to be reshot, then those need to be paid for too. He must stipulate all these details for the folks he swindles. And I can see the change to commercial as Ruthie's land is next to the old spring's hotel property. He must be thinking of some type of inn or hotel. Great land to do it on."

"Okay, but what do you make of the light industrial for the old Carlson's piece?" I asked. "That's some type of manufacturing, isn't it?"

"Usually is," Caleb replied. "But what would he be manufacturing? If indeed it's him. I can't see him getting involved in setting up some shop. But I could see him leasing that property out to some other developer. He gets the land rent, the money from the state for the right of way, and probably some cut of the product profits. But he'll have to give some type of explanation in order for it to be considered. It seems it might be good to have a reporter at the zoning meeting tomorrow night, wouldn't you say?"

"It would seem that way," I agreed. "Both of us, or just one?" I asked.

"I'll go," Caleb said. "I'll hang to the back and just look like we always go to the meetings. I'll also let Andy know I'm coming so it won't come as a surprise."

"I'll let Daddy know too," I added. "He'd be a good one to ask a few questions as a concerned citizen."

"Yes, he would," Caleb said. "And I know you wouldn't have to twist his arm to be there."

"He's so fired up now. Any time he catches sight of Norman, he acts like Lieutenant Columbo. You know the way Columbo just kind of appears and asks a normal question," I said and smiled a little sadly. "And then he calls me at night, and we discuss what he thinks it meant. Daddy truly wants Norman to pay for what he's done, like we all do."

"I know," Caleb said. "But we have to keep our heads about us and not let emotions lead the way. So tell me what you have planned for Ruthie."

"I've been rehearsing the interview with her. I thought it might be nice to chat with local folks on TV as long as Norman wants me up there. You know, there's always time that lags and you need some fill in. I'll have her standing by the edge of the stage so I can just pull her up."

"You have to be careful, Ethel. We can't think that Norman would just walk away from us with no retaliation," Caleb said as he looked over the top of his glasses at me.

"I know." I sighed. "I will find a way to end this. Now, back to work, or we'll have to give the paper out for free today."

And so we went to work and got the paper ready by eleven. I bundled up and delivered papers to our regular spots—the inn and the stores and Ruthie's. Most folks were busy chatting about the weekend and if we were going to have more snow. A few folks asked about the derby, and I told them there was news coming out next week. I let them know there were at least one hundred entries, and they changed the conversation to the cost and how many folks in town did we think would be in it. Good-natured conversations from who's got that kind of money to pay for the entry fee to how were all those folks with all their fancy gear going to feel when a local from Piney Bluffs won the purse. A few asked me if Daddy was entering. When I got back to the office, Caleb was on the phone. He let me know it was Frank and motioned that I go home early since it was Friday. I acted out the charade that I had no car as Charlie had driven me to work. He fished in his pockets and threw me his keys and mouthed Sadie will come for me. I gave a little salute that he returned with a smile, and out the door I went.

Being a bit of a detective myself, I decided to take a spin by Tubby's to see if Norman and Mike were still in town. There were several cars in the lot, most likely folks getting supplies to prepare for ice fishing tomorrow. I didn't see Norman's jeep, so I kept on going and took the long way home. As I drove along, I wondered again how this had happened to us. But more so, how was I going to be Piney Bluffs' Joan of Arc? I knew everyone was behind me, and I had proclaimed that I would be the one to bring Norman down. However, I was missing the divine guidance that should have made itself known to me by now to show the way. Where was it? Was it going to come from Momma? And if so, could she just give me a sign and not wait too long? I was really hoping that when all was said and done, I wasn't going to be feeling the heat from my proverbial burning at the stake.

All I felt now was a little tug at my belly button. I stepped away from my folk heroine status for a moment and thought what this baby would bring to Charlie and the mommy me. There was no better place to live and bring a child into the world than Piney Bluffs. The quality of life here was made from the compassion and generosity of its people and the respect we had for the land and the water and what it provided. Even the newcomers who had moved here within the past few years saw what we had. The world was changing. That was a given. But here we had the ability to slow that change if only ever so slightly. And if keeping the likes of Norman at bay or totally out of our lives was what it took to keep us that way, then that was what I had to do.

I had always told myself I was going do something that would make a difference. When he first interviewed me, I had told that to Caleb when he asked if I had a vision. At the time, I had never thought that Piney Bluffs was where it was to happen, but now I realized that this was exactly where I needed to be, doing exactly what I was doing.

38

I pulled into my driveway to the watchdog woofs of Mutt and Jeff. I saw Charlie's face in the kitchen window, looking puzzled at Caleb's car. He looked even more puzzled when he saw it was me. He called out to me.

"I was just about to come and get you. Is everything okay?" The look on his face made me melt. He was so concerned and came out to the car to walk me to the house.

"I'm fine, Caleb, let me go early since it was Friday, and we were done for the day." I welcomed his arm around me as we walked as one to the house.

"You're sure?" He kissed the top of my head and pulling my lapels closer around my neck. "You should have your storm parka on with its hood to keep you warmer."

"I am fine, dear, really." I secretly loved every moment of attention that he gave me.

"How is Caleb going to get home?" Charlie asked.

"Sadie will come and get him," I said. "Or if you'd like to take a hungry pregnant lady to dinner, we could drop it off tonight."

"All right, why don't we call Jackie and see if she and Andy want to join us?" Charlie suggested, and I went to the phone to call.

"Hey, Jacks, how are you?" I asked as my friend answered her phone. I heard crying and banging in the background.

"Well, if you define great as two teeth coming in with drool the length of spaghetti and a newfound hunger for homemade applesauce that can only be communicated by banging anything loudly on the floor, then I guess things are fine," she snapped. "And you?"

"Charlie and I are going out for dinner and wanted to know if the two or four of you would care to join us," I tried to console my friend, letting her know she was not forgotten.

"Well, it's just three as Andy is closing the diner tonight. But if you think you could stand the drooling and the banging, I'd love to go. I can hardly wait until I can be an adult again. What's it like, can you tell me?" Jackie snapped.

"It's all bonbons and candlelit dinners." I swooned with a little la-di-da in my voice.

"Sounds just divine. Diner or the inn? Better yet, the diner. Mom has a function tonight, a winter soiree for some of the new folks in town. And I don't think she would want the heir to the throne to meet his subjects just yet. I'll meet you at the diner in a half hour with the little terrors, okay?" Jackie said. "Plus I want to know more details of what's going on with all this Norman stuff," she added.

"Sounds good to us. We'll see you then. And yes, I will fill you in," I replied and hung up. "Okay, let's go. Jackie's bringing AJ and Jack, and we're meeting them at the diner."

"Do you want to call Caleb first to make sure he's still there?" Charlie asked.

"Good point," I said and picked up the phone and called *The Bugle*. "Hi, Caleb," I said as he picked up the phone.

"I thought I told you to go home early," Caleb chided me.

"I am home. We decided to go for dinner. So we're going to meet Jackie and the kids at the diner and was wondering if you were still at *The Bugle* so we could drop your car off," I said.

"That's great. I was just going to call Sadie and have her come and get me. She'll be happy not to have to go out in this cold. See you in a bit." And Caleb hung up.

"All set, Caleb's still there. Let's go, honey." And with that, back out the door we went leaving Mutt and Jeff sitting at the door. "Good boys," I turned and said to them as they just about wagged their tails off at my acknowledgment of their job performance.

"I've got good news to tell you, but it will have to wait till later," Charlie announced as we walked to the cars. "That developer I met with today has quite the project for O'Connor and family."

"Really, oh, that is so wonderful," I exclaimed as I hugged him fiercely. "Where is it? Will you have to travel far?" I knew he had gone up to Bar Harbor to meet with the guy. And he had said that the project wouldn't be up there, but having him any distance away troubled me more than it used to.

"Actually, it's right in town," Charlie said. "Now that's enough, into the car, and off you go. I don't want you standing out here, freezing." And with that, he ushered me into the car, buckled me in, and closed the door. "No speeding." And he wagged his finger at me.

"But I want to know more," I called out to him through my closed windows, and he just waved to me as he got into the truck. He could be such a tease. My, but this was wonderful news because depending on the length of the project, I'd hate to have him far away as we got closer to my due date.

"Wave bye to Daddy," I patted my belly, speaking softly. *You are only the size of an orange now from what I'd read. It's nice to know I've got you to talk to. There will be so many things to tell you about our beautiful part of the world. And then I will have to tell you about Momma.* What will I say when I really don't know much about her other than the fading pictures in Daddy's house and the stories he had of her. I could share the letter that she wrote, and perhaps, that would explain. But it won't give much of what or who she was. And who was that? Daddy always said that she was going to be something, but he never went any further than that. There will be time. For that, I am certain. Time to learn and live and find yourself in this world.

39

Saturday morning came, and Charlie was out early to finish up a kitchen-remodeling job. He had kissed me and told me to stay in bed and rest. But that had never been my style, pregnant or not. So not long after he left, I got up and took my cup of tea and settled into my chair with feet buried in Mutt's furry undercoat. I had my notepad jotting down those unanswered questions. The least of which was what had happened to Bill? I knew Caleb was contacting Frank in Boston, but I wondered if the Browning brothers could help us track Bill down. There had to be more to it. I made a note to call Russell Monday morning.

I kept running the derby's "moment of truth" through my mind. I was on the stage reporting on the contestants as they came in. Norman was off to the side getting ready to present the trophy and prizes to the winner, and I had Ruthie doing the "woman on the street" interview. And then what? Something, a jaw-dropping moment, but what?

The thought of Mike was interesting. I hadn't known him long enough to find out what his passion for life was. Sports was a given, and his sarcasm was what gave him his edge. He was good at what he did, that much I did know, although the world of reporting was evolving and sports shows were coming into their own. Maybe he saw this as his way into TV time. But fishing? He clearly knew nothing about it. It didn't make any sense. Remembering back to his appearance at the inn the day of Jackie's wedding, I shook my head. It looked like he had chosen fishing equipment as you would a

Chinese dinner menu—a fly-fishing pole from column A, saltwater boots, and a freshwater reel from column B, and for free, the hat of your choice. Nothing had made any sense that day either. I dared myself and made another note on my pad: Call Mike. What was the worst that could happen? So he swore at me and hung up or never returned my call. At least I needed to try.

I must have nodded off because I awoke as my footstool began to bark. Mutt and Jeff went to the door, tails wagging. There was a quick knock, and I got up to answer the door.

"How's my girl?" Daddy was standing there, smiling. In his hand was a bag from Miss Ruthie's and a Styrofoam cup with a tea tag dangling down the side. "Got time for a break with your old man?"

"Oh, Daddy," and I hugged him as I closed the door behind him. "Come on in. I was just sitting and making a to-do list for work."

"Looks like you were napping to me. I can see it in your eyes. You had that same look all through freshman year of high school. I thought you'd never wake up!" And he set the bag and my tea on the coffee table. He took off his coat and laid it on the couch. Jeff sniffed at the pockets until Daddy reached in to get their treats. "Okay, you two, you know the drill." And with that command, Mutt and Jeff sat down and lifted their left paws for their treat. Happy with their bones, they settled down on either side of his feet.

"Coffee, Daddy?" I said and went to fill the coffeemaker.

"If it's not too much trouble. What's the matter with your coffee pot?" He eyed the Mister Coffee that Charlie's parents had gotten us for Christmas. "That thing make coffee that tastes any good?"

"Always the skeptic, aren't you? Well, you be the judge. It'll be ready in about three minutes." I sighed and came back to my chair, my furry footstool coming back to his place away from Daddy. "So what brings you out here so early?"

"Can't a man visit his daughter without a reason?" He began to rip open the bag and displayed a cinnamon-and-sugarcoated doughnut and a chocolate-dipped almond claw. He held them up. "Pregnant women get first choice."

"Oh, you know those are my two favorites." My eyes went from one to the other. "Tell you what, I'll cut them in half, and we can have some of each."

"And that's why you'll be a good mother," Daddy said as I got up to get a plate. I poured his coffee and brought it back with me. "So?" And I watched as he took his first sip.

"It's all right, I guess." He relented and took a bite of the almond claw. "I just don't like its sound. It would make me think there's a cow pissing on a rock somewhere in my kitchen. I like that *blup blup* the percolator makes."

"A cow? Oh, Daddy, how I love you. But you are not to talk like that around your grandson." And I smiled as I tasted the cinnamon donut. "This is even better than I remembered. Good thing you only brought the one. I could've eaten six of these."

"What do you mean I can't talk like that in front of my grandson? I'll talk to him anyway I see fit, and if I can't say cow in front of him, then you're not the person I thought you were," he said, emphasizing "cow" grinning foolishly at me.

"What am I to do with you?" We sat sipping and enjoying a quiet moment.

"I've been fixing up your old room. Painted it and hung up some of my model planes. Do you think he'll like that?" And his eyes glistened as he looked at me for confirmation. "Wasn't sure if I should get a crib. Didn't know if you'd let me babysit."

"Well, you've been busy, and I think he'll like it fine. And yes, you will be the number one babysitter. Didn't you read that in the fine print in your father-daughter contract?" With that statement, he smiled.

"Okay then, I'll go get that one I saw in Portland. It had fish carved along the edges. I think he'll like that." And you could see the excitement in his eyes, but then it was gone. "I've been thinking lately, all these changes in town, in our lives. Not going to be the same as when you were a little tike."

"I know." I searched his face. There was something more he wanted to say to me. "What is it, Daddy?"

255

"What are you going to tell him?" he set his lips in a hard line as he looked back at me.

"Tell him about what?" I asked.

"About your momma," he replied quietly.

"Well, I thought I'd leave that to you." I looked at him across the top of my cup. "Daddy, what do I truly know? A few lines in a letter and fading pictures? I only know what you've told me, and truthfully, there's never been too much. I've had to create a world of make believe when it came to her—of what I thought she would have said or how she would have held me when I cried. I have no idea how hard it has been for you to have loved someone and lost them at one of the most meaningful times of your life. I've seen the pain in your eyes, those times when you were quiet, when you were angry with me. I don't know what I could say to him." And we were both quiet.

"I had just graduated from high school and was waiting to go to basic training. I had a job delivering for Pappy's. She was from Oxford, going to school at Keene to be a teacher. She had a live-in maid job at the inn with Jackie's grandparents. And she was the prettiest girl I'd ever seen." And he began to tell me a story I'd never heard before. "I remember the first time I saw her. Her honey brown hair was in braids, and she was wearing shorts and red tennis shoes. She was carrying a basket of laundry out the back steps to put on the line to dry. And I was carrying in a box of kitchen supplies. We bumped into each other. Her basket went over spilling the sheets all over ground, and my pots and pans broke through the damn flimsy box. We both landed on our butts and looked each other and started to laugh. I can still see hear her to this day.

"I asked her out right then and there, and we had our first date on a Tuesday, her only day off. We packed a picnic lunch, and I took her fishing. She even caught one," he continued with the most peaceful look I had ever seen on his face. "We went fishing every Tuesday. It was almost the end of the summer, and she was going back to college. We were getting pretty serious, and I thought she'd be thinking of breaking it off. But she wanted to keep up and told me to write her when I found out what my military address was going to be. I thought once I was gone that'd be it. I never thought in a million years that she'd write back. But she did. I kept all of those letters too. That's what got me through basic and then the rest of my tour of duty. Oh, she was so scared that I was flying.

"I told her I just worked on those planes and only flew them to make sure the commissioned guys were getting a good ride. I was still in when she graduated and found a job teaching fifth grade back in her hometown. When the class studied geography, she would show them all around Europe where I had been stationed and even read my letters to her class."

"Daddy do you still have those letters?" my voice was so quiet I wasn't sure he even heard me.

"Yes, Ethel, I do. My hitch was up, and I wrote that I was coming home in the beginning of June, but I wasn't sure of the date. It was June tenth, and on my ride home, all I could think of was when I was going to get up to see her. I didn't have to wonder too long. As the bus turned the corner up to Pappy's, there she was, waiting on the porch, sipping an orange Nehi. Four years had changed her from pretty to beautiful. I asked her how long she'd been sitting there, and she said every day for a week. She'd drive down when school let out and sit there until the last bus of the day had driven off. I asked her to marry me that day. She said yes, and we got married that summer, August 1. We didn't have much, lived in an apartment near her parents. We made plans for her to enroll that fall for her master's degree. Her goal was to be a principal. She felt that education was the most important gift you could give a child. But then she discovered she was pregnant for you, so she withdrew. She stopped teaching, and I got a job down here at the airfield. We moved down here into our house. You were born that next April, and then she was gone." He looked at me as a tear fell from his eye. He put his hands up to his face and held them there for a moment. When he took them away, he was smiling at me. "So do you think you could tell him now?"

"Daddy, why have you never told me this? This is so beautiful." And I came and sat next to him on the couch and held his hand.

"I guess I didn't know how." He looked like a weight had been lifted from his shoulders.

"Are any of Momma's family left in Oxford?" This newfound information made me want to know more.

"Well, she was an only child, and I remember her daddy had passed away while I was in the service. I never met him. I saw her momma for the wedding and a few visits during the holidays. She got pretty sickly after your momma passed and died when you were about four. I used to take you to see her couple times a year when I could get away. She loved to see you. She made you a little gray rabbit with a furry tail that you had until it fell apart. Do you remember her? You called her Gammie, couldn't say your r's until you were about five." He let this information settle on me. "And I'm not sure if there's anyone else. It was hard to get to know people once she was gone."

"I'm trying so hard to remember, what did she look like?" And my mind ran back through the memories of my younger years. I thought I could almost remember the feel of a furry tail. Was that what it had been?

"I'm trying to remember myself, but it just won't come. Been too long now. There's a box I kept with all kinds of things from your momma. I was never sure when the time would be right." He let out a heavy sigh. "I'm so sorry that I've waited this long to tell you."

"Can I see the box today?" I was excited to see what was in there. Who were these people from Momma's life? And where did they fit in my life?

"Why don't you and Charlie come over for dinner tonight, and I can get the box out. Mr. Striper's been missing you anyway, sits in your favorite spot in the sunroom and looks around. I also want to make sure that the little guy's room will be to your liking." He looked at me hopefully.

"Of course, we'll come over. I have to check on your housekeeping skills anyway," I said and squeezed his hand. "What do you want to have?"

"Well, I'll put a pot roast in the oven when I get back home, and if you want to come over early, you can finish making the meal." And he gave me an impish look.

"Had this all figured out, didn't you?" I shook my head.

"Pretty much, yes." He chuckled.

"All right then, you get out of here and go put that roast in. Soon, as Charlie gets home, we'll be over," I said. "And, Daddy."

"Yes, Ethel?" He stopped at the door and looked back.

"Thank you for solving this puzzle for me." I came to the door to give him a hug.

"I may have solved this one, but I think we just got started on a new one. That's what life's all about, figuring out where all the pieces go." And he kissed my forehead and walked out the door to his old Chevy truck.

I stood and watched as the soft billow of smoke from his cigarette drifted out the truck window as he drove away. Daddy was right. We had just started a new puzzle, and I could hardly wait to open the box and get started. First though, I had this other puzzle to finish, and I needed to find those few remaining pieces. It seemed like it should be simple, only a few empty spaces left. But I just couldn't get them to fit. Not yet, but I would.

40

Monday morning at 6:30 and I was at my desk. Charlie had asked what I was up to, and I told him I had to find answers to my questions. And it had to be today. He shook his head and told me to be careful. He was off to Portland to meet with another contractor about this new project. The weekend had flown by, and we never had the chance to talk about it. Oh well, tonight would be time enough. I was just hanging up the phone when Caleb walked in.

"Got a lead on a juicy story? Or is the pregnancy making you an early riser?" Caleb remarked as he hung up his coat.

"Neither of the two. Just plotting to overthrow your majesty's kingdom." And I smiled as I thumbed through my Rolodex. I was looking for the *Herald*'s number so that I could call Mike. I had already put a call into Russell, but apparently, New Yorkers didn't get into work at 7:00 a.m. I had left a message on their machine and hoped I would hear from one of them. Finally, there it was, and I used a pencil to bookmark the *Herald*'s number and turned my chair to face Caleb.

"Did you get any information from Frank on the whereabouts of Bill or anything about him before he met up with Norman?" I was hoping for answers.

"He was going to check and get back to me today," Caleb replied.

"How about Mike? Did you ask Frank about him too?" I was disappointed and kept writing as I talked.

"No, wasn't sure we needed to." And Caleb took the cover off his typewriter and turned it on.

"Well, I'm going to call him," I said.

"Who, Frank or Mike?" Caleb looked up and seemed somewhat confused about who I was calling.

"Mike, of course." With that, I reached for the phone.

"Hold on just a minute. Tell me what bee got under your bonnet this morning." Caleb seemed exasperated with me.

"I've done a lot of thinking this weekend, and things just don't add up." I put the phone back in its cradle.

"Like what for instance?" I had his interest now, and he turned his chair toward me.

"Like how Mike knows nothing about fishing but Norman tapped him for this event," I said, checking off that item on my list.

"But he doesn't have to know anything about fishing to produce a remote location shoot for TV." Caleb shook his head. "The topic may change, and there may be some details germane to that event, but the mechanics of production are the same."

"Yes, but that's just it, how long has he been producing TV shows and still writing for the *Herald*? You watch the Boston stations like we do, and I've yet to see his name appear in the credits. And another thing, the way he acted. Granted, I was only with the man for a month or so, but his demeanor when they stopped by that day. *Uneasy* isn't the word, *preoccupied*, maybe." I grew more intense as I added one more question to my list.

"So you're just going to call and ask him what he's doing working with Norman?" Caleb lowered his voice as he always did when he was trying to talk me down from the ledge. "Going to be a bit awkward working with him during the derby if he tells you where you can put your questions."

"Don't think I haven't thought about that." I narrowed my eyes. "But I've got to ask." And with that, I picked up the phone and dialed.

"Sports desk, O'Brien here," the Irish voice husky from cigarettes answered.

"Hello, Mike," I said, surprised he answered on the first ring.

"Speaking, who this?" he said, and I could hear him pacing.

"It's Ethel Koontz O'Connor from Piney Bluffs," I said, hoping I wasn't going to need much more to jog his memory.

"Don't tell me somebody took all of the fish? You really should be calling forest rangers and not the *Herald*." His sarcasm never failed him as he tried to diminish any importance that I might have in calling him.

"No, I think we'll have enough fish." I rolled with his insinuations.

"Then why are you calling?" he demanded.

"I have a couple of questions. And I'm hoping you'll give me straight answers." I could hear the pacing stop.

"This sounds serious coming from a fishing reporter in No Place Maine." He was still trying to joke, but I could tell his attitude was changing.

"My questions are about Norman and you." And I listened while Mike processed these words.

"Really, and what makes you think you should have questions about Norman and me?" I could hear him fiddling with something on his desk, probably the baseball he had caught at a Sox game. It was one of his favorite paperweights.

"Reporter's instinct," I replied.

"Oh, the vast experience that you've had now, for what? Maybe ten years? Must be hell keeping all that talent cooped up in that piss hole of a town," he continued to bait me.

"Well, I was going to give you all of the credit for molding that instinct, but I guess you know better than me about instinct. You either have it, or you don't." I waited for his next retort. I was trying to keep my cool under his relentless insinuations.

"So what's your damn question, Ethel. I haven't got all day for this nonsense. Unlike Piney Bluffs, there is news happening in Boston every second that we are on this phone." And he got the conversation down to business.

At this moment, I knew I had to get his attention. Did I start with what I knew and see how that news settled in, or did I begin by asking questions about his newfound talents in the production business? I wished we were face-to-face so I could watch for a reaction, if any. When I thought about it as Caleb had said, Mike's experience wasn't my concern. It was Norman that I needed to know about and how much Mike knew about his charade. There was no easy way to start, so I began by telling him our experience with Norman and what we had discovered thus far. I stopped short of telling him of our plan for exposing Norman on the day of the derby. I wanted him to keep thinking of us as small-town folks without a clue of what to do. As I finished, there was a long silence.

"Mike? Are you still there?" I could hear the baseball's thud on the desk.

"That's a crock if ever I heard it." And I could imagine him shaking his head at me. "You should be writing fiction instead of reporting the news."

"So either you don't know about Norman's shady real estate deal-ings, or you don't think there's anything wrong with what Norman's been doing?" I was hoping the questions would have caught him just a bit off guard, and he might give me an inkling as to what he knew. And if he was in on the deal, had I scratched the surface to see if his humanity was retrievable?

"I know what the score is with Norman," he scoffed at me. "There's nothing illegal about what he's doing, and you should know that with all of your *vast experience.*"

"All of those people who were swindled. You don't think some-one should care about that?" I kept at him.

"What a bunch of bleeding heart bullshit." He sounded exas-perated with me. "He's a businessman. And I admire that, wish I had known him long before now."

"Well then, it sounds like you must be in for your piece of the pie," I conceded. "Too bad, I thought just maybe I would uncover some evidence of morals and ethics in you, but I guess not."

"Never mind about my morals and ethics. That crap doesn't pay your bills. You should just be happy he's brought these shows your way. He could just as easy move his operation to another nowhere town." And it seemed that Mike was chuckling. I could imagine that smug look on his face.

"I won't bother you any longer, Mike." I was trying to control my anger.

"Good, 'cause I got lots to do to get ready for your little derby," he was dismissing me. "And don't be thinking you can bring him down either. You are way out of your league in this thing, Ethel."

"I don't know about that, Mike. There just might be someone out there who has a sense of justice." I realized my threat was pretty hollow, and I didn't push back too much. "And it's never too late to switch which side of the river you fish on. Never know how it can change your view."

"What is it with you and the fishing hooey," his exasperation was no longer contained. "I won't embarrass you by telling Norman about this before the derby. But know this, this will be the last time he does anything for your town. So make whatever profit you can, 'cause this river is about to dry up. Hey, how do like that one?" And with that, the receiver banged in my ear.

"That went well," Caleb observed. He had rolled his chair alongside of me during the conversation and had heard the entire exchange.

"As expected," I sighed and shook my head. "I don't think he realized what we know about Norman, that I'm certain of. Most of it he put aside to we're a bunch of do-gooders and don't know anything. But I'm not sure how to take his last comment."

"What was it again?" Caleb asked.

"He said it's the 'last time Norman does anything in our town, so make whatever profit you can'. He did say he wouldn't embarrass us by telling Norman. Don't you think that's odd?" I was musing over the comments. I had taken notes while we were talking, thinking now I should have had my tape recorder going.

"How do you mean?" Caleb asked again.

"Well, I guess if it were me, I would run right to Norman and let him know what we were saying." I clasped my hand together and rested my chin on them as I looked down at my comments.

"Norman has a lot to lose if he cancels now. All of the preparation, not to mention the notoriety it brings for him. He knows we've been building a fan base with this derby and the other events that have come before. Even if he knows we know, he'll just smile through his greed. That's the trouble with folks like Norman; he has no remorse for what he does. And it seems like he's found a partner in Mike," Caleb shook his head. "Too bad."

The phone rang to break our thoughts.

"*Bugle*," Caleb answered. "Hey, Frank, what have you got?" And as Caleb started his conversation, I turned back to my work and thought about what information Frank could have for us. I couldn't wait until Caleb got off the phone.

I tried to distract myself for a bit and looked at our schedule for the next month. Right now, we were less than thirty days away from the derby. And there were stories that would be running each week and then daily up to the day of. Most of those were already in draft and could wait for the final entry counts from Norman. But before that, we had the Planning and Zoning meeting tomorrow evening where Norman would be presenting his case for the change to the most recently swindled Carlson property. As well, Miss Ruthie would be there to change her zoning to commercial for the sting property. I wished I could be there, but knew it best for just Caleb and Daddy to go.

And then after that, we needed another *Fishing Weekly* to hit our outlets here and the surrounding towns. We had begun to distribute editions to the larger bait and tackle outfitters in Lewiston and Auburn. Although our disdain for Norman was very real, so was our town's need for the revenue this derby would bring. The *Weekly* had performed as Caleb had predicted, but the derbies were compounding our reputation and popularity. The previous shows that Norman had produced were small in terms of coverage. This one was being telecast live with coverage during the day by WBZ. Spectator attendance alone was going to be a huge boon for our town's businesses. Business owners were ready with special products for the day. While we had spoofed about that in the last *Fishing Weekly*, business owners had actually played into them and were now waiting for the big payday.

It didn't take long until Caleb hung up from Frank. He jotted down something and accented a dot with a heavy hand of his pen.

"Well, I didn't see that one coming." And he turned to face me.

"Didn't see what?" I asked, eager for answers.

"Frank said they did a search on Bill's background, and prior to 1970, he didn't exist." He let that news settle on me.

"What do you mean he didn't exist? How can that happen?" I was wide eyed as my mind raced.

"It means exactly that there wasn't any Bill Rushford until 1972. Had some history in small market radio stations and then met up with Norman around 1975. Probably met him on location in one of those nowhere towns, and Norman liked what he saw," and for the first time in a long time, Caleb began his ritual to lighting a cigar. I watched as he sliced the end and wet it then put a light to it and puffed as it caught. The gray smoke rose slowly above his head. "Surprised though that Norman didn't check too carefully into his background. But I suppose if he was working in business, he didn't see a reason to completely vet him."

"Hey, I thought the doctors told you to cut that out," I scolded him. "So what does this mean?"

"I'm not inhaling, it helps me think. Let's see, usually when a man, or anyone for that reason just appears, it's either because they're hiding from a former life, or they're planted in a situation for a particular reason," he leaned back with his hands behind his head and puffed. "I'm guessing he was planted. But why?" The plume of smoke rose and briefly dissipated from the draft by the window.

"And then why did he disappear again?" I was finding all of this hard to believe. "This is something from a detective novel. What have we stumbled on?"

"What indeed. You see, I think he was planted because he went just as quickly as he appeared. Well, not that four years is quick. But whatever he was to do, his job must have been over," and Caleb continued puffing. "And if you remember, Norman stumbled a bit when we asked what had happened to him. Frank wasn't able to find anything in San Diego either, so that leads me to think all the more that he had a purpose for being with Norman."

"It's got to be something bigger than just real estate swindling," I said.

"Definitely much bigger," Caleb agreed through clenched teeth.

"But how will we know what part we play in this?" I couldn't believe this was unfolding.

"We might not ever know, depends on what it is. Norman could be just a small part of a bigger whole that Bill had to investigate." Caleb shook his head and shrugged his shoulders.

"But that seems like a long time, if he's just a small part in something." I tried to think what it could all mean.

"Ethel, think back to that interview. Was there anything that didn't look like it belonged?" what Caleb was asking seemed like trying to recall ancient history.

"That was so long ago. I was just out of college, hadn't been here but a few months. I remember thinking though that it was just the perfect setting for a sportsman," I said and mentally walked through the interior of the cabin and tried to remember the pictures and fish on the walls. "That's it, just perfect."

"How about your interview," he continued. "Were there things he didn't want to answer?"

"No, he was very open and honest, very concerned about the environment and how I seemed to be one of the only one of my generation who got what this was all about." I was sitting on that porch like it was yesterday, fumbling with my tape recorder, listening to the soft voice. That voice now, that turned my stomach.

"Where did Bill stay?" Caleb questioned. "In the house?"

"You know, I really can't say," I said. "He came to meet us at the runway. He and Daddy spent time together after lunch while I did my interview. And then he drove us back out. And that was it. I wonder if Daddy remembers anything? It would be a long shot. But I'll call him if you think it will help," I couldn't imagine what we were going up against now.

"I don't know that it would, but maybe," Caleb didn't seem to want to dismiss it. "I can't think that we are sitting on the biggest story of *The Bugle's* existence, and we can't even get a whiff of what it's all about." Ashes from the cigar were starting to rain on the floor as Caleb continued to talk and smoke.

The phone rang. This time, I picked up.

"Good morning, *Bugle* office, this is Ethel," I said as I turned to a new page on my pad, pencil ready.

"Oh, Ethel, how good to hear you. This is Russell. How are you feeling?" And the bubbly voice of Russell Browning filled my ears.

"Russell, good morning, I'm feeling fine." I smiled as I imagined his fluffy red hair moving as he talked. "I'm so glad you returned my call."

"Well, I had spoken to Caleb last week, and he filled me in on what's been happening. And we just can't believe it." You could hear the disbelief in his voice.

"Russell, can I put you on hold for a moment? I have another call. I promise, I'll be right back." I pressed the hold button. "So, do we let Russell know the latest?" I looked at Caleb.

"No, not now. But ask him if he found anyone who can give us legal help. That one I contacted in Boston wasn't willing to come out here." Caleb was contemplating the possibilities and I knew he didn't want to let out all of the information before he had a handle on it.

"Hi, Russell, I'm back. Were you able to find us an attorney who can practice in Maine?" I got right to the point with him.

"Oh, yes, have just the person for you. He's out of Boston but can practice in all of New England." He sounded happy that he was able to give us the help. "And you don't have to worry about the fees. We have him on retainer for us when we do business in New England, so there. His name is Ben Wallace, and he'll be coming out tomorrow. What with the zoning meeting, we thought it might be good for him to be there."

"Oh, Russell, you and Robert are too good to us." I was elated that we had someone on our side.

"How could we not come to your rescue? After all that you and Piney Bluffs have given us?" And I knew that if he had been here, he would have been patting my hand. "By the way, we've made our reservations at the inn for the derby, so we can see how the drama unfolds. Just in case you need the assistance of two bumbling fishermen, we are at your service."

"Oh, that will be just great. It's always good to have extra folks in your corner." I could have almost predicted that Russell and

Robert would be here. There was a lot at stake here for everyone. The *Roads* publication was doing well, and even notoriety could increase circulation.

"Okay then. If there's nothing else, I've got to round up my brother and get to the agent's meeting for ten. You call and let me know if there's anything else we can do," he said and added, "And, Ethel, you can do this. We know you can."

"Thanks, Russell, I appreciate the accolades. Bye for now." And with that, we had a lawyer and the support of the Browning publishing house.

"We have a lawyer, going to be here tomorrow and stay for the zoning meeting," I announced to Caleb.

"Great, zoning regulations are a bugger, and if someone thinks they can railroad something in, they'll go right at it," Caleb shook his in confirmation of the Brownings' help.

"Well, all of this excitement has made me hungry. I'm going to Ruthie's for a coffee and muffin. What can I get you?" Caleb had gotten up and put his coat on.

"Muffins and cigars. Your doctors are not going to be too terribly pleased with you," I kidded him. "But I would love a tea and something healthy."

"Don't you worry about me, you got enough on your hands to worry about." And he smiled as he started to close the door behind him. "Just figure this whole thing out before I get back, won't you? Save me a lot of time." And with that, he was off to Ruthie's, still puffing away. He was happy to be in the hunt for the story. And for that matter, so was I.

I got up to stretch and look out the window. The January morning sun cast a sparkle to the snow-covered surroundings. Picture perfect but only for those who didn't know the whole story. Piney Bluffs was not immune to the downside that exposure and growth had brought. The people who discovered our beauty were not all devoted to the preservation of our resources. Everyone had an angle. Progress, they say. Judging from other areas in Maine, we had been spared some of the glaring new structures that had begun to dot the landscapes. They seemed awkward like the new kid in school who was trying to fit in. Sometimes, they were accepted, and some never were. Who would guess that in a little more than thirty days, this puzzle would find the last piece, the piece that would make this scene truly picture perfect again.

41

Tuesday morning seemed to take an eternity waiting for our lawyer Ben Wallace. He left a message on our answering machine that he would be in to see us around one. That didn't leave too much time for the day's edition of *The Bugle*. Caleb and I went through the stories and put the paper to print around 11:00. I was out delivering the papers by 11:30. My last stop was the diner. After I dropped my bundle on the counter, Andy Sr. motioned for me to sit down at the counter with him.

"You shouldn't be out delivering what with this weather and all," Andy said and gave me hug with those burly arms. "Here's some tea." And he set a steaming cup in front of me.

"Oh, Andy," I said. "I'm fine. I'm only four months pregnant, not dying." I smiled. "So are you all set for tonight's meeting?"

"I guess. Should be an interesting one. Charlotte said she's had a couple of calls over at the town hall asking for the meeting's time." Andy and I both chuckled.

"I bet she gave them the third degree," I said.

Charlotte was the town clerk and knew everything about everybody's business. And what she didn't know, her sister-in-law Dottie, our postmistress, did.

"Well Ruthie will just be going through the motions for her piece of the bait. But I'm not sure about Norman. I can't imagine what his light industrial usage proposal will be." I took a sip of my tea and looked back at Andy. "He does have to tell you what it's going to be, doesn't he?"

"Well, yes and no," Andy went on to explain. "He has to acknowledge the constraints of the zoning regulations for our town. And he'll need to answer questions if anyone asks them. But he won't really need to get down to the specifics until he starts with the initial site and building permits. And if as we think, he's going to sell it to some sucker with extra cash in his pockets, then it could be a while until we truly know. At that time the new owner will need to reopen the permits to disclose the plans for the property. Whatever he submits tonight as potential businesses would still need a majority vote by the board after tonight's meeting when they go into executive session. If they vote no, it stays residential. But there's something that he doesn't know, and I've been meaning to tell you."

"Well, good morning, or should I say good afternoon." And it was the voice of Norman. I turned to see him sliding into a booth behind us. "Hope Tuesday's special is still meatloaf, Andy. I been thinking about it all the way here." Norman had been making weekly visits for a couple of months now, and as always, his ingratiating style was annoying.

"Yes, we still have meatloaf on Tuesdays, same as we did last week and the week before," Andy said with a forced smile and got up from his stool to go back to the kitchen.

"How's things going for the derby, Ethel?" Norman said and turned his attention to me.

"Going along quite well, thank you," I said rather coolly. "How about on your end, registrations coming as expected?"

"Yes, indeed, got almost one hundred entries, and we've still got a few weeks to go. I expect we'll reach nearly one hundred fifty," he beamed as he spoke. "Got some big names coming in for this, some former winners of the Canadian winter derbies. You won't believe what this will do for this town."

I did some calculations and quickly came to ten thousand dollars to fifteen thousand dollars, with more to come in the next few weeks. And he'd had the nerve to ask our merchants for five thousand dollars for the grand prize!

"That's what you keep saying, Norman, is how much this is going to do for this town. Isn't it just a flash in the pan kind of day?

Kind of like that saltwater fishing trip that you'd take if you were on vacation. You had a lot of fun, but you're never quite sure if you'd go back there again." My voice was louder than usual as I was tiring of his speculations about what this was going to do for the town. Granted the money was great, but for one day? What would the fishermen take away from here? Would they be back? Or was this just another notch in their jigging pole? Would it be a "been there, done that, and now what?" kind of adventure?

"Ethel, you got this all wrong. This town needs the derby and the rest of the events that we've planned for this year. These will be repeat visitors, and Piney Bluffs has got to meet this challenge. Expansion will be the name of your game. Lodging, restaurants you name it, people are going to want it when they're here. This town has to recognize its potential and grow." Norman was talking like the salesman he was, selling the dream of false hopes. And it was making me sick. Literally.

"Everything all right out here? Meatloaf's coming up soon." Andy had come out of the kitchen and stood beside me, his brow furrowed with that look of concern.

"We're fine," Norman said with that salesman smile. "Ethel and I are just having a discussion on things and what's good for this town. But we pretty much agree, now don't we, Ethel?"

"No, we don't, Norman, not now and not ever." I was fighting the wave of nausea that was coming over me. "I'm sorry, but I'm really not feeling well. You'll excuse me, won't you?" And I headed to the bathroom of the diner.

"Of course, are you all right?" his voice was dissolving behind me as I hurried to the ladies' room and fumbled with the doorknob. Not a moment too soon as my tea and breakfast quickly departed as I vomited. When I was through, I looked in the mirror. The face that looked back at me was tired and confused. Cleaning myself up as best I could with brown paper hand towels, I replayed what he had just said. He talked about the rest of the events for the year. I seemed to recall him mentioning that when he and Mike first came to the office. But hadn't Mike said this was the last time he was going to be in Piney Bluffs? This wasn't making sense. Was Mike counting on

Norman pulling the plug on the rest of the year's events? It had really only been a day since I'd spoken to Mike. I suppose they hadn't had a chance to talk and for Mike to let Norman know that we were suspicious about something. Unless Mike knew something else. And what had was Andy going to tell me? Well, that conversation would have to wait. But now, my head was still spinning, and I really needed to get a grip. Ben was due at the office in less than an hour, and I wanted to be ready with information for him. I left the ladies' room and walked past Norman on my way to the door. His head was down reading *The Bugle*.

"See everyone later," I spoke to everyone and no one in particular. I opened the door to the cold air. It felt wonderful on my face. I took in a deep breath and immediately felt better. I almost wished that I could walk the short distance back to *The Bugle* in order to stay outside in the cold for just a while longer. Instead, I got in my car, put the window down, and drove around the green once and pulled into a space near the office. A shiny black Cadillac with Massachusetts plates was parked in front. Ben must already be here. I hurried up the stairs and opened the door to find Caleb sharing pleasantries with a man.

"And here she is now. Ethel O'Connor, I'd like to introduce you to Ben Wallace, our attorney," Caleb said and rose to help me with my coat.

"It is so nice to meet you," I said and offered my hand. "And thank you, Caleb." I wondered what had brought on this momentary return to chivalry.

"It's good to meet you as well. Russell has told me so much about you." He stood to take my outstretched hand.

"Andy called and said you'd had a conversation with Norman. Are you okay?" This explained his valet service of my coat.

"Yes, I'm fine. I've been comparing what Norman and Mike have said, and well, it just doesn't add up." I took my seat at my desk and turned to face Ben. A rather handsome man, he looked to be as tall as Caleb and in his midforties. His dark hair had just a trace of gray at the temples. And he was dressed in slacks, a suit jacket, and a turtleneck all in varying shades of charcoal and all very well tailored.

"Ben was just beginning to share his story of how he became the attorney for our friends," Caleb explained to bring me into the conversation.

"As I was saying, I was attached to a firm in New York in the entertainment division when I met Russell and Robert about ten years ago. I'd been on the fence about becoming a partner or breaking away from the city altogether. They were pretty persuasive, made me an offer, and here I am, happy as hell to be away from the city. I live out in Rockport and can be in Boston in less than an hour." Ben smiled. His relaxed manner bespoke a man who was satisfied with where he was in life. "I've helped authors from all over New England navigate the legal pitfalls of the publishing world. But don't worry, I still retain a full knowledge of the law. Your case is particularly interesting to me and even more so now that I'm here in Piney Bluffs. This is a gem of a spot."

"Well, it seems like we owe Russell and Robert our gratitude for bringing you here to us," Caleb said.

"We haven't gotten through this thing yet, so you might want to hold back a bit on the thanks," said Ben, but that look in his eye showed confidence within.

We spent the next hour talking about the circumstances of Norman from day one to our plans for a sting. Ben asked for many details of what and when as he jotted down note after note. It was almost three when he checked his watch.

"I'm going to get over to the town hall to look through the land records before they close." He straightened up his notepad. "Can I leave some things here with you?"

"Of course," Caleb said. "You can use the table in the back room. I'd let you have the student desk here, but it would be better if you were able to work without the interruption that could happen if folks saw someone new in the office. Not that we have anything to hide. I just want to make sure that anticipation doesn't give rise to speculation."

"Understood completely." Ben chuckled. "I know how small towns can be. I'm thinking of staying over tonight. Can you recommend a place?"

"The Inn of course. It's my best friend's parents' place. The food is excellent, and the views of lake are great," I offered. "I'll call Mrs. F and get a room reserved for you. How's that sound?"

"That sounds just great. I want to make sure I get all the information I need, so if it means spending a day or two here, then that's what I'll do." And with that, Ben handed some binders to me and was off to the town hall.

"I like him," said Caleb.

"Me too," I agreed. "Boy, do I wish I was going tonight." I walked to the back room and placed the binders on the table.

"You had trouble with a five-minute conversation with Norman. I can just imagine how you'd react when he starts telling what he's going to do with that property," Caleb noted.

"Jeez, a girl can't have a moment. I am pregnant," I said and started to leaf through the binders.

"Oh, now you're using the pregnancy card," Caleb replied. "What are you doing in there?"

"I'm just seeing what our attorney has up his sleeve," I said and pulled up a chair to the table. "Holy smokes, he's been doing his homework."

"What do you mean?" Caleb asked and I heard his footsteps as he left his desk to join me.

"I mean, he's got an entire file on Norman. And his attorneys and his most recent land deals, IRS files too. Who is this guy? Does he know Frank?" I was marveling at the amount of information that he had been able to accumulate in just a few days.

"Remember, he played with the big boys in New York, so I'm sure he still has connections," Caleb remarked as he too was now paging through the binders that Ben had put together.

"He's been very busy. Look, he's even got notes on Ruthie's bait property," I said as I scanned his section titled Land Acquisitions.

"I get the feeling Ben's going to be some force to reckon with," Caleb said. He was reading sections on Norman's law firm, Anderson & Anderson.

"I'm starting to feel better about this already. Oops, I'd better call Mrs. F for his reservation before I forget." I returned to my desk and started to dial the inn. I made the call and talked with Mr. F for a bit and secured the room for Ben for the next two nights. He said they were happy to have the business during this slow period after the holidays. He also said they were looking forward to Derby week as there were almost booked up.

I reflected on what Mr. F had told me. The derby was going to be a big help for the town, which was certain. And having other events was just as likely to have good turnouts too. But couldn't they happen without the villainous hand of Norman's conducting them? The more people learned about Piney Bluffs, the more they loved everything that it represented and the more they wanted to come back to all of this. But all of this would change if there continued to be more.

I remember when I was about ten and had eaten three bowls of chocolate ice cream and ended up with a stomachache and not being too fond of chocolate ice cream thereafter. Daddy had said "too much of a good thing is never a good thing." So too would Piney Bluffs need to learn not to wish for that extra bowl of exposure. Too much would make us want everyone to forget they'd ever heard of Piney Bluffs.

Somewhere there had to be a balance, as in all things. Who held the scales to weigh the truth and fairness? Was I to be our Lady Justice armed with those scales and her double-edged sword of reason and justice? Right now, my sword was getting heavy. The first skirmish would be tonight. The battle had begun.

42

I was home, taking off my coat when the phone rang. My watch had gotten hung up in my sleeve, so I was struggling with it when I answered.

"Hello," I said, still trying to untangle myself.

"Are you okay?" It was Charlie. "You sound out of breath."

"Oh, I'm fine," I replied. "God help me with a child if I can't even get out of my own coat. There now, I'm finally free. Whew." I all but whipped the coat around the room to free myself from its knitted cuffs.

"What happened today? I know that tone," and that's why I loved this man.

"Oh, I had a run in with Norman at the diner. But I think he got the message," I said, not wanting to get into too much detail.

"What did he say? Are you sure you're all right?" he pursued.

"Yes, yes, now what time are you coming home?" I was done with Norman at least for the moment and wanted my full attention on my home life.

"Well, that's just it. I'm going to stay here in Bar Harbor for the night if that's okay with you," he said. "Another snow storm is coming up the coast, and I really don't want to start back now."

I realized I'd been so caught up in the day that I'd forgotten where Charlie had gone. This developer had wanted him to finalize the details at his office and then would continue down here with preliminary site work and permits.

"Sure, honey, that's fine. Mutt and Jeff will keep me company." I looked down at my two furry children who were wagging their tails at the mention of their names. I was a bit disappointed, but it was only one night. "How did it go today?" We hadn't talked a lot about this new project, but I knew it was going to be a sizable enough job as his dad and brother would be needed.

"He loved my plans. Now all he has to do is tie up the purchase of the land, and we'll be good to go." His voice was full of excitement. In the past few years, Charlie had made a name for himself with the homes he had designed and built for folks. But this project, as he said, was going to put him into another category of builders.

"Where is this going to be again?" I asked.

"Somewhere along the river. He didn't quite say. I know part of it is in Piney Bluffs. The seller contacted him and told him there were zoning issues that needed to be settled first," he continued. "He wanted this to have the rough style of a log cabin but the amenities of an upscale hotel. There will even be a section for spa treatments. Mr. Maloney is very committed to this project and at the same time to the preservation of the natural resources around it. He said this piece of land is just beautiful."

"Maloney? Why does that sound familiar?" I asked, momentarily diverted at the mention of the name.

"Not sure, he did tell me he is third-generation Maine. His ancestors came down to Maine after they had immigrated to Canada from Ireland during the potato famine. He's a feisty one," Charlie said.

"Something about that name, oh well," I said. "Maybe it will sound familiar to Daddy. I might take a ride over and see him."

"Isn't he at the zoning meeting?" Charlie asked.

"Yes, he is, how could I forget that," I said as I glanced at my watch, 5:45 and the meeting started at 6:00. "I'd best be getting ready to go."

"But I thought you were going to stay home and let Caleb and your daddy handle this?" Charlie's concern was coming through the phone, and I knew what was coming next. "Ethel, you promised me.

You've got to think of yourself and our son. You need your rest. Don't put yourself in a stressful situation."

"I'm fine," I said. "Will everyone please stop thinking I'm dying? For the love of Pete! I can sit in the back row, and no one will know I'm there."

"Ethel, please don't go," Charlie was pleading with me, but in his heart, he knew I was going. "At least have your dad come and get you so you're not driving around in the snow."

"Charlie, please, the weather's fine here," I said hurriedly. "I've got to go now. Daddy's probably there already. I love you."

"I love you too, but I wish you'd stay home. Please be careful," he said.

"I will, now, bye. Call me later." I quickly hung up the phone, grabbed my jacket, and out the door I went. I don't know why I had ever thought that I shouldn't be there tonight. I just hoped I wasn't too late.

Cars lined the street around the town green as I pulled into a spot near *The Bugle*. I hurried across the street to the town hall and went inside. I checked my watch, ten after six. The lobby was empty as I walked down the hallway to the community room. The doors were closed, and I waited and listened first before entering. I could hear Andy asking a question. The responder was Ruthie. I opened the door a crack to see who was there.

The community room was painted a light green that had dulled over the years. The pendant lights hung from the ceiling in a row down the center of the room. The one in the rear where I stood had burnt out long ago. The riser at the front of the room had an American flag in one corner and the Maine flag in the other. The moose on the flag seemed to come to life as the heat floated up making the flag flutter from time to time. Some folks fidgeted in the creaky wooden seats as they tried to listen in polite silence as Ruthie continued.

All seats faced forward with the zoning board members seated at a long table on the riser in the front of the room. A smaller table off to the side was for the zoning applicant. And there sat Ruthie, calm as could be, not a paper on the table, hands folded in front of her. She still had her bakery uniform on with her heavy-knit sweater pulled around her. Daddy, Caleb, and Ben were seated near the back. About half of the seats were filled with folks who could either be interested in their town's politics or just nosey. Most still had their coats and hats on as the heat was just beginning to rise from the radiators. I saw Norman seated by himself in the front off to the side. He was looking through some papers but was keeping an eye on Ruthie.

I opened the door and quietly slipped in and stood by a corner post in the dimly lit rear of the room.

"Well, like I said, the land will need to be changed to commercial so I can sell it easier," Ruthie said, quietly looking at Andy. "Lately, I noticed there seems to be more interest from people wanting to start a business than buy a home. And this piece is so close to the springs that it might make a nice little inn or something like that."

"But why after all this time?" Bubba asked. Bubba was another member of the committee.

"I'm getting on in years, and the price this land will fetch will give me some retirement money. Never was much for putting money away, always was something I needed for the bakery. Have to keep up with all of my customers wants. You know how that is, Bubba. Costs money to do that. So this is my opportunity." Ruthie was so earnest, and most of what she was saying was true. Even though her father had been a doctor, he practiced with a country attitude of pay me when you can or barter with what you grow. He was very well loved but died penniless, save for that piece of property that Ruthie inherited and had been paying taxes on all these years.

"Does anyone have any more questions for Miss Ruthie?" Andy asked and scanned the room for a raised hand. Seeing none, he added, "Thank you, Ruthie. That will be all for tonight. As a reminder to everyone, all matters heard by the zoning board this evening will be voted on during the closed session that will follow at the end of tonight's public hearing. The results will be announced at next month's meeting."

No one said a word against her application. Ruthie got up from her chair and walked to take a seat a few rows back. She looked up, and our eyes met briefly, and she raised her hand to wave hello. Daddy's head turned and saw me, and he shook his head in that "wait till I get you home, young lady" attitude. I just smiled back at him.

There were mutterings among the attendees before Andy read the next application filing.

"Next applicant is Norman Williams," Andy announced. "Application is to change the zoning from residential to light industrial on property at 78 Old Forest Road. Property is bordered on the easterly side by state forest. An emergency access road is maintained by the state to access that easterly section of the forest. Size of the property is five acres, and there are three streams that flow to Bluff Creek. Norman, come forward and take a seat at the side table if you please."

"Thank you, Andy." And with that, Norman was seated at the table. He placed his papers in front of him and looked over to the other two board members with a smile. "And good evening to you all." Bubba and Reverend Ezra muttered good evenings. And with that, Andy began.

"Norman, will you please explain what you propose to manufacture on this property should the zoning category be changed?" Andy had opened what looked like a general statutes volume and placed a slip of paper to bookmark the page.

"Well, I'd like to keep that purpose as close to the needs of the folks in this town and those that come to visit," he began.

"And so that would mean?" Bubba questioned further.

"Fishing poles and canoes," Norman replied proudly. "I think Piney Bluffs would benefit from its own line of poles and the like. And with the streams, it would be a natural place to test the poles and the canoes. We could even have fishing and boating clinics." And his eyes shone bright to the board and to the audience.

What did he just say? Was he playing the town the way he played the folks he swindled? Didn't that just sound perfect for us?

Who was going to object to that? Conversations started in the audience at this news.

"Quiet please," Reverend Ezra asked. He was the secretary and sergeant at arms for the board.

"You think you'd be able to compete with the other big names?" Bubba asked, referring to LL Bean and Old Town, two of Maine's top manufacturers of canoes, not to mention their fishing poles and gear.

"I have no doubt that there will be a market for these. I plan to have a prototype of the fly rod ready for the derby as a grand prize." And he looked at each person in the audience to meet their eyes with his sly smile. He hesitated on me as he scanned the room, and for an instance, his look changed as his eyes narrowed.

"What you going to do with the house and the garage?" Bubba asked.

"Oh, I'll keep those while I'm building the manufacturing space. At some point, they might come down. It depends on how things go." Norman seemed to be just thinking about that as he was asked the question. "Why, will the house and garage have to stay?"

"No, Bubba was just asking if you intended to use the house as a residence because you would then need to apply for additional zoning categories at the time when both activities, residential and light manufacturing, commenced," Andy replied as he was now leafing through the book in front of him. Norman made a note of that comment but maintained his smile.

"When do think you'd start this building?" Reverend Ezra asked. He was the third member of the board.

"Soon, as my builder says it good to go. Most likely in March or late April after the frost has gone," Norman said. He looked relaxed by this simple line of questioning.

"When can we expect you to pay the fee to the state?" the question came from a man seated near the front. All heads turned toward the man who had asked the question.

"Excuse me, I'm sorry, I don't believe we've met. I'm Norman Williams, and you are?" Norman's eyebrows knitted together as he asked the question.

"I'm Commissioner Joseph Barnes of the Department of Environmental Protection for the state of Maine." And he stood. He was dressed in the green uniform of a DEP agent. His nameplate caught the glare from the lights.

"Welcome, Commissioner Barnes," Andy said. "It's not often we have a visit from Augusta. But it is customary that a representative from the DEP would need to be in attendance when land abutting state property is slated for zoning changes. Would you please continue on the subject of fees."

"Certainly. The Carlson family has been the sole owner of that property since this area was first settled in the 1850s. And as such, they were exempt from the road access and maintenance fee that is associated with land bordering state forest. State statutes provide that when such a property is sold to someone outside of the family, the new owner is responsible for said fees." As he finished, he walked toward Norman and handed him a piece of paper.

"What's this?" Norman asked, his eyes widening as he read the paper.

"It is your bill, Mr. Williams," the commissioner replied. "The fee is calculated based on the number of feet of the property's boundaries. Our boundary is two acres, which calculates to eighty seven thousand one hundred and twenty square feet. We divide that by four, as it is only one border. The fee as published in the statutes is ten cents a foot. This totals to two thousand seven hundred and eighty dollars. Monthly."

"Monthly?" For the first time, I saw a crack in Norman's salesman façade.

"Yes, monthly," came the confirmation. "Here is the information on where the payments can be made." And with that, he handed Norman another piece of paper.

You could have heard a pin drop as all eyes were on Norman. He scanned the paper, and when his head lifted, the face of the salesman was back.

"If I could just confirm for a moment. The Carlsons were paid a monthly access fee by the state, isn't that correct?" The persona of the honest fisherman was back.

"Yes, that is correct. As a continuous ownership by a family, they were paid a monthly fee. This was established as an incentive during the late 1800s, the time when the state of Maine was encouraging people to settle in our state. Some folks were paid a one-time fee while others who purchased property near state land received payment as a good-neighbor incentive. Within the statutes, it specifically affirms that payment by the state ceases on the sale of the property to a non-family member. Your lawyers should have come across this during their title search when you bought the land."

"Yes, it seems they should have." Norman was busy writing, knowing full well his lawyers had never stepped foot in Piney Bluffs. "Strange the Carlsons never spoke about this and how it would change."

"They probably never knew it," Mr. Barnes replied. "For them and their family before them, the money has always been there. The transfer of the land from father to son never needed a title search, just a recording here in the land records. They wouldn't have had any knowledge that things would change when they sold to someone outside of the family. Is there anything else, Mr. Williams?"

"No, thank you, Commissioner Barnes. I will have my attorneys look into this." Norman put the bill with his other papers. His movements were very deliberate, and you could tell he was holding his anger at bay.

"Well, don't have them look too long," Barnes replied. "Interest is calculated at one and one half percent of the total owed on a monthly basis. You have been in possession of the property for one month at this time. Payments are due on the first of the month. You should have received your initial notice in the mail a week after the sale was finalized."

"I never received any such notice," Norman said indignantly.

"I have the return receipt here in your file, so you must have seen it," Barnes said as he flipped to a green postcard that was stapled to his folder.

"Mr. Williams, I accepted that for you as you had asked me to do when you started with all of your transactions at the post office," Dottie's small voice was heard, and all heads turned toward her as she stood straightening her uniform. "It came just as the commissioner said, but you haven't stopped into the post office, so I was holding it for you." She pushed up her glasses with a forefinger and sniffed.

"Well, I stand corrected," Norman said, and he all but glared at Dottie who had taken her seat. "Apologies for my lack of attention to this detail. I assumed that all correspondence would be forwarded to my business address."

"State regulations dictate that information concerning a property that has state of Maine access must be sent to the owner at the property address," Barnes continued, reciting the letter of the law. "However, as it appears that you were unaware of the fee associated with owning this land, I have the authority to waive the interest for the first month. Tonight's proceedings will be recorded in Augusta as part of the property's accounting. If there are no additional questions, I'll be leaving."

"The board has none at this time. Norman, do you have any other questions for Commissioner Barnes or for the board?" Andy was being very businesslike with Norman. Norman shook his head no. Mr. Barnes left the room, and Norman got down from his seat. The conversations started again until Andy announced the next applicant.

Norman nodded his good nights to the board and walked quickly down the center aisle. He held himself upright and stiff. He glared at me and mustered a terse smile. I waited a moment and then went to follow him. The front door to the town hall was just closing as I got there. From the corner of my eye, I saw another man in the opposite darkened corner slipping out the side door. He didn't seem familiar to me. Who was he? I would worry about him later. The door was almost closed, and I snuck out just in time. I stood in the shadows and heard Norman talking with Mr. Barnes.

"Just what the hell is this all about?" Norman was in Mr. Barnes's face with his finger. He wasn't loud but almost hissed his statements. "Where did you get your information, and how the hell did you end up here tonight?" Here finally was the other side of Norman.

"Mr. Williams, calm down," the commissioner answered, holding his hands up in front of him to keep Norman back. "All zoning applications that deal with state land are forwarded to state offices. As your zoning chair stated, it is the state's responsibility to administer the laws for our land. It would seem with all of your real estate transactions in the state, you and your lawyers would have come across this by now."

"What are you inferring? How do you know what I do?" Norman's hiss was rising in tone, and he turned to look toward the town hall to see if anyone was coming. I slipped behind one of the large arborvitaes by the steps.

"Mr. Williams, as I said, the state has a responsibility to all residents to see that laws are upheld. We even protect your rights." The commissioner had his hand on the door of his car. "Any additional questions can be answered at our offices in Augusta. Here's my card." He handed Norman a business card. Norman took it and ripped it in two and threw it on the ground. "Good thing this isn't state land. That would be a two-hundred-and-fifty-dollar fine for littering."

"You haven't heard the last of this. My lawyers will get to the bottom of this." Norman turned away from the car and started to walk toward his.

"I'm sure we haven't. But keep in mind the law is the law whether you like it or not." With that, Mr. Barnes drove off, leaving Norman sputtering as he walked.

"Things not going your way, Norman?" I had made my way toward him, and he looked surprised to see me standing there.

"You, you've got to be behind all of this," he hissed at me. "Mike told me you were going to be trouble."

"Really, and what did he base that on?" I spoke with an innocent tone, hoping to draw more information out of him.

"You have no idea who you are dealing with or what I am capable of doing to your little town," Norman continued and pointed his finger at me. "You'd better watch it or—"

"Or what?" Daddy's voice came from behind Norman. He must have gone out the side exit when he saw I'd left. "You're not threatening my daughter, are you, Mr. Williams?" And Daddy had moved to stand beside me.

"Well, hello, Ed. Ethel and I were just talking about the derby now, weren't we, Ethel?" Norman's sly smile had returned as he deflated at the sight of Daddy.

"In a manner of speaking, I guess we were." And I forced a smile back.

"Well then, I'll be going, long drive back home." Norman quickly walked toward his car. At the sound of the ignition, we turned and walked back to my car.

"Thanks, Daddy." I hugged him and laid my head into his shoulder.

"You are just damned lucky I came out looking for you, young lady." Daddy kissed the top of my head.

"I could've handled myself," I replied and quickly changed the subject. "So that was quite some turn of events with the land fee, wasn't it?"

"Andy knew about that all along. He stopped by to tell you and Caleb the other day, but you had gone to the doctors. Seems he had a call from Commissioner Barnes a few weeks after the sale of the Carlson property hit the record books in Augusta," Daddy said. "Because we're bordered by state land in several parts of town, the zoning board receives quarterly reports on who owns what and any restrictions or fees that go along with it."

"It was just wonderful to see Norman squirm," I said. "But how about the fishing poles and canoe factory? Doesn't that just seem too tailor made for us. Who would object to something like that?"

"That's just it. No one would. So that's why the zoning board will most likely approve the zoning change. But remember, whomever he sells it to will need to reapply for the permits to actually build something. That will be a hurdle for another time. And with the new information about the state fees, well, he'll have to do some fast talking to make someone buy it soon," Daddy as always, made it sound like it would be all right.

"Well, I'd better get home. I'm tired," I said as I had begun to relax while talking to Daddy.

"Good night, Ethel." Daddy gave me another hug. "We're going to get him."

"I know." I waved to Daddy as I walked to my car. The night seemed a little brighter as the moon shone the way to my car. As I drove home, I felt a little kick from within.

"Hi, little fella. We've had quite a day, didn't we?" I rubbed my hand where I'd felt the kick. "You just wait until you get here. This is going to be just the best place in the whole world to be a little boy. Momma's going to make sure of that. Just a few more things to do, and then we'll be ready for you." And with that, I turned the radio up as Aretha sang "Baby, baby, baby, I love you." Yes, just a few more things to do.

43

"What's the surprise muffin today?" I called out as I opened the door to Miss Ruthie's. After the zoning meeting, I had thought about her all night and wanted to talk before I started work. I unwrapped my scarf and loosened the belt of my ever-shrinking coat. The warmth from the bakery's ovens began to take away the chill of the morning. In my heavy sweater and corduroy slacks, I felt almost too warm. These days, I was never sure if it was the pregnancy or me.

"Aren't mothers-to-be supposed to get lots of rest?" Ruthie came out from behind the counter and wrapped me in a cinnamon-infused hug. "How are you doing today? Look at those dark circles under those pretty brown eyes." And she took my chin in her floured hand and turned my head from side to side to have a look.

"I'm fine," I emphasized to her. "But how are you? That wasn't too tough on you last night, was it? I got there after the meeting had started. Did Norman talk to you before the meeting?"

"Don't you worry about me. I've been taking care of myself for a long time. And as to Norman, he did stop by yesterday just to check in. He bought a coffee, schmoozed a bit, and then was on his way. No hurry in his step. Never really mentioned anything about what would be next once the zoning board approved the change. But I expect that he has plenty to keep himself busy after last night's twist on the Carlson property. I just loved the look on his face. And when Dottie ever got up and all but waved the letter in the air." She chuckled as she busied herself with a cup and set a tea on the counter. "Now sit and let me make you some kind of breakfast."

"I don't have time for a lot," I said as I eased onto the stool and shrugged off my coat.

"You'll have time for whatever I make you, and that's that." Ruthie smiled in her motherly way and went into the back to fix something for me.

"Are you sure you're okay?" I asked her again.

"You know, one thing I realized last night is that some of what I said is true. I really have never put too much thought into retiring and what I was going to do for money." Ruthie came back out to the counter with two muffins. "Here you go, the last of my wild blueberries, just enough for today's surprise muffin."

"These look scrumptious! And you can't retire, not for a while yet. You can't deprive EC of your delicious treats. How will the child grow up?" I said in mock sadness.

"Oh, I've got some years left in these old hands, so don't you worry. Now you enjoy your muffins, and let me get back to work." She patted my hand and left me to my breakfast and my thoughts. As I cut one muffin in half, the steam rose giving me hints of cinnamon and vanilla along with the essence of those wild blueberries. She traveled to Blue Hills every summer to pick them. Then the baking would begin. From berry buckles to fresh pies and muffins, her customers were delighted. The overflow berries were carefully processed and frozen for days just like this in winter when it seemed that spring would never arrive.

Listening to Ruthie made me want more than ever for this land deal to fall through with Norman and then let her sell to the real buyer for the amount of money that was rightfully hers. She had earned the right to live a comfortable life in her retirement years whenever that would be.

I placed a decadent amount of fresh butter on each half and watched as it slowly melted into the muffin's blue tinged texture. The first bite was just the best. I always tried to get some of the streusel topping and butter in one satisfying mouthful. I was lost savoring the flavors when the door opened sending a cool breeze in to wake me.

"Maybe we should move the office in here. At least you'd be in on time." Caleb came in and sat on the stool next to me.

"I still have ten minutes, such the slave driver," I said through a mouthful of muffin.

"You leave the poor child alone, Caleb," Ruthie said as she came out from the kitchen. She poured a cup of coffee for him and set it on the counter. "And I suppose no one was making breakfast at your house either?"

"No, I snuck out before Sadie had her latest concoction ready. I just barely made it out with my life!" Caleb chuckled.

"You better watch out. Someday, she'll make something that actually will end your life! And we won't feel none the worse for your sorry butt, making fun of her all these years. Why the woman is a saint," Ruthie said, shaking her head side to side. "You men don't know how good you've got it."

"Oh, I know what I have. Sadie is what makes my life worth living. And I'm sure you both know that by now." Caleb smiled at the two of us. "Are you going to eat both of those muffins?" And he reached to grab the other muffin from my plate.

"By all means, I'm willing to share, but you're buying lunch," I said, and Ruthie brought out another plate for him. "And I am very hungry today after last night's victory."

"Yes, it was quite the turn of events for poor, dear Norman. I suspect his law firm is getting quite the earful this morning, if not last night," Caleb said as he started to butter his muffin.

"What did Ben have to say? Did you two stay for the rest of the meeting?" I asked.

"We left right after Norman walked out. I saw you talking with him. Didn't look like a friendly conversation," Caleb commented.

"He was blaming me for all of last night's actions," I said. "Daddy was there in the shadows and came out just in the nick of time before Norman's anger got the best of him."

"He didn't! He harms a hair on your head, and I will show him what the large oven out in the back is truly for!" Ruthie was mad, and the color in her cheeks was beginning to show.

"It's all right, calm down. Daddy just told him to be on his way," I said. "It was fun to see him squirm like a worm on the end of the hook. But back to Ben, what did he have to say?"

"As we have said all along, everything that is happening is within the confines of the law. But he is interested on how he is going to tackle the land fee payments," Caleb said. "Our only hand to play is the public embarrassment on national TV. And then I'm not so sure of that. He could sue us for defamation of character."

"Defamation of his character indeed. He just makes me want to spit," I said. "There has got to be something else."

"Ben said he'd be in later this morning before he left. I imagine he'll have some kind of a plan for us," Caleb stated as he finished his coffee. "And now if you don't mind, I think we have a paper to run."

With that, we paid our bill and said good-bye to Ruthie. The morning passed uneventfully until Andy stopped by.

"Good morning, you two. Although I doubt for old Norman it's not a good one. And to make his day even worse, I have the votes from last night," Andy said as he placed his report on my desk and took a seat. "It was unanimous, no change in the zoning for the Carlson property. It remains residential."

"Wow, I thought that proposal would go right through," I said.

"Well, it did sound like a good plan from him, but he's not the one who's going to be staying here building canoes and fishing rods," Andy answered. "We've got to be careful what happens in Piney Bluffs. We know we need to grow, but we can wait until the real owner comes to us with a definite plan. Listening to him, fishing poles and canoes sound idyllic, just what you'd want to see here. But who's to say whoever he sells it to won't start something that doesn't fit."

"He's going to be one very unhappy man. But I thought you wouldn't have your vote ready to announce until next month," I said.

"We'd been asked by Commissioner Barnes to move up our vote. Seems the state doesn't like to lose revenue," Andy said. "They're out almost two months' worth plus interest now. While it doesn't seem to be a whole lot of money, that fifty-four hundred must be earmarked for somebody's line item. I called Barnes this morning to let him know the official zoning decision. I hope Dottie's ready for another tirade from him when he gets this latest correspondence." He held up the envelopes that were addressed to the property owners.

"This is going to put Norman into quite the state. He's not used to being denied. I'll be curious to see what his next move is," Caleb said.

"I see Ruthie's got the change she or should I say Norman needed." I handed Andy's report to Caleb.

"If we only knew who his intended buyer was, we could tip them off," Andy said. "Maybe that's something your lawyer could find out."

"Wouldn't hurt to ask. He's coming in today before he leaves town," Caleb replied and looked at the clock. It says 10:30. Ben had said he wanted to leave by noon.

"Well, I got to be heading to the post office now and get back to the diner before the lunch rush," Andy said as he got up, and he went to the door. "I got some nice turkey pot pies for lunch with a side of cranberry compote. Want me to save one for you?" And he gave me that broad smile as he waited for my answer.

"Sounds great, seeing as how someone stole half of my breakfast," I said as I nodded my head toward Caleb.

"Make that two, and we'll see you about 12:30," Caleb chimed in.

"You got it. See you then." Andy was out the door.

"Don't you wish you were a fly on the wall at Anderson & Anderson law offices this morning with Mr. Norman?" I said.

"Yes, I do believe someone's head is rolling at this point," Caleb replied. "I'd hate to be the legal assistant who thought he'd done his due diligence on this property."

"And I'm sure that something so old as the particulars of this granted payment to the original owners wouldn't show up in most records. The payment must be recorded as it comes from the state, and I bet that's what got him interested," I said.

"He'll be lucky now if he can sell that property. Those fees will have to be disclosed to the new buyer. I can't imagine someone paying those fees on top of a mortgage," Caleb commented.

"I'm sure he'll sell it based on the story he'll tell a buyer about how much money they could make with whatever manufacturing idea they would have," I said, disgusted with both the thought of his deceitful ways and what could be a potential bad business for our town.

"Well, we can't speculate all day, I guess," Caleb said. "I'll go pay a visit to Dottie and get the mail, and you can stay in where it's warm. I'll be back in a jiffy."

"No, that's okay, I feel like a walk. This baby boy of mine is kicking up a storm. Maybe a little walk will settle him down," I said as I got up and reached for my coat.

"All right, you just be careful on the icy spots," Caleb said.

"Oh, I'll be fine," I replied and finished putting on my hat and gloves and was out the door.

Even though it was late morning, the chill of day seemed to keeping people off the street. I waved to someone on the other side of the green, but with all of our winter garb on, it was hard to tell who it was. Oh how glad I will be when it's warmer, when the derby is over, and when I have this baby. I felt a kick in my side, which I considered a "me too, Mommy" comment from my womb.

"Hi, Dottie, how are you doing today?" I asked. "Did anyone send us some sunshine? Or better yet, some warmth."

"I tell you, Ethel, this is going to be my last year in this damn cold." She shuddered as the draft from the door swept across the room. "I mean look at me, what would the US Postal Service say about the way I'm dressed? I have my long underwear on under my flannel-lined pants. I've got my shearling-lined boots on and a turtle-neck under two sweaters. About the only government issued item I have on is my earflap hat!" She was quite the sight. Her usual pressed post office garb had been put aside today for her self-preservation. The hat was the crowning touch with the fur-lined flaps resting on her curly gray hair. They made her glasses tilt even more to one side than usual. I had all I could do not to laugh out loud.

"What happened to the heat?" I asked, noticing that it was colder than usual in the post office.

"Oh, the damn furnace is on its last leg, and I think it finally went. I've been moving these space heaters all around to keep some heat going, but it's no use." Dottie raised her hands up in exasperation. "I put in a USPS-259 form in the summer to get the funds sent up for the repairs. But so far, all I get when I call is, 'Your request is in process. Please allow six to eight weeks for response from your local disbursement agency.' By the time the disbursement agency gets around to me, I'll be frozen to death!"

"So did Norman call this morning asking about his letter from the commissioner?" I asked.

"He's was in this morning at 8:30 to get it," Dottie replied. "He didn't waste a lot of time, and he was none too polite either. Thought he had better manners than that, but I guess I shouldn't be surprised with the likes of him."

"In this morning?" I asked. "Why he couldn't have gone all the way back to Blue Hill last night and then in here this morning, not the way the roads are."

"He didn't. He stayed at the inn and was griping," Dottie said. "He thought he should've been given a special rate seeing as how he's bringing in all of this business with his name attached to the Derby."

"I bet Mrs. F set him straight on that," I replied. "Did he have anything else to gripe about? Did he take anything else out of storage area?"

"Nope. He did ask for something that wasn't here, though," Dottie continued.

"And that was what?" I continued to ply her. Dottie loved to gossip, but you had to work at it sometimes.

"Something from a company up in Bangor, had letters in the name," and you could see she was trying very hard to come up with the name. "Had an *M* in it as I recall. Damn, must be the cold getting to my brain. Wait, I remember now, MCC of Bangor. Yes that was it."

"Well, here's your mail." She got *The Bugle*'s mail from our slot and placed it on the counter. "Nothing too exciting, usual stuff. You stay warm."

"And you too," I replied, going out the door.

"I'll try, but don't be surprised if you find me frozen stiff here tomorrow," she replied and stomped her feet and flapped her arms as I went out the door. I finally could release a smile and shook my head as I watched her through the window still flapping and stomping.

Caleb was on the phone when I got back from the post office, so I set the mail on my desk. It was as Dottie had said—the usual, payments for ads, and letters to the editor. I was beginning to open one when Ben walked in.

"Good morning," I said, placing the letter back on the desk. "How are you?"

"Good morning to you too. Doing just fine, had a wonderful breakfast at the inn," he said.

"Yes Rocky's talents when it comes to all things food `are hard to beat," I said. "Have a seat. Caleb and I would love to know what you've been able to find out." Caleb hung up the phone and turned to face Ben.

"First, I want to tell you who I almost had breakfast with this morning," Ben said.

"Oh, who's that?" Caleb asked.

"Norman," Ben replied. "I was seated at the window, and he walked toward me almost about to introduce himself so it seemed. Then he must have remembered me from last night and that I had been with Caleb. He stopped and told me to stop wasting your money because I would never win," Ben finished.

"He seems so sure of himself," Caleb said.

"Yes, he does," Ben answered. "And I'm afraid I can't give you much better news after reviewing all of the information." He had taken a seat across from me and opened his briefcase.

"Nothing huh?" Caleb said.

"Well, if you wanted to publish a list of all of the properties he has purchased and what he has sold them for, he'd probably get a Realtor of the Century award. On the surface, it is plainly that, buying and selling property." Ben shrugged his shoulders. "It's the story behind each of those sales that would have him beheaded for his deceit if we were living in different times. However, in the present day, if people were willing to come forward to have him investigated, we could build a case. But that would take money on their parts, and that was the reason Norman got involved with them in the first place. They needed the money. But I'll do some more digging once I get back to the office. He's got to have slipped up somewhere along the line."

"Is there a way to know who he has lined up for a particular property?" I asked. "I'm interested to know if the buyer for Ruthie's property could be contacted."

"That may be hard to find. Only legal name and path to chase is the name on the current deed, and that would be hers, so not much there," Ben said. And he doesn't use a realtor, so you wouldn't even be able to find a potential buyer through the deposit contract."

"What if we did a hypothetical call for say, insurance? You know we could call his lawyers saying we were the insurance company looking into the property selling date for coverage for client, Ruthie. And then we could say we'd like to let the potential buyer know about our service, and then maybe they would give us the name. What do you think?" I asked as my mind was racing to find some way to get that name.

"Hold on, Ethel," Caleb said and held up his hand. "This sounds illegal, misrepresenting yourself. What do you think, Ben?"

"Yes, it is illegal if you get caught," replied Ben. "You need to consider the risks and benefits of this knowledge."

"The risk doesn't seem very high. It's just a phone call. But the benefit is that Ruthie will get the money she deserves if we can get to the buyer first before he signs with Norman," I said, my voice raising in pitch.

"Well, as your attorney, I would advise against it. But as an acquaintance, I would say nothing ventured, nothing gained." Ben smiled at me.

"Aren't you supposed to be keeping us out of trouble?" Caleb's voice showed concern for our legal assistance that was giving me the go-ahead for something illegal.

"The choice is mine," I said. "And I'll take your information under advisement. Aren't those the words you would use, Ben?"

"Yes, they are." Ben chuckled. "I'm not sure why Russell thought you needed me, Ethel. It seems you could handle most anything yourself."

"Please don't tell her that," Caleb pleaded. "I've told her more than once before that I'd be enlightening her son all about the time she spent in jail." And Caleb, though concerned, knew there wasn't much he could do to stop me once I got going.

"I am trying to follow another seemingly dead end, and that's Bill Rushford," Ben said. "I still think there's something that would help us if I could find out who he really is. And I do have my friends at the IRS looking into Norman's tax records. Remember, that was how the gangsters were brought down in the twenties."

"Bill's disappearance and Norman's reaction the first time we saw Mike with him was uncomfortable at best," Caleb said. "That's one story I'd like to know the end of."

"Well, let me see if I can add a chapter or two to the story by the next time I see you," Ben said, and he put on his coat and closed up his briefcase. "I'll give you a call at the end of the week with an update. And, Ethel, you be careful. I don't want to have to go to court defending you for some sting operation."

"Oh, I'll be fine. I'm not a silly schoolgirl," I said. "But you can't blame a person for wanting to help a friend."

"That I can't," Ben agreed. "In the few days that I have been in Piney Bluffs, I get what Russell and Robert find here—the sense of loyalty and honesty. This isn't found in many places."

"And that's what we're trying to protect. Thanks for your help, Ben." Caleb rose to shake his hand.

"The pleasure is mine. I want to find a way to get this guy myself now that I know all about him," Ben replied. The door closed behind him, and Caleb and I sat back down at our desks.

"Well, that's that, for the moment at least," I said.

"Yes, it's like a chess game waiting to see what the next move will be," Caleb said. The phone rang, and he answered. "*Bugle*, Caleb here." And with that, we were back to normal for a moment, pushing all of this aside and focusing on the work of *The Bugle*.

44

What time was it? Seven o'clock. I must have fallen asleep. I remember coming home after work, feeling a little tired. I had changed into a sweat suit, my long bathrobe, and knitted slippers. I sat down after feeding Mutt and Jeff who had obediently curled up on either side of me. And now I heard their soft woofs.

"Who's there, guys?" I asked them in almost a whisper. They had made their way to the door. Now a low growl came from their throats. I didn't hear that often. I felt my breath catch. I hadn't heard a car, but then I'd been asleep. Footsteps on the deck and now the doorknob was turning. Why hadn't I locked it? Charlie was always after me to keep the door locked when he was gone. I reached over to the fireplace tool set and grabbed the poker. I clutched at my bathrobe. The only light shone from the fire fading in the fireplace. I swallowed hard as I gripped the poker. The dogs continued to growl as the door swung open, inviting a rush of cold air in.

"Easy, guys, have I been gone that long that you forgot me?" And there stood Charlie in shadows of the dimming fire. He reached down and roughly petted their heads.

"Charlie O'Connor, you scared me half to death," I said as the words rushed out, and I quickly went to his side. I buried my head in his chest and hung on as his strong arms held me. I inhaled the faint scent of his aftershave as his down jacket warmed my face.

"What's the matter? What's got you so spooked?" He lifted his head back to look at me.

"It's their fault," I said and pointed my poker at them. They sat wagging their golden furry tails, happy that Charlie was home. "Why did they growl? Didn't they hear your truck?"

"Different vehicle. Dad came up to the meeting too. We exchanged vehicles. He needed the truck back home, so I have the four-wheel drive for a few days," he explained as he relaxed his hold and kissed me deeply, holding my chin. "There, now that's what makes the long ride home worth it. How are you feeling? What's been happening?" He took off his coat and hung it on the hook. He went over to the fireplace and added some more logs. He took the poker from my clenched hand to adjust the logs.

"Oh, I'm fine, just a little tired," I said with a yawn that turned into a shiver. "I need to make some tea." And I filled the kettle and set it on the stove to heat. "Are you hungry? I completely forgot to get something ready."

"That's okay, I stopped at the diner, and Andy put together a few things for us," Charlie said, pointing to a bag on the counter.

"What do we have?" I said, suddenly feeling famished as I peered into the bag. The kettle started to whistle. I put in the tea bag in my cup, and we sat down to see what kind of a feast we had.

"Let's see. There's some lobster stew for you and the meatloaf special for me," Charlie said as he opened the containers. "And here's some of Ruthie's sourdough sunflower rolls."

"Oh, it's still hot, and it smells like Andy used some sherry," I said as I dipped my spoon into the thick stew. The spoon brought up a chunk of knuckle meat surrounded in creamy peach-colored liquid. The taste was smooth with that little kick from the sherry.

"That looks good, but not as good as this meatloaf and gravy with the carrots and turnip mash," Charlie said as he picked up the first meaty forkful and offered it to me.

"No, thanks. I've got all I need right here," I said, and we settled into our dinner by the glow of the fireplace. Charlie was nonstop for a while with the plans about the Maloney property. Maloney said the purchase was being held up for town regulations, but just as soon as it was his, Charlie and his dad could get to work. Together, they had designed a larger-than-life log cabin. The individual rooms were suites, and Maloney had hired a designer from Boston to coordinate the interiors. The grounds would have walking trails, gardens, and places for fishing. All in all, it would be a property that would combine nature with a new style of vacation living.

"This is going to be the beginning of development in and around Piney Bluffs. Maloney has already said that if this does well, he has ideas for other types of shops that would fit in with the needs of the customers and the landscape," Charlie explained.

"Like what for instance?" I asked

"All kinds of things—clothing shops and sporting equipment, maybe a café or an ice cream shop. There's a lot of land, and he aims to use it," Charlie answered. "And he wants me to do the building." Charlie's eye shown with both pride and excitement at the potential this partnership would bring.

Next, it was my turn. I filled him in on what happened at the zoning meeting and how Norman reacted to the commissioner's information.

"You should have seen him," I said. "He looked like he would explode one minute, and then he was back to the Norman that we have all grown to hate. I would say he is one cool character, but I think that's giving him more than his due."

"I'm surprised his lawyers didn't know anything about that clause," Charlie said.

"Andy knew and had told Daddy, Caleb, and Ben about it just before the meeting. But he thought that even the Carlsons probably never really knew much about the money or if it would ever stop. That knowledge was passed on from father to son. So when Mr. Carlson told Norman they got a payment each month from the state, I'm sure he rubbed his hands together with an 'oh goodie, even better,' attitude," I replied.

"Going to serve him right," Charlie said.

"Yes, it will," I said. "But there was someone there that night that I never really saw."

"What do you mean you saw someone you didn't see?" Charlie questioned.

"I was standing in the back of town hall, and there was someone else close by the door. I didn't think about it much; he was in the shadows. And when Norman's case was done, I turned to look again, and he was gone," I replied.

"No car or anything," he asked.

"Well, I'm not sure. Once I went outside, I never thought much about it because I was trying to hide and listen to Norman's conversation with Barnes," I said. "And then when he was done with the commissioner, he tried to intimidate me."

"He what!" Charlie was angry. "Why didn't you tell me? I'm going to find him and show him—"

"Easy, honey. It was just the words of a man who is starting to see we aren't the country hicks that he once thought we were," I said and reached out to hold his hands. "It's okay, Daddy was there and told him to be on his way."

"I should have been there." Charlie was shaking his head, looking at me. "I'm so glad this new project will be here. I don't know what I would do if something happened to you." And he got up from his chair and gently pulled me up from mine and held me in his arms. His flannel shirt felt soft on my cheek. He softly kissed my lips and looked into my eyes. "How I love you. God bless that day we met on that bus."

"I know." I kissed him back and exhaled a sigh of relief. And then there was a little kick. I brought Charlie's hand to my belly. "I think our son is agreeing with us too." We chuckled and headed up to bed, Charlie's arm around me, dogs bringing up the rear.

As I settled into bed, I thought, *Almost done, just a few more weeks, and Norman will be a story to tell.* I just hoped I would get the ending right.

45

As I looked out *The Bugle*'s window, I was amazed at how our town had been transformed in the past few days. Trucks had rumbled in and set up the area all around Tubby's Bait Shop, taking us from a cozy village to something that resembled an outdoor television studio. From technicians to day laborers, they moved like an army of ants about our town green in preparation for the main event. The crews operated like well-oiled machines. Undeterred by the cold, they had arranged generators and tractor trailers with precision and surprisingly an attitude of respect for their surroundings. A main stage had come to life with the flick of a switch as one semitrailer's entire side rolled up. A banner proclaiming Winner's Circle was hung at the far side of the stage. In the center were electronic scales, tubs for the fish, and a digital clock that was counting down to the derby's start. To the left of the stage, there was a broadcasting area where microphone stands were in place, and soon, sound checks would be made. A banner hung from behind and proclaimed, "Another family fishing event brought to you by Norman Your New England Fisherman." *New England fisherman my swollen pregnant foot,* I thought.

They had rolled out portable aluminum grandstands for the spectators and set them along both sides of the stage. A center walkway was being marked off with signs directing participants to the steps that led to the weigh-in area. The path would start at the lake's frozen edge and end at the front stairs of the stage. It was empty now, but on derby day, it would be full of fishermen anxiously waiting for their catch to be weighed and to know if they would take home the five-thousand-dollar purse.

There had been even more activity from the fishermen who had been arriving in town since Sunday. Rooms at the inn and Big Bob's camp were full. The school had given permission to be an overflow parking area for RVs and trailers, and at last count, there were almost fifty. Andy's Diner, the inn, and Miss Ruthie's, as well as other restaurants in and around town, had enjoyed the economic midwinter boost by filling the bellies of the hungry fishermen. Conversations between residents and visitors had been lively and full of anticipation as to who would win the grand prize. Friendly bets were being made between locals and out-of-towners. All in all, the atmosphere around town was more like that of a summer country fair than midwinter in February.

No fishing had been permitted on the lake during the week. But the fishermen had walked all over the ice to find their spots and plan their strategies. Along with their tactics came the elaborate trappings of the professional ice fisherman. We were used to a fire on the edge of the lake, a few tip-ups or jigging poles, an auger, and maybe an ice shanty. However, most of our shanties looked like former outhouses. These fishermen had motorized augers, and their shanties resembled small cottages complete with porches, windows, and heat. Some even had small kitchens.

The networks had sent out crews last week to check on locations and power availability with Norman. He had set up a mobile office in a trailer next to Tubby's. Banners were hung on both sides of the trailer advertising, "Piney Bluffs' 1st Annual Ice Fishing Derby," 'Manager's Office'. There was a constant stream of people going in and out for registration or some type of business or another. Mostly, he had stayed away from us save for a final check on the headlines for Friday's edition. We had assured him that we would include the full schedule of the day's event. He also gave us a piece to run, thanking all who had made this event possible. His story looked like one that he had cut and pasted from previous events. Not much on specifics but long on his bio and what this experience would mean to our town for years to come as our annual tradition. He had no idea of what our annual tradition would celebrate the day we ran Norman out of town.

Mike O'Brien had called only once. Two days prior, I had answered the phone and heard his unmistakable voice.

"Ethel, this is Mike," he all but growled over the phone.

"Yes, what can I do for you?" I replied in a matter-of-fact way.

"Just checking to see if you have any questions," he said in a way that made me think he hadn't wanted to make this call.

"Oh, I've got lots of questions, Mike, but I don't think you're ready to give me the kind of answers I'm interested in," I said snippily.

"All right, then let me make this short for the both of us. The broadcast coordinating team will be down the day before the derby to talk to you. If you got any questions, ask them." He hung up.

I made a face at the phone and hung up. "Another witty repartee with your former employer," Caleb noted.

"He is such an ass," I said, shaking my head.

"I believe that was established some time ago," Caleb responded.

"I just hope he stays far away from me on Saturday," I said. "I'll never regret staying here and not taking that job with him."

"Well, I'm glad of that, but you did miss out on all those Sox tickets." Caleb shrunk away from me for what he assumed would have brought a jab to the side or a pencil thrown in the air.

"Trust me that was the only perk that job had going for it."

It was true. I had never regretted staying. Life here had just seemed to fall into place. Some of my friends from college had been in touch and told about how they had moved away and found their dream jobs. But they always talked about wanting to move home again when the time was right. I was lucky I had my dream job, and I was home. Someone had once said, love what you do for a living, and it will never be work. And that's what it was. I loved what I was doing and the people I was doing it for. That was something I doubt that Norman would ever be able to say.

The day before the derby was like watching the beginning of a concert. All of the instruments in their discord of tuning and the noisy conversations of the audience could be compared to the fishermen restringing jigging poles, laying in their food supplies for the day, sharpening the blades of their augers, and the last-minute to and fro of people scurrying about town. Tomorrow morning, Norman the conductor would tap his baton, and the performance would begin.

For his rehearsal, he was hosting a reception from four thirty to seven o'clock tonight at the inn for the fishermen, reporters, and local business owners who had contributed toward the prize money. We were going to see how "our New England fisherman" worked the crowd.

"I wonder what we'll find out, if anything," I said.

"He'll be very smooth, I imagine," Caleb said. "But it will be very interesting to see him operate. It will also be interesting to see some of the professional fishermen who work this circuit. Did you see the gear and the outfits on these guys? Some of them have every inch of their jackets covered in sponsorship logos."

"I know. Daddy said for some of these guys the tournaments are their only source of income," I noted. "Must be good money judging by their rigs but also must be very competitive."

"You're right on that. And if you get a sponsor, so much the better for the fisherman as they will pay registration and transportation fees. But I hear it is a cutthroat business. And I wouldn't put it past Norman to play favorites if it was to his benefit," Caleb added.

"Ben hasn't come up with anything in that respect, has he?" I asked.

"He says Norman covers his tracks well if there is anything. Ben has been looking at some different angles of how he might run things to his advantage, but so far, nothing. He's trying to track down some more leads on Bill Rushmore and why he vanished into thin air." Caleb shrugged and put his pipe in his mouth.

"You're not going to light that, are you?" I questioned him. "Your doctor won't be too pleased, not to mention Sadie."

"I'm not lighting it. I'm just chewing on it," he answered. "It helps me think."

"Oh really, is that the story you're using now?" I chuckled. "What are you thinking about?"

"I'm thinking about what Rocky might have made for tonight," Caleb said and clasped his hands behind his head and leaned back in his chair.

"I hear that Sadie leant him some of her favorite recipes for tonight," I snickered as Caleb glared at me.

"You really know how to hurt a guy," he said.

Just then, the door opened, and a tall man entered. It looked like he was one of the broadcast coordinators with the Portland affiliates name on his jacket.

"Hi, Ethel, that's right, isn't it?" he said as he looked at me and then down at the clipboard he clutched with his huge leather mittens. He had on a plaid earflap hat with the flaps up, his bushy red hair sticking out from all sides and a mustache to match. Between the hat, hair, and mustache, his face was all but lost. His bright-green parka had WPOR embroidered across the back. He looked like a circus clown who was on a winter vacation. All that was missing was the red nose and the big feet.

"Yes, I'm Ethel. What can I do for you?" I asked and stifled a laugh.

"I'm Brad from POR. Can you come down to the stage for a final microphone check? We want to get all this done before we break up for the night." And with a flourish, Brad checked an item off his list.

"Let me get my coat, and we'll go," I said, getting up and grabbing my coat from the rack.

"Oh, you're pregnant," he said with a surprised look on his face.

"Yes, I am. Is that a problem?" I asked.

"No, it's just that I, ah, you're not going to deliver during this thing, are you?" He was so uncomfortable with me it was laughable.

"No need to worry, Brad, I've got a couple of months to go." I chuckled as we went out the door.

"It's okay, we'll just do head shots and not so much of the full-length type," he added.

"It's really fine with me if you show that I am pregnant," I said and then called out. "If I'm not back in time to close, I'll see you at the reception, Caleb."

"Okay, let me know if you need anything," he said as the door closed behind us.

We walked for a bit in the quiet, and then I broke the silence.

"So, Brad, do you do a lot of these remote locations for Norman?" I asked, trying to see where I could get a little more dirt on him.

"No, this is my first one," he replied. "But our station's been televising his events when he has a big derby. Usually, it's summer derbies. This is the first ice derby."

And our conversation continued about all things broadcasting on our way down to the stage. Brad didn't seem to know much about Norman and wasn't too much of a talker. I finally gave up and went through the checks that he needed as the sun began to fade into the pale of a winter's afternoon. I looked at the time, almost 4:15. So I said good-bye and headed up to the office and finding it in darkness, I went to my car and drove up to the inn.

"Hello, my sweet Ethel," said Mrs. F as I came through the door. She got out from behind the desk and gave me a big hug. "You look wonderful. Pregnancy certainly agrees with you!" She twirled me around like she had when Jackie and I were kids.

"Well, I'm not so sure I'm as light on my feet as I used to be," I said and steadied myself on the edge of the desk.

"Are you okay?" Her motherly concern now raised her eyebrows as she looked at me.

"I'm just a little hungry, I guess. Either that, or my twirling days are over." We both laughed as she walked with me into the Tavern Room. The reception had just started, but the room was already full. The championship trophy was the centerpiece for the table that was laden with an assortment of Rocky's finest. He had made skewers of shrimp, chicken, and beef with sauces to compliment. There were hot lobster puffs and cheese squares. Rocky's take on a brownie consistency but with a cheese taste. And of course, there were bowls of clam chowder and fish stew. My cousin Edie was busy ladling the soups into bowls and gave me a smile as I passed by. I saw Daddy and Caleb standing by the bar and went to join them. Norman was busy holding court near the trophy, stopping to pose with anyone wanting to take his picture.

"So what have you found out?" I asked as I put my arm through Daddy's.

"Not much of anything. Caleb's going to do some in-depth reporting just as soon as he gets a drink," Daddy said and kissed my head. "How's my girl? Are you okay? I know, you're hungry. I can tell that look. Had that since you were six." And he made me sit on the bar stool while he went for a plate of food.

"I did notice a small group of pros standing off by themselves," Caleb said. And he indicated their direction with a tip of his glass toward them.

I followed the line of sight and found six or seven men standing in a group. All were dressed basically the same in their jeans with lightweight parkas with their sponsors' names displayed across their backs. Most had a beer in their hands, some were holding coffee cups, and all were eyeing the trophy.

Daddy returned with a plate of goodies that we immediately dove into. The lobster puffs just melted in my mouth, which I chased with sips of the savory fish stew. I was just about to talk to Jackie's dad who was behind the bar when I heard the clank of silverware on a drink glass. I turned and saw Norman at center stage, glass in hand, smile on his face. People silenced, and he began.

"Thank you all for coming," Norman began. "For tonight and tomorrow's derby would not be possible without all of you. To those of you in this wonderful town of Piney Bluffs who have opened your doors to the derby. And to the fishermen who have traveled from near and far to be a part of this derby. Here's to all of you, and may the best man win in the hunt for the prize of five thousand dollars!"

At the mention of the amount, the crowd erupted into a cheer. I watched the group of pros, and they were applauding but not as enthusiastically as the rest of the participants who were either folks from neighboring towns or our own residents. It seemed to me that the pros were the group to watch.

After that, the crowd milled about the food table and took their own pictures with the trophy. Two little boys, Bobby and Rodney Kramer were noisily asking someone to please take their picture. The youngest competitors finally found someone to take their picture with Norman and the trophy. Happy to have that they next turned their attention to the food table and as only little boys could began to devour anything in sight. They were quite amusing, and Caleb took their picture and told them it was for *The Bugle*. Excitedly, they ran out the door saying, "Wait till we tell Mom."

Norman had gone over to the group of professionals and spoke to them while most listened intently, save for one guy who was looking about the room. As much as I didn't want to be around Norman, now was my opportunity to introduce myself to those who I might be interviewing.

"Hello, everyone. I'm Ethel O'Connor. I'm the assistant editor for the paper here in town, and I will be one of the newscasters for tomorrow's derby," I said and held out my hand as the group looked up, almost surprised at my intrusion.

"Hi, there, I'm Bill Crawford, and this is Bob Konoski, Sammy Tessler, Snowshoe Ted Bussey, Tommy Bard, Randy Jones, and Little Jim Charette," said Bill, the man who had been looking around. The men shook my hand all around. Not much else was offered, but then it was Norman's turn.

"Yes, we really have Ethel to thank for all of us being here," Norman piped up. "When she was a cub reporter, she flew up to my camp and did an interview with me. She told me all about her wonderful town and the bounty that the rivers and lakes held. Right then, I knew at some point it would be a wonderful place to have a derby."

Oh great, I thought. It wasn't enough to see how badly things had developed, but to make me face the fact that it was I who led Norman here, oh I just wanted to scream!

"Now I'm sure Ethel has some last-minute stories to finish up." Norman put his hand on my shoulder to remove me from the group

"Well, it was nice to meet all of you," I said, quite annoyed at the way I had just been dismissed, thus ending my conversation with the group. I walked back to the bar saying hello along to the way to some of the business owners in town. Big Bob and his sister Bertha were standing close to the food table stuffing one lobster puff after another into their mouths as a newscaster from WPOR tried to interview them. Miss Ruthie and Grandpa Lewis were laughing with two fishermen. In spite of our problem with Norman, this was a way of putting Piney Bluffs on the map. A regional fishing event with media coverage was like money in the bank. This one deposit would grow with interest for years to come. Just then, I felt a tap on my shoulder. I turned to see the Browning Brothers dressed as dandily as ever in their après fishing attire.

"Oh, Ethel, look at you, now give me a big hug," Russell cooed to me and wrapped his cologned arms around me.

"Save enough love for me too," and now it was Robert's turn for his greeting.

"It's so good to see you two," I said, taking both their hands. "Come on over and say hi to Daddy and Caleb." And I led them over to the bar.

"Hello, Robert, Russell." Daddy shook their hands and clapped them on the back. "What are you two drinking to chase the chill tonight?"

"Hi, Eddy, I'll have a port if Jack's got any, and Robert will have a Manhattan," Russell replied and turned to Caleb.

"Caleb, how's the rag business?" As Jack handed Russell a glass of port, Caleb and he clinked glasses as a greeting.

"Doing well, how about your business? Selling anything?" Caleb took a sip and waited for the reply.

"No. We're just resting on our laurels from the sales of the *Weekly*." We all chuckled over that.

"Really, what's going on?" Robert asked.

"Not much to tell," I said. "Ben's been up a couple of times, but so far hasn't turned up much of anything that we didn't already know."

"Look at him, he is such the ass," Russell snorted as he made the comment looking at Norman glad-handing all that he could.

"What time should I be ready to fish?" Robert inquired.

"Six is the shotgun start, but we start televising at five," I replied. "But don't tell me you two are fishing?"

"Well, yes, Big Bob promised that he would show us just what to do. And that he wouldn't laugh as he usually does when he's with us," Robert said with a giggle.

"I'm just going along for the hot toddies. You can fish. Now, young lady, you'd best get to bed early. We want those lovely brown eyes to sparkle," Russell said as he patted me on the shoulder.

"Oh, don't worry about me. I'll be going shortly, I've just got to chat with a few more folks before I leave," I said and bid them all good night, looking for the group of pros.

I spotted them on the other side of the room near the door. Bill Crawford, the spokesman for the group, was off to the side with Norman having a conversation. Norman's look was very serious, and Bill, although cool when he had introduced the others to me, now appeared somewhat like a child that had just been scolded. As soon as Norman turned around and saw me looking at them, his demeanor changed, patting Bill on the back and shaking his hand. He was quite the chameleon—no, more like an actor. I wondered if he ever got back to whom he really was.

The pros thanked their host and headed out the door together. I moved toward the door grabbing my coat and leaving a couple of steps behind them, hoping I hadn't been seen. There were lots of people coming and going, so the traffic helped to hide my exit. Thinking they were alone, their conversations were full of bravado on who was going to win. But then Bill silenced them.

"You know what the old man wants, so remember who's winning tomorrow," he said in hushed tones. "You all clear on that?" They said their yeses and continued walking to their van, got in, and drove away.

I stood almost frozen out of the light of entrance. What did that mean? The old man had to be Norman. But "Remember who's winning"? So, somehow this derby was going to be rigged. But how? I walked to my car and got in and drove home all the while thinking of how many ways you could fix a fishing tournament with thousands of people watching the live broadcast. It seemed I was going to have a lot more to worry about than sly real estate transactions. While the outcome was still unknown, this was indeed a day that Piney Bluffs would never forget.

46

Derby day was finally here. It seemed like the middle of the night when Charlie had kissed me good-bye and told me he'd see me on TV. Then he promptly rolled over and went back to sleep. As I walked to the car, I could feel a sense of relief waiting in the wings like an actor about to deliver the closing lines of a play. Whatever the reviews, today, it would finally be over. The curtain would come down on the last act. And the classic story of Piney Bluffs' triumph over evil would close to a packed house.

It was four thirty in the morning, and it was cold. The temperature couldn't have been more than twenty. As I got out of my car, I thanked God that I was just able to fit into my knee-length parka and pulled the hood closer around my head. I had worn thermals under Charlie's flannel-lined pants, the legs of which I had stuffed into my insulated storm boots. Thinking about it now, it was probably a good idea that they weren't going to do full-length camera shots of me. Although I doubted glamorous would be how participants, fishermen or anyone else, would be described today. My breath seemed to freeze in midair as I walked to Tubby's bait shop. The warm glow of lights showed the inside of the shop packed with fishermen buying their last-minute supplies. I stayed outside for a moment and went out onto the deck. The first rays of dawn were beginning to break into the cloudless sky, and the stars were disappearing as if someone was turning them off one by one. The dim light was instantly gone when I heard "light check," and the area was awash with light. The technicians had been at work, finalizing the staging area and connecting the floodlights, and now it looked like high noon in the summer.

The news station vehicles had arrived. The Boston and Portland stations were going to televise a continuous program from the shotgun start at six to the noontime weigh in.

WPOR had teamed me with Bruce "Bulldog" Baxter, a sportscaster with the station for as long as I could remember. The nickname bulldog referred to his having attended Yale. He was a husky red-faced man who always looked like his tie was too tight. But his sports reports were more than just the scores or highlights. He always seemed to find an angle in the story that came back one way or another to Maine or Yale. He affectionately called them his Bulldog's Bones.

I went over to the POR trailer and knocked on the door. I heard steps, and the door flew open in my face.

"Are you here with my coffee?" Bulldog asked as he gave me a once-over.

"No, actually, I'm your co-anchor. I'm Ethel O'Connor," I replied, dismissing his assumption of my identity.

"Sorry about that," he apologized. "Come on in." He motioned for me to enter the trailer.

"Nice to meet you." I offered my hand as I removed my gloves. The inside of the trailer had a counter with a makeup mirror and a clutter of makeup items. A table held papers and coffee cups with folding chairs piled on the floor. Looking through to the driver's seat, there were compact control panels with a technician already busy at work connecting to Portland.

"Same here," and he continued with his makeup. "Station tells me you're the assistant editor for the paper here. Any television experience?"

"No experience, but I know a lot about fishing." And I watched for his reaction.

"Good, the fishing knowledge will keep you talking when there's no action. And don't worry about the other stuff. You've got a pretty face, and your voice seems to be good," he said. "Keep out of my way. Don't get nervous, and you'll do fine. Where'd Norman find you anyway?"

"I interviewed him early on in my career, and his assistant Bill Rushmore had come to fish in Piney Bluffs a number of times. Norman came to us with his derby idea a while ago," I answered, taking in his comments. "Sounds like you've known him for a while."

"Norman and I go way back when he had his television show. I had the POR job too, so I was a semi-regular announcer with the show," he said as he sat at his makeup area talking to me through the mirror. "I stayed with him until it got ugly. The show ended, and that was it. Stayed with POR all this time, and I love it."

"What do you mean until it got ugly?" I asked, hoping for more information as another layer of Norman was revealed.

"Maybe ugly's too strong," he said, finishing up and removing the tissues from his neck. "It was always about money. Norman thought he deserved more money, and the station didn't. It was like a lot of shows. They had their moment in time, and then the viewer's whim changed to something else. Ratings fell, and it was time to go. They didn't pay out the end of his contract, so he begrudgingly flew off into the sunset. I hadn't heard from him in years, and then out of the blue, a couple years ago, there he was with his new angle for televising derbies. It's been okay, gets me out of town and meeting new folks. Good stories for when I get back in the studio. And good money for Norman."

"How's that?" I asked.

"Well, he gets the towns to put up the money for the purse. The station's advertisers pay for television coverage of the event. The fishing equipment companies sponsor all of the rest. So at the end of the day, he walks away with all the registration fees and any other grease that lands in his palm, if you know what I mean," he continued, giving me quite the education.

"Our registration fee is one hundred dollars, and we have more than one hundred entrants, so that's ten thousand dollars without doing too much. So what other grease is there?" I asked, fascinated with this underside of our so-called family fun day.

"The sponsors pay him to have their products splashed all over the sets and to be part of the giveaways," he explained. "And some of these pro fishermen slide a little something his way so they have an even better position in some of the events. Like today for instance, you see everyone grouping up by the edge of the lake?"

"Yes," I said as I looked out the window of the van and down to the ice recognizing the fishermen I had met last evening.

"Who do you see in the front?" he asked.

"The pros," I said. "It's ice fishing for crying out loud, what does position have to do with it?"

"Exactly my point," he said. "Position has a lot to do with it. These guys have been here, what, the whole week? And they have been scouring every part of this ice. Even though it's ice, they tell me fish still have the same habits as when there's just water, so they'll be in the same hiding spots. For the guys who get there first, they have a greater potential for a win than the guy that steps out on the ice last."

"And I thought I knew a lot about fishing," I said.

"I'm sure your knowledge about fishing is how to catch them, but this is all about the business of fishing. It's starting to grow, and in the next ten years or so, shows like this are going to be big," Bulldog continued. "And Norman will be right there with his hand out, waiting for his turn to come around again."

"I have to thank you for my education," I said.

"Listen, you seem nice like a nice young gal, and this seems like a real nice town. Just be careful, that's all I'm saying," he said and smiled at me. "Now let's have you sit down and put a little makeup on for your television debut. Although with your pretty face, I can't say as you'll need too much."

"Bulldog, did you ever know Bill Rushford? He was Norman's assistant for a while," I said and reached for some foundation.

"I recall the name, but can't say as I could pick him out of a crowd. I've met the new one, O'Brien. He's quite the character. Don't think he'll be too long for this business," Bulldog answered.

"How's that?" I asked as I had found the right shade and started to smooth it on. It felt a lot heavier than what I was used to. I made a face.

"Don't worry, I know it feels like paste, but unless you have something on, you'll look like the underbelly of a pike." He joked. "Mike's just too independent and doesn't kowtow to Norman like he's used to. But then who knows, with the cut he gets, must be worth his while. He's still at the *Herald* too, so he's making out okay."

"He gets a cut?" I asked and finished with some rouge and eyeliner.

"Sure, Norman gives fifteen percent. That's if you hang in until the end, although most get out," he commented and started with hairspray on his thinning hair. "Sorry, not too much on top, but what I've got needs to stay in place."

"What's the end?" I continued with my questions.

"Forty-five," a voiced called out and knocked on the door at the same time.

"Well, we'd best get a little practice in. These last forty-five minutes go fast. You look great, Ethel. You'll be fine. Just follow my lead." Bulldog stood and motioned for me to stand as well.

And so my questions ended, and we began our practice of where to stand and how to look at the camera. Bulldog was a lot like Caleb. A well-seasoned newsman who was happy to share his craft and not at all worried about the pretty face of a newcomer. We decided that due to the cold, we would take half-hour shifts at the mic. And of course, he would open, but I could join him and be there to smile and hold my mic.

"Twenty," the voice and the knock came again.

"Let's go, Ethel." And with that, we walked out into the cold. It seemed all very professional now as we worked our way to the back of the stage, albeit a tractor trailer. A small city of technicians with light and soundboards were sliding switches back and forth. As we came out to the front, we were met with the glare of the spotlights. I remembered what Bulldog had said and looked out to the very back of the audience so as not to be blinded. A mic was thrust in my hand. What seemed like miles of cable were lying in coils next to us awaiting our moves. They told us we had enough cable to go two hundred feet. That meant we could go out onto the ice and do interviews with the fishermen. The cameras were equipped with battery packs and would be at our sides as well.

"Is my mic on?" I asked Brad, the technician I had met yesterday.

"Not yet," he replied. "We'll do sound checks in a minute." And he was gone to the back of the stage. His red hair seemed even bushier today. Still in his green WPOR jacket, he moved around the set with precision-like movements.

I looked out at the ever-growing crowd. The bleachers were full with people bundled almost beyond recognition. I heard a couple of "Hi, Ethels" and waved in the direction of their voices. I was trying hard to observe the actions of the pro fishermen to see if they were showing any signs of, well, anything. With all that I had learned last night, coupled with what Bulldog had said this morning, I was sure I would know it if I saw it. And the "it" was what I was now going to hang my hat on. From being the mastermind in fixing the winner of the derby to the money that made its way to his pockets, Norman was not going to get away with "it" today. The land swindling was going to take a backseat. There were now bigger fish to fry. I had six hours to scrutinize and find the loose cog in the workings of what seemed to be yet another well-oiled money-making machine in the world of Norman.

Gas-powered augers roared as they were getting their last-minute checks. Larger sleds were in place and checked for supplies. The anticipation was building as more people lined up for the six o'clock shotgun start. Spotlights shown on the eager faces of the fishermen. Bulldog and I took our places on the stage. The cameramen were in place by the clock as it neared the end of its countdown. Norman made his way through the crowd, shaking hands as he went. He was dressed in a bright-red parka with a Russian type fur-lined hat atop his balding head. He was all smiles and waves to those gathered in the crowd as he climbed the stairs to the stage. He spoke to the Boston newscasters as he came across and then gave a handshake and a clap on the back to Bulldog as he made his way to the microphone. He gave me a glance and a quick smile. I couldn't wait until the smile turned to shock and dismay. Mike appeared at the edge of the stage, clipboard in hand, looking around judgmentally at the goings-on.

Our eyes made contact for a moment without any hint of recognition from either of us.

"Good morning to you all, and welcome to the 1st Annual Piney Bluffs Ice Fishing Derby," he said as he spread his arms out and waved to the cheering crowd. "Let's get right down to business. So here are today's rules. All entrants must have a Maine fishing license and no more than three holes per person. All fish must be live at the time of weigh in. The ice must be cleared by 11:30 as weigh-in begins at noon. First prize goes to the one who has the most overall weight for five fish. And courtesy of one of our sponsors, FineLine, there will be a one thousand dollar prize for whoever catches the biggest fish. Also, Tubby has announced that he will give a fifty-dollar gift certificate to Tubby's Bait and Tackle shop to whoever catches the first fish. Any questions?" And he scanned the crowd side to side for any response.

All eyes now went between the clock and Norman. He reached into his coat and took out the starter pistol. He looked over at the clock as the digits fell to zero, zero, zero. The crowd grew silent as Norman raised his arm over his head, gun in hand, and then he fired the shot. The sound pierced through the cold air. The crowd cheered, and then all you could hear were the cleated boots rushing over the ice and the excited voices of the fishermen as they made their way to stake their claims on a section of ice. They seemed to scatter like so many marbles thrown out on the floor going every which way. Some went far out to the center of the lake with their sleds in tow or pushing their ice shanties. Others stayed close and walked out about twenty or thirty feet. The augers were starting, and holes were being drilled. Tip ups were in place as hooks were baited, and the wait began.

Bulldog's broadcast welcomed all of the early-morning viewers to the derby as he set the stage and brought Norman in for the first interview. Norman went into his greeting of how happy he was to be bringing the viewing audience a family sporting event in the wonderful town of Piney Bluffs. As much as I wanted to show my disgust, I had to remember that I was on the air and needed to be all smiles. This portion of the broadcast lasted about five minutes, and then Bulldog finished up another five of the background of the event and timetable for the day. And then it was time to go back to the studio. He had explained that there would be regular intervals for the updates on the local news and weather. I was learning that television was a matter of timing. It seemed that more than television was about timing as well. Piney Bluffs had put their faith and trust in me to execute the timing of our plan. The day would go quickly, and I prayed that when the hands of the clock signaled the end of the derby, that we would have our victory.

During the second break, we had discussed where I would begin. We agreed that I would be out on the ice and interview a Piney Bluffs resident. We wound our way through the crowd until we reached the edge of the lake with the help of Brad who was laying out microphone wire like it was oxygen lines for deep-sea divers. The cameraman was following close behind.

"I'll give you the cue when we're five seconds to airtime," he said and cautioned me. "Do you see who you're going to talk to yet? You only have about thirty more feet of wire."

I looked around and saw Daddy and Uncle Ellsworth standing between three holes. They were just about within my range. I walked out and motioned for them to come and join me as I hurriedly explained that they would be my first interview. They held their cups of coffee in the red tops from their thermoses and were dressed in their full-length coveralls, earflap hats, and insulated boots. They would be good on TV as they looked like the typical ice fisherman.

"I'll let your father do all the talking. That's what he's good at," Uncle Ellsworth said as he blew on his coffee and looked over at Daddy.

"Oh, like you don't know how to open your yap," Daddy replied back to him.

"Okay, you two, no fighting," I scolded.

"Ethel, five," Brad held up his hand and counted down. He pointed to me at the end of the count, and I began.

"Good morning. My name is Ethel O'Connor, and I'm on the ice with two local fishermen, Eddy and Ellsworth Koontz." I smiled into the camera. "Gentlemen, tell me who do you think will win today?" And I held the microphone up for Daddy.

"Oh, I think it'll be a local guy, for sure," he said. "We know these fish and these waters. These professional guys don't have a chance."

"That's right. They got all their fancy sleds and shacks. Don't matter to the fish," Uncle Ellsworth said, surprising me by talking.

"How's that?" I was beginning to enjoy my conversation with my dad and uncle, almost forgetting that we were on TV.

"They're coming in with their fancy lures and bait, but you got to use what the fish like," Uncle Ellsworth explained.

"And what would that be?" I asked.

"Well, now, Ethel, you know I can't tell you that. That's a family secret." Daddy and Uncle Ellsworth just smiled right into the camera.

Our conversation continued for the full ten minutes of my first airtime. Brad came around to the side with a five-second warning, and I wrapped up.

"Whew, that was over so quickly," I said to Bulldog. He had been waiting to the side.

"You were wonderful!" he said. "I thought you said you didn't have any experience. Couldn't prove it by me."

"Thank you. I was wondering if I would be able to pull it off," I said, shaking my head in disbelief. And then I heard the muffled clapping of gloved hands.

I turned and gathered at the edge of the ice were Ruthie, Caleb, Jackie, Andy, and Charlie.

"You were fantastic!" Charlie said and gave me a big hug. And the rest of my friends came in and gave me hugs as well.

"Bulldog, I'd like you to meet some of the best friends in the whole world," and I began the introductions.

"Ethel, five minutes. Where to this time?" Brad had my wire coiled and ready to go. I waved to everyone, and we were off to my next segment.

"I'm going over there." I pointed to Bill Crawford who was walking in from his spot on the ice. We made our way over to him.

"Hi, Bill, I'd like to do a little interview with you or some of the guys, if you don't mind," I said as we fell in step with him. He was walking with a purpose, so his response didn't surprise me.

"Yes, I do mind, and we don't have time for this crap." He kept on walking.

"Well," I said to Brad. "Things must not be going his way."

"The pros are always like that. If you ask me, they shouldn't be allowed in these competitions. They always win," he said.

"They do?" I asked, hoping for more information and how this business seemed as crooked as a dog's hind leg.

"Sure, oh, some amateur might win the first or the largest, makes them feel good. But these guys always finish in the money," he added.

"How do you think they do it?" I asked.

"That's what I'm here to find out, Ethel," Brad replied, and I took a step back and looked at him.

"What did you just say? Who are you?" I looked through that bushy red beard, thinking that I almost knew who it was.

"You knew me as Bill Rushford," the man answered. "But my real name is James Summit, and I work for the Department of the Interior Fishing and Wildlife Division."

"Bill? The Department of the Interior Fishing and Wildlife Division?" I was incredulous. What was going on?

"There's not a lot of time to talk right now. You go on in ten seconds. So you'd better find someone to talk to soon," he said.

"Ahh, okay, over there. There's a couple of kids from town, let's go," I said and hurried to where they were standing. As I got to them, I saw they were the Kramer boys. They had been at the reception last night. Their father had passed away in a lumber camp accident last year, and folks in town had been trying to help out their mom Suzy in any way they could. They were bundled in their pint-sized coveralls, hand-knitted scarves, and hats with mittens that were already soaked from the water.

"Welcome back to WPOR's coverage of the 1st Annual Piney Bluffs Ice Fishing Derby. I'm Ethel O'Connor, and I thought you might like to hear from some of our younger fishermen. Hi, guys! What's your names, and how's the fishing?" I hoped I had picked the right kids and that they would provide some good dialogue like there used to be on those TV shows like *Art Linkletter's*.

"I'm Bobby Kramer, and this is my little brother Rodney. And we ain't caught nothing yet." The two boys looked away from me and right back into the hole.

"Nice to meet you two. You only have one hole to fish from. How come?" I asked, anticipating any number of answers.

"Well, we didn't have any power tools. But Mr. Koontz came over and made one for us," Bobby continued. "Besides, we only have one license. Rodney doesn't need one 'cause he's only ten. So he couldn't win anyway, and I only have one tip up, so one hole is all we need." He was so matter-of-fact that it made me chuckle.

"That's great," I said, and I looked over to see Daddy waving. "But who bought your entry fee, that's a lot of money for you two."

"Mr. Carponoski from the Bait and Tackle store told us we'd won a kid's contest. He picked our name at random. Do you know where that is? Is it near Piney Bluffs? Anyway, here we are, and I sure hope we win." Bobby smiled up at me with such sincerity that it almost broke my heart.

"Bobby, look, I think we got something!" Rodney screamed as the flag on the tip up started to quiver and then sprang straight up, signaling a fish on the line.

"Yippee, we got one! Do you think we're first, do ya?" Bobby was excited but was very careful as he wound the reel on the tip up.

"I think you may just be the first," I said and was hoping beyond hope that indeed there was a fish on the line and that they were first.

"Look, look, we got one. We're first, we're first!" Rodney yelled and jumped up and down as his brother pulled the pickerel out onto the ice. Fishermen who were close by came over to the boys to congratulate them.

"Hold it up for the camera, boys," I said. "And I'm getting the signal from our crew that yes, you do have the first fish. Congratulations!"

"Oh boy, oh boy, we won, we won!" the brothers shrieked together with the exuberance that only children can have. I saw Brad, no, James, hold up his hand for five seconds.

"And that's part of today's excitement with Rodney and Bobby Kramer here in Piney Bluffs. Now back to the studio." I switched off my mic and took a moment to enjoy the boy's win. They were running to the stage to show that they had caught the first fish. You could see them continuing to jump up and down when they were handed their gift certificate. Bobby carefully folded it and zipped it into his overalls. Then they came running back down to put their catch on their stringer and put it back in the water to keep it alive.

"Okay, Ethel, time to switch. That was a wonderful segment on those boys. People at home have got to be loving every minute of this. Now you go get off your feet and get warm. I'll see you in thirty minutes," Bulldog said and waved me off the ice.

"Come on, honey, let's go sit down," Charlie said as he linked his arm through mine. He had followed me to my interview with the boys and was waiting for my break.

"But wait, I have to talk to Brad," I said and turned to see him, trailing off with Bulldog for his segment.

"Come on, have something to eat. Who's Brad?" Charlie asked and led me up to Tubby's. He had brought me a cup of hot chocolate and a piece of Ruthie's banana oatmeal bread. We sat at one of the outside tables that had kerosene heaters near them to offer some warmth. The sun was up now, and it was above freezing. It felt good to sit down, but I had to get back to James.

"Charlie, Brad is Bill, but he's really James," I said in hushed tones. "He's here to find out who and how they're fixing these tournaments.

"What? Slow down, Brad is who?" Charlie looked at me like I was completely off my rocker. "Are you sure you're not just cold?"

"Stop it, I'm not crazy. During the last break, he told me. He is with the Department of the Interior Fishing and Wildlife Division and is here to find out how these derbies are being fixed," I said. "Keep your voice down. I don't know who's in on this."

"Fixing the derby, how do you know that?" Charlie asked.

"Last night, when I was leaving the inn, I heard the pro fishermen talking about the 'old man' and that he had told them who was going to win. I just haven't had a chance to tell anyone about this. And then to have James tell me that same thing two seconds before we go on the air, well, it's just wild," I relayed to him.

"But I thought this was all about land deals, not fixing fishing derbies," Charlie said.

"It was until I heard about the fixing. And now with James working on this too, well, this is the help we were looking for," I said, my mind racing ahead to what I needed to ask James. I had to keep up with what Bulldog was doing, but I needed to find out as much as I could from James and how I could help.

"You be careful," Charlie said and gave me kiss.

"I will. Tell the others that the plans have changed," I said, happy to see that Bulldog had come over to Tubby's for his segment. I waited while he was describing the shop and owner and that in the next segment they would go inside to meet with Tubby. At the end, Bulldog went inside to get Tubby ready, and James stayed outside.

I hurried over to him and explained how we'd been trying to bring a case against Norman with the land swindling. I told him I was going to try to bring these accusations to the public's attention today on national television. He said he knew about that as he had been at the zoning meeting. He had been the man in back of the audience that night. And he answered the question about his sudden disappearance from Norman's employ. He explained that he had gone undercover with Norman several years ago. The department had suspected him of conservation mismanagement of the land that he had been gorging his pockets with. He had, as we suspected, promised the owners that the land would be held as it was. But in the end, with the help of his legal staff, had been able to ignore federal conservation and wildlife regulations and plunder some of the finest land available in the northeast. He had paid the fines without so much as a care to natural resources or the wildlife that inhabited those lands. I remembered back to the taped interview I had done with Norman when he had gone on and on about how we must be so concerned with wildlife and natural resources. What could have turned someone into such a monster?

"What do you think happened to him? When I first met him, he seemed so different," I asked James.

"Money was always behind everything. I found that out right away. He had that wonderful caring appearance, but money was always in the driver's seat. Came from his poor upbringing as much as we can figure," James said. "He was orphaned, raised by a so-called aunt who was only after the state aid that came her way for taking care of him. Most of that went to her drinking and not much to his upbringing. Sad, really. He clawed his way into the business and never looked back on the dirt-poor life. A person has two paths to take in life, and unfortunately for him and all of us, he took the evil way. With all that money, he could have done so many good things for people."

"But what can you do now that you haven't been able to do before?" I asked. "Can't his lawyers get him off again?"

"Not this time," he explained. "Whatever method they are using to increase the weight of the fish is detrimental to the wellbeing of the fish since they must be live at the time of weigh-in. So in essence, he is participating in harming a protected species."

"Our fish are protected?" I asked.

"Yes, during the winter months, fish are considered a protected species. And as such, however, increasing the weight of the fish is unnatural," James explained.

"What can I do to help?" I asked, finding this information unbelievable.

"You've got the right idea about the national exposure. But you wait for my cue. I've got some other help out here as well, so just know you're not alone. I'm not sure how this thing is being fixed, but I have my ideas. This may come down to the final moments of the derby, so hang in there with us," he said and checked his watch. "Got to go, time for Bulldog's next segment."

He turned to find Bulldog who had been talking to folks on the deck and ushered him into the building and arranged people in the shop. His segment began, and I took this time to look out over the ice. The local fishermen were having a great time. They had fired up their grills, and the air was filled with the aroma of sausages, venison and more than likely fish that weren't going to be on the winning stringer. They were visiting back and forth with one another with the good-natured competitive jabs and conversations.

The professional group was just the opposite. There was a sense of seriousness or was it that someone was watching them. I had wondered what Bill had been up to when he gave me the brush off earlier. But I could see nothing that looked wrong or out of the ordinary in their setups. They were all grouped together with their holes but set away from the other fishermen. There was one ice shanty in the middle of their area, and I noticed that each of them took turns going in and out of it. Answering nature's call and having something to eat were my first inclinations, although I was sure that there was something in there that they were using to insert into the fish for weight gain.

"You're looking very serious, my dear." I turned to see Russell and Robert. They were decked out in the warmest-looking attire I could ever imagine for ice fishing. New York designers must have been working overtime to outfit these two. They had matching navy blue down jackets with plaid overalls. Their boots were well insulated and had some type of exotic fur around the top cuffs. Their gloves looked like waterproof leather that would have been the envy of any fisherman.

"Hi, you two," I said as I gave them each a hug. "I thought you were going to have ice fishing lessons with Big Bob? What happened?"

"Well," Robert started. "Russell had to have just one more scone with his tea at Ruthie's, and then they began to chitchat about her cookbook. So we missed our meeting time, and you know how Bob can be with us. He doesn't like a tardy client. But we're having a fabulous time despite that. We talked to your dad and uncle. They seem to have quite a few good ones on their stringer. Could be one of them is the winner."

"Nothing would make me feel better than to have one of them win," I said.

"How's everything going with you know what?" Russell all but whispered to me. "Was Ben able to find anything that can help?"

"Ben's been great, but Norman's lawyers have got him very well protected. But it's going to be quite the finish, so make sure you're here till the end," I whispered back. "Say, how about I do my next interview with you two? I think it would be great since you're regular visitors and can tell folks how much you like Piney Bluffs. You could also plug Ruthie's."

"We'd just love to, wouldn't we, Robert?" Russell said, smiling to his brother.

"Of course, we would. Do we need makeup, dear?" Robert asked, patting at his pudgy chin.

"You look fine, both of you," I said and positioned them on the deck with the lake behind them. "Now I'll be right back."

They were a joy to interview and oozed everything that was good about Piney Bluffs and all of the places they loved to go. Time with them flew, and then it was back to studio.

The morning seemed like it had just started when the whistle blew. All eyes looked toward the stage. Norman was there with the clock ticking down.

"It is now 11:30. Stop fishing, and make your way to the staging area. Weigh-in will commence at noon," he announced. His face and tone were serious. No emotion other than a slight smile on his face.

The results of my morning had me no farther ahead on how this was being fixed. Norman had kept to his trailer and had appeared only once to talk to folks around Tubby's shop. Mike was reserved and seemed to have the task of arranging things on stage. I had walked around out on the ice talking with the fishermen when I wasn't on air, and for the life of me, I couldn't see how anything was wrong. I had to assume that it went on inside of the ice shanty. When I tried to talk to the professionals, I'd been met with a rather cool reception. Catches were kept below the ice, and no one was showing me anything. My hopes were pinned on James and the others, whoever they were. All I could do now was wait on stage with my microphone, ready to recognize "it" at the right moment.

The weigh-ins began as the fishermen lined up. Mike was there to enter the totals on the board for each contestant. Norman took each one's catch and weighed each fish individually and then together. Some folks hadn't caught anything and took their place in the reserved seating area to wait till the end. Bobby and Rodney came along with their stringer and had a total weight of twelve pounds. The smiles on their faces were what this derby was all about, and Caleb had been there to take pictures of our local favorites. Bulldog and the other broadcasters kept on with their steady broadcasting banters as the contestants took their place at the weigh-in area. Daddy and Uncle Ellsworth were last before the pros. I still couldn't figure out how they were going to do it. How would they know how much the top weight was before they weighed their fish? I watched as the weigh-ins continued. Top weights so far were eighteen to nineteen pounds. Uncle Ellsworth's was twenty, and Daddy's was the top at twenty-one. Daddy also had the single biggest fish so far. The crowd cheered at the announcement of his fish's weight. They all wanted one of their own to win. Then the pros started. Of the eight of them, their weights ranged from sixteen to twenty and a half. Bill was the last to weigh in, and what do you know, twenty-three pounds. The crowd groaned at the realization that a Piney Bluffs fisherman hadn't won. Norman got up at this point for the trophy presentations.

"Thank you all so very much. I hope you've had as much fun today as we've had." He was smiling like the Cheshire cat, and I was losing faith and thought for sure that he would get away with it once more. I looked around for James but couldn't see him anywhere. "Now to present the trophies and the prizes."

"Hey, mister, can we help?" the small voice of Rodney came from the bleachers. Clearly, this was not what Norman had intended. But the crowd with their applause got behind the children, and he relented to having them up on stage.

"I am happy to announce that the prize for the largest fish goes to Piney Bluffs native Eddy Koontz," Norman said and stood as he waited for Daddy and then handed the check to him as the cameras rolled and the flashbulbs from the cameras popped. The crowd cheered and applauded as Bobby and Rodney held up the fish holding by either end. They were just so pleased with themselves to be on stage and better yet on TV.

"And the grand prize of five thousand dollars goes to Bill Crawford." Norman smiled and put his arm around Bill as they posed for their pictures. He tried to encourage the crowd to applaud; however, it fell flat after the previous cheers for Daddy.

The boys again took hold of the all of Bill's fish, but because he had caught bass and pickerel, they didn't want to get their hands cut on the fish's teeth, so they held up the fish by their tails. And then it happened. One by one, small lead weights began to drop out of each of the fish's mouths. The crowd immediately cried foul. The cameras were focused on Norman and Bill. Their smiles quickly turned to the dismay as they watched the weights drop as if the fish were blowing lead balloons. James, minus his red hair and beard disguise, came from backstage showing a badge. Bulldog and the Boston newsman without delay began to have a field day with this breaking news story.

"Norman Williams and Bill Crawford, you are under arrest for contributing to the harm of protected species as designated under the federal laws of the Department of the Interior," James said as he turned Norman around to place the handcuffs on him. As James pinned his arms behind him, weights dropped out of his sleeves, leaving no doubt in anyone's mind how the fixing was done. Appearing at his side was Mike O'Brien and a Maine state trooper with another set of cuffs for Bill. From the edges of the stage came other troopers who took the rest of the professionals and announced that they were all being held as accomplices.

"We'll, just take this," Mike said as he took the check from Bill's manacled hand. Didn't see that coming, did you, Ethel? You never know when you've made a friend for life. Don't you forget that."

My mouth opened in surprise at the realization that Mike hadn't been part of Norman's horrible way of life.

"Mike's been working with me on this for a while now," James said. "We contacted him as soon as we became aware of the weight fixing."

"This is going to make good press all around, wouldn't you say so?" Mike said. "I'll bet if you did a piece, I could get you a spot in expose on this. That's if you're still talking to me."

"I guess I could find the time to talk to you. And what time does that piece need to be in?" I shook my head and smiled.

"But hey, who won?" came the yells from Rodney and Bobby.

"The winner of the 1st Annual Piney Bluffs Fishing Derby goes to my daddy, Eddy Koontz," I said as I stepped up to the microphone and handed Daddy the check and pulled him to stand near the trophy.

"I can't think of a better way to end this derby than to accept this check on the behalf of Piney Bluffs. I'd like to use this to start the Stephanie Koontz scholarship for any of our young men and women who attend college in the pursuit of fishing and wildlife studies. Education had been my late wife's passion, and with this scholarship, her passion will never die," Daddy was so happy to announce this and gave me a hug.

The crowd was on its feet, applauding in appreciation. I was so proud of Daddy and our town. With the help of two innocent little boys, we had defeated a foe that seemed unbeatable. It had indeed been a good day to have gone fishing.

Epilogue

The cry woke me from what seemed like a short nap. The early August morning already had the feel of heat and humidity. I slipped out of bed and looked back to see if Charlie was still sleeping. He had been up for EC's last feeding and was now in a deep sleep. I padded across the hardwood floors and down the hallway to the nursery. Mutt and Jeff slept like sentries on either side of the crib. They raised their heads briefly to acknowledge me, and their soft wagging tails thudded on the braided rug beneath them.

Eddy Charles O'Connor had been born on the Fourth of July right on schedule. The remainder of my pregnancy had gone surprisingly well. But I had spent the last two weeks in the hospital before delivery after my blood pressure had bottomed out one day, and I passed out at my desk. I had been busy, and it was chalked up to a lack of food that day, and nothing to worry about.

I looked down at that sweet face. I thought that he almost smiled. Most likely, it was gas—at least that was what Jackie had told me. She said he was too young to smile, but I liked to think it was a smile. I picked him up, smelled that sweet baby smell of powder and lotion, and cuddled him in my arms and sat down in the rocking chair. His crying stopped, and he closed his eyes and went back to sleep, at peace once more, if only for a moment.

Peaceful was how you could describe Piney Bluffs after our misadventure with Norman. James had been able to make the charges stick to Norman for his harming of protected species. The professional fishermen were also charged with being accomplices. Even though there would be no jail time, there were hefty fees levied on all of them. The television coverage had sealed their fates. Norman's reputation was now so soiled that there was no chance of him ever regaining any of the promise that he might have had in the new future of sports-fishing programs.

In the end, Charlie's project with Maloney had turned out to be Ruthie's property. Maloney had many inroads to land and site developments. The sign of true man of his word showed when he heard of how Norman had tried to swindle, and he would have been one of his marks that he gave Ruthie the actual value for her property. The construction was going well, and The Lodge at Piney Bluffs was scheduled for opening during the winter holiday season. Ruthie had even been asked to have her baked goods as part of their breakfast menus.

I wrote that story for the *Herald* and submitted it to Mike. It ran with my byline in their special on the Norman Williams expose. Since that time, I had written other pieces for the *Herald* and continued a renewed relationship with Mike. We even brought him back here and gave him the proper introduction to fishing. He still didn't quite appreciate the calm and quiet of fishing, but he did say he could understand how we felt about it and about our town. I had also been contacted by WBZ. They had seen my segments on derby day and had offered me a part-time broadcaster's position when they were on location. I had accepted, but we agreed it would be after EC was a little older.

Sitting here, I thought of Momma. It would have been so wonderful to share the joy of our baby. But that was not to be. Daddy, however, was funny. He stopped by every day to see his namesake. While he was a little unsure at first, he was now becoming the expert at diaper changing and feeding his grandson. I loved to listen at the doorway as he would tell EC the stories of fishing and how he would teach him to be the best little fisherman that Piney Bluffs had ever known.

Looking around at the nursery, my eyes hit upon the box. Some months ago, when Daddy had told me the story of how he and Momma had met and he had given it to me, he said that she kept special things in there, but that he had never opened it. One thing had led to another, and as much as I was curious to see what was in it, it had never seemed like the right time. Putting EC back in his crib, I went to the shelf and took down the box. It was an old wooden box, no bigger than an egg carton, with the inscription Souvenir of Maine carved in the top. My hands felt the worn letters as I waited. How many times had Momma's hands been in the same place as my hands were now? What had she put in there? Were there remembrances of special times? Was there another letter? And was this the time that I should open it? My hand was on the lid, and I had to use both of my thumbs to push the top up. The smell of old wood hit me first as I gazed at the contents—letters tied with ribbons, a silver dollar, a small book dated 1944, and pictures also tied with ribbons. My past was waiting to be opened with a slight tug of the ribbons.

At that moment, EC cried out. I looked between my son and the box that held another glimpse into my mother's life. I held my breath and pushed the lid back down. I placed the box back on the shelf. I went back to the crib and picked up my son and walked toward the shelf. With one hand on the box and my son in my arms, I felt the feeling of completeness. There would be time for my dream, my family, my own.

The next installment of the
Gone Fishing Trilogy

Gone Fishing

THE LINE

Look for it Spring 2018

Available at bookstores everywhere, or
online at Amazon, Barnes & Noble, the
Apple iTunes Store, or Google Play.

Follow me on Facebook @
Jane Herr Desrosiers
gonefishingthehook
http://www.gonefishingthehook.com/
Email: janeherr51@att.net

CHAPTER ONE

"That's it, we're going," I blurted out.

"Going where?" Charlie looked up from feeding EC. Our baby boy reached out to bring his bottle of juice back to his hungry mouth.

"Oxford," I said firmly. "I've been going through Momma's box and I need to have answers!"

Daddy had given me that old wooden box about a month before Eddy Charles was born. It contained letters, pictures, a silver dollar and a small diary book for 1944 measuring four by five inches. The silver dollar seemed to have a simple explanation for its presence in the box. It was a Canadian George VI, and minted in 1950, the year I was born. And the fact that Momma's family was from Canada brought that item to certain closure. The red leather diary had only a couple of entries in tiny writing beginning in June which was the beginning of World War II. They read, 'sad days for all.' Another page, "who will heal the wounds". Those two passages spoke to me of her compassion and made me wonder what she would have thought of our involvement with the Vietnam war.

The letters and pictures however had been the greater source of interest. I had been reading and rereading the letters and looking at the pictures for the past year. The letters were yellowed with age and most of them had been from Daddy when he was in the services. And while I cherished the unfolding love between them, it was the other letters in a different penmanship, that had piqued my interest.

CPSIA information can be obtained
at www.ICGtesting.com
Printed in the USA
JSHW052309010422
24366JS00001B/4